Seafarer Page

Third Book of the Aethereal Knights' Tales

Seafarer Page

Copyright © 2021 by William Cornelison

Cover Illustration by Hannah Werner

Printed in the United States of America

ISBN: 978-1-7343415-5-3 (Paperback)
ISBN: 978-1-7343415-6-0 (ebook)

First Edition

10 9 8 7 6 5 4 3 2 1

Seafarer Page

Third Book of the Aethereal Knights' Tales

William Cornelison

Warring Magic Books

The Aethereal Knights' Tales

Outlander Page

Mountaineer Page

Seafarer Page

The Siren Knight's Wave

* * * * * *

* * * * * *

~ Chapters ~

There exists in everyone a light magical,

a light that brightens the world with wonder.

Its rays reveal the myriad paths one may take

and promise adventure and excitement wherever they go.

But after taking it so far, the light begins to dim,

and the world's color comes to dull.

It is an inevitable fate.

But one cannot ignore the darkened shades of the world,

for they are a part of it.

Accept the darker shades and foster the light.

They complement each other and complete the canvas.

And when it comes time to strive for a change,

remember to not betray yourself.

~ First Chapter ~

Routine

With the passing of a season came the birth of another. Winter came to an end in the kingdom of Vermalio, bringing, with the sighting of the first flower in bloom, the start of spring.

It was business as usual for everyone in the capital, Brigadier, but the townspeople were more eager to work now that the sun came out much sooner. Merchants set up their stalls and shops, mothers let the light into their homes to wake their children, soldiers took their shifts in better moods, and everyone began their errands earlier than usual.

Little changed for the pages in the Estrine Chateau. The bell hanging above the fine mansion rung the same time three times as it had every dawn.

And as she had every morning, Veronica awoke to the first deafening *gong* that rang throughout the chateau. Energetically tossing the blanket off of her, she sprang out of bed and jumped right into her morning routine.

She performed fifty push-ups, fifty sit-ups, and fifty squats to get her blood pumping so she may take on the new day. Afterwards, she undressed and slipped into the small wooden tub in the corner behind the partitions. It was already full of nice, warm water, courtesy of the servants who came in while they still slept. There was never enough time to enjoy soaking in it—only to get clean and get out.

She shared the water with her roommate, after all, so she could not keep its warmth all to herself.

Cheryl always slept through the bell's ringing, but she always woke up around the time Veronica dried off and dressed. That did not seem to be the case this morning; she was still curled up in the bed across from Veronica's, head buried beneath her pillow.

She always pushed herself so hard when it came to her training.

But she would wake up, even if she did not want to. On their shared nightstand sat a pitcher of cold water, one which Veronica dumped on her head whenever she slept in. She never missed the opportunity when it presented itself.

Maybe it was not the best way to do it, but it always did the trick.

There was still some time before that, though, so Veronica held off on her little prank to finish suiting up. Once dressed, she took her brush from the nightstand drawer and tended to her hair in front of the tall mirror beside the window.

Veronica stood at five feet tall, just barely shorter than the mirror. Her hair was long and golden, the damp locks glistening in the morning light, and easily became untangled with a tug of the brush. With the sunlight gleaming through the window, her clear, big blue eyes shimmered; their reflection made her think of the ocean back home.

Once her hair was nice and straight, she reached back to braid it into a ponytail.

The red tunic and sturdy chainmail consisting of the upper half of her uniform still fit her rather well, but her black leather pants felt somewhat tight around the hips. She made a mental note to visit the maids later for another fitting.

With everything taken care of, she glanced back at her sleeping roommate, ready for a little fun. At least, until she saw her already up.

First stretching her arms above her head and grunting, then rubbing the sleep from her eyes, Cheryl looked up at the girl creeping over to the nightstand for the pitcher. "Not this time, Veronica."

Though she tried to hide it, Veronica was a little disappointed that she did not stay down for a few more seconds. She straightened herself before facing Cheryl with a guilty grin. "Good morning, sleepyhead," she said with a giggle failing to hide her mischief.

"Morning, morning." The groggy girl stood and stretched again, trying to keep herself from getting comfortable and lying back in bed. If anything, her roommate's little pranks were an excellent motivator. "I'll meet you in the banquet hall. Save me a bowl, will you?"

"'kay!"

Leaving her roommate to prepare for the day, Veronica stepped out the door and made her way through the girls' wing. A few others were about and beginning their day, but the spring sunlight did nothing for their fatigue. She thought to cheer her peers up as she crossed them with a friendly "Good morning!" before going on her way.

A few of them looked grateful for the kind greeting; others were only more tired after being exposed to her sunny disposition.

It was much brighter on the chateau's main level. The windows around the foyer entrance gleaming with the sunlight gave off a gloriously inviting impression, which always struck Veronica as odd. Tempting as it was to go out and smell the flowers, she needed to eat before the lessons began.

She always made it to the banquet hall before most other pages. It gave her free choice of which table to sit at, but she always chose the one in front of the lone stained-glass window. The colorful light beaming through the glass was too irresistible to stay away from. No one else liked to sit there for some reason, so there was always time to get food.

As per the norm, the servants bringing out the gruel greeted her as kindly as she had them. Some of them often said how her smile always made their mornings worthwhile. They were a very sweet bunch, and they always allowed her to take hers and her roommate's servings.

This morning, they even gave each of them an extra biscuit. When Veronica tried to mention it, the woman who served the food gestured for her to keep quiet, to which she smiled and nodded. That happened on occasion. Veronica always worried they would get in trouble, but they always assured her it would go to waste anyway.

As promised, Cheryl was down by the time Veronica carried their trays to the table, and they met each other there.

She donned the same uniform every page wore, and it accentuated her muscles well. Cheryl was a tall one, needing many fittings done over the years and constantly in need of new clothes as she grew. The latest sets she got only a few months earlier looked to be lasting. It always made her happy when they did. That wild brown bedhead of hers was tamed into a bob that almost reached her shoulders. Her hazel eyes still looked tired, but she kept moving and kept them open even when she sat to eat.

A big smile drew on her face when Veronica placed her food in front of her. She inhaled the aroma, sounding more awake afterwards. "Nothing like a good meal to get the morning started. Thanks again, Veronica."

Veronica sat across from her friend and gave a silent prayer to the gods as thanks for the meal before partaking. Both of them started with the biscuits so they would not chance getting caught with extra food.

"It's nice of them to do this for us," Cheryl stated. "We'll need all the energy we can get to train for next month."

"I know you like to test your limits for the war enactment, but it worries me that you strain yourself so much beforehand."

The Estrine family, who was responsible for training the pages to be exceptional squires, always held a major trial for them every year one month after the first day of spring. It revolved around the pages being split into two armies to be put against one another. Magic spells kept the warfare simulated with no risk of fatalities, but that did not make the trial less important.

Everyone was evaluated on their abilities, cunning, approach, and, most importantly, whether or not they win the war enactment. Doing well in the enactment was the best way to get recognition from the knights who came to witness it.

And Cheryl realized that as well as anyone. "Better to overdo it than to not give enough." She was rather fond of that saying. "And I won't be the only one pushing myself. You know how competitive everyone gets."

"Yes, that is true."

"You should be putting more into your training too."

"I always give it my best. You know that."

Cheryl sighed. "Yes, but you need to give more. This is your fifth year in the chateau, Veronica. Most pages already get picked to be someone's squire by this time."

"I can't help it if the knights choose someone else."

"I'm just trying to look out for you while I can."

"I know, and I love you for that," said the cheerful girl with a smile.

Their relationship had been like that since they met—both thinking of each other, both worrying about one another.

More pages came while they talked, eager to get whatever nourishment that would sustain them until the midday meal. The tables were all filled except for the one Veronica and Cheryl sat at.

They were talking about the fun times they had during the Flame Festival, where everyone came together to celebrate the end of the year and endure the cold together by dancing around a great bonfire.

Veronica noticed her friend's focus trailed from their conversation to the group of boys across from them. A few of them were staring them down before she started glaring at them.

"Never mind them, Cheryl. They are just having their morning meal, same as us," Veronica insisted, keeping her smile big and bubbly.

Cheryl tried to respect her wish and turned her attention back to the topic when Veronica reminded her of how she danced at the festival. She forgot how she wanted to forget that. While Cheryl thought she looked ridiculous at the time, Veronica knew she had fun then.

It was easier and more amusing to see her laugh from embarrassment than it was seeing her worked up for the entire meal.

Those boys at that table, some of them liked to bully Veronica, and Cheryl never let that go.

Many pages in the Estrine Chateau, unfortunately, had similar opinions about Veronica. They thought her strange, "suspiciously kind" some have explicitly said. They looked at her as an outsider, someone not to be trusted. And some of them acted on that thinking.

As much as she wished they would stop, Veronica never wished it never happened. After all, it was how she and Cheryl became friends.

When she became tired of talking about the Flame Festival, Cheryl began scarfing down her gruel. She always did the funniest things when trying to get out of an awkward conversation.

After finishing their gruel, the two pages brought their dishes to the servants and left. They always took to the training grounds after they ate to get some exercise in before the lessons.

They pondered on what they would do with the time as they crossed the hall leading to the back of the chateau. Soon, they came to the exit and stepped out into the open fields.

The fields were glorious this morning, the sunlight glistening over the beds of grass short and tall. A gentle breeze occasionally brushed across the area, making the greenery sway. The birds, returning from their migration, graced them with their chipper songs and danced whimsically in the air.

It was a wonderful day to train under the sun.

Some servants were still bringing barrels of weapons and other training tools out of the old shed and setting them up along the beaten path from the chateau gate.

Instead of taking a shaved sword from one of the barrels and getting right into sparring, Veronica walked up to the man carrying out supplies. "May I help?"

The servant, recognizing her, gladly accepted her offer.

Many serving the Estrine family were familiar with the kindly girl who took the time to help others. The servants were unsure about accepting her help when she first became a page, but grew to appreciate the generosity when she proved capable of balancing her deeds with her responsibilities.

Cheryl helped as well so that they could spar sooner. Everything was set up faster as a result.

"I didn't realize you two were so eager to train, Page Alivvrn, Page Evaleen."

A tall man walked up to the girls from behind. He wore armor with the Estrine family insignia on the shoulder plates. It was Sir Storn Stog, one of the instructors who taught the pages combat skills. His presence surprised Cheryl, who winced when she got a look at his flat, chiseled face. He rarely arrived before his pages did.

The two pages stood straight and greeted him with a firm "Sir!"

"Since you are here, run three laps around the chateau before you leave for your lessons. Be back by the time my pages arrive."

They obeyed and ran along the wall of the chateau once he finished speaking.

Neither Veronica nor Cheryl took part in Sir Storn's lessons. Being fifth- and fourth-year pages, respectively, they were expected to be responsible for their own combat training. Those who failed to meet the expectations set for them were punished with long, arduous courses, and the Estrines always knew when their pages were slacking off. But they could not disobey him since pages were meant to follow their mentors as soldiers should with their superiors.

They kept going at their fastest even when they were well out of sight. They could not hover around the chateau wall when moving past the front; tall hedges and bountiful gardens stretched from the main entrance to the gates. It made completing the lap all the more trying.

A few servants were in the yard tending to the plants. They were careful to avoid them.

Some pages arrived at the training grounds when they completed the first lap, prompting them to pick up the pace. Nearly everyone was there after finishing the second. By the time they completed the third lap, the last page in the group showed up with a look of surprise, perhaps wondering why someone was already tired.

Sir Storn seemed pleased with himself for whatever reason.

Before they could leave, he ordered the two to join his pages in warmups and give fifty pushups. Everyone managed well enough, even the ones who were not supposed to be there, which set the knight's countenance to a wrinkly frown.

Veronica tired out after the exercises but tried not to let it show. She kept herself composed when Sir Storn called on her to demonstrate a few maneuvers for the younger pages.

As instructed, she first demonstrated how to quickly unsheathe a sword. She then approached Sir Storn and dropped her weapon against his in a downward swipe, followed by a horizontal swing, then held her sword to effectively block the knight's counter.

The movements were quick and precise, but they did not impress the instructor. He moved to correct her stance using the flat of his sword, tapping where the faults were. There were quite a few, according to him.

"This is why I don't like Lord Estrine letting his pages run around unsupervised," he quietly mumbled, then looked to Veronica and Cheryl. "That'll be all. Off with you before your instructors send the hounds after you."

They did as he said before he changed his mind. They left the other pages behind as they were taking practice swords and began their warmup repetitions.

The air inside the chateau was still cool. It granted them a little relief on the walk to their first lesson of the day.

"Once again, Sir Stoneface goes out of his way to work us ragged."

Veronica did not entirely agree with Cheryl, but she still let out a laugh hearing the nickname she gave him. "He is supposed to be strict, just like the other knights and scholars who instruct us."

"Yeah, but he doesn't get on the boys' backs like he does with us."

"I'm sure you are imagining things."

"You always say that..."

They arrived at their etiquette lesson as their cultural instructor called out the pages' names. Lady Deva did not like it when her students arrived almost late, but she allowed them to join the others when they greeted her with a proper bow.

Learning etiquette was sometimes as strenuous as combat training. Pages were required to carry themselves in a respectable manner and respond to everything properly. They were to listen to every word from Lady Deva without interrupting or speaking out of turn. Unsightly and unbecoming character and actions were corrected and, if uncouth enough, punished. More often than not, those punished were ordered to work under the servants.

The lessons and discipline served to better prepare the children for the future. Knights were expected to be respectful, upstanding servants of the kingdom. Giving their lives to protect their people did not permit them to act as they pleased. Any knight worth their shield would present themselves in a manner worthy of praise to earn favor from the people.

Veronica liked and agreed with the principles Lady Deva taught, and felt ashamed of those knights she saw who behaved as though ordinary people were beneath them.

The lessons appealed to Cheryl, too, because Lady Deva taught the girls the same way as she did the boys. Nobles and commoners alike, the girls all knew some way they were told to behave that differed from the boys. But a lady knight was not expected to behave in any way different from her male peers.

"A soldier is a soldier, regardless of their sex," their cultural instructor had often said. "There is no reason for me to teach you any differently."

After practicing etiquette, Lady Deva had the pages review the various languages she had been teaching them. Many did not see the point of practicing the Abioan or Brungonian languages, and some were definitely not fond of learning Pternite. One page was so bold as to ask why they needed to do so, earning himself a punishment assignment.

"Communication is key to everything," she deigned to answer.

Many people speaking those languages came to Vermalio. If they met any of them, through means peaceful or otherwise, being able to speak their language would be an immeasurable help if they did not understand Vermalian.

Every language had its challenging words and phrases, but they were fun to learn. Abioan sounded elegant when correctly pronounced. Brungonian required a lot of annunciation. And Pternite had a different sentence structure than the other languages.

They were all expected to learn each language perfectly before a knight chose them for their squire.

Following the etiquette lessons was incite on the ways of war with Lord Tamsilac. The elderly Estrine taught them the differences between strategy and tactics, the desired course and the means to fulfill it.

Lord Tamsilac always emphasized the importance of using the environment to their advantage. It was why he extensively taught them about geography and the weather while going over old war stories.

A lot of pages liked learning from him. His stories were always interesting and never strayed far from the lesson plan. Whenever a new page joined his lessons, he asked them where they were from, then regaled them with knowledge of their region even they did not know about and tested his pages' wits by asking them what they could do in said place during this or that situation.

On occasion, he would get drowsy during a lecture, but he always got back to the point.

After the lectures were finished and their instructors dismissed them, the pages would scamper off to their next lesson. Many were preoccupied well past midday. Once pages had two years of experience in the Estrine family's care, like Veronica and Cheryl, they were free to train themselves after the lectures however they saw fit.

Cheryl always became antsy after the lectures were done.

She headed straight for the training grounds for a nice workout, same as ever, and as always, Veronica followed to help.

First, per Veronica's request, they stopped by the stables to tend to their mounts. The pages learning from the Estrine family were taught everything, including mounted combat. They were responsible for caring for their horses and helping the stable hand keep their abode clean.

The stables lay past the training grounds into the field. It was simple in structure compared to the impressive chateau but wide enough to house over a hundred young horses. Several pages often shared a single mount since there were only so many available. But not every page took proper care of their mount despite the promise of punishment for such negligence, and so Veronica convinced her friend to put her restlessness aside to ensure their four-legged friends were well cared for.

Then, after taking them out for a run, they returned to the training grounds for the sparring session they missed out on earlier.

Both girls favored the sword and knew how to use it. Cheryl fought quickly and aggressively, hacking and slashing with her weapon in both hands. Strong as she was, there was no need for her to hold back against the swift and deft Veronica. Every move she made, Veronica glided past it fluid as water, allowing her to get the drop on her taller rival.

Had it been their first time sparring, Cheryl would have been stunned in trying to follow those snapping reflexes, but she had seen what Veronica was capable of time and again.

The exercise continued until they thought it time to stop for a breath, then they began another round. When they were not sparring, they did simple things like push-ups or sit-ups, seeing who could do the most without stopping.

After a while, Veronica decided to go back inside.

"What? You done already?" Cheryl teased.

Veronica laughed a tired laugh. "Not all of us are as enduring as you."

"All right then. You rest up. I'll see you later."

Cheryl dropped to do another exercise the moment she stopped talking, and not long after was challenged by other pages. She seemed to notice how they approached now that she had finished her time with Veronica. But she did not turn them away; a little swordplay with her seemed an appropriate punishment for such rudeness.

I'm sure she'll have fun with them, Veronica thought to herself.

Veronica walked back to the chateau, wobblily and a bit unbalanced. It was refreshing to walk through the cool breeze after getting covered in sweat.

Upon entering the chateau and stepping out of sight, though, she shed her fatigue in favor of an upbeat attitude. The constant training was tiring, to be sure, but she was happy to go through it. It made her a better warrior, after all.

Her exaggerated fatigue was but a ruse. As close as they were, Veronica and Cheryl were still rivals. There would come times when they had to oppose one another, as they had before, and the best way to confront her was to catch her by surprise. Hiding how much she could take was but another prank in Veronica's bag of tricks.

And since Cheryl knew how impish she could be, it was best to have as many tricks as possible.

Besides, she had another reason to step away.

Veronica was careful to take an alternate path as she returned to her room. When the soldiers serving the Estrine family found an experienced page wandering the halls, they tended to give them tasks as small as polishing their boots or weapons to ones as important as delivering letters. Although she liked to be of help, there was someone she had hoped to see.

After years of practice, she had gotten good at sneaking around patrolling guards and servants to the point she would tease them. Of course, she never did anything more than give them a fright—perhaps startle them by making water bead from the ceiling and tap the back of their necks, but nothing more than that.

It would have been troubling if someone caught her using her powers so frivolously.

Soon enough, she returned to her bedchamber and found her expected company making herself at home. No one was seen inside when she opened the door, but she still felt her presence. A little focus was all it took for her to see her guest: a phantom.

The power she possessed gave her magic sight, the means to see the flow of energy in the world. Most would only recognize the flow as the rest of the world faded, but Veronica's magic sight was special. She could perceive the mystical phenomena and the material plane in unison. And, unlike anyone else, she could also interact with phantoms of the dead, lingering spirits that have left behind regrets.

Seeing the world through her magic sight was different than looking through normal eyes. The plane of phantoms appeared somewhat darker, as though dusk was upon them. It was without the sun's golden light. Instead, a serene veil of blue enshrouded them, accentuated by these flickering ghostly embers that floated aimlessly about.

And by the window was the silhouette of a teenage girl. She was leaning against the windowsill, staring drearily outside, the ethereal embers complementing her beautiful red hair. Although her form was somewhat transparent, she interacted with the space around her as though she were truly alive.

The phantom glanced at the door, her sharp eyes resting on Veronica. "So, done getting your arse handed to you?"

Veronica smile. "You watched me spar with Cheryl."

"If you can call it that," the phantom scoffed.

Veronica knew this phantom well. She met her during her first year as a page in that very bedchamber one solemn night. The moment they met—the phantom's surprise when she realized someone could see her—was still fresh in her mind.

Veronica walked up to the window to see what she was looking at before she entered. "Did you have any luck today, Rubi?"

The phantom sighed. "Not a bit."

Interactions with the dead were common for Veronica. For as far back as she could remember, she had conversed with phantoms, heard their stories, made friends with them, and ultimately worked to help them find peace.

She offered to do so for Rubi as well, but Rubi rejected her help time and again. She had been trying to find the cause of her death on her own for five years. For her, this was a trial she had to complete through her effort alone.

All she knew was her name—and even that took some time to recall—and the fact that she used to be a page herself. Phantoms only held on to mere pieces of their former lives, if anything. Their memories either returned in time or were unearthed after learning something in connection with them.

Rubi made herself comfortable flopping onto Cheryl's bed. She stared at the ceiling, portraying a tired irritation.

It only made sense that she felt at home there. After all, the bedchamber was as much hers, at least in life.

"What did you do today?" Veronica asked her spectral roommate.

"Took a trip to the palace."

"Oh? Were you searching for someone you might have known?"

"No, I tried to possess the king so I could rule Vermalio with an iron fist."

Veronica laughed. While that might not have been the intent, there was no mistaking Rubi's sarcasm for anything serious.

"Is that so? I suppose it did not go well."

"Oh no, it did. But I got grossed out possessing a man, so I abandoned the idea."

"Perhaps the queen would suffice," Veronica jested.

Now Rubi chuckled. "Sure, if by better you mean surrounded by high-strung, tight-minded, heel-licking pains in the arse who always want their favors granted. Thanks, but no thanks."

She had a crude sense of humor, but one that sometimes tickled Veronica in a way she would not expect. "Rubi, how terrible," she teased.

"You should hear what the guards here have to say about their lord."

For as much as she disliked making fun of people, Veronica could not help letting out another laugh. The soldiers certainly have said some colorful things in response to Lord Estrine's strict regulations.

Rough around the edges as she was, it was not hard talking to Rubi. She spoke candidly about everything. Getting her to open up was challenging at first, but being a phantom, she had no one else to turn to. No one else could hear her woes or acknowledge her existence.

And Veronica was happy to.

Simply exchanging words was, at times, more helpful than doing anything else. Having someone to talk to was often a moment of relief in a time of stress and angst. And it worked both ways.

"How about you? Any luck in your search?"

A weight dragged her lips downward, but Veronica strived to keep the smile on her face. "Not yet, no."

The dream of knighthood led her to become a page. But what drew her to the Estrine Chateau was not its reputation or the promise of being introduced to reputable knights. Six years ago, a faction of the Renegades, the rogue militia threatening the current reign in Vermalio, infiltrated Brigadier and turned it into a battlefield. Innocent lives had been cut short, including that of Veronica's older brother Wallace.

"Do you still think he's here?"

"I do."

No matter how many times she was asked, her answer remained the same. She could feel it. Her brother was still present, somewhere, lost and unable to find peace.

It's been five years, Veronica, she sometimes imagined someone saying to her. *Accept reality. Wally is gone. You can't see him anymore.*

But the reality she knew was not the same as theirs. Phantoms did not always appear at the moment of death. Some lingered in silence, outside the perception of the plane of phantoms, for months, even years at a time, until finally being able to move around on their own. But they always remained tethered to the place they died in until they discovered what regret they left behind.

And phantoms could search for just as long to calm their angst.

He was there. She just did not know where yet.

"Then you'll find him—without a doubt."

Coming from anyone else, that would have passed as mere encouragement. But Rubi did not say anything she did not mean.

Those few words brought Veronica enough comfort to keep with her search for a few years more. "I do hope so."

The two talked a little more about what they did since they last met until Rubi decided to take her leave and continue her search. Once again, Veronica offered to go with her, but again Rubi turned her down.

"I'm fine on my own. Go work on your form or something." She moved toward the door, but stopped to face her again. "And if you try to follow me again, I'll make your reflection look like a goblin whenever you look into a mirror."

Of the few things phantoms were capable of affecting in the material plane, their grasp on mirrors was riveting. Although incapable of touching physical bodies, phantoms could easily distort the light that mirrors captured to show almost anything.

Veronica did display the shock and fear her phantom friend was hoping for, but then found herself thinking what she would look like with green skin and long, pointed ears. Before she could think about how much weight her words carried, Rubi phased through the door.

A little curious, Veronica looked to her mirror and leaned in a little, in case she decided to give her a little preview. But her complexion did not change.

After fixing her hair up a little, she left the room to find something to preoccupy herself with until the evening meal.

~ Second Chapter ~

Peers

Before the evening meal, Veronica decided to visit Lady Abeel Estrine, the instructor who taught pages the principles of magic. She did not attend her lessons as of late, wanting to focus on her swordsmanship.

The young mages practiced in the east wing, inside of a spacious chamber lined with protective spells. Given how late it was, Lady Abeel would not be there. Pages were already passing Veronica by as they left the sorcery room.

But Veronica kept going. A few looked her way with curiosity, perhaps wondering why she was there.

She walked past the sorcery room, eventually coming to an ornate door at the edge of the wing. There were markings around the doorknob that, although appearing impractical, supported a spell that prevented the uninvited from entering. It waned when Veronica reached for the knob, though, and the door opened without protest.

Lady Abeel was inside, sitting comfortably at her desk while examining her notes. She dressed in her favorite kimono, a garment from the western empire of Pterna. The mature woman looked Veronica's way when she entered, brushing the strands of her brunette hair from her eye.

"Ah, Veronica. Good evening."

The page bowed her head. "Good evening, Lady Abeel. I hope I am not intruding."

"Nonsense, dear," answered the noble sorceress. "Come in, come in."

Veronica shut the door behind her and approached Lady Abeel with a spring in her step. She got a quick look at the sheets of parchment on her desk; magic circles were drawn on them, each with markings for various binding spells. No magic had been applied to them, save the one Lady Abeel held between her fingers, which she reduced to ash with a sparking fire spell. Another failed attempt, sadly.

Veronica looked past her shoulder at one of the talismans she was appraising. "I don't think that's the right sigil."

Lady Abeel glanced at the one Veronica pointed to. When she found the sigil, she covered her mouth to stifle a laugh. "Oh my! This would make a barrier as solid as jelly." She faced Veronica again with an impressed smile. "Good eye, dear."

The praise made her giddy.

Her knowledge of magic met the Estrines' standards. She was also a good study, quick to pick up facts and eager to apply what she learned. But her notably exceptional knowledge was not the reason she did not attend Lady Abeel's lessons.

"Do you suppose I could try one?"

"Not these, no. I need the pages to see with their own eyes what—" The noblewoman paused when her gaze noted a particular talisman with a simple-looking design. Upon reviewing it, she shook her head and sighed. "Someone is being reserved again." She looked back to Veronica and handed her the talisman. "Give this one a go."

Veronica took the parchment and laid it on the floor. She sat before the talisman, then took a deep breath and cleared her mind, ridding herself of unnecessary thought. Once she was ready, she reached out and focused on the energy within her.

To cast a spell, one needed to heighten their focus so that the mind resonated with their very life energy—their valsara. When that happened, they could compel the ethereal forces that made up the world, and use them in a form that depended on a person's ability.

Her valsara was stable, her mind and spirit balanced, but all Veronica got out of the effort was an unsavory headache.

The talisman was supposed to support a simple illumination spell. Done properly, a sphere of light would appear and brighten up the dim space. But once more, much to her disappointment, nothing happened.

For all her knowledge, what she could do with it was sadly limited.

When she saw that she had given up, Lady Abeel gave her shoulder a sympathetic pat. "It's all right, dear," she comforted her, as she had done in their past sessions. "Why don't you show me how the magic you do know is faring?"

Veronica shook off her disappointment and stood, eager to answer her request. In the corner of the room was a vase holding three delicate chrysanthemums, the flowers kept fresh by the water inside. With but a pull from her rising hand, the water slowly rose to the rims of the vase, trailing out the sides so as not to damage the delicate arrangement. Three long strings of water flowed up and converged into a sphere. A few drops fell upon the petals as the sphere floated over to Veronica. It stretched out like a snake and morphed into one as it circled her. The snake bit its tail, then gradually smoothed out into a simple ring while the girl spun around inside it. Then, as she thrust her arms out, the ring fractured and broke apart as it floated higher into the air, the pieces stretching out into soaring doves; the droplets that fell off flew back to form the plumes in their wings.

Lady Abeel normally did not permit magic to be used in her private quarters, but she trusted Veronica to be careful. Her control was so precise that not a drop of water fell out of place without her consent.

The demonstration came to an end when the doves soared over Lady Abeel and circled the vase, breaking apart bit by bit until the water trailed back into its container.

The smile on the noble sorceress' face was that of a proud parent's gentle praise. "Excellent as always, Veronica."

The page smiled as well, grateful for the kind words. But her dissatisfaction remained buried under the surface.

Her talent for bending water to her will only reached such heights because she had been practicing all her life. While she loved what she could do, she wanted to learn to use other kinds of magic. But for some reason, she could not perform even the simplest of spells. It was why she did not need to attend Lady Abeel's lessons. It was enough that she regularly reported to her.

"You seem to be as chipper as ever. There is no trouble with your abilities as of late, I hope."

"None, ma'am."

"That's always good to hear."

Lady Abeel had turned back to her talismans when the shrill whistle of her tea kettle called for her attention. She neatly stacked the parchments before setting them down, and walked over to a small hearth in the corner. She picked up the kettle hanging over the fire with a thick mitt and carried it to a stone counter where several ornate teacups sat.

"Do you have the time to join me for tea?"

"Certainly, milady. I would be delighted."

Veronica walked over to where Lady Abeel stood so she could pour the tea for her. The Estrine mage went to her desk after the page filled her cup, and Veronica took a seat on an empty stool.

When they were comfortable, Lady Abeel offered the pleasantry of asking about the page's training, to which Veronica said all was going well—the expected and only response.

These private sessions of theirs often went in this direction. Lady Abeel always inquired about Veronica's power, asking what she did with it, to speculate on its potential. Veronica complied, although she chose to omit the times she used it to pull pranks. Pages of her level were expected to track their progress and seek ways to surpass them on their own; the knights evaluated their martial skills, and Lady Abeel their magic.

It was not all formalities. Lady Abeel also enjoyed hearing about Veronica's daily life and the letters she received from her family. It always put her in fine spirits listening to her delightful stories and knowing she was well.

Whenever they spoke, Lady Abeel paid close attention to more than her words, but also her expressions, her posture, and how readily she answered her questions. It was as though she was studying her. But their discussions were always pleasant, so Veronica never minded. Whatever she needed to know, she honestly hoped she found it.

Soon, it came time for the teacher to bid her student a good day, as there was still much for both to do before the day's end.

The days went by steadily with the pages hard at work. Never did they remain idle. Not only would it prompt the Estrine knights to reprimand them, but they would fall behind their friends and rivals.

Like soldiers at war, the pages were competing against one another. The most impressive were often the first to be chosen as squires, after all, and they all wanted to get closer to knighthood.

But work without rest left the worker a mess.

After the lessons ended for the day, Veronica and Cheryl returned to their bedchamber for a short break. They made their plans for the remainder of the day, often aligning them so they might be together, while relaxing. During that time, Cheryl reviewed the history and tactics she learned that day, and Veronica played with the water in the pitcher on the nightstand.

Cheryl sometimes worried about her friend using her power so frivolously. While unfamiliar with the laws of magic, she knew from watching apprentice mages that constant use of their power left them weak. Every magic user had a limited reserve of energy; the more spells they used at a time, the more time it took for them to recover. Using too much magic could often be dangerous, even life-threatening.

Simply playing with a small mass of water never gave Veronica any trouble. And it never made her weary, no matter how much she reshaped it in the air. What became a simple effort after years of practice always helped her to relieve stress.

After their rest, they made their way to the training grounds.

There were not many pages out exercising at that time; most were third- or fourth-year pages performing repetitions with swords. Cheryl thought to join them, but Veronica coaxed her to follow her to check on their horses.

The verdant fields behind the Estrine Chateau stretched for miles, without any stone buildings of the city to obstruct its majesty. Small copses peppered the landscape, islands in the sea of brilliant green. Along the trampled earth at the chateau led a path into the eastern hills; it was not until they scaled to the top of the first that they saw a glimpse of Brigadier's wall encompassing the free landscape. And upon skidding down it, they came across the stables.

Veronica went inside, excited to see the horses. Nearly every stall inside was occupied by the majestic creatures, all of them healthy and well-fed. One of them, a steed of dark brown fur, leaned over to sniff her hair. Its strong breath tickled her face.

"Hey, Geor," she greeted the steed with a laugh. After petting him, she noticed Cheryl still lingering at the stable doors wearing a look of unease. "Come on, Cheryl. They don't bite."

"No, they don't bite *you*," Cheryl rebutted.

"Don't tell me you're still afraid of horses," said Veronica while stroking Geor's long face. "You've been handling one for four years now."

Knowing full well she could not stay there the whole time, Cheryl tentatively stepped inside. "Mine's the one horse that won't try to bite me or trample me or—" She jumped when she heard the horse nearest to her whinny, then gave it a dirty look as though believe it to be taunting her. Her cheeks colored an abashed pink when she heard her friend giggle. "I'm just not good with horses!"

She had said so time and again. If she had not been responsible for taking care of her mount, she would likely never step foot into the stables.

She would be missing out, Veronica always thought.

Their mounts were housed in the back of the stables, where the stableman usually dwelled. It was a straight path to there that would not seem so long if Cheryl walked the pace she usually had. The confident, self-reliant girl lingered behind Veronica like a timid child afraid of being spirited away from her elder sister. But she did not mind being her shield.

When she first learned she had to take care of a horse, Cheryl would not go near the stables. It had gotten so bad Lord Estrine threatened to send her to another facility unless she got it under control.

She was conquering her fear, slowly but surely.

They were almost to their horses' stalls, but Veronica would not need to go farther to meet hers. Someone else was leading her chestnut-haired mount, Amber, outside.

A girl about their age held the reins, and stopped in her tracks when she saw them. Long blonde curls flowed down her head, the golden bangs hanging orderly over her lively green eyes. "Ah, Veronica, Cheryl. Good day," greeted the girl with a prim voice.

"Hello, Sashan." Veronica looked at her with her usual cheery expression, but strained to keep her voice from cracking. She glanced down to the reins in her hand, then up at Amber.

Many children were taken under the Estrine family's wing, much more so than in previous years. The family had space aplenty for them, but recently, they lacked the horses to pair with each page. Several had to share their mounts—such as Veronica with Sashan.

"Would you mind making way? I have a run to make."

"Ah— Yes, of course."

Veronica stepped aside to let Amber and Sashan through. Cheryl remained where she was, as though she were the one who needed to stand her ground, but she made way so everyone could continue their business. The golden girl walked by with composure enough, but in her valsara, Veronica sensed a spiking hostility when they crossed. Her smile slipped when she could no longer see Sashan's face.

Cheryl watched Sashan leave, then turned to Veronica when she was out of earshot. "Is she still mad?"

Veronica nodded.

Sashan used to be very friendly toward Veronica, but that changed some time ago. She reacted to her advances coldly, remained distant, and when Veronica went after her to ask what was wrong, she slapped her outstretched hand away. Distain boiled in her eyes, and hate flared in her valsara. It was as though she became a different person. Or that she was looking at someone else entirely.

The strange thing was that Veronica could not think of anything she did that might have upset her. She racked her brain trying, but in the end, she still did not understand. And she wanted to.

But unless Sashan let her in, they would not get anywhere.

"Guess you can't ride for a while. Darn shame. Let's get out of here."

"Not so fast," Veronica grabbed her friend's arm as she moved to leave. "We came all the way here. Let's check their stalls first."

Cheryl hung her head, discontented, but agreed.

Their work in the stables was simple. The stableman took care of the horses' feed. As for the pages, they were responsible for keeping their horse's stall clean and ensuring the beasts were well-groomed. Shovelling dung was no pleasant task, and if not attended to timely, it proved to be arduous work.

Some pages occasionally shirked the work, some with thoughts fixated on training, others just scoffing menial labor. And whenever that happened, the stableman informed Lord Estrine, who punished them promptly for the disobedience. Cheryl knew of pages that were sent back home for refusing to go near dung. "Stuck-up arses," she called them, and Veronica had to agree.

There would doubtless be orders given to them that were far more unsavory than cleaning up after a horse. And soldiers were expected to comply no matter what they were.

Sashan was still out with Amber after they finished. Instead of waiting, they returned to the training grounds, which elicited a heavy sigh of relief from Cheryl, to practice their swordplay.

More pages were outside now, raring to tussle with one another.

The sight of combat got the bushed Cheryl excited enough to rush down the hill for one of the blunt weapons. Any chance to better herself as a warrior, she took it.

Veronica followed behind, greeting a few pages still warming up. She approached a barrel holding the shaven swords they used to train and reached out for one when someone else grabbed it, trotting off before she could react. Paying it no mind, she reached for another, and her fingers tapped the hand of another who stopped to look her way.

"Oh! Hello, Veronica," the boy greeted.

She knew him, vaguely. They met briefly months ago. The boy was new to the chateau and had a difficult time finding his way, so Veronica showed him around.

"Hello there. ...Shay, was it?"

He smiled. "You remember."

Returning the smile with her own, she pulled her hand back so that he had a pick of the sword he wanted.

"No, please," Shay insisted as he, too, pulled back. "You first."

Instead of continuing the cycle, Veronica went first. When Shay took his, she asked him to spar.

The two took an unoccupied spot. Upon crossing their swords, a formality that some did to wish each other a good fight, they lurched backward and took their stances.

Since the sword was light in her grasp, Veronica held it in one hand, and moved it steadily as she went in for the first strike.

Shay aptly blocked the forward thrust and pushed his opponent back. But Veronica fought the force repelling her, maintaining her footing. She read the younger page and moved in again, making him wince with a deceptive feint before artfully sliding her dull blade at his exposed side.

Again, they crossed their swords for another round. Shay became wise to the deceptive attacks and took the offensive. His foe moved around the waves of his sword, having her fun with him, then she parried and poked his chest with the sword tip.

The boy struck her as timid and a bit clumsy, but he was quick to learn from the mistakes he made, something that showed as they kept sparring.

He held up a hand to yield when he had enough.

"Is that all you got?"

Another page approached them when Shay stopped for rest, this one a tall boy looking down at them with small blue eyes. Veronica thought she recognized him but could not quite recall from where.

The tall boy shook his head at Shay. "What, you like the taste of dirt? Is that why you let this girl knock you down?" He watched as Shay scrambled back onto his feet, eyes flared with scorn. "You wouldn't get back up if someone with more meat on their bones put you there."

Adrenaline still pumped through Veronica's veins. Her gentle smile stretched a tad, her slim brows narrowing for a confident gaze. "Oh? Might this be a challenge?"

The tall boy shot her a smug look, an eyebrow arched. "Ha! No, it would be a warm-up." He waltzed over to Shay, ripping the sword from his hands. He waved it at Veronica—a challenge if ever there was one.

Wasting no time, they crossed swords, but instead of moving back, Veronica's new opponent went right for a strong swing at her torso. She leaped out of the way well before the dull blade made contact. The way he held his weapon told her where it would travel. Instead of taking advantage of his exposed right side, Veronica decided to have her fun watching how he moved as he swung haphazardly at her.

"Stay still, you gutless wench!"

His words were uncalled for but expected. In the thrill of battle, pages—as much as knights—often hurled insults and taunts at their opponents.

Veronica never had the urge to do so herself. Competition was about seeing who was the better adversary, and in a sword fight, words only dulled their focus. But the custom did have its uses: allowing her to determine how worked up her foe was, for one.

The path of his sword was simple to determine, the boy much too eager to prove himself the better. And when she allowed him to get close, she brought her sword against his. Gliding metal along metal, she ran her blade clean against his chest.

Stagger backward did the boy, looking at Veronica with the eyes of a wounded pup.

While she gave him a sincere smile for the good fight, he bore a vengeful scowl. He looked ready to go another round, but when he felt the eyes of the other pages rest upon him, his arms shook angrily. Fed up, he threw the sword on the ground.

"Not worth fighting a cheating witch."

The words stung, but not as much as they used to. Many boys she bested often resorted to accusing her of using magic to give her an unfair advantage. Their complaints fell on deaf ears, though, and eventually, they just started saying such things to spite her.

She understood the frustration of failure, and dismissed his words as but a child's griping.

With that, Veronica picked up the pilfered sword and returned it to Shay, who accepted it with a sweet smile. Although he appreciated her kindness, his eyes revealed a slight wariness.

"Shall we try again?" Veronica was not afraid to ask.

"You're sure you don't need to rest?"

It was a warm day, befitting the dawn to spring. The sun was shining brilliantly. Sweat beaded and rolled over her skin, sticking to her tunic, the more she fought under it. Her muscles were warm and urged her toward the cold ground when she slowed. But instead of caving, Veronica wiped the sweat from her bow and smiled at him.

This was as much endurance training as it was sword practice.

Another group of pages called to Shay before he could give an answer. They seemed to be friends of his, judging by his excited reaction. He looked back to Veronica meekly, appearing to expect some backlash for his next course of action. "Please excuse me."

But Veronica only smiled and nodded. "See you later."

Shay left to join his friends, and she began looking for new competition. And it seemed Cheryl was doing the same.

Cheryl was only ever unoccupied in the training grounds when her opponents became tired of losing to her. Seeing an opportunity, she rushed up to Veronica, holding her sword high.

The air screamed upon the blade's fall, ringing against Veronica's ears. Her eyes perking wider open, she swiveled out of the way, evading the shrill whisper creating the sword's path.

"Ah!" Cheryl clicked her tongue. "You always see it coming. How do you do that?"

Surprise attacks in the training grounds were Cheryl's way of testing her friend's impeccable reflexes. She could scarcely get past them in a proper fight and craved the chance to land a good blow.

But Veronica moved like a river around stone.

The only answer she gave her friend was a sly smile.

Not caring to leave it at that, Cheryl raised her sword again. Veronica lifted hers for them to cross.

Their sparring matches were thrilling, and they continued until they could not ignore gravity pulling them down.

Not many pages remained in the training grounds to practice after Veronica and Cheryl clashed; fewer and fewer remained with each round they went without pause. They only noticed as much when they stood again to find no one around.

Daylight still glimmered above. There would be time for more exercise later.

For the time being, they returned inside to rest and rehydrate.

Only the servants were permitted to collect from the wells owned by the Estrine family. If the pages wanted water, they had to visit the stations set up on the ground floor. The system was reasonably efficient and gave the pages opportunities to recuperate after tiring sparring sessions and long study periods. Cheryl and Veronica went to the station closest to the rear gates, where stood a line of children waiting for their share.

Cheryl folded her arms, scowling. "What're they here for? I didn't see any of them breaking a sweat."

"Everyone needs water, Cheryl."

"Yeah, I guess…"

The line moved steadily along.

The girls talked to each other about their techniques to pass the time. Cheryl always tried to get Veronica to tell her how she got so reflexive. She was subtle about it when they first met, and became less so over the years. Veronica always said there was no secret—she simply knew how to react. But Cheryl was never satisfied by that answer and insisted there was more to it. She made many peculiar guesses to sate her curiosity: that she danced around flying arrows as a child, that she practiced swordplay blindfolded before coming to the Estrine Chateau. All she managed to get was a laugh out of Veronica every time.

Some of the others in line seemed amused by Cheryl as well. They stifled chuckles under their breath.

"Oh, I got it! You drink enough to make your muscles fluid as water."

The whispered laughter stopped then.

Veronica shook her head. "You eat and drink more than I do, and you're no more agile than me."

That response silenced whatever retort Cheryl kept in reserve. When she got her thoughts in order, she playfully nudged her friend with her elbow. "I'm agile enough to keep up with you."

Veronica giggled. "And I've got the bruises to prove it."

Soon enough, they were at the front of the line. Veronica let Cheryl get her water first, seeing how worked up she got during training, cursing her opponent more than the boys had.

She did not realize how parched she was until she saw the maid lift the ladle from the water bucket and pour her a cup. Her dry throat tightened when she saw Cheryl bring the cup to her lips.

When the maid handed her a cup, Veronica bowed her head and thanked her, eliciting a smile from the servant.

There was nothing quite like a drink of water after so vigorous a workout. Although proud to feel her muscles burn and her tendons grow sore, she would not have been able to continue without the cool feel of revitalizing liquid passing her lips. A sip was all it took to make her feel at ease.

She did not chug her water down like Cheryl had. She liked to take slow sips, savor the cold liquid brushing down her throat.

They remained nearby, discussing what they should do until the evening meal while enjoying their drinks. Veronica suggested that they go to the library to review their Abioan or Pternite. Cheryl complained, but she changed her tune when her friend said it would impress Lady Deva.

While their talked, someone bumped into Veronica's arm, knocking the cup she held against her collar. She let out a shout when the water spilled and looked down at her soaked clothing.

The cool splash along her neckline certainly gave her a start. It was not how she thought to cool down.

"What was that for?" Cheryl shouted at the culprit. "I saw that—you did it on purpose!"

The boy who passed them looked back at what happened, pretending he did not even notice. His countenance was one of apathy and without regret. "What're you crying about? The little freak can just brush it off."

"And you think that makes it okay?"

"Not like it bothers her. Look, she's not saying anything."

"You bloody—"

"Leave it be, Cheryl."

Veronica would not look back to see if her friend obliged lest she catch a look at the boy. She did not want to know his face or his name, or even let his voice linger in her pool of memories. That space should instead be reserved for important things.

"But—"

"It's just water. Nothing to fret over."

Rather than remain and wait for a response, Veronica walked away. It was in her best interest not to engage in petty behavior. Hers was the only set of footsteps to echo through the hall for a time.

The silence was welcoming; it allowed her to still the unsteady feeling bubbling in the back of her mind. It did not last long. The loud shout from behind was most definitely Cheryl retaliating against the individual Veronica chose not to identify. While threatening, what little she heard did not seem like it would result in a fight, so she focused instead on returning to her bedchamber.

Water trickled down her body, falling from her chain mail in a tired *drip, drip*. It happened in tandem with her steps until what little remained clung to her tunic and stuck to her chest. Walking around in wet clothes was very uncomfortable.

She moved a little more briskly once she entered the girl's wing.

A few pages crossed her path now and then. Some of them attempted to grab her attention with a few friendly words. But Veronica just kept walking. She heard the malevolent jeers laced within them.

Her fellow pages only began speaking to her to taunt her.

Whatever they were saying, she did not know. She drowned out their japes so as not to lose focus of her chamber door.

When she was in the privacy of her own room, she drew her palm across her forehead and took a deep breath. It was a taxing effort shaking off the mean-spirited things they had said and done. She did what she could to see the best in people even when they behaved with hostility, but sometimes it was not enough.

Their words left an impact. *Witch... Freak...* And their pranks done out of spite were humorless. *Well, I suppose I'm not one to talk.*

A moment to recollect herself was all she needed. She removed her chainmail, then pulled off her tunic. The moisture spread along her clavicle had all been swept away with but a brush of the hand. Her breastband absorbed the moisture that bled through the tunic rather well, so there was no need to worry about that. All she had to take care of was the tunic itself.

Moving water over stone and skin was simple, but her power could not easily guide it once something, like cotton, had absorbed it. The best she could do was wait for it to evaporate. Waiting there until dinner sounded appealing, but she doubted her tunic would dry in time. And she did not feel like leaving to ask the servants for another change of clothes.

Pages were given a single change of clothes every day. A new uniform was given to them each morning, and the old one was always taken away during breakfast for cleaning. One of the many responsibilities they were given was taking care of their appearance, and punishments were dealt to those who constantly ruined the uniforms they were graciously provided. The Estrine family commanded respect, and having their pages look as presentable as possible attributed to that. Only when their attire was wrecked or dirtied from training were they given another change.

She doubted she would get anything—apart from a brief lecture—for moderately wet clothes.

Veronica tried imitating the maids when they attended to wet laundry and waved her tunic. Then she swatted it with her arm.

Her back was to the door when it opened again. Stepping inside was Cheryl, who quickly shut the door when she saw her friend without her top. Veronica stopped hitting her tunic when she noticed who entered. She greeted her roommate with a smile. "I'm sorry I left you back there."

Cheryl shook her head. "I get it. I wouldn't want to stay near that gutless toad either ... except maybe to wring his fat neck."

"Tell me—"

"I didn't, I didn't," Cheryl insisted.

A sigh of relief escaped the kind girl's lips. It would not have been the first time Cheryl assaulted another page for mistreating her friend, but Veronica always felt guilty whenever it happened. Every time she got in trouble for it, she thought it was her fault.

Cheryl pulled up the chair at the desk they shared and sat down facing the back of the chair, her arms resting atop its head. "You shouldn't put up with how they treat you."

This was a conversation they often had. It was what she said to her when they first met.

Veronica remembered that time well. It was her second year in the Estrine Chateau. She had been getting along well enough in her training and education, pushing herself to the limit, shaping herself into a proper warrior. But it was a lonely time for her.

She made many friends she thought would be with her until their next step toward knighthood. But they came to avoid her, treat her like she did not exist, and ultimately shun her. Even her roommate at the time made excuses to kick her out of their shared chamber.

She often went to the hidden pond behind the chateau to be alone. It was the closest thing she could find to remind her of home. She thought of the wharves of Harnola—its crystal ocean waters, the sturdy boats she used to sail on, the shimmering beaches, the gulls that tried to steal from the fishmongers, the manse where her family resided. She did not return home for the summer, having herself asked to remain in Brigadier, so that she could continue her search. She missed her family, all of her family.

Her tears trickled into the pond, sorrowful ripples forming in the murky water. She rather wished they had been tears made to flow from nostalgia instead of the pelting of mudballs she endured at the training grounds.

There she sat, alone and forlorn, until a tall girl walked through the bushes. The girl looked upon her with pity and said those same words she would come to repeat years later, then kneeled beside her to help clean off the mud.

When next she looked at the water, it was clearer than it had been earlier.

Veronica was grateful for Cheryl's kindness, looking after her like the sister she never had. She always looked back to that time with a smile.

"I know."

A smile from her always had a calming effect on Cheryl, but her response left her worried. This was a dance they had performed many times, and almost nothing changed afterwards. She always managed to retain her faith in others even after being harassed, and smiled and laughed as if those bad things never happened.

There was a time when Cheryl used to ask if she ever got mad at those who bullied her. She was never given a whole answer.

"How to put this..." Veronica would respond before trailing off into deep thought. It was not that she never got upset, rather that she was unsure how to express it. Thoughts tried to form beneath the deep pool in her mind when she focused on her tormentors. But they failed to emerge from the dark depths, remaining muddled and incomplete. She sometimes attempted to grasp whatever bubbled forth, but whatever she caught had dissolved before she could make sense of it.

She did not like being bullied. The names they called her were disgusting. The petty games they played were feckless, asinine, and often cruel. But she saw no point in imitating their behavior.

She could not make anyone like or respect her. And she could not make them stop treating her like she did not belong. All she could do was strive to become her best self—and hope others might do the same.

Knowing well her friend's thoughts on the matter, Cheryl did not push it further. Instead, she was just there for her. "What was that thing you always said?"

Facing her friend, Veronica graced her with a gentle smile. "We need to build each other up, not destroy one another."

Simple words though they were, they left a good impression on Cheryl, a big, goofy, amused smile on her face. "You're something else, Veronica."

~ Third Chapter ~
Reversal

The next morning was as bright and sunny as the last, and the routine was the same as ever. The servants rose early to ensure a smooth transition into the new day for everyone else. The guards continued to maintain the peace. And the pages made ready for the trials they would face.

Veronica performed her regular morning routine—she chose not to prank her roommate, for once—and attended her lessons, same as always. Yesterday's shenanigans behind her, she looked forward to what the new day would bring.

The etiquette lessons were as stimulating as ever. They usually had the pages focus on developing linguistics and social behavior. On occasion, though, Lady Deva was requested by her in-law, Lord Dragnal Estrine, the head of the Estrine family, to have her pages demonstrate what they learned. The request typically involved a gathering or a visit from a noble with important business. Whenever that happened, the pages served the guests instead of the hired help.

But none of that happened this time. Instead, Lord Estrine merely paid a visit to her lecture hall to evaluate their progress.

The procedure was simple. Each page needed only to approach Lord Estrine when called and respond to him accordingly. Keeping a straight spine and proper posture throughout was key to earning his good graces. When speaking, one must do so clearly, concisely, and with the utmost respect. Their answers were also to be quick and avoid creating unnecessary discord. And, as they were to be soldiers, it was vital that they move swiftly, but not lose their composure in rushing themselves.

A lot of pages felt queasy when their turn came to introduce themselves to the man who would ultimately decide whether they were fit to be squire to a knight.

One would look at Lord Estrine and think nothing impressive—in their first encounter. He was a petite, hirsute man barely as tall as the average-sized children, with a full face that often sported a jaunty grin. He resembled a kindly fishmonger Veronica once followed (uninvited) on a voyage. The man commanded respect, though, and it showed when he furrowed his brows and let out from the pit of his gut a shout of thunderous proportions.

He was much stricter, and therefore much louder, than usual. It was likely due to the nearing enactment. Leaders and teachers had many roles, including inspiring their juniors. Inspiration and motivation came in many forms.

Butterflies fluttered in Veronica's stomach, even when she walked away with his stern nod of approval and brash dismissal.

Others were not so fortunate. In every instance the proud lord found something unacceptable, he made his disapproval known, bellowing his loud, fervent disapproval that made their ears ring.

Compared to that, in addition to Lady Deva's heightened expectations due to her uncle's presence, the following tests on tactics and geography appeared tedious.

But while everyone else froze and choked up before Lord Estrine, Cheryl faced him with composure befitting a soldier. She stood firm against the storm that was his booming voice and answered his harsh criticisms with agreement and obedience.

And she still had the energy to train, rather fiercely, even after that.

Even when it came time to rest and enjoy a meal, Cheryl scarfed down her food with great vigor. A lot of pages ate quickly to keep their gruel down, but whenever she did it, it was to get back to business without further delay.

Veronica sat with her friend at their usual table, watching her shovel food into her mouth. "You have quite the appetite today," she commented.

Cheryl pulled away from her bowl for a moment, looking at her with an arched brow. "I do?"

It was humorous that she did not notice. When wandering in one's own world long enough, it could be easy to lose track of reality, even one's own actions.

"You are always so energetic after an evaluation."

Cheryl wiped the gruel from her under her lip. "No, I'm not."

"Oh? I must be imagining things then."

Veronica looked down to her food, but did not yet partake. She played with her gruel, stirring the dark broth into a little whirlpool with her spoon. She lifted her spoon only so her friend would stop staring at her, and stopped it just before bringing it to her lips when Cheryl went back to eating.

Then, seeing her chance, "Oh, Lord Estrine, sir! A pleasure."

Cheryl leaped to her feet when she heard the man's name, dropping the spoon that dangled from her lips, standing straight and proper. She looked around for him, then scowled at her friend when she realized he was never there.

Veronica relished in her startled reaction, laughing with abandon and kicking her legs under the table.

The flustered girl pinched the space between her brows. She blamed herself for believing it more than her impish friend for making the joke. "How do I keep falling for that?"

A giddy smile was Veronica's only answer.

Cheryl was an honest sort, always one to share her feelings about others. She lashed out at pages for improper behavior, and while minding her manners with her elders, she would later voice her complaints to Veronica, who always listened with rapt attention. But when it came to Lord Estrine, she had nothing but respect for him, even when he called out every fault, minuscule or imagined, and covered her face in spit.

Though she had her fun teasing her, Veronica understood why she looked up to him so.

It was Lord Estrime who admitted her into his family's training curriculum when she came to Brigadier. He introduced her to the role of knighthood, taught her how to wield a sword, and, throughout her stay, had been like a father to her.

It was no exaggeration to say he gave her hope again.

But that did not make her different from the other pages in the chateau. On the contrary, Lord Estrine was all the harder on her because he made her a page. He expected the most from her—that made her happy.

He knew she could be a great knight, and it made her want to surpass those expectations.

After their meal, Cheryl thought to return to the training grounds, but Veronica convinced her to instead go with her to the library. They had not gone yesterday due to a trivial inconvenience, so she reluctantly agreed.

The library resided in the third level of the chateau. Guarding it were two mighty doors of a fine redwood with depictions of a tall, heavenly willow tree masterfully crafted on each one. The doors slid open with a push of the branch-shaped handles, granting entry to a room as spacious as the vast banquet hall. The shelves were all organized to create straight paths that joined together. In those shelves were a myriad of books, organized by subject, then alphabetically. Most of the Estrine family's collection consisted of rewritten copies of war stories—some from the perspective of individual soldiers, some from the historians—as well as documents about important periods, people, and events. There were enough books to almost completely cover the walls of the grand space.

Cheryl ran toward the section of war stories to prepare for Lord Tamsilac's next lecture. Veronica, meanwhile, went to the center shelves, where awaited the books about famous places and foreign lands.

There was this one book she found the year prior that she was absolutely fascinated with. It contained a bounty of knowledge about countless places from all over the world. Every page held information so expressive that it felt like she was there when she read about it. She was especially fond of the section describing the southern seas of Saemior.

Veronica perused the shelves for the book, but sadly could not find it. It was rather odd. She had been checking the library every week for the past year and never managed to find it. Cheryl seemed vaguely interested in it when she showed her, even if she had never heard of it. None of the other pages she asked, or rather, those willing to answer, seemed to know about it either.

Unfortunate as it was, the book likely had been lost by someone who borrowed it. Such incidents were why the librarian no longer allowed books to be taken out of the library.

The silence carried her disappointed sigh along the rows of resting books before a raucous *crash* snuffed it out.

Alarmed, Veronica immediately rushed to where she heard the sound come from and came across a pile of books crumbled before one of the shelves. On the floor, lying on his back after falling, was the librarian himself. The middle-aged man attempted to get himself off the ground, stopping midway and rub his back.

Veronica kneeled beside the librarian with an outstretched hand. "Are you all right, sir?"

The librarian let out a sigh of relief that someone came to his aid. "Yes, yes. Not to worry. Nothing is broken." He took the girl's hand and was pulled off the ground, barely needing to move a muscle. "Oof... A strong one you are. Thank you, Veronica."

"What happened?"

"Oh, it's just an old shelf, my dear. Too much weight after too long and—well, this." The librarian gestured to the mess of books slid into a pile in front of the shelf in question. "Very unfortunate, really. Very unfortunate."

The librarian wasted no time in collecting the books. He had bent down and began gathering them into his left arm. The little slope along the collapsed shelf consisted of dozens of books. It would take him a great deal of time to finish.

"Let me help, please." Veronica had already crouched down to do so before an answer was given.

The librarian said nothing but looked her way with a kindly smile.

The books were endowed with hundreds of pages each, giving them a fair girth and heft, but Veronica and the librarian gathered them all into piles with little trouble.

She glanced over the title of each book, still eager to find the one she had been after for the past year. It was unlikely she would find it there, even if the sorters had mixed up a few. What they collected were majorly records of knights and noblemen and the exploits that made them famous. While they were fascinating reads, especially the one about the Ivanstronge family and their diplomatic work with Ederea, they only told about a few corners of the world.

There were many wonderful things about the world they lived in. Being a soldier of Vermalio, she would likely only get to experience them if she were sent to fight in a war. Having a book, a record of one's experience and knowledge, to read was a grand means of expanding the world as she knew it.

Veronica followed the librarian to his study at the front of the library. They placed the books atop the desk where he greeted the inhabitants of the chateau—and made sure they did not make off with any of his treasures. They continued going back and forth between shelves and the front desk, gathering every fallen book. On occasion, the librarian would stop to look over one of his books, inspecting it for damage. His gentle handling showed how much he cared about them.

The books soon piled up into a tall wall atop the front desk. Veronica looked up at them in awe, surprised at how high they stacked up.

"Thank you kindly, dear," said the librarian with a puff of breath after setting the last of the books down.

The page faced him with a delightful smile. "It's my pleasure, sir."

"What brings you to my humble library, if I may ask?"

"My friend and I are merely looking for a few reads."

The librarian offered a smile and nodded. "Anything in particular? Perhaps I may be of assistance in retrieving it."

Her face beamed with pure delight. "Actually, there is one I have been interested in for a time. It is a rather large book called Foreign Outlands."

His thick eyebrow arched, and he lifted his hand to drag his finger against the wiry stubble on his chin. "Foreign Outlands...? Hm, I do not believe I recognize that name."

The smile Veronica wore thinned. "Are you certain?"

"I believe I would recognize such a redundant name. Sorry, my dear."

It was disappointing, but nothing could be done about it.

"It is quite all right, sir."

"Perhaps there is something else I may help you find."

To that, Veronica shook her head. "No, thank you, sir. I enjoy taking the time to peruse your shelves."

She left the librarian with a cheerful smile on his face after he dismissed her, and went to find her friend.

It kept hitting her how peculiar it was that Foreign Outlands spontaneously vanished. Finding that the librarian knew nothing of it turned her mind in a few perplexing directions. His reaction was interesting. She might have been mistaken, but it almost seemed forced.

He must be embarrassed about losing it, the poor fellow.

Deciding to leave it at that, she focused on searching for Cheryl, curious to see what she found. She always found the most peculiar stories when they visited. It was one reason she loved coming with her so much.

The evening meal the next night was a lively one. Every member of the Estrine family was present in the banquet hall to dine with an honored guest of theirs.

A squadron of knights patrolling the region of Everspeak returned to Brigadier to rest and replenish their supplies. Their leader, an old friend of Lord Estrine, accepted the gracious offer to stay at the chateau during their respite. He sat at the grand table with the Estrine family, partaking in fine cuisine while the pages fed on gruel.

Many of the pages looked upon the family and their company. Some were salivating over the food they ate, aglow with jealousy; others were simply curious of the company. The knight put away venison and wine as if he had not seen such food for years. Beside him was a young man at least seventeen years of age, his squire.

The pages at Veronica's table quietly complained how unfair it was that the boy who came of age got to eat actual food. Someone suggested that was a benefit of being recognized, particularly by someone who knew the right people. And a few others thanked their lucky stars that their evaluations went well, otherwise they would likely be serving the Estrine family and their guests.

Veronica did not engage much in conversation, and often looked to her friend catering to their hosts.

Cheryl was not the most articulate, but she performed exceptionally well during her evaluation, even when being so callously chastised. And yet she was still made to serve at the Estrine family's table instead of being allowed to recuperate from the day's training. It was moments such as this that Veronica wondered how much he expected from her.

She pondered on that while those who shared her table socialized with one another.

The other pages spoke about many interesting things. They did not look directly at their bowls, hoping that would make the gruel taste less unappetizing. And they always looked past Veronica when they spoke to one another, never paying her any mind.

But it was no bother. When around a group of her peers, she could listen to the rumors they whispered among themselves. She often found out about phantoms roaming the city through said rumors.

Nothing they shared pertained to potential phantom activity, though.

It was but ordinary gossip—talk of which boy fancied which girl and vice versa, Sir Storn being a golem, anything they overhead from the servants about their masters' secret endeavors.

Fascinating as the topics were, gossip of such nature often did little more than hurt the reputation of others. Veronica did not care for it.

A loud *ka-clunk* disrupted the orderly atmosphere in the banquet hall. All eyes turned in the direction of the Estrine family's table. One of the pages serving them was on the floor.

Veronica stood and walked over to get a better look.

The Estrines were startled by their page's fall, but they did not rise to help him up. And the guest looked upon him with a look akin to disgust. The other servers teetered between moving to help and staying put on Lord Estrine's order.

If he were a servant or civilian, he would have instead barked at them for not acting sooner. But seeing as he was a page, the Estrines adhered to their rules and waited to see if he could help himself up. Pages, soldiers in training, were not to be coddled, especially not over minor injuries.

The boy worked his way on all fours before tumbling again, a hand clinging to his ankle.

Veronica stepped around the shattered glass and spill of wine to get to him. She leaned down with her hand held out to him, and recoiled when it was slapped away.

He did not want help, that much was clear, but it was also as clear that he could not support himself on that leg. Even the Estrine family recognized it. The eldest of their bunch, Lord Tamsilac, took his walking stick in hand and made his way to the stubborn page.

"Consarn it, boy! You can't do *everything* on your own." He brought the stick closer to his head and struck it firmly onto the ground. "Grab hold, now, and let's get that leg looked at."

Although not wanting to admit that he needed help, the page could not defy an order from an Estrine. He clung to the walking stick and climbed up it to stand again, relying on it to support his left side. Lord Tamsilac then hobbled off with him to the medical ward.

The Estrine family's guest sneered at the page as he exited. "Clumsy oaf," he called him.

There was no comment from the others at the table. They had often seen their pages ignore injures they incurred for the sake of their pride or to continue their training. It was irresponsible, but there was no need for them to say so; the shame the pages felt often did so in their place. Perhaps that was why they neglected to mention as much to their guest.

While she pitied the boy, Veronica focused on how she could help. She bent down to pick up the glass and save the servants some trouble when—

"Page Alivvrn."

She stood at attention when addressed by Lord Estrine. "Sir!"

"Since you are so eager to help, you will take his place."

"Yes, sir."

By command of Lord Estrine, she left the banquet hall only to return from the kitchen with another pitcher full of grape wine. The broken glass on the floor had been cleared away by one of the butlers, who was still there soaking up the spilled wine with a rag. She was careful not to get in his way as she walked to the visiting knight.

The guest flashed her a disturbing scowl, perhaps to have a little fun with her. Veronica had seen him do so with others at the beginning of the meal. He seemed dissatisfied when she did not so much as flinch while pouring the wine.

Whatever impression it left, he simply went back to drinking. "Make sure you keep my squire's mug full," he said upon coming up for air.

Veronica nodded and took a glance at the squire's mug. When noting it was still full, she walked over to the pages at attention along the table. She stood beside Cheryl and looked up at her, eliciting a goofy smile from her.

The pages who served the Estrine family worked well past the evening meal. When the tables had been cleared and cleaned, they were permitted to eat their dinner in the kitchen. The corner in the back of the room did not have much space for the pages or the chairs they sat in, but it was enough for them to rest.

And it certainly did not keep them from venting their grievances over the company they served. The knight, Sir Dels, was not as courteous or reserved as his hosts, or as restrained with his words and eating habits. He guzzled down quarts of wine until needing to be carried back to his room—a sight unbefitting of a gallant knight.

Everyone agreed that their least favorite part of the evening was getting sprayed on by the man's liquor-laced spit whenever they got too close. They doubted that he was trained to be a knight by the Estrines themselves.

Veronica had the pleasure of joining them since she could not finish her meal. It was enjoyable to be in their company and share in the conversation for a change. One of the girls even laughed when she tried not to sound too rude about how she described Sir Dels, thinking it part of a joke.

She was in good spirits by the time it came for them to get on with their night.

A few of the first-year pages were tired, so Veronica offered to clean their dishes for them. And while she was scrubbing them in a large basin, the others piled their dishes into the water, smiling and patting her on the shoulder making their escape. By the time she caught herself to say she could not do them all, they had already left.

Cheryl remained behind to help. She first offered to drag them back by their hair, but after being pled by Veronica not to, she instead settled for helping with the workload.

Veronica tried to convince her friend to let her handle it herself. Even though the dishes were not difficult to clean, the amount put upon her would keep her busy for some time. So, of course, Cheryl did not listen.

Gratitude fought guilt to remain in the center of Veronica's thoughts as fatigue came to etch itself over Cheryl's mien. She worked herself ragged to ensure the Estrine family's meal was exceptional and had pushed herself throughout the day.

When Cheryl's mind began to err, Veronica managed to persuade her to go back to their chamber and rest.

The lingering sunset dyed the horizon in a brilliant amber light by the time she finished cleaning. The halls were faintly lit in the late-day glow. It would be curfew soon.

Veronica walked leisurely through the quiet hall, humming a song that reminded her of home. It helped keep her in higher spirits after a long day of work. And accompanied with the majestic rays that preluded a calm twilight, the melody had a soothing effect that put her at ease.

Singing and humming were activities she enjoyed a great deal ever since she was small. She had not been doing either frequently since coming to the Estrine Chateau. Knights were expected to be the most upstanding people in the kingdom, the picture of strength and sophistication.

No one ever told stories of a knight who sang.

She found solace in the moments she was alone because they meant she could sing the songs she had while growing up. They were more vibrant than the weathered memories she strived to preserve.

She stopped just as the verse was about to reach its conclusion when she heard something that did not follow the melody. There was noise coming from down the nearby hall tucked away from the dwindling light. She took a few steps in that direction—there was a shout. Perhaps someone tripped and hurt themselves. Believing they needed help, she walked down the hall and into the shadows.

It was strange how an atmosphere changed when the light had been peeled away. There were moments when the darkness had a comforting effect, providing a gentle embrace, especially in a space familiar and comforting. With the glow of the moon and the glimmer of the stars, it was something serene.

But that was only when one had been given the impression of safety.

The shouting continued to echo through the hall, registering in Veronica's ears as a troubled cry. She heard another voice as she moved to hurry. This second voice was not as startled but clearly upset.

"—n't listen, do ya?"

Although she had gotten close enough to hear them clearly, there was not enough light to make out who was there. Her vision shifted to magic sight, allowing her to see their valsara, which revealed the movement of their bodies. The two were rather close to each other, to the point where their energy converged. The shorter one—a girl, Veronica assumed from the voice—was afraid. Her valsara flickered in the direction opposite of the one over her, rejecting their very presence. She wanted to get away, but could not. The valsara of the other flared maliciously. It laid bare an unsteady yet forceful mind filled with aggression, arrogance, and—

Veronica gasped as her vision returned to normal, her eyes adjusted to the darkness. The squire to Sir Dels was standing above a girl, a fellow page. He had her against the wall with her arms pinned over her, his other hand over her throat.

The squire cocked his head in Veronica's direction.

"What is this?" she asked in a shrill voice. She did not wait for an answer before moving in to pull his hands off of the page. "Unhand her this instant! This is unaccepta—"

The hand around the girl's neck let go only to grab Veronica by the collar. He brought her closer and spat when he spoke. "Stay outta this!" His breath rolled over her heavily with the scent of liquor. It threw her off balance as he shoved her away.

Veronica caught herself in the stagger and rushed back up to the squire. "I will not. You cannot treat people like this."

The squire hurled his fist at Veronica, barely missing as she brushed it aside with her forearm. She did not want to get violent; he was not in his right mind. Even so, she could not let him do something so vile to her. She repulsed his punches as they came and taunted him with rough jabs to the chin until his focus drifted, the passive hand letting his captive go to grab Veronica by the ponytail. He only noticed what he did when his first target shoved him from behind.

He fell on Veronica, crushing her under his weight. When he tried to get up, the other page wrapped her arm around his neck. He gagged and spat on Veronica some more, but managed to fight back and stand.

He then ran backward to smash the page against the wall.

The page fell to the ground and held the back of her head as the addled squire hobbled back to her. He smacked her face, then grabbed her chin to make her look up at him. "Thought I'd have some fun, but now I'm gonna make it hurt."

Veronica had her eyes on what was happening as she struggled to regain her focus. He was supposed to be a young man, an exceptional youth learning the ways of knighthood. But what she saw was a grabby boy treating the girl in his claws like a doll.

Was that supposed to be the visage of chivalry? It was vile. It was wrong. It was *sickening*.

Veronica pulled her mind out of the mire and picked her body off the floor, arms shaking, fists closed tight. A fierce emotion overtook her, bringing her back to the squire in a hostile rush. She wrenched his hand away from the page's neck, then rammed her fist into his jaw, knocking him on his backward, with an angry snarl.

The brute groaned as he struggled to get back up. He glared at Veronica almost as aggressively as she had at him. "You got a lotta nerve, wench!" He closed in, ready to throttle her, but before he could, Veronica grabbed hold of his wrist again.

He then crumbled back onto his knees, spasming, squealing pitifully. There was barely any more force applied to his wrist than when she pulled him off of the girl, and yet what she was doing now left him tortured by pain.

"I bet you didn't know your body is mostly made of water," Veronica taunted the brute. "And I can control water!"

He looked up at her with such fright that she doubted the drink had much effect left on his sick mind.

There were many things Veronica's power allowed her to do. Manipulating water, controlling its flow, making it move and take the shapes desired were simple feats for her. Water was, indeed, what the human body was mostly made of, but it was molded into a solid mass; she could not move it as she wished. But at some point, she learned that when she made direct contact with someone's bare skin, she could use the water in them to twist and wring their muscles from the inside.

The more he struggled against it, the worse the pain became, as he quickly realized.

"Listen and listen well. I don't like pigs like you. We're not here to amuse you, and you don't get to treat us however you want. The girls here are to be left alone. If I catch you like this again—" She paused to have her power make knots of his muscles, and watched him as he writhed in agony. "—I'll pull your arse out of your throat."

When she believed the message got through, she released him, leaving the sniveling mess curled up on the ground.

The page she rescued watched the entire thing, something Veronica realized when she turned back her way. They locked eyes for a moment, at which the girl winced.

Feeling affronted, Veronica clicked her tongue and walked away.

The girl would gain some distance before the brute got up. The pain inflicted by Veronica's power lingered even after she let go, and most of her focus was on his arms and legs. They would be stunned for a while. By the time he recovered, he would alone.

There were a number of times when Veronica lost her temper and used her power on people like that, twisted their muscles until they could not even stand. There was never lasting damage. Water in the muscles was too solid for her to rend them. At most, it taught others not to mess with her.

Like that girl. She recognized her. She had seen her use that power on someone before.

After going so far down the hall, Veronica's pace began to slow. Her eyes fluttered and her head swayed. When she was stable again, she turned this way and that, looking very confused.

Huh? ...What am I doing here?

She had lost her train of thought. There was sunlight, dim as it was, peering through the windows not too long ago. The windows were not there either. The halls looked different.

Her hand moved to caress her scalp and nurse the headache she only now realized she had. Then the other rubbed her elbow, feeling a little sore.

"I must be more tired than I thought. Best to get back to my chamber." She rubbed her hand until she started walking down the hall again. "Cheryl must already be asleep, the poor thing," she said with a giggle. "I should be quiet so I don't wake her."

~ Fourth Chapter ~

Unease

The pages behaved more aggressively the following day. They called Veronica out while she was sparring with Cheryl, claiming something about needing a handicap and not fighting honorably. While she did not understand what they were referring to, it was nonetheless a smear on her honor. And a knight would not stand for such disrespect.

She gladly obliged in challenging them to prove them wrong.

Each page went a round against her, but they did not have much time to act. Veronica remained steady when they performed the courtesy of crossing swords, then struck quickly when the round started. The first page caught unawares wound up with her blunt blade jabbed into his chest before realizing she was there. Those that came after were confident they could outmaneuver her. They moved quickly and with purpose, but Veronica always nimbly evaded their attacks before they could connect and countered.

She noticed her opponents' swings were guided by a striking hostility. It made predicting their movements easier, though their malignant valsara made her jumpy.

Her skill did nothing to deter them. They kept going, one after another, believing one of them could wear her out and swat her down. But soon, they ran out of challengers. They had enough.

Losing a sparring match was something everyone could come back from; were it not so, the Estrines would give them lectures on humility and admitting defeat. When they lost to Veronica, though, they would not seek a rematch so soon.

The hostility in their valsara told her everything they would not. They would not be satisfied with finding a way to best her fluid swordplay. They wanted to crush her, humiliate her, make her wish she never learned to swing a sword.

It was not simple jealousy, but not quite spite either.

And she confirmed as much shortly after beating her last opponent.

He picked himself out of the dirt, grunting, with shoulders rising and falling from ragged breath and hands balled into tight fists. He seemed hostile enough to charge at her once more. But while the temptation was visible in his eyes, hesitation repressed it, which only further stoked his fury.

"Bunch of tricks—that's all it is," the page groused. "That's the only way you can beat anyone."

It was the same puerile insult her adversaries always used. There was more to it, though, when he made mention of someone whose name evaded her.

"What are you saying?"

"Quit the innocent act, witch! Every page in the chateau knows what you did."

As he went on, his words began to pass her by, overshadowed by a vague sense of déjà vu sweeping over her. It was from that feeling alone that she realized what this was about.

Upon seeing the girl's eyes widen in disbelief, the page assumed he was getting to her and started to make low blows. She lowered her gaze, appearing daunted and submissive, but not from whatever he had said.

The anger emanating from him, it made her feel like she was under attack. Or rather, that he was retaliating.

When she finally understood what was happening, she heard the rabid page finish by saying, "You don't deserve to be a knight!"

Cheryl had enough of standing on the sidelines and letting him torment her friend. She took her practice sword firmly in hand and threatened to beat the insolent page into paste. She likely would have had he not run away with his tail between his legs.

The other pages watching scattered when Cheryl swung her sword their way. The knights overseeing them did not get involved but remained on watch in case they needed to intervene.

After letting out a few haggard breaths, she turned back to her sulking friend. "What gives, Veronica? Why didn't you do anything?" She was still rather huffy and looked at her as her brothers used to when disappointed in her. "You can't keep letting these arses walk all over you like that. Stand up to them! Say something back!"

"It happened again..."

"Huh?"

"It happened again, Cheryl."

It did not take long for her to figure out what she meant.

As kind and tolerant as she was, Veronica was not without anger. There were instances, rare though they were, where she could not look at someone and think the best of them. A frightful rage overtook her when that happened, clouding her mind and guiding her hands. The most frightening thing was that every time it happened, whenever she lashed out at others, she never remembered what occurred afterwards.

Cheryl had seen that side of Veronica several times before—enough to know that part of her was the opposite of the gentle, altruistic girl she called her friend.

It frightened Veronica every time she realized she had undergone this reversal. It was as though a piece of her time was lost, brief and unnoticed though it first was, only for it to be forced upon her by the reminders of angry pages. And the things said alarmed her beyond belief. She preferred solving issues peacefully if at all possible. To lose her composure and assault someone made her loathe herself.

Cheryl glanced aside and tried to think of what to say. "He mentioned that knight's squire. Did he do something?"

"I don't know. I can't remember."

"It had to have been bad, though."

It was uncharacteristic of Cheryl to worry about saying just the right thing. She only did so when her friend was deeply troubled. Rather than fret over it, though, she cupped Veronica's shoulder and spoke from the heart. "Look, I don't know what happened, but I know you, and you don't do anything to anyone without a reason. I don't care about that squire. I'm on your side, no matter what. Got it?"

Veronica lifted her head to look Cheryl in the eye. She was always so sure of herself. No hesitation. No uncertainty. It was comforting to know that was included in her encouragement as well. "Thank you."

A warm grin spread over Cheryl's face. "Thank nothing. Come on, let's spar some more."

The two continued to practice their swordplay together until their muscles were on fire, and then some. Fighting through the fatigue was strenuous yet exhilarating. They relished in knowing they could keep going even when their bodies shook and their breath burned their throats.

They stopped only when their legs gave out. They took some time to let the midday air cool their bodies, then got off the ground to get some water.

The day was rather brutal. After the pages came at Veronica with their harsh slander, the knights gave her task upon task upon task to complete, promptly. Shining swords, polishing armor, scrubbing floors, delivering messages—she did it all while more was piled onto her.

The knights did not really believe anything in the pages' accusations. They put all of their pages to work whenever they saw the opportunity. Allegations of misconduct and actual misconduct were often all the same to them when all there was to go by were words, although if it sounded more like bellyaching than anything, the accusers were put to work instead. It depended on the knight making the order and the page following it.

In Veronica's case, they relied on her good nature to help them with menial tasks, and had more opportunities than usual because of the constant accusations.

Pages were but soldiers, and thus had to follow the instructions of their superiors without question. Failure to do so resulted in disciplinary duties or remedial lessons. So Veronica completed her tasks dutifully and to the best of her abilities.

There were times when another page would cross her path, often to impede with her given task. Some found it funny to kick over her water bucket when she scrubbed the floors. When she organized equipment in the storerooms, those attending to disciplinary work either pretended to trip over them or blatantly knocked them to the ground.

She was not oblivious. She knew they went out of their way to get in hers. But Veronica did not dwell on it.

She always picked up the bucket and fetched more water, not bothering to rely on her power to clean the spill. She only mentioned what a shame it was that the equipment fell over before putting it all back.

When apologies were made, genuine or otherwise, she assured them there was nothing to worry about before getting to work. Otherwise, she refused to dignify the snide remarks made at her expense with a response. Encouragement would only feed their egos. And since they would not stop, she refused to encourage them.

The Estrine knights who caught them in the act, on the other hand, did not think twice about engaging them. They gave the culprits a firm swat to the head before reprimanding them. "Setbacks hurt more than just the one who has to clean up after," they said before making them set things right. Veronica still helped them when it happened despite their intentions. It got rid of the mess faster, allowing them to continue their business.

After a while, a few knights asked her to give them some exercise.

The knights typically ordered pages to spar with them when they wanted to test their stamina. The trained militants had more strength, skill, and finesse than the children who strived to reach their level. A fight between them was but playtime for the knights.

Facing a single knight would be all it took to tucker most pages out. Four had their turns with Veronica, who kept on her toes in every round. She was as capable of reading them as she had the pages, moving quickly and fluidly to counter them. But her opponents had well-trained reflexes and were just as ready to meet her attacks. She handled herself well, though matching them was still hardly a simple feat.

She had little energy left when the evening meal came along. It took some effort merely to lift her spoon. When she noted as much, Veronica could not help let out a dry laugh. She grew accustomed to being worn out from a day's work to the point it went unnoticed. It had been some time since she complained about fatigue.

Upon finishing her meal, she immediately returned to her bedchamber. She stood at her door for a few seconds after unlocking it, staring blankly into space. She went under one moment, and upon coming to, she stepped inside, drew the door closed, not bothering to relock it, and let her hand slip from the handle as she stumbled over to her bed. The moment she was close enough, she flopped into the blankets with her face in the pillow.

It felt nice to lie there, in the comfort of darkness and silence, and not have to worry about anything else for the day. She could have fallen asleep right there had she forgotten she was still in her uniform.

Just a few moments, she told herself, unwilling to move yet.

She rested a few minutes more until she felt she was no longer alone.

Veronica scarcely lifted her eyes open enough to see any light that crept in from the hall. A turn of the head let her see that the door remained closed. No one had entered. She thought she was imagining things for a moment, but as her mind continued to work, she realized what this presence she felt was.

She switched to magic sight and took a look around, finding the phantom Rubi sitting casually on Cheryl's bed.

"Rough day, huh?"

Veronica smiled upon seeing her phantom friend and groggily lifted herself up to sit. "It was certainly more eventful than usual."

"I bet." Rubi looked perfectly relaxed, but the air about her seemed oddly tense. "It would probably have been less so if you fought off those oafs."

Veronica blinked. "You were watching me?"

"How could I not?" she stated while shaking her head. "Hard to look away from someone who won't stand up for herself."

She was tired enough to forget that was what the phantom told her the last time this happened. Whenever she was present when someone teased her, interfered with her duties, or outright attacked her, Rubi would appear and reproach Veronica for not responding in a manner more befitting her roommate.

Veronica could not help laugh whenever she said such things.

The smile budding on her face, her cheeks all rosy, brought Rubi to scowl. "Don't say it."

They went through this pattern a few times now.

It was clear what Rubi tried to do: rile her up enough for her to lash out at the phantom, which would hopefully inspire her to do the same with those who wished her ill. She never allowed Veronica to help her with her problems, and yet Rubi chose to pry into her life often.

"It's because you're so hopeless," she always retorted.

She liked to act tough, but Rubi was very nice. As unfortunate as it was that they did not meet when she was alive, Veronica was glad to have gotten to know her now.

Veronica lay back on her bed and stared at the ceiling. "I'm not like that, you know."

"Yeah, I know. You don't care what people say or do; you still want to help instead of hurt."

Veronica nodded. "Yes."

"It's fair game if they target you, though."

"That's of no concern to me."

Predictable as their back and forth had become, they still tried to push their points across to the other. Rubi spoke her piece irritably, and Veronica remained patient and listened to the phantom's argument before giving her rebuttal. Both wanted the other to see from their perspective and thought of the other's as harmful.

"I defend myself when they try to lay a hand on me."

"Yeah, but not from their insults."

"Words are mere breaths. They cannot harm me."

"That's not what I saw out there. It looked like they hurt you pretty badly."

Sometimes, they would stump each other and be unsure of how to respond. It was irksome, but they would not get anywhere if they became angry and let the argument get out of hand. They both wanted to make progress.

"...I was distraught, true, but it wasn't really from what they said."

"You were doing fine until they came along. Whatever it was, you could have stopped it. And you didn't."

Maybe that was true. Instead of recoiling before the pages who slandered her and giving them what they wanted, she could have defended herself. But without the memory of the moment in question, whatever she said would not have sounded convincing, even if they were willing to listen.

The reality of her situation was simple: they did not like her, they did not trust her, and they did not want her there.

When did it all start again? She did not know anymore. Perhaps it was because of her power; no other child brandishing magic had the control that she did. Perhaps it was because she had been caught talking to herself before; the phenomena caused by phantoms and her conversing with them could easily be linked together, and cast suspicion on her.

Her reversals were a likely cause. They have been occurring since she came to the chateau.

Whatever the reason, it mattered not. She reached for knighthood to help people. As a soldier, that help would likely lead to the opposition of another, someone after a desired end that harmed the ones she would help. Surmounting the efforts of the pages siding against her was but the first trial she faced to prove her valiance.

She already made up her mind to be a knight. Nothing was going to keep her from that, not even the wishes of others.

"I have to focus on my training. There is no point getting worked up over their silly games. If they want to play them, I cannot stop them. But I cannot afford to play along, nor do I want to."

The silence that lingered in wait for a response went on, this time for Rubi. Veronica expected further argument regarding how she did not wish to engage in uncouth behavior, rather than what she said instead.

"So that's how it really is," Rubi said with a slight laugh. She stood from the bed and stepped over to the window, her eyes on the moon brushing up from the horizon. "I guess I get it. We came here for a reason, after all."

Veronica picked her head up and held it up with her hands. "What was your reason?"

Rubi shook her head. "Still don't know."

It was to be expected. Had Rubi uncovered anything about herself, she would not have been as aloof as she was. Veronica vividly remembered the vigor she showed when she remembered her own name—the delight in her laughter, the way she leaped about and cheered herself.

It always brought her joy to know a lost soul had taken a step toward the peace they sought.

But to hear she still had no luck, Veronica wished she had not asked. She felt guilty about reminding her. Being teased by her was preferable to seeing her despondent. For as much as she tried to act fine, completely concealing angst and dread was impossible for a phantom. How the flickering embers wavered around her visage revealed enough to Veronica to see how she felt.

Before she could apologize, a faint creek hit her ears. The door opened for Cheryl, who crept inside slowly. She looked to the bed her friend lay in and smiled when their eyes met.

"Still awake, huh?" She closed the door behind her and pulled off her chain mail. "I thought you would have fallen asleep by now."

Her friend's entrance reminded her that she had yet to get out of her uniform either. The metal rings of her mail dug into her back until she sat up. She mimicked her friend's movement and slipped out of her the mail.

"Do I really look so tired?"

"More than you have in a while. Did the knights give you a rough time?"

"No more so than they normally do."

"Sorry I couldn't help you out. Lord Estrine needed me to take something to the palace."

That response almost pulled Veronica entirely out of the mist of fatigue permeating her mind.

"To the palace? Really?"

Tasks given by the Estrine knights were typically within the chateau. If the pages ever left the facility to follow orders, they seldom went too far into the city. The fact that Lord Estrine ordered her to do something made Veronica even more curious.

Cheryl looked to her with a broad grin. "Yeah. He had some message for the captain of the guard, needed me to take it to him."

"Wow, that's amazing. What was it like there?"

"About as classy as it is here, but there is a lot more space and fancy décor, and knights in white armor patrolling the whole place!" Cheryl plopped onto her bed. Her earlier excitement still flickered in her eyes. "I always wanted a look at the place, ever since I came to Brigadier."

Many shared that sentiment. The royal palace was the very center of the kingdom, the heart of Vermalio. Authorities gathered from across the country to pay respects to the king and queen and ask for their favor. Being allowed into the palace was an acknowledgment of one's power and renown.

Everyone in the capital looked to the royal palace at one point in their lives wanting to know what went on within. Many even went to the cathedral just to find the best view of the palace.

Pages were rarely, if ever, permitted to go to the palace. It was little wonder Cheryl leaped at the opportunity when summoned by Lord Estrine, especially since she had her first chance taken away for getting in a fight beforehand.

The chance was given to Veronica when she arrived in Brigadier five years ago, but she declined to go. She did not want to go there for another apology and best wishes from the royal family. The day she first entered the royal palace, she decided, would be to accept her knight's shield.

"Lord Estrine must really trust you."

Cheryl glanced up at her friend as she was pulling off her boots. "You think?"

"The Estrine Chateau cooperates with the royal palace to ensure Brigadier is safe and prosperous. Lord Estrine must send messages to the palace periodically. It's a very important task, and he asked you to do it."

She looked about ready to offer a modest rebuttal, but caught herself and gave the matter some thought. Information was a valuable asset, something she learned early in her training. And Lord Estrine put that asset in Cheryl's hands for her to deliver.

The already wide smile on Cheryl's face spread further until stressing her cheeks, turning them a giddy red. "You know what this means, right?"

"A good word from him."

"Heck yeah! Next time a knight comes looking for a squire, he'll mention me. I'll be on my way to knighthood and all the closer to finally getting my chance at those dastards!"

Veronica nodded. "You'll have knights fighting over who gets to take you with them."

"Oh, this is great! But I can't slack off now. I need to train even harder to make sure he's watching me." Cheryl put the boot she slipped off back on and went to the door.

"Cheryl, remember curfew?"

"Huh?"

She had gotten so excited that she forgot the time. The first ring of the evening bell repeated the reminder in place of Veronica.

"Ah, right." She chuckled awkwardly. Instead of relaxing again, she walked to the dresser to take the pitcher in hand. "I'll just get some water then. You rest up. Be back in a minute."

And she was out the door again.

The smile on Veronica's face remained even after she left. Her fatigue did not drag her down as much anymore after being exposed to such pure delight. She turned to the window and found herself alone, the phantom also having taken her leave. Feeling the need to take Cheryl's advice, she readied to turn in for the night.

Everyone had been very busy the following week. All was well in Brigadier until people began falling ill from a terrible sickness. It spread fast, consuming the entire city in less than a day. For some, the symptoms were meager, a light coughing and sudden cold flashes. But others suffered high fevers, delirium, and muscle weakness that left them bedridden.

Numerous people in the Estrine Chateau became infected as well. Pages, servants, and instructors alike were ailing and unable to care for themselves.

It was common for illnesses to form and spread around the transition from winter to spring. The nobles had stockpiles of potions and remedies stored away in anticipation of this frail time of year. But the medicine did little more than comfort the ill this year, treating the symptoms without remotely affecting the disease.

It was easy to see how many had fallen ill simply by looking at those passing by. Few people roamed the halls of the chateau. Manpower became scarce, so the pages ceased their training regimen to compensate.

Veronica helped however she could. For a time, she had been in the kitchen preparing ingredients for the soup made for the ill. Afterwards, she loaded coaches with boxes of potions, the drivers tasked with distributing them to the infected. At the end of each day, she reported to Lady Abeel the current stock of supplies she and the servants needed to make more medicine.

When allowed to rest, she returned to the kitchen, where the servants prepared and provided hot tea for the pages who worked so hard. Most of them found it too bitter to keep down, but they steeled themselves and begrudgingly swallowed. The maid who prepared it was perfectly clear that it was not an invitation, but an order, to drink. Keeping them healthy was as important as caring for those who already fell ill. There would only be more work, and fewer to attend to it all, otherwise.

Veronica nursed her tea in a corner away from the others. Many pages were still agitated with her after her latest reversal. Hostility seethed from them the moment they laid eyes on her; it made her skin crawl. They would not cause her any trouble, not with other people still about, diligently working.

It was a little lonely without her friend to accompany her.

While she wondered how Cheryl was feeling, someone decided to approach her. Veronica noticed their valsara, which was unusually tame, before looking up, and was surprised by who it belonged to. It was Sashan.

Veronica's breath caught in her throat before she could offer her a greeting. They just stood there staring at one another, Sashan more coldly, Veronica with unease, until Veronica faked a cough. "Good day, Sashan."

The fellow page did not return the greeting. Uncertainty reflected in her eyes as she stared at her. It looked like she wanted to speak but could not quite find the words. She did make up her mind about something, though. Her hand drew up to the cup in Veronica's hands, and she held it steady to refill it with the kettle she had in hand.

It would not be a lie to say she was surprised by the kind gesture, not after she had been so curt to her previously. But Veronica would not reject the offer. She took back her cup and brought it to her lips for a drink. She looked back to Sashan for a moment, expecting something from her, but returned her attention to the tea washing down her throat and slowly warming her body.

Veronica kept sipping until the bitterness became too much. She knew what she had to say, but there was hesitation again to form the words. It would have been rude not to, so she gave herself a little push before letting it out. "Thank you."

It took a moment before Sashan gave her response. "Yeah. Sure." Her words were dry, partially empty, but came out easily. "Wouldn't want you getting sick."

That was never a concern for Veronica. She never remembered a moment in her life when she had fallen ill from anything. The only time she so much as sniffled was when her nose became irritated by cold weather.

But Sashan did not know that. And that she concerned herself with her at all completely stunned Veronica. She barely gave her the time of day whenever they passed each other by. When last they really spoke, Sashan was foaming at the mouth and warned Veronica to stay away from her. She remained civil for the sake of decorum but exuded an undeniable aggression regardless.

"You ... care if I get sick?" Veronica could not help inquiring.

"It's not—" Sashan paused, her thoughts in a gentle frenzy. She groaned, stifling herself, then took a deep breath and looked back to Veronica upon exhaling. "Listen, I just wanted to thank you."

"Thank me?"

She did not want to elaborate, but she relented. "You really helped me before, when that boy threw himself at me."

"What boy?"

"I'm trying to be nice—don't be coy!" Sashan shook her head, again stifling herself for the hostility, and cleared her throat. "I'll not be calling that squire a man. He doesn't deserve the courtesy."

Mention of a squire, given the recent aggression from the other pages, undoubtedly meant the one serving Sir Dels. Veronica blinked, again surprised. No one mentioned there was anyone else there when it happened. Did they not know as much as they led on?

That was not what concerned Veronica. "Did he hurt you?"

"Just a few bruises, luckily. He had some muscle on him. It was hard to get out of his grip. It would have been worse if you hadn't come along."

Veronica was speechless, but not because she saw her during the reversal. She said she helped her. No one ever once expressed that when they angrily reminded her of something she did not realize she did. It was shocking but also a relief to know. It meant Cheryl was right. Something did trigger the reversal, and it involved Sashan's strife.

Whatever she did, it helped the girl who kept her distance from her, enough for her to approach and express her gratitude.

"I am glad you are okay."

"Thank you." That, she said genuinely. A gentle kindness began to emanate from her, and it washed over Veronica. She looked friendlier, more open.

"So ... you lashed out at him for what he did. Did Marc offend you somehow?"

Veronica withheld from answering immediately. There were a number of times she had undergone a reversal and caused a disturbance. She heard many names and unsavory accusations—mainly the use of her power.

But she did not recall that name.

"Marc...?" she hesitantly repeated.

Sashan blinking and arching her eyebrow made Veronica feel a lump in her throat. "Marc. The boy you paralyzed with your magic." Her words were less than courteous. And when they did not invoke a favorable response, Sashan looked to Veronica with an unfriendly gaze. "The one you shoved into the dirt and kicked like a dog." Her voice grew sharper the longer she remained silent. "Are you seriously saying you forgot what you did to him!?"

Telling the truth was always something she believed to be right, but looking at Sashan as she was, Veronica knew honesty would not leave a good effect on her.

"I can't believe you forgot what you did. Are you *that* heartless? You don't feel a shred of guilt for what you did?"

"It's not that—"

The kettle in Sashan's hand trembled. Deciding she did not want to hear any more, she flicked open the lid and hurled the tea at her. Veronica winced and held her hands up, her power invoked on reflex and causing the heated water to part at her sides, nary a drop touching her.

A shriek was heard from behind.

Sashan tensed up and dropped the kettle when she realized what happened. When Veronica turned around, she saw that half of the tea had soaked a maid. She covered her gasping mouth with both hands, horrified at what she had done.

Fortunately, the tea was only lukewarm. The maid looked down at her dress aghast, a massive wet mark forming over her midriff and down her belly. Livid, she went up to Sashan and seized her by the wrist.

"Come with me, young lady!"

Veronica got in front of the maid before she could take a step. "Wait, please! It wasn't her fault."

"I don't care why she threw it, and I don't care why you were arguing. You both can discuss this with Lord Estrine."

Arguing with her any further would get them both in more trouble. Rather than waste her time and patience, Veronica followed her while Sashan was dragged like a misbehaving child.

~ Fifth Chapter ~
Empathy

Veronica and Sashan waited in silence outside of Lord Estrine's quarters, as instructed by the maid. They stood at attention so they would appear presentable for their superior when he returned.

It was difficult to stand beside Sashan when Veronica could feel the tangible hostility she exuded. It tempted her to take a step away, but Veronica did not move. She was told to remain exactly where she was, and, more importantly, if she did move, it would only anger Sashan.

If she wanted to be a knight, she had to appear resolute, undeterred by others. While she could not force her countenance to appear indifferent, she could be patient and endure the rage that made her skin crawl.

They were not made to wait long. Lord Estrine walked down the hall with a guard in tow, relaying instructions to him as he returned to his quarters. When the guard went on his way, Lord Estrine looked to the pages with a less than pleased expression. "So you two are the ones causing mischief." He took out a key to unlock his doors, then opened the way for them.

The girls followed Lord Estrine inside without a word and stood before his desk as he dropped the documents in his arm over it. He sat down and began writing on a piece of parchment.

"I am sure I do not need to remind you two that we are in a strenuous situation. So explain to me why you are taking up my time instead of aiding the servants or the ill."

Sashan left no chance for Veronica to speak first. "I did not wish to cause trouble, milord. I did not intend to harm the maid. But I cannot tolerate Page Alivvrn any longer. This girl is a scoundrel."

Veronica did not say anything in response. She just looked down in shame when Lord Estrine looked her way. He expressed bewilderment, not quite sure what to take away from what he heard.

"She attacked my friend in broad daylight some time ago and had the gall to claim that she did not."

"I did not say that—"

"She has done this for years now, beating her peers and then acting like it never happened. Dozens of other pages have seen her do it before, and whenever it is brought up to the knights, no one believes them. 'That page? Nonsense,' they say. 'She's much too gentle.' But she's not. She is nothing but trouble."

Veronica offered nothing in response to the accusation. She would admit to not remembering whether she attacked someone or not, but she did not believe that it never happened. The anger that the pages exhibited, it was not just frustration born from envy or spite. It was genuine, tinged with alarm and fear, just as Sashan's was.

The gaps in her memory frightened her, and that unease showed in her troubled gaze. She tried to keep her eyes locked with Lord Estrine so as not to show disrespect. It made her look pitiable.

The nobleman looked at her with heavy eyes and furrowed brows as he weighed the information. He then turned to the furious Sashan. "And when did this beating take place?"

"A ... a few ... months ago, milord."

"A few months ago. And I am hearing of this now?"

That harsh tone, the one that was usually followed by a frightful bellowing, made Sashan flinch.

Lord Estrine let out a tired snort, then faced Veronica again. "Page Alivvrn, is this true? Did you assault her friend?"

Veronica's throat closed. She did not know what to say. The honorable duke's voice growing heavier let her know that his patience was at an end. He was in no mood for distractions. Sashan expected her to admit to her actions, and Lord Estrine demanded the truth from them. But she could only give one answer.

"I am truly sorry, but ... I do not remember that happening."

While she did not wish to upset Sashan, Veronica had to answer Lord Estrine promptly and truthfully.

"I understand that I have upset Sashan, sir, and I would like to understand how. But I truly do not know of what is she saying."

It would have been more appropriate for Veronica to face Sashan and say her piece to her directly. If she thought that it would not have shown disrespect to Lord Estrine, she would have done so.

He did not appear any less agitated after hearing her side. The quill in his hand kept moving when his eyes drew away from them for a moment, quickly finishing a document. "Page Alivvrn, return to your duties. I will speak to Page Passeri alone."

Sashan looked back to Lord Estrine, aghast and humiliated. This was likely the outcome she expected, having known of the times others have spoken out against Veronica, but that did not stifle her frustration.

"Lord Estrine, if I—"

"You may not! I have enough to fret over without impudent children causing disturbances in my home and harming my help."

"Sashan did not scald the maid, sir!"

Both Sashan and their superior looked to Veronica when she spoke up, perturbed for reasons their own.

"It was me. I parted the tea with my power and splashed it on the poor women by mistake. It was my fault." She chose to omit the part when Sashan threw the tea so focus would not be brought back to her.

That did not sway Lord Estrine. "Then you can take over her duties for the remainder of the day. Now leave!"

Nothing would be gained if she continued to press the matter further. Lord Estrine had made up his mind. It would only change for the worse unless his orders were followed.

Understanding that, she clenched her fist over her heart to salute him and went on her way. As she left, she could feel Sashan's valsara flare vehemently, her anger yet growing.

Upon stepping outside and closing the doors, Veronica slumped against them. Her situation went from bad to worse. All she wanted was to set things right with Sashan. And as they kept meeting, she began to wonder if that was possible.

She did not know what to say, what to do, but she could not leave the matter like this. Sashan was upset and hurt by her actions; whether she remembered doing them or not was irrelevant.

How could she approach this? After what happened, if she were to try speaking to her again, Sashan would reject whatever she might say.

Remaining there only conflicted her, so Veronica stood straight and returned to her duties.

The servants were still hard at work when she returned to the kitchen. There was too much for them to focus on to pay her any mind. Veronica reported to the head maid and explained she was back to help. Too busy toiling over the large pot of soup she was making, she brushed the girl off with the instruction, "Go help restock the larder."

She dutifully performed the task given to her, all the while passing ingredients the cooks needed to them as they came. The men were very appreciative of her help, and expressed that generously when they asked her to deliver the finished soup to the quarantined pages.

Even with the other servants helping her, she still had dozens of bowls to deliver. Most of the ill were moved to different bedchambers so they would not infect the healthy. She carried two or three bowls on a tray at a time. Balancing them without spilling anything took some effort, as the bowls were filled to the brim. But it became easier with each delivery.

She brought the bowls to the pages, wished them well, and left to continue her task.

She felt terribly for the ill, even the ones who bullied her. They were weak, suffering, afraid of what was going to happen to them. If there was more she could do to help them, she would have. But she did not understand what made them so unwell, and she did not know any magic that could ease their pain.

When finished with her task, she took one last bowl with her back to her bedchamber. It was not for her. She would eat with the other healthy children later.

It was not easy convincing the servants to let Cheryl remain in their bedchamber after she showed symptoms. But Veronica did not want to be separated from her. She wanted to be the one to nurse her friend back to health. A selfish whim, perhaps, childish even. But if she could, she had to do it.

It would have tormented her not doing anything when she needed it.

This late in the day, the halls were completely empty. Pages well and ill were resting uneasily in their bedchambers. Those still awake were troubled by anxious thoughts breeding uncertainty. It was strong enough for Veronica to feel it in the air, even without consciously using her magic senses. The hard day's work was nothing like training, but it tired them enough to drift off to sleep before long.

It impressed her how arduously everyone worked to help those around them in such trying times. It further reinforced her belief that the people—pages, knights, servants, commoners, nobles all—were truly benevolent at heart.

Even Sashan, who still detested her bitterly.

Veronica did not want to dwell on that for now. It would not do to show her friend dismay when she was in the worse position.

A gentle *knock, knock* at the door, and Veronica let herself in. Cheryl was where she had been since she last saw her: in bed, buried under her blanket, her head wedged beneath her pillow. While she looked to be sleeping, her valsara was active enough to show she was conscious.

Veronica circled the bed and found her were eyes half-open. They peered off into space, revealing terrible fatigue. She had been drained of all strength since yesterday morning. Fighting off the infection was taxing on the body and a strain on the mind. But some of her color had come back, and the groan she let out proved that some of her energy had returned.

Cheryl pulled her head out from under the pillow. She rubbed her scalp, then her eyes. "Am I better yet?"

Veronica giggled as she placed the bowl onto her nightstand. "Not yet, I'm afraid." She stepped away only to take the chair from their desk, bringing it in front of Cheryl's bed for her to sit. She took the bowl back in hand and dipped the spoon into the soup, stirring it a little.

Cheryl scowled as she pushed her arms against the bed to sit up. "I told you before! I don't need you to spoon-feed me."

When Cheryl first got sick, she was so weak that she could barely hold a spoon. It trembled so much in her hand that the soup spattered all over her bed. Veronica went to help her when she noticed, and then—

"You said that, yes, and then shortly afterwards, you accidentally spilled it all over me."

When it happened, Cheryl leaned in to pick up her bowl, hold it in hand and bring it closer to her mouth. Then the bowl slipped from her grasp, and the soup slung at Veronica's tunic. The piping hot soup made her dance about in a panic as she tried to brush off it and cool her skin.

There was no response from Cheryl, who looked away, embarrassed by her previous blunder.

"Tell you what: if you can take this spoon from me without dropping it, I'll give you the bowl."

Cheryl looked back to her friend, an eyebrow raised, suspecting a trick. Veronica smiled as she pulled the spoon from the bowl. It did not inspire any confidence from Cheryl. That giddy smile told her she took enjoyment from this.

Rather than let her, Cheryl propped herself on her elbow and reached a hand out for the spoon. It trembled as it stretched out toward Veronica.

The muscles in her arm tensed up in fighting to keep it still. She made it up to Veronica's elbow before coming to a stop. Her arm could not stretch any farther, and Veronica was not inclined to bring the spoon any lower for her.

She would have to sit up if she wanted to take it.

Her eyes irately narrowed as she glanced down to her elbow. She recognized that she might not be able to do it. But Cheryl was wonderfully stubborn. She always kept going until she could not anymore. Her elbow swiveled backward until her palm was all that held her up, and she gradually brought herself to sit up again.

It delighted Veronica to see this. She had not been able to do as much just yesterday.

But that was all she could do before toppling over, landing in her friend's lap.

"This is so embarrassing..."

Veronica put the spoon back into the bowl and then the bowl onto the nightstand so she could help the poor girl back into bed.

"Want to try again?"

Cheryl scowled at her and growled under her breath. "Just get it over with."

Amusing as her bashfulness was, it was unnecessary. Veronica picked up the bowl again as Cheryl got comfortable. The agitated look she received when faced her, a bitter scowl twisted from aching and nausea, almost made her snicker. "This is only awkward for you because you are making it awkward."

"Easy for you to say... You're not the one in this position."

She stirred the soup along the bowl's rim, then picked up the spoon, carrying a taste for the ill page. Cheryl turned away for a second, squishing her cheek against her pillow, looking every bit the pouty child, then she relented and opened her mouth for a sip.

"I did the same for my brothers and mother when they were ill."

Cheryl did not look directly at her while she was being fed. She slurped up the soup and swallowed, then muttered, "That's different..."

"Why? I've always thought of you as family."

Veronica's response kept her from retorting before the next spoonful was brought to her mouth.

"Stop looking like you're enjoying this."

"I don't enjoy you being unwell."

"Uh-huh..."

The smile she wore was kept thin and gentle for her sick roommate. But Cheryl knew the subtleties in Veronica's smiles and what they usually meant. There was the smile she had when going about her day, the smile for when she had her favorite treat, the smile for after she tired from exercising, the smile for when she was about to pull a prank on some unsuspecting person.

Then there was the smile she saw now—the one she had when she saw something precious. Cheryl would not have forgotten that one. She had a laugh and commented on how smitten Veronica was when she saw a baby crying in its mother's arms. Her eyes were not aglitter as they were then, but the smile was very much the same.

This was a rare instance for Veronica to see Cheryl vulnerable. She did not think any less of her, but she did like the fact that she could take care of her now that she needed it.

Cheryl turned back into her pillow when she was full.

Veronica wished she would finish, but she did not push her to. That she ate more than half the bowl, more than she had the previous night, showed she was getting better. That was enough for now.

"I will be back to check on you later."

When it looked like Cheryl would fall asleep again, Veronica stood with the unfinished bowl.

"H-Hey."

She stopped while putting the chair back where she got it, looking back to the bedridden girl. She looked back to eyes hesitant but needing.

"Could you ... sing that lullaby for me again?"

Her timid request brought Veronica's smile to change. It always touched her when she asked her that. She knew how much Veronica liked to sing and how uncertain she was about her talent for it since she always did it in secret. Cheryl was the only one in the chateau who heard her sing, and the only person who asked her to.

She could not deny her, especially since she was unwell.

Delighted, Veronica walked back to Cheryl and softly sang:

Come along, follow me, to a world unknown,
where our heartfelt dreams come true.
Close your eyes, take my hand, keep hold of faith,
and fly with me to paradise.

The serenity of her voice soothed the weary Cheryl, her eyes slowly drifting shut, until she let it carry her off to sleep. She looked so peaceful, a world away from trouble. Her sinuses were stuffed and made her breathing raspy, but she was finding some comfort in rest.

Veronica leaned down to tuck Cheryl in. When she looked comfortable, she then went to the window and bowed her head, offering silent prayers to Lady Sundralla, Lady Cural, and Great Gaia for their mercy and blessings for the ailing people.

Once she finished, she quietly left, eager for something to eat herself.

The plague continued to slam Brigadier for the next week. More had fallen ill with each passing day. The symptoms of the newly infected were worse than those who fell victim first.

Tending to the sick became more arduous with less to take care of them. Supplies for medicine were running low. The Estrine family and the royal palace's Master of Lev sought help from within and even outside of Everspeak, but theirs was not the only region assailed by the plague.

If things continued as they had, the only means of fighting the illness would be willpower and prayer.

The pages were kept ignorant about their medicine shortage. The adults feared that if they knew, their hope would fade. The only reason Veronica knew was that she overheard a worrisome discussion between two servants who feared for the ailing children.

Their fears nearly became her own. But she knew not to panic. Just as soldiers had to press forward in battle, they could not stop treating the ill. They had to face this crisis with valor, come what may.

Cheryl's symptoms were somewhat stable lately. She found it easier to work knowing that.

When she was not distributing the meager portions of medicine they had left, Veronica assisted Lady Abeel. The Estrine mage relied on her students to aid her in her search for a cure, but the last of them had fallen ill three days ago. Veronica was the only one left to help.

And Lady Abeel was showing signs of fatigue herself. She refused to take long breaks or let her thoughts stray from her work, even for food and sleep.

When she was not experimenting for a cure, Lady Abeel used whatever resources she had left to concoct remedies. It came as a surprise, at first, to see her mainly work with natural concoctions and not lace them with healing spells.

The potions Lady Abeel brewed, according to her, were less effective on the illness than regular medicine. She often said not every problem could be solved with magic, and this unfortunate development reinforced that belief.

They still needed to find something that would solve their problem.

It was late in the day, and Veronica was still working with Lady Abeel to meet the demand for medicine by tomorrow. The page was permitted to leave and rest some time ago, but she did not want the laborious mage to be alone toiling throughout the night. Rest could be prolonged for a while longer if it meant finishing that medicine.

She had been pestling the leafy ingredients into a gooey paste. Once it was ready, Lady Abeel poured the paste into the cauldron over the hearth. It sat until coming into a slow boil, then she added a few agents into the concoction and stirred.

While she was doing that, Veronica scooped the last batch that sat out to cool into vials.

After all of the pestling, Veronica could feel the joints in her arm ache when she lifted it to pour the medicine. It stung, but it was tolerable. There was still more work to be done.

A brief but firm knock at the door spooked Veronica, nearly causing her to spill the medicine she was pouring; she managed to whisk it back into place with her power before it touched the floor.

The knob turned and the door opened, a sign that the one entering was welcome by Lady Abeel and unaffected by the enchantment on it. His armor revealed him to be a knight, but it was not the same as the uniform of the knights serving the Estrine family or even the city guard. It looked grander than anything even the Estrines themselves donned.

Lady Abeel turned away from her cauldron, her tired eyes suddenly lighting up when resting on the visitor. She dropped the ladle into the stewing medicine. "Charlie?"

The blonde man shut the door behind him. "It has been some time, Sister." He glanced at the page in their midst, his red eyes smoldering under the glow of the lanterns, then set them back on Lady Abeel.

"Indeed. Although, I wish you came back under better circumstances."

"Better than helping my family? Nonsense."

He walked to the cauldron and took a peek inside. Veronica watched him as he did, curious by his presence.

"Father informed me of the situation. This concoction isn't working."

"Sadly," Lady Abeel answered. "But it is the best we have to alleviate the symptoms."

The knight lifted the ladle and watched as the liquid dripped back into the cauldron. The medicine's consistency changed entirely after heating, becoming fluid as water.

"You said you came to help."

"Yes."

"I am pleased to see you again. But your being here may only endanger you. There are more ill here than anywhere else in the capital."

"Your concern is appreciated. But I would not risk burdening you all with another to nurse back to health if I did not think I could change the situation." The knight reached into the satchel at his waist, taking out a small vial. Inside it was a thin, wiry-looking plant.

"What is that?"

"A rare plant I found in the south of the kingdom. Malute ivy. The doctors in the region think it poisonous."

"I take it that you had a look at it yourself?" shrewdly asked the sorceress.

"They did not understand its properties very well, but I saw something in it." He opened the vial to have the plant rest in his palm. It was a deep green with slivers of its plucked branch turquoise. "In the amount they used, it became poison. That is only because the medicinal properties of this plant are so rich. A handful of leaves alone would overwhelm a grown man, resulting in death." He plucked a single leaf from the plant, putting the rest back into the vial. The underside of the small leaf had slivers of turquoise too, and it almost looked see-through in the light. "This, however, should be enough to be used as medicine. If we add this to your recipe, I believe you'll see better results."

It was hard to believe, even after hearing his reasoning. Knowing that the plant may be poisonous did not inspire much confidence.

Their precious resources were dwindling. The medicinal herbs they had left were all they had to give the ill a fighting chance. And he was suggesting adding a poison to a life-preserving batch of medicine.

Veronica could see this man had the best of intentions, and he had given his hypothesis some thought. What he suggested, however, would gamble with the lives of many suffering people.

The skepticism Lady Abeel expressed was understandable. "You are certain of this, Charlie?" But she wanted to believe her sibling, and she recognized that their options were limited.

"I used it on myself when I fell ill on the road, just two days earlier. If it didn't work, I doubt we would be having this discussion."

A startling statement, but he spoke it with such certainty.

That seemed to be enough for Lady Abeel. She looked to the knight with a tired smile and shook her head. "You reckless fool," she said as she snatched the leaf from her brother. She then crushed the leaf in her hand and sprinkled the potentially dangerous flacks into the cauldron.

The knight looked like he wanted to retort, but as he remembered it was not just him and his sister, he chose instead to keep a dignified appearance.

While Lady Abeel stirred the medicine, the knight took a piece of paper from her desk and quickly wrote something down.

"Is this one working with you, Abeel?"

She turned from the cauldron, almost looking to have forgotten that Veronica was there. "Actually, she was just stepping out to rest." The way she looked to the girl let her know it was an order in the guise of a pleasant response.

"Then she can deliver something for me before she does." The knight folded up the note and handed it to Veronica. "Take this to Lord Estrine."

She took the note with her left hand, allowing her right to make a fist over her heart, saluting the knight. "Right away, Lord Charleston."

The slight raise of his slanted eyebrows let her know he was surprised that she knew of him. She smiled as she stepped out, following his orders promptly.

While unsure at first, the way Lady Abeel addressed the knight let Veronica know who he was. The sorceress occasionally spoke with her about her brother over tea.

Lord Charleston used to be a combat instructor in the Estrine Chateau. He almost always remained in Brigadier, leaving only rarely to visit old friends he fought beside in the war against Pterna. But five years ago, he became the new Champion of Duty.

Lady Abeel often said how proud she was of him for earning the right to become one of the king's Six Champions, and more importantly, for accepting it. Many knew of how the previous Champion of Duty disgraced his title, as well as the Estrine family name, by aiding the Renegades, an extreme and malignant group that worked to overthrow the king. By becoming the new Champion of Duty, Lord Charleston was striving to erase the smear on his family's name.

Even before coming to the chateau, that was something Veronica had come to understand. She was not ignorant of the name of the previous champion, or the harm he caused.

She sometimes wondered what sort of person had been given that esteemed title. And right now, she was helping him with a gambit that could save the ill.

Lord Estrine seemed intrigued when he received the note. Perhaps he did not read any mention of the risky ingredient Lord Charleston planned to use. Whatever the case, he read the note calmly and dismissed Veronica when he was done, an order to relay a response not given.

There must have been a plan, but a humble page was in no position to know. She followed her orders, as any soldier did.

Peaceful slumber had been hard to come by as of late. The moon still hung high with the stars, veiled by thin clouds, when Veronica awoke in a fright.

She felt groggy, and her head spun. It could not have been more than a couple of hours of sleep. And yet her mind was alert, wary, anxious.

A turn of the head showed poor Cheryl still sound asleep. She snored louder than usual, a harsh, congested sound, not at all like the cute noise she normally made.

Her snoring was not what startled Veronica. She was not sure how she knew, sound asleep as she was, nor did she know what could have made such a noise.

She had never heard such a frightful cry before in her life. It was not from a nightmare, and yet the air was still as could be.

Perhaps it was nothing more than her tired mind playing tricks on her—a punishment for the pranks done with the use of her powers. But she was not swayed by such reasoning.

Curfew was still in effect. If she left the bedchamber, there would be consequences. She understood that, but she could not stay put.

Veronica climbed out of bed, quiet so as not to disturb Cheryl, then put on her uniform minus the chain mail. She carefully unlocked the door, and stepped out unheard.

The stone floors of the chateau were freezing, and feeling them press against her bare feet shot chills up her spine, shocking her fully awake. It occurred to her to go back and fetch her boots, but she did not want to risk alerting anyone. Sound carried through the halls like a flute.

She just wanted to find out where that cry came from and return to her bedchamber before she got caught.

Leaving the girls' wing was easier than expected since nearly everyone asleep. She was in the clear until making her descent down the stairs. The halls on the ground floor were patrolled regularly even throughout the night. If she made one wrong turn at the wrong time, they would spot her, chase her thinking her an intruder.

But fortunately, she had something the average intruder would not.

Her magic senses were very keen. When fully utilized, she could see, hear, and feel nearly everything that was happening around her. If she could sense the guards coming, she could evade them.

And a good chance to prove that came along. Upon utilizing her magic sight, she caught a glimpse of someone's valsara turning the corner and crossing into the foyer. She kept to the shadows and slinked back up to the stairs as the guard made his approach. She observed him thoroughly scan the area, making note of everything, and then glance toward the stairway.

For a moment, she thought he suspected something, that she had been caught already, feeling his presence linger for so long. But the guard started walking again. She finally breathed when he was gone.

When the coast was clear, she descended again, but stopped near the bottom steps. An uncanny feeling brushed over her, weighing against her muscles for a moment and then suddenly releasing. It was cold, unnaturally so. And it came from down the hall the guard just went down.

Following it was a bad idea, but she did so nonetheless. That uncanny feeling—it was the same as when she woke up, when she heard that cry.

Her steps were quick and quiet, careful not to alarm the nearby guard. It gave her a start whenever she sensed him stop. She did the same in case it was to listen. At one point, another guard crossed his path. They did not stop to exchange pleasantries but acknowledged each other as they passed one another.

The one Veronica hid from walked away as the other walked toward her. The hall was a straight path with no doors at its sides. And it was too long for her to go back to avoid being seen. What was she to do?

Perhaps rely on the trick of a friend.

As he made his approach, Veronica expanded her area of influence and pulled in the water in the air, bring it around the guard. It could not be too much for the water to be seen, only enough for him to feel it brush against him.

One of the phantoms she met—a young prankster who died of pneumonia—taught her how to mimic the chilling presence of a phantom using her power. Collecting the water vapor into a thin veil, she could drape it over someone without it lingering too long and give them the impression that someone was there.

A swift pull brought the vapor over the guard. He stopped in place and flinched. The rattling of his modest armor gave away his fright. Confusion and uncertainty bubbled in his valsara, rippling from fear. But he did not back away. Startled but ready to act, he kept a hand on his sword as he went back the way he came to see what it was.

Veronica peeked around the corner to watch him. What someone would do afterwards was always a mystery.

He seemed to think someone was watching him, teasing him—how humorous to witness. He turned the corner at the end of the hall, looking irately in both directions.

When he seemed to be ready to turn back, Veronica gathered more water vapor and brought it over him from the hall opposite of the one the other guard went down.

"W-Who's there? Show yourself!"

Led astray, the guard rushed down the hall he felt that ghostly sensation from, eager to find and apprehend the culprit.

Sneaking out of her bedchamber and tricking the guards in the dead of night offered a different thrill than the little practical jokes she pulled.

It was not something she wanted to make a habit of feeling. As fun as it was, it could get her into more trouble than it was worth.

When the coast was clear, she moved down the hall, only to pause again at that uncanny feeling weighing on her once more. It was stronger this time, a forceful current washing over her. And it made her think—

A bloodcurdling scream ripped through the hall. She jumped from the terrified sound, but then ran down the hall she misled the guard down to see what was wrong.

The guard former rushed her way. Though the child's presence surprised him, it was of little consequence when he was alerted by distress.

When they reached his comrade, they found the man had fallen over and backed himself against the wall. His eyes were wide as saucers and shook terribly. His armor rattled in the rhythm of his trembling body, and he babbled repetitive syllables cut off again and again by horror.

They looked to the darkened corner the man's terrified gaze froze upon and were bereft by the same horror. The guard tore himself away from the ghastly sight to help his quivering friend onto his feet. Distraught, he struggled to keep a hold of himself so he could question him on what happened.

Veronica could not turn away from what they had found. She wanted desperately to, but she could not. Her hands remained cupped over her mouth, quieting her startled and broken gasps. Tears formed, traced along her fingers, and fell to the ground.

~ Sixth Chapter ~

Unforgiven

Word of the tragedy quickly spread and shook the already unsettled chateau. Unrest and anxiety polluted the air as yet another danger presented itself.

One of the Estrines, Lord Tamsilac, had died. It was not the plague's doing. No malady, no matter how deadly, could cleave a man's torso open. It was a horizontal cut that tore him open and spread his blood all over the wall like paint from a brush. His staff, it turned out, was a scabbard for a hidden sword, which had been drawn and broken in two.

Someone had infiltrated the Estrine Chateau and killed the former head of their family.

Veronica was, so far, the only page who knew of this. The Estrines did everything in their power to keep the spread of information limited to her and the handful of guards and servants it reached. They could not have further unrest in their home, especially when they had yet to find out who committed the horrid act.

She was explicitly instructed not to mention this to any of her peers.

Even if permitted, she was not sure if she could.

The disobedient page was to be punished for leaving her bedchamber during curfew, but Lady Abeel convinced her father to be lenient in light of what she had seen. So instead, she was merely confined to her bedchamber until further notice.

Veronica could not relax. The first thing she did when back in her bedchamber was pray to Lady Cural, the guide of souls, to grant Lord Tamsilac safe passage to the Elysium. After that, she lay in bed with troubled thoughts.

Prayer usually made her feel at ease. That it did not this time only upset her all the more.

The following evening, she could not sleep. She nodded off briefly now and then as she contemplated what to do. This was not something the Estrines could handle themselves. But would they believe her if she told them?

The world continued to shift between moments of absolute darkness and blurred reality, time lapsing when her mind forced itself to rest. It happened enough times for her to lose patience and stop trying.

Moonlight gleamed through the window. The moon arched just right for it to shine down on her. It had such a majestic glow, almost magical. Watching it—mercifully—erased the anxiety keeping her from taking a proper rest, as if Lady Luneste, the goddess of the moon and bringer of the night sky, tried to soothe her.

"Veronica."

A voice came from nowhere. For a moment, she thought it was Lady Malute, the goddess of misfortune, Lady Luneste's mischievous twin, come to prank her. But Lady Malute never had her fun under the watch of her orderly sister.

It took her a moment to realize who the voice belonged to, bringing her to trigger her magic sight. She sat up and saw Rubi had entered.

The phantom girl was kneeling beside her bed, staring at the weary Veronica. She backed up only when she knew she was seen.

"Rubi? How come you're not sleeping?"

Rubi narrowed her eyes. "I'm a phantom, remember?"

"Oh, yes. Sorry."

The dead were only at rest when they were at peace.

"Is something the matter?"

"I should be asking you that. I felt your spirit scream from the other side of the city."

Rubi went over to Cheryl's bed and sat atop the girl sleeping in it. Having done things like that to amuse herself since no one could see her so often, it became something of a habit, and one made more entertaining since Veronica could see her do it. Although, the look on her face did not suggest she was there to play around.

"I heard. Someone's dead, huh?"

Veronica nodded. "Yes. Killed. ...By a phantom."

She still could not believe it herself, even after seeing it with her own eyes. An unearthly energy lingered where Lord Tamsilac had been cut, precisely like that of the phantoms. If it were only a form of magic, Lady Abeel would have been able to detect it after examining his body. She could not find anything, but Veronica did.

"Huh..." Rubi did not seem too surprised.

"How can this be? Phantoms can't make contact with people like that."

"Every rule has exceptions. Some of them are unexplainable. All I really get is that something is allowing that phantom to move between planes, even if not completely."

It seemed Rubi understood little more than Veronica.

A phantom attaining a physical state was unprecedented, but as it was with other phantoms, when they came into contact with people, they behind left traces of their energy, sometimes enough to form trails. And the energy lingering on Lord Tamsilac was immense. There was no other sign of the killer whatsoever. It came, then it was gone.

There was no mistaking now that the cry she heard hours earlier belonged to that phantom. It screamed—for help, out of rage, for some reason. She heard it as she had the others she found. It was different, but she still heard it.

"I have to help it."

"How?" Rubi retorted. "You don't even know what became of it."

"I'll think of something. I have to. If I don't, then..."

It would kill again.

Whatever it was there for, it would not have acted without reason. Phantoms came to be as they were because they had something they needed to do. For whatever reason, it sought to kill Lord Tamsilac, and somehow attained the power to do it. Once the need arose again, it would be on the hunt for another.

"Then I'll look into it." Rubi stood up again. "I don't need sleep, and you do. You can't do anything for anyone if you don't look after yourself, so rest up and leave it to me for now." Her smile beamed with confidence.

It was rare for Rubi to offer help directly, partially since there was little she could do without a body. But this was something another phantom would be able to do better than someone who could only interact with phantoms. Their planes differed in more ways than a mortal could recognize.

As much as she would like to resolve this quickly, it would do Veronica little good to go after the killer phantom now and further exhaust herself. She returned the smile given to her with one of gratitude. "I appreciate this, Rubi."

"Don't mention it."

"Just please be careful."

"Hah! Let it come. I won't go down without a fight."

Veronica laughed with her. She felt a little better after seeing Rubi leave through the door, and soon managed to find sleep again.

The morning passed slowly. The halls were depressingly quiet, as they have been since people began falling ill. But this was the first time Veronica allowed herself to focus on that.

She had instead been focused on Cheryl once she awoke.

Cheryl was always surprised to find her roommate there when she woke up. She did not mind, at least not until it came time to eat again.

Her recovery was going poorly, so she had not the strength to resist Veronica's insistence on spoon-feeding her.

Upon noon, Veronica had to leave her roommate and return to aiding Lady Abeel. She did so reluctantly. It was challenging to hide her concern for Cheryl's condition. Her color was fading again, and she was beginning to develop a fever. If her condition became critical, the medicine would not help anymore.

Before she stepped away from the bedchamber door, Veronica closed her eyes to give another silent prayer, this one to any god that would be willing to listen and offer compassion.

And when she arrived at Lady Abeel's study, she found something amazing. The noblewoman was working diligently over her cauldron to prepare more medicine. The tools and ingredients around the room showed that she was using the same process as they had been, but there was one notable change. Veronica walked into the room just as Lady Abeel plucked a leaf from the Malute ivy Lord Charleston brought and dropped it into the mix.

It gave her the same start she had when last she saw her do it.

"Ah, Veronica. Good timing. Come here and stir this."

The page followed her instructions and took the ladle from her hand, allowing Lady Abeel to step away and hastily tend to the batch that had been cooling. She poured the ready concoction into vials, filling them only halfway.

That concoction had a different color to it. It was a brighter green than the batches Veronica had seen previously.

"Lady Abeel, is that batch the same as this?"

"That it is, dear."

"Then the ivy is safe after all?"

Lady Abeel kept her focus primarily on filling the vials to the proper level and overlooked the other brief questions asked of her. There was little for her to spare in fulfilling her task while fighting the fatigue weighing on her. The little rest she allowed herself was barely enough to keep her going.

When the cauldron was empty, she wiped the sweat from her forehead and looked back to Veronica with a smile. "It's more than safe like this. It could be what saves us."

"Really?"

"I tested the batch we made before on the worst cases and kept watch over them to study responsiveness. There were no negative side effects in the passing hours, and when sunrise came, I found their symptoms diminishing. By the afternoon, their conditions improved significantly. At this rate, they'll make a full recovery.

"My brother was right. This plant's properties are miraculous. It only killed people because they took more than their bodies could handle. Even a single leaf is too much for one man, but when mixed into another concoction and thoroughly dissolved, it can make medicine that can heal dozens of people."

That was incredible. The medicine they had been using so far did little more than reduce the fevers and relax the muscles. But now they had a cure. It was so hard to believe.

The weight over her heart finally lifted. There was hope again. Her prayers had been answered.

A brief reminder from Lady Abeel warned her to keep stirring. Their hope renewed, the noblewoman and page continued to work until enough medicine was made for everyone in the chateau.

The Malute ivy still had half of its leaves, but at the rate they used them, they would run out before all the ill in Brigadier could be given their medicine. That might have been why Lady Abeel tried to limit how much she put into the vials.

Fortunately, there was a plan to acquire more, but that would take time. Until then, they had to use the Malute ivy sparingly.

Even as the day came to an end, Lady Abeel insisted on continuing her work. Veronica worried for her. She had clearly not slept recently. The death of her grandfather and the chaotic state they were in troubled her so. Convincing her to rest took some effort, but she was gradually worn down by the child's innocent pleas to consider her own well-being.

She promised to get some much-needed sleep after determining who needed the miraculous medicine most.

With that, Veronica took her leave—or was about to at least. It might have been selfish, but she turned to make another request before stepping out the door.

"Lady Abeel, would it be acceptable if I took a vial with me? My dear friend has been getting worse since this morning, and I worry how she is faring now."

"The medicine should only be for those in the worst condition right now." She did not look away from the list she had been examining, paying no attention to those big, sad, sparkling blue eyes looking her way. The document kept her attention for a bit longer, but then she added, "Be sure she drinks every drop."

Veronica offered the noblewoman a big smile, even if she did not see it, and bowed her head. "Thank you, milady!" She eagerly went to the small crate they stored the medicine and took a vial, then bowed to Lady Abeel again before taking her leave.

She wasted no time in returning to Cheryl to give her the medicine. And not a moment too soon. The poor girl had become as white as a sheet, and her skin was terribly hot to the touch. She was awake, thankfully, but could not even lift her head to greet her.

Veronica sat beside Cheryl and cradled her head while slowly pouring the medicine into her mouth. While she struggled to keep it down, Cheryl drank it all, gagging from the foul taste.

"Gods! ...You are so lucky you don't have to drink this swill."

Veronica giggled. She sounded better already.

Veronica awoke that night with a fright. She leaped from her blankets, turning this way and that, suddenly breaking out in a cold sweat.

She heard it again, the terrible cry from the night before. It was louder this time, clearer. The malice it carried still echoed in her head.

The phantom was on the move, in search of another kill.

Veronica did not even think about curfew this time. Someone was in danger. That phantom would strike them down if she did not act now.

She slept in her uniform that night, suspecting that the need to act would arise. Silently, so as not to wake the recovering Cheryl, she stepped outside.

Trying to remain unseen would cost time. Instead, she heightened her focus to locate the phantom. Its screams kept resounding throughout the chateau. They frightened her, but she did not waver.

It was on the ground floor again.

She raced through the hall as fast as her legs would allow. Upon coming to the stairs, the screams grew louder. The force of its rage rattled her. It was stronger than anything she ever felt.

They came from the rear gates.

The halls were clear, without any guards on patrol. The phantom's voice was rising. Perhaps they heard pieces of it. Given that it could phase between planes, that did not seem unlikely.

It was getting louder. She could almost make out words.

Something had drawn her attention before she could make them out: a weak moan at the end of the hall. Veronica followed it and found a woman lying against the wall. It was Lady Deva.

Veronica rushed to her side and bent down to inspect her wound. There was a terrible gash in her side, deep. Her corset was stained crimson. The same malignant energy left by the phantom lingered on it. Her breathing was rough and ragged, but she fought to control it and raised her head to meet Veronica.

"Stay calm, Lady Deva. I'm going to get help."

Lady Deva took her hand from her wound and grabbed Veronica's wrist before she could stand all the way. Her grip was strong and would not allow resistance. "No... Look there."

In the direction she gestured to was a shattered window letting in the cold night air. Few glass shards had fallen to the floor; most of them had flown outward, suggesting that it was broken from the inside.

"Charlie... It's after Lord Charleston," Lady Deva gasped. "Help him, please!"

Veronica wanted to protest; she could not leave her behind when she needed help. Her wound was severe. But the phantom had its sights on another. Its scream shook the air as she contemplated what to do, this one different than the ones it let out earlier.

It was determined to engage the one it was after.

Lady Deva's hand slipped from the page's wrist, having needed to cup over the wound again. Veronica stepped over to the window and saw footsteps in the grass. They led along the wall to the gate.

Lord Charleston was not running away. The phantom had to be after him and not Lady Deva, otherwise it would have finished her where she lay. He must have tried to lead it away from her while reentering from the locked door by the gate.

They did not understand their foe. It left a trail of its energy, eerie blue wisps of unstable emotions, in stalking its target down the hall, never bothering to phase through the walls. Either it knew what he was up to, or the phantom still had limitations it could not violate.

But it would not give up until it had what it was after. If it caught him, it would kill him and vanish again until the next hunt. Now was the best chance she had at stopping it.

Reluctantly, she faced Lady Deva, whose eyes begged her to do as she asked.

"Stay awake, milady."

She hurried down the hall, following the energy trail left behind in the phantom's wake. There was more lingering than an ordinary one would leave behind. It almost looked like the wisps were consuming the halls. They left no physical marks, but the terrifying anguish in them made the air crushingly heavy.

There was so much. It must have been festering for years.

They began to concentrate as she neared the gate, a form inhuman coming into view. It was massive, nearly taking up the entire hall, its broad head almost touching the ceiling, and its body thick as stone. Its head moved to the side for but a moment, giving her a look at how long it was, a heinous set of fangs sprouting from its maw.

Rarely had Veronica seen phantoms of the like—their humanity completely buried beneath layers of chaotic emotions, unrecognizable as they once were. And this one was consumed by anger, anger born from pain.

The degraded phantom lashed out at someone before it. It reached out its mangled claws to keep him from stepping out the rear exit, forcing the door shut and smacking him to the ground. It raised its claws high, ready for the final blow.

"No!"

Desperate to act, Veronica used her power to gather water from the air into one great geyser erupting from the floor. It knocked the phantom back just in time. She took advantage of its disorientation and slipped by it to get to Lord Charleston. The champion lay on the ground, his hand gripping his right shoulder. His sword had been torn from his grasp and had fallen beside him.

It was difficult to see someone of his caliber in such a state, but he faced a foe he could not harm or see well.

"You?" he exclaimed. "What are you doing here?"

There was not the time to offer a proper answer. The phantom was not done yet. It got up and faced Veronica, directing its rage at her for standing in the way. The malice was oppressive, but she would not run. A knight did not abandon those in need.

"Stay behind me, milord." Veronica picked up the sword on the ground and drew her hand along the blade, gathering water around it.

The water compelled by her power could touch whatever she could see. And used in this manner, it could harm the intangible. If it struck a weakened phantom, their spirits would give out, exorcizing them.

It was not how Veronica liked to put phantoms to rest. Their regrets did not leave them. They would leave the world tormented by their failure to uncover why they had yet to move on, what they had left behind. Forcing a phantom to depart, it was no different than killing a person.

But there might not be a choice. This phantom, maddened by the pain it had suffered in life, pain that tormented it for time immeasurable, had succumbed to and been swallowed by terrible anger, and acted to blindly kill.

"I know you are angry, and though I don't understand why, I cannot allow you to harm this man." It may have been beyond reason, but she had to try to reach it. "Be calm. I can help you."

Her words fell on deaf ears. The enraged phantom stood back up and roared, ripping the very air apart, before charging at her.

The enemy was immense, but Veronica stood her ground. She brought the sword against the phantom's claws, holding them back with brute force alone, then drew it along and sliced through its arm. The water along the blade moved back into place shortly after being pushed. To keep it unbalanced, she gathered more water into her outstretched palm until it burst, forcing the phantom back.

It turned its face to her again as it picked itself up. It was without eyes, blinded by rage.

"Why are you doing this?" she continued to try reasoning with it. "Why are you after the Estrines?"

The degraded phantom rose slowly, enfeebled by Veronica's power. The opposition only made its anger grow, allowing it to fight the effect.

"—!" Its heinous snarling began to sound like words for a moment. They kept falling to pieces before forming anything understandable.

Her words were not what forced some humanity from it, that she knew. It was its own resentment trying to be voiced.

"X— Xanlir!"

Veronica froze. Of all the things to come from its mouth, she did not expect to hear that name.

Xanlir, the man who killed her brother.

It made sense now. Xanlir was of the Estrine family, the traitor who sullied their name. This phantom was also among those who died by his hand, and it sought revenge for its murder.

The pain—it derived from betrayal. And as it charged again, she felt how deeply the pain had ingrained into it. It was as though someone was crushing her heart in their hand.

She fought through her empathy for the phantom to block its attack, then cut through its other arm. Again she forced it back, waving her arm, water forming into a whip lashing at its torso. "This man isn't Xanlir!" she shouted. "You're attacking someone who did you no harm. Please, you must understand. There is nothing to gain from doing this but more heartbreak."

Saying and hearing that accursed name riled it up more. It refused to listen and got up, shedding the water soaking it, to go back on the attack.

It brought more force down at her, more desperation to take its kill. It rammed her with its long head, throwing her onto the ground. As its lacerated arms regenerated, the enraged phantom hurled them at her. Veronica rolled out of the way, quickly getting into a kneeling position, and thrust the sword up to pierce its neck. Quickly flicking the weapon away from it, she then kicked her left leg into the sturdy torso and brought it down to go into a spin, smacking her blade against its face.

Were it a living monster, it would have already been slain. But the phantom's damaged form continued to regenerate. The only sign that her attacks were doing anything was the way it trembled in getting back up.

It would not stop. The degraded phantom was determined to break through her and get to the man it unjustly blamed.

She could not allow it. Lord Charleston did not deserve its wrath, and his family did not deserve to suffer another loss. Although it pained her, she knew she had to be the one to bring the phantom's suffering to an end.

When it again drew near, Veronica stepped forward, taking the initiative in the fight. She leaned low as the phantom towered over her. Swiftly, she guided the sword into an arcing swing, tearing through its torso.

Overwhelmed by the continued abuse, the phantom fell to the ground.

Veronica stood tall over her fallen foe, breathing uneasily. Fighting her empathy took more of a toll on her than the physical exertion.

She knew what she had to do. She knew that it had to be her. But knowing that did not make it any easier.

She vowed to help the phantoms she met, for there may have been no other who could. Exorcizing them like this, it was far from helping them.

But no matter how much she wished it, she could not help everyone. She had been warned time and again before becoming a page that, as a knight, she would have to help some over others, that she would not have a choice.

This was the first time she understood what her father meant.

"Please..." Nevertheless, she had to try. The phantom was too weak to resist anymore. If she could get through to it, then she had to try. Who else would for them? "Stop this. I beg of you, listen. I can help, but only if you let me."

She looked down to the degraded phantom, the moister in her eyes nearly forming tears. There was so much anger enshrouding it, pushing it, making the pain grow. It had completely shut out the world and made the anger its cradle.

No matter her words, no matter her compassion, no matter her sadness, it refused to listen. It only cared about breaking those it was angered by. And it would not stop getting up to try.

There was nothing more she could do.

Veronica fought the weight of her heavy heart to lift the sword, preparing to strike it down. "I pray that you may forgive me."

She dared not look away from the phantom she was about to exorcize. The deed was to be carried out by her; it was her duty to see it off.

"Stop it, you two!"

Veronica halted her sword just before swinging. She looked past the degraded phantom, following the sudden outburst. It was Rubi.

Rubi looked on at the scene with budding frustration. One who saw her would think she stumbled upon a friend causing trouble. "What are you two doing?"

Veronica was about to answer when she noticed her enemy turning the other phantom's way. She did not fear it going on the attack. With how much she harmed it, it could not do much very quickly.

It only set its sights on Lord Charleston and anyone that got in the way. That it paid her any heed took Veronica aback.

"Have you two become so dense that you forgot what the man who killed you looks like? Really, Charleston's an arse, but nowhere near as bad as him."

She was admonishing it, rather crudely at that, and did so familiarly. She knew the phantom—phantoms? Why was she talking to it like that?

The degraded phantom fought to get up, bringing Veronica to retreat a few steps back, but she did not stop it. The anger, it was waning. It carried its monstrous form toward the phantom girl, approaching her like a wounded puppy.

Rubi was not afraid of it at all. She even walked up to it in a huff.

"Always causing trouble... And you, I would have thought—" Rather than continue berating it, Rubi paused to sigh. "No. No, I can't put that on you. ...You've both been through a lot."

The degraded phantom raised its head to her level. "Ru...bi...?"

She gave it a kind smile. "It's nice to you two again."

It lowered its head to press against her, letting out a hoarse but sad, broken sound that could only have been sobbing. Rubi wrapped her arms around it in a gentle embrace.

The ethereal light around the degraded phantom slowly dissolved, its form diminishing with the subsided rage. As it broke apart, the one form became two.

They were children who died about the same age Rubi had. They laid their heads into her shoulders, each caressed by one of her hands. For the first time in a long, long while, they left bare their pain, bawling into her.

"It's okay," Rubi reassured them. "It's over. It's over now."

Seeing the threat had gone, Veronica let her power rest, the water around the sword reverting into vapor and returning to the air. She lowered her weapon and watched as the eerie blue surrounding the two phantoms flickered, turning radiant and golden. Their transparent forms began to fade.

They had found their peace.

Rubi held them in her arms even as they began to disappear. "I'll see you two soon." The two phantoms looked at her with broken smiles until vanishing, flickers of golden light lingering in their place. Rubi closed her arms around herself, capturing some of that light. There was genuine happiness in the smile she gave them, and when they were gone, that happiness went with them.

Veronica wanted to comfort her, but her work was not yet done.

She turned back to Lord Charleston, who stood again only by leaning against the wall. He looked upon the scene with caution and confusion. Whatever his eyes allowed him to see, it was not enough to let him know the threat was gone.

"Are you all right, Lord Charleston?"

That the page would ask that meant they must have been safe. Even the first-years in the Estrine Chateau knew better than to leave their back exposed to the enemy.

"Don't waste time on me." He walked past Veronica, only to hobble and lean against the wall. "Deva is down the hall, injured. Get to her at once!"

For him to respond that way, he had to be okay. She did as was instructed and hurried down the hall.

Lady Deva was still breathing when she got to her, though it was soft and difficult to control. More blood had seeped from her wound, soaking her dress and sticking to the floor. "Please excuse me, milady." Pressed for time, Veronica tore a long strip from the noblewoman's gown and used it to dress the wound. She made sure to wrap it around her tightly to restrict the blood flow as best as she could.

"I-Is Charlie—"

"Yes, do not worry. Lord Charleston is safe."

She said nothing after that, her concentration only on staying awake.

"Hold on, Lady Deva. Hold on..."

~ Seventh Chapter ~

For Them

Help arrived for Lady Deva not long after the conjoined phantoms vanished. The guards who found her with Lord Charleston and Veronica were baffled by their conditions. No one had heard any noise to suspect a confrontation, let alone one of this nature.

The improvised compress helped slow the blood loss until she was brought to a more suitable place to treat her. There, Lord Charleston gave her something to dull the pain and mended the wound himself. Everything had been done to keep her comfortable so she may recover.

Alas, the poor woman never made it to see the sunrise.

The deaths of Lord Tamsilac and Lady Deva were difficult for the family to process, and would be difficult to hide for much longer. An entity unseen, unheard, and untraceable had taken their lives and sent the survivors into disarray.

They did not accept it when they were told the threat was gone, but somehow, Lord Charleston managed to convince everyone that it was the case.

There were many questions about Veronica's involvement, having been at the scene of both murders. If she were to tell the whole truth, it would have been dismissed as a child's wild imagination, as it had been many times before, and perhaps even an excuse for a coverup. All she could say in her defense was that she felt something was wrong and she left her bedchamber to find out what for herself. They were aware that Veronica privately studied under Lady Abeel, who testified that the page's magic senses were more than exceptional, justifying her concern.

It was not that they believed she was somehow involved in the deaths. There was much about the situation that they did not understand, and they were desperate to find a plausible explanation. When unable to do so, people became paranoid and erratic, willing to believe almost anything.

Were there a reason to suspect she had a hand in these heinous acts, Lord Charleston would not have allowed her to walk freely. He lost his wife, after all.

With the situation resolved, as much as it could be, Veronica was escorted back to her bedchamber to rest until morning.

Someone was there waiting for her. Rubi stood at the window, lost in thought as she stared at the moon and bathed in its radiance.

Veronica waited by the door, wondering whether she should speak up or not. Her very spirit projected a melancholy she never felt from the outspoken phantom before.

Even when she put on a brave front upon turning to Veronica, she could not quite bury her feelings. "Hey," she said huskily. "You're not hurt, right?"

Veronica smiled, if only to help her feel better. "I'm okay."

Rubi lowered her head and glanced away, appearing embarrassed if not ashamed. It took her a moment to look back her way. "Listen, I—" she paused to swallow some lingering disgruntlement. "Don't ... hold it against them, okay? They weren't really themselves."

"I understand." Veronica approached the phantom and sat on her bed. She patted a spot beside her for her to sit. Clearly, she came to get something off her chest.

Hesitance kept her lingering at the window for a moment more; she did not want to leave its glow. But she relented and sat beside her.

"Did you know them?"

"Yeah... Those two were always so kind, soft even. I never imagined they'd become so hateful. But I can't hold it against them." She turned toward Veronica before continuing. "I don't condone what they did, but really, I'm glad they stayed together all this time. They've always been dependent on others. If they were alone ... it might have broken them.

"Still ... I'm surprised I'm not more like they were, after we were killed by the same man."

Veronica's eyes widened. "You remember."

Rubi nodded. "The spot they died on was close to mine. I never thought to look in the Estrines' crypt because, well..."

There was no need for her to say more. Most phantoms had a crippling anxiety about entering places like crypts and graveyards. It was not so much a phobia, more like trying to face a terrible trauma. Though they knew they were dead, phantoms did not look forward to looking at the spot where they died. Many required Veronica's help simply for that reason.

"Anyway, I decided to follow those people laying Lord Tamsilac to rest, see if I could find out anything from the energy on him. And I found much more than I expected."

A rush of mixed emotions welled in Veronica's chest. She leaned toward the phantom, who seemed unsure of how to process what she had learned herself. "Rubi, who are you?"

She looked Veronica in the eye for the first time with purpose. "My name is Rubella Ivanstronge. I am the fourth daughter of Duke Riverin and Duchess Rauva Ivanstronge of Cragfill. I came here to train as a page and earn my knighthood. But I was killed, by a man everyone loved—the same man who took your brother from you, Veronica."

A prick at Veronica's heart made her wince, and the welling emotions turned to lead. Mention of that man always made her retreat to a place inside herself she did not like to be. She never knew about the others who were killed along with Wally that fateful day. When she first heard about it, sadness had all but drowned her, keeping her from hearing anything but the name of her lost brother.

She stared at Rubi for some time, her big blue eyes shimmering as old memories resurfaced. "Rubella... You were one of my brother's peers!"

Rubi smiled bittersweetly. "So he actually talked about me. I never really believed it, but since you know of me, it must be true."

"Rubella—"

"Just Rubi," she stated firmly. "I never liked Rubella."

"Okay. Rubi, do you know what became of Wally?"

She did not respond right away. Her gaze turned back toward the moon. "He and I were next to each other when we died. Not even inches apart... I haven't seen him, any of them, since we were killed. The two you fought to protect Sir Charleston, they're the first."

Veronica tried to hide her disappointment; it was not her fault that she did not know. Rubi saw through it the moment she looked back at her. Her smile became sympathetic and offered her the comfort to turn the lead in her chest to air.

"You said that he's still here, so he must be. He'll turn up."

"Thank you, Rubi." She tried not to dwell on her lost brother and instead pay attention to the phantom beside her. "So ... you found what you were on your own after all. You were right; you didn't need my help."

Her pride beamed through the sympathy for but a moment. The smile did not keep. Rubi did not seem very confident about what she had done. "Yeah, I found out who I am. I know how I died." She looked down at her transparent hand and watched the ethereal light encompassing her gleam and ripple with her every movement. "But I'm still here. I can't move on yet."

"How come?"

"There are still huge gaps in my memories. Pieces of my life are missing—important pieces. It's not my death that's keeping me here. Something else is. And I have to find out what."

Their lives being inexplicably cut short were usually reasons why phantoms emerged and remained. Sometimes, the shock of what killed them was so strong that they could not move on without accepting it. But as it was with the conjoined phantoms, that was not always the case.

Emotions could be very powerful things. Anger was what kept the conjoined phantoms there. Something else must have been doing the same for Rubi.

But this phantom, this young girl was strong and stubborn. She kept going and kept herself together for over five long years in search of the answers she needed. And the clenched fist and resolute stare she made showed that she would keep going until she finally found it.

Now Veronica gave a smile to uplift Rubi. "I know you will."

Her resolve reestablished, Rubi stood again and walked back to the window. The moon kept her attention a while longer, its light mesmerizing. Perhaps she did that in life to settle her restless thoughts. She then turned to Veronica, her eyes almost pleading. "Is it all right if I stay the night?"

"Of course," she said with a nod. "This is as much your room as it is ours."

With their minds in better places, the two bade each other good night. The page, reeled by these volatile events, tucked herself in and fell asleep watching the phantom gaze out the window.

The new medicine had wondrous effects on the infected. Their symptoms gradually diminished, their strength returning, and within days, many made full recoveries. With its effects proven, the medicine was soon distributed throughout all of Brigadier.

Life slowly returned to the capital with each person cured.

While the demand for the medicine was greater than expected, the Estrine family continued their diligent work to ensure said demand was met. Several pages and servants were tasked with making the medicine once an appropriate recipe had been formulated. Since she had been helping Lady Abeel the most, Veronica directed them to ensure each batch was perfect. The sorceress herself had fallen ill after pushing herself to the point of exhaustion. She did not appear to have been infected by the plague, but her family, not wanting to risk her health further, had her rest for the time being regardless.

As they worked, Veronica often looked to the vial containing the main ingredient, something guarded at all times by a senior knight. They had very few Malute ivy leaves left. There was only enough to make five more batches, which would last them another day or two.

She did her best to focus on their current progress instead. Their goal was to help as many people as they could. If they made any delays, more would succumb.

Another batch had finished cooling while she was lost in thought. As she went to pour it into the vials, someone tapped her shoulder to get her attention. She recognized the page as one of Lady Abeel's magic students, although she did not remember him by name.

He whispered into her ear that she was expected in Lord Estrine's quarters and that he came to take her place.

Veronica explained the situation to the knight guarding the Malute ivy and went on her way.

The halls have been getting livelier with each passing day as more recovered. More feet beat against the floor as bodies rushed through the halls. The faces of those Veronica passed by were not as grim and downcast as they used to be. Everyone seemed hopeful again.

It was good to see everyone in higher spirits. They were not exactly happy but definitely in better moods than they were when the plague first hit. And that was enough for now.

Not many lingered in the hall leading to Lord Estrine's quarters, likely so they did not get scolded for loafing around. The path to its doors was clear. After reaching them and giving them a soft knock, she opened one, stepping inside to find not Lord Estrine, but Lord Charleston instead.

The Champion of Duty sat in one of the chairs set for guests instead of the empty seat behind Lord Estrine's desk, and stood when Veronica entered. He looked to her with a countenance stoic and austere. His valsara was much the same, though grief still trickled through his remarkable composure.

"Lord Charleston, sir." Veronica stood at the door to await further instruction, as was expected of her, but she forgot to offer a salute as she appraised his valsara. "You summoned me?"

His stare became somewhat harsher, as if he could tell what she was doing. "Veronica Alivvrn, correct?"

"Yes, sir."

Lord Charleston gestured for her to approach, which she did promptly. He looked down to her as she stood at attention, eyes hard and cold, like the veteran knights Veronica once met in Harnola.

"Sit."

She did as she was told and watched the champion walk over to the window.

"There is much I have to ask you about. That ... thing that struck down Lady Deva, for instance."

Veronica suspected that had something to do with his summons. He watched as she fought the conjoined phantoms, and he kept his eyes on her as the rest of his family questioned her. He knew perfectly well she was not ignorant of the situation that night.

Shame kept her from looking directly at him. She felt she was partially to blame for his wife's death, leaving her when she did. "You may not believe me if I tell you."

That response made his gaze harden. "Try me."

He insisted on a real answer, no matter how ludicrous it might be. Understanding that much, Veronica steeled herself and looked Lord Charleston squarely in the eye again.

"Well ... what attacked you and Lady Deva was a phantom."

"A phantom," he echoed skeptically.

"Yes, milord. A phantom."

The champion made no other retort.

He looked at her as if she were an intricate lock, determined to get her to open up and reveal what she kept hidden.

Seeing this as a silent command to continue, Veronica swallowed and said, "Truly, I was quite surprised by it myself. I have seen phantoms my entire life, and never once have they managed what this one did. They should not be able to materialize into our plane. I believe it was the phantom's immense anger that allowed this aberration to occur."

The stone-cold stare fixed on her did not falter in the slightest. There was no surprise or irritation, only the cynicism he held up while evaluating her words and demeanor.

Veronica would not tell a lie if she could help it, especially not to someone as revered as a champion. Given her reluctance to admit the whole of what she knew, though, even if it was surreal, she accepted his skepticism as well deserved.

Her face was an honest one, contorting to match what she felt. What Lord Charleston wanted to know of her intent had been perfectly exposed for him to see, as well as her discomfort from having to say what often got her teased and admonished in the past.

Lord Charleston stepped up to the chair behind the desk, putting his hand against the headrest. "How did you know where this phantom would be?"

He did not ask that to humor her. He had been there himself and saw, albeit rather poorly, the threat that nearly ended his life. He did not know what his attacker was, and would not pretend to know what it was not.

"I could hear it cry out, at least when it made itself known. When it hid away, I couldn't sense it, so I couldn't track it before—"

Veronica lowered her head and looked away from Lord Charleston again, disheartened.

The champion's eyes fell half-lidded at the reminder as well, but he closed them completely to upkeep his stoic appearance. "You came to my aid and left Lady Deva's side, why?"

So as not to further disrespect him, she looked him back in the eyes, her own reflecting the grief she felt. She may not have been family, but Lady Deva devoted herself to teaching the pages to be upstanding servants to the kingdom.

And she was very grateful for her dedication.

"She knew the phantom was after you, so she sent me to help."

The man took in those words, then let out a long, heavy sigh. "Then you have nothing to regret." He opened his eyes to look forcefully at Veronica, though not without a shred of kindness. "A soldier follows orders. Had you disobeyed her, you would have earned her contempt."

Those words were meant to inform as much as comfort, and they did. Veronica's shame had been brushed away like cotton on the wind. She looked to him without any more lingering doubt.

No one grieved for Lady Deva more than Lord Charleston. If he said as much, then it had to be true.

He stepped around the desk again, leaving the empty chair be. "Still, a phantom... And it came after me, my family, fueled by an immense anger—anger toward Xanlir."

Hearing that name brought another prick to Veronica's heart. She bunched her pants in her hands to try and ignore it. But it did not go unnoticed by Lord Charleston, his eyes ever observant and keeping watch of her emotional cues.

She tried not to notice her own actions, if only to look less pitiable. "What became of it?"

"It is at rest now. I promise it will not endanger your family anymore."

"And what of you?"

"Huh?" Veronica's eyes opened wider after blinking.

After coming around to Veronica's side, the champion brought himself to the chair beside hers, and sat with her. From there, it stopped being a professional matter of a knight questioning a subordinate. He looked to her as someone he wished to understand.

"Xanlir's betrayal has taken much from many, I am sure you know. Your youngest brother, Wallace Alivvrn, was killed by my brother's hand." He paused a moment not to let that hang in the air, but to maintain his own decorum by clearing his throat and keeping his voice composed. "You were expected to be sent here to follow in your brother's footsteps. But after that day, your father, Marquis Brian Alivvrn, rejected your admittance into our training facility and denounced the Estrine family for taking his son away. Yet here you are, five years later."

Veronica remembered that time well.

News of the attack on Brigadier reached Harnola within a day. And after a week's time, a more informative version arrived, along with Wally's body. Her parents tried to shield her from what happened, but she saw it for herself. The last time she saw him, he was so upbeat, full of energy and vigor, and could even go toe-to-toe with the guards in swordplay. But then he was brought back home: pale, cold, and still.

She could not believe it. Her brother was gone—the last of her brothers who would come home regularly, play with her, tell her stories. She tried shaking him awake, just in case he needed a little nudge. But it did not work. He was gone. Dead.

She locked herself in her bedchambers and cried for days on end. She rarely ate or spoke to anyone. The only thing she did was pray to the gods for her brother back.

Finally, the tears stopped flowing, and she began to think of what she would do without him.

"Why did you come here?"

Veronica had become lost down memory lane in reliving that painful time. Lord Charleston did not strike as a patient man, but he took days to grieve before choosing to question her. He understood the pain of loss, and allowed the time for her to process her thoughts.

It was true; her father did reject the Estrines' hospitality after what happened to Wally. Knighthood became a curse he did not want her to bear. But when she picked herself up and left her bedchambers again, she implored him to reconsider. Of course, he dismissed the matter at first.

So she asked him again, and again, and again, and again.

But he would not have her endangered by the Estrines, or anyone who hid behind a knight's shield and waited to stab them in the back.

And she would not have him deny her.

Her father did not understand why she was so insistent on this. He kept denying her every day, and every time he did, she went to the guards' rest area and asked them to help her train.

Wally used to teach her sword techniques when he came home, prep her for what was to come. Because of that, because of her loss, they did not hesitate to oblige.

When her father saw her training, he knew what it was for and demanded that she stop. When she refused, he punished the guards who enabled her and let it be known that she was not to touch another weapon.

But she always managed to convince them to help her despite the consequences.

After catching her with a sword so many times, he recognized her progress. His daughter showed much promise, more so than his lost son. And she was committed to refining her skills for more than just herself.

When next she implored him to let her be a page at the Estrine Chateau, he did not refuse her outright. Instead, he asked why she was so set on this.

As she found the path back to the present, Veronica lifted her head to look at Lord Charleston, and answered him as she had her father. "All of my siblings have been taught the ways of knighthood by the Estrine family. They have grown into the wonderful people they are now because of the discipline instilled in them." In thinking about her brothers, she placed a hand over her heart. "When I became the only Alivvrn child left at home, I thought of the ways I could be close to them again. In truth, I did not know whether or not I looked forward to when I would join them in knighthood. But after Wally died, after I grieved for him, I realized that it is what I must do."

That hand over her heart closed, capturing and holding dear the wishes she made. She placed it back in her lap as resolve filled her stare.

"I do not blame your family for the sins of Xanlir, Lord Charleston. And I dearly hope that, someday, Father will come to forgive Lord Estrine and renew their friendship. It is because I believe your family is just that I wished for you to be the ones to instill in me the discipline my brothers learned. And with that discipline, I shall become a knight—for Wally, for Father, for all of those who lost family to the Renegades, including you."

Those last words coaxed Lord Charleston's eyes to widen ever so slightly. That was something that truly surprised him.

But it was only natural that Veronica considered him one of those who suffered at the hands of the Renegades. His brother was swayed to betray his family and walk a path of conflict and despair. For as much as they denounced him, she knew the Estrine family grieved for the fall of one of their own.

The teachings of the Natural Orthodoxy equated a man falling into sin to the death of their self. One became something else entirely when they chose to forsake their loved ones, their values, their loyalty, their humanity.

After weighing everything said to him, Lord Charleston retook his stoic countenance and stood from his seat. "Discipline is but the armor and weapon of a knight. What makes a knight worthy of their shield is what carries and guides them: their character and will. Remember that."

"Yes, Lord Charleston."

"Now, come."

The champion led the page out of Lord Estrine's quarters, his business there finished, and locked the doors behind them with a simple brass key.

"And Page Alivvrn, be sure to exercise control of your power. It will serve you well."

"Yes, Lord Charleston."

With that, he dismissed the page, and they went their separate ways.

As more recovered and fewer became ill, Brigadier came to see the end of its plight. More of the Malute ivy had been secured and brought to the capital, as orchestrated by Lord Estrine. The result: numerous people that were in agony and on the verge of death were saved.

Their nightmare had come to an end.

Though it was not without loss, they could once again greet the new day with hope instead of fear. Time would tell how everyone recovered from the impact.

The pages who worked throughout the epidemic were granted some time for themselves. It was a rare opportunity, so they did not waste it, though many wanted nothing more than to spend that time resting.

With so much time put toward helping the ill, Veronica had too few opportunities to check on her mount. She went to the stables to rectify that and took Amber on a nice, long run. It was grand to be riding atop a horse, feeling the wind brush against her face and through her hair.

Amber had so much energy from being cooped up she ran through the fields like her life depended on it. She was generally docile and liked to prance about at a relaxing pace. Veronica could hardly blame her for being so excited. Perhaps she worried it would be just as long before her next run.

After the horse ran herself—and her rider—ragged, Veronica led Amber back to the stables to get her watered. Amber was very appreciative of the water and eagerly drank from the trough.

Veronica stroked her hand along Amber's chestnut mane, captivated by her charm.

She then took notice of the sweat along her brow and effortlessly brushed it away. It surprised her that sweat would cling to her forehead when the wind brushed against it so frivolously. It made her realize how thirsty she was too.

She dabbed her palm against the surface of the water in the trough, then pulled up, drawing some into a small sphere in her palm. She held the sphere in both hands and brought it to her mouth for a drink.

When Amber had finished, Veronica brought her back to her stall. Although tuckered out, the horse seemed reluctant to follow, tugging her reins back toward the exit.

It made Veronica giggle. "Come now. You'll only exhaust yourself if you overindulge."

The horse followed her and returned to her stall without much fuss. Veronica delighted in seeing the beautiful creature trot inside and nosh on some hay, but also noticed she was almost out. Not wanting her to go without, she walked over to the corner where the stableman stored the hay.

She stopped in place when she noticed someone else had the same idea. Sashan walked in her direction, carrying a bundle of hay. She stopped at the sight of Veronica, looking at her with a hard scowl and struggling to keep her demeanor by repressing her rage. Despite the attempt, Veronica could feel her hostility pricking at her skin. She feigned ignorance of this and tried to give a pleasant smile, if only to be friendly.

"Good day, Sashan."

The fellow page did not deign to return the greeting. "I take it Amber already had her fun."

Veronica nodded. "Y-Yes."

"She'll need to be groomed then. I shall handle it."

Without another word or even looking her way, Sashan walked past Veronica, not intent on keeping up the pleasantries.

"Sashan."

Veronica tried to speak with her, but she ignored her and kept going. She still felt guilty about getting Sashan in trouble and wanted to apologize. Her pleas for her to wait and listen were ignored, so Veronica followed Sashan. She raised a hand and placed it on her shoulder.

That connection eviscerated the sluice holding her emotions at bay. They flooded up Veronica's arm, its full force stabbing her.

Sashan dropped the bundle of hay in her arm and struck at Veronica. She might have only intended to swat her hand away, but in the process, the back of her hand smacked her cheek. Veronica tottered backward a few steps and cupped her cheek, looking at her peer aghast.

"Don't look at me like *you're* the victim," Sashan hissed. "You know what you did. You know who you've hurt!"

Her voice screamed pure rage. Her stare was feverish, as if she saw her as a threat. A terrible contempt exuded from her valsara. It left Veronica petrified, unable to say or do anything in response.

Having let her emotions out, Sashan took a breath to regain her composure. She leaned down to pick up the hay she dropped. "I tolerate your presence because I must," she said upon standing again. "If I have to speak with you, if I have to work with you, then I will. But do not act like you deserve to be forgiven, witch! Unless it is necessary, keep your distance."

Not caring for whatever response she may have, Sashan walked away.

Veronica remained where she was, caressing her cheek. Horror tinged the guilt in her, coaxing it to spread, these terrible feelings clustering in her chest.

Rather than stay and allow them to grow, she ran outside.

~ Eighth Chapter ~
Determination

Sunlight glimmered through the roof of the leaves to reflect off the water of the secluded pond. The water shifted to and fro in a manner that almost appeared restless.

It moved to the pull of Veronica's power. The troubled girl sat on her knees beside the pond, trying to let her thoughts flow unhindered by turbulent angst.

Clearing her mind proved difficult in times when it was not necessary to keep on her toes. It was not until she came upon the small body of water that she could unwind. Simply breathing in the moist air helped her calm down. She kept taking slow, deep breaths until the pond was still again.

Her thoughts again steady, Veronica's eyes lifted open to stare at the clear water. She saw her reflection and looked back into her half-lidded stare.

Those words Sashan spoke wounded her. The bitterness they carried left her shaken.

Time and again, Veronica withstood such bitterness, but her skin had not grown any thicker for it. It only left her to wonder how many more times she would have to endure it.

Dwelling on that would not do her good. Understanding that, she stood before the pond. She lifted her arm and held out her hand, pulling upward, bringing a long whip of water to sprout from the pond.

Her pull bent and twisted the whip, swerving it through the air, its end drawing through loops made from its body without touching them. It came to resemble a tree as the knots of water merged together, and as the line linking it to the pond was severed, Veronica pulled her hands to draw the water outward. The mass hovering above the pond now shifted into a butterfly.

A smile drew between her cheeks and her eyes widened in delight. The slivers of sunlight reaching the water made it gleam as dazzlingly as her ocean-blue eyes.

She always admired the beauty her power allowed her to create, no matter how much she used it.

When the butterfly flapped its huge wings, shimmering droplets scattering to the air, she pulled her arms closed again. The butterfly, following her whim, receded into a condensed sphere. Her hands gently clasped together, and when she held them up and pulled them apart, the sphere of water split in two, each half forming an elegant eagle that flew in opposite directions. The raptorial birds circled her, and Veronica spun to follow in their aerial dance.

As the eagles ascended, flying circles around one another, Veronica extended her reach to them and squeezed her hands closed. The masses of water split again and plummeted, her power cradling them just before hitting the ground and carrying them upward to form dolphins.

The dolphins swam together through the air, playfully moving in seemingly unpredictable patterns to keep her attention. One broke from its pod to approach Veronica and kiss her cheek.

She fondly remembered how spirited the dolphins that swam by the ships of Harnola harbor were, how they liked to greet and play with the voyagers. During a voyage when she was five, Veronica met a friendly young calf that sprayed her with its blowhole. How surprised it was when the giddy child collected the water and sprayed it back just as gently.

It was such a friendly creature, so eager to get along.

The dolphins slowed until coming to a stop, just hovering in the air. The only movement made was from their bodies rippling steadily.

Her mind was clouded again with thoughts of those who have shunned her. She did not understand why others her age disliked her so. She was kind and genuinely cared about those around her, but it was not enough.

Why was it so hard for her to make friends?

She merged the masses of water back together, slowly pouring it all back into the pond.

"Stopping so soon? I barely got a look."

Unbeknownst to her, Cheryl had been watching her exercise, though it seemed not for long. She had been recovering well since taking the improved medicine, and finally managed to walk from the chateau on her own.

Veronica turned to greet her friend while the water seeped back into the pond. "Cheryl! Are you feeling better?"

She gave a confident smile. "Much. You didn't think a little malady would keep me down, did you?"

"Not at all," answered Veronica with a little giggle.

For as much as she would have enjoyed testing that confidence by reminding her of her vulnerable moments, she was much too happy to see her fully recovered.

Cheryl stepped from the shrubs and walked up to Veronica, a look of sympathy in her eyes. She knew her well. The only times she came to the pond were to swim and to forget about her troubles—and it was not the best weather for a dip in the water. She cupped her friend's shoulder, giving it a little squeeze.

Veronica appreciated the gesture, though she still hung her head. She wanted to show that appreciation with a smile, but she knew Cheryl would have none of that. She always insisted that she did not need to put on a façade for her. If she was genuinely unhappy, she did not want her hiding it.

"What happened?"

The mark made by Sashan's hand had long since faded.

"It was nothing." Veronica did not think it necessary to burden her with the anger that would come from knowing about their altercation.

Of course, Cheryl would be upset no matter what. She never tolerated it when someone hurt her friend. "It's not nothing. Come on, Veronica. You can tell me."

"Really, it was nothing. Times have been rather strenuous lately. I am just not myself because of it."

She could insist on that until the kingdom fell, and Cheryl would not believe her. Nothing so small upset her like that.

But Cheryl chose not to pry since Veronica would not confide in her. She gave her shoulder another squeeze before letting it go. "Build each other up, not destroy one another, huh?"

She understood the reason behind her silence, which made Veronica smile again. It was nice to have someone who understood her so well.

"I wish you would do something besides take it."

"It's sweet of you to worry."

"You only fight when left no choice—of course I'm going to worry."

"I do not believe getting into fights will protect my dignity. Besides, you know the Estrines prohibit it."

"Yeah, they do, but it doesn't stop anyone from doing it. You know that as well as anyone."

"I will respect their rules as much as the knight's code. And I will not betray my own beliefs either."

As a page, a knight-to-be, she was expected to fight. And she would, for the right reasons. To better her skills. To protect herself and others. She would even spar with others for sport; she had come to find a thrill in fighting with those that knew how. But she never felt it right to fight others simply to get back at them.

Cheryl sighed, finally relenting. "Guess that just means I'll have to stay by you so you keep out of trouble."

Veronica giggled, then put her hands on her hips. "Oh, you'll keep me out of trouble, mm? I did not realize I was the one constantly being called out by the Estrines."

Her teasing made Cheryl's face tense up, but she quickly relaxed when she realized her friend felt well enough to poke fun. She met that big smile with a somewhat uneasy one. "Come on, let's head back inside."

Veronica nodded and followed Cheryl back to the chateau.

The plague that terrorized Brigadier gradually subsided over the weeks, and the last of the infected made remarkable recoveries. The crisis finally passed, allowing order to be restored.

With the aftermath and requests for aid from neighboring towns in the region being handled by the palace, the Estrine family could reorganize and revise their plans for the pages. Spring was the season when they underwent the most rigorous training and the harshest trials.

The unforeseen setbacks forced them to make considerable changes. But there would be no cancelling their most important event.

The long-awaited war enactment was rescheduled to allow for preparation and the chance for expected knights to arrive. This test of cunning and resolve was too important to permit otherwise. Through the enactment, the Estrines reaffirmed their standing as the kingdom's most prominent page trainers, and the pages demonstrated their prowess before scores of renowned knights who might choose them to be their squire.

It was an opportunity none could afford to miss. That was why, after news of the enactment's date was announced, Cheryl had been training nonstop to make up for lost time. She wanted to be ready for anything that would come.

Cheryl had been working hard since the dawn of spring, but now that the enactment was so close, she pushed herself beyond the limit. To ensure she did not work herself ragged, Veronica trained with her.

The midday sun gleamed down on the two as they sparred in the training grounds. They were drenched in sweat and fought to control their breathing. Fatigue from their consecutive bouts made their muscles melt like butter. They were sore all over from various wounds. And still they wanted to go on.

"That's thirty-two to fourteen," Veronica stated, ending in a gasp. She looked to her foe and pointed her blunt sword at her, one-handed. "Shall we make it thirty-three now?"

Cheryl tightened her grip on her weapon and flashed a tired grin. "Don't get cocky. I'm just getting started!" Her legs were a little wobbly, but she still stood tall.

Both pages lowered their swords and approached each other for their weapons to cross. When their blades met, Cheryl pressed hers against Veronica's firmly to taunt her and remind her of her strength, while Veronica held hers steady against Cheryl's and looked her confidently in the eye.

"Ready...?" Veronica stated.

No one watched over them to supervise their clashes or direct them on when to begin. They remained that way until one of them broke their connection to start. No moves were made right away, both combatants testing the other's mettle and patience.

And patience was something Veronica understood well. Her confident stare never wavered from Cheryl's. And though her arms were hot and sore, she knew it was the same for her foe, who exerted force just for intimidation.

Deciding to take the initiative, Cheryl drew back her sword, "En garde!" and quickly hurled it at her foe. Veronica followed her motion perfectly and blocked the swing to parry. It was not enough to throw Cheryl off balance; she recovered immediately, blocking her foe's next swing and shoving her away.

Taking a few quick steps back sent spasms down Veronica's jellified legs, forcing her to go on the defensive. For as skilled as she was, going over forty rounds of swordplay without rest did her no favors. Her arms and legs slowed, and the loss of speed brought on a loss of power.

While Cheryl's strength also waned, she was exceptionally stubborn. She refused to admit defeat and insisted on continuing until she got more wins than her sparring partner. Her endurance and persistence made her the page she was.

And she was not willing to settle for the strength she had.

Cheryl rushed in and threw her sword into a blinding flurry. Veronica was just as quick to block every single swing. She swept the attacks away before they would reach her head, her neck, her belly, her sides, and waited for the right moment when her energy burned out.

Once she found her opportunity, she stepped forward into a clean thrust, jabbing her blunt sword into Cheryl's right shoulder.

Veronica watched her topple into the grass, and tried not to do the same herself. It was thanks to her reflexes that she managed to hold her own, but even with them, she could barely keep up. Her muscles, her lungs, even her tendons burned in her efforts to last against Cheryl's insatiable thirst for combat.

Her body tensed up upon seeing Cheryl rise for more, but the proud fighter slipped back down, her legs unable to support her.

"Perhaps ... a small break is in order?" Veronica tried to say through her heavy panting.

Her sparring partner had just as hard a time getting her words out. She gave a shaky nod and said, "Y-Yeah... Sure..."

Thankful for that response, Veronica dropped to her knees and fought for breath, her free hand held over her chest. Now that she had come to a full stop, she could feel the sweat trickling along her skin, sticking to her uniform, hanging from her brow and nose. It felt uncomfortable, but she did not have the energy to so much as brush it off.

With every drop of sweat shed, she could feel her mouth getting drier. There was not even saliva for her to swallow.

The day did not start warm but quickly became so as the sunlight stretched far over the land. Training underneath the dazzling rays was always trying, but it seemed much more so today.

Lady Sundralla must desire to test us to have her radiance shine so brightly, Veronica reasoned.

Catching the attention of the goddess of luck and bringer of the morning sun made her giddy. For her to test them so, it must have been a sign that she may yet favor them.

"Gods..." Chery groaned. "How do you do it? It's like you know what I'll do before I even do it."

Veronica raised her head to give a smile. "If that were true, you wouldn't have won fourteen rounds. Your reflexes are improving."

"Not fast enough, they aren't." The determined girl pressed her arm to the ground again and this time got to her feet, standing tall.

While Cheryl was impressed with Veronica's deft hand, Veronica admired how quickly Cheryl recovered. Defeat from anyone left her unsatisfied; she wanted to be strong enough to take down any who got in her way.

Though only the gods were invincible, Cheryl wanted to come close.

Seeing her still on the ground, Cheryl reached out a hand to help Veronica up. Upon grasping her hand, she pulled her up onto her feet and greeted her with a broad grin.

"Might we stop for a drink?" After such a rigorous workout, anyone would need to quench their thirst.

Cheryl nodded in agreement. "Yeah. Come on."

The two walked back to the chateau together. Cheryl took the lead until noticing how slowly Veronica trudged behind. She slowed down, waiting for her to catch up.

The air had been notably dry as of late. It left Veronica more winded than usual. That became evident in how heavily she breathed, how she struggled to take in all the moisture she could.

Days like this made training all the more taxing.

Cheryl noticed her plight and tried to help her take her mind off it. She took a deep breath through the nose, humming with delight. "Mm, the air smells great today, huh?"

Veronica smiled and nodded. "Yes... Rather fragrant indeed."

"The flowers must all be in bloom for it to smell this sweet."

Veronica did not notice that at all. She only said what she felt was appropriate.

She never told her friend that she had no sense of smell. The aroma of flowers tickling her nose was a sensation foreign to her. No matter how faint or pungent a scent may be, it would always pass her by.

When she first found out, she thought there was something wrong with her. But as she grew, she came to see it only as an inconvenience.

It made her uncomfortable to talk about it, though, so she instead just agreed with whatever Cheryl described and reacted appropriately.

"This really is a good day to train!" Cheryl said with glee and a smile to match it. "After we drink up, let's come back out and spar some more."

"Okay!"

Later on, when they returned to the training grounds, they found several more pages had gathered there. They were all lined up at attention for Sir Storn to direct.

Cheryl tried to avoid getting caught up in their affairs, and grabbed Veronica by the arm to lead her back inside, but the knight noticed them and called for them to join.

Reluctantly, Cheryl let go of her friend's arm, and they did as ordered.

With the day of the war enactment drawing closer, Sir Storn tasked himself with preparing the pages with a final evaluation of their skills. He stated that it was his duty as their combat instructor to ensure they had not gone soft from the time spent recovering. The enactment would test their physical prowess as much as their wit, coordination, and reactions. To see whether or not they were still able to participate, he would lead the pages through various exercises.

The pages sparred against each other one-on-one as a start. Sir Storn critiqued their performances as they did, just like when they were going through the regular training regimen. He was as blunt and critical as ever. But at least this time, he was not jabbing them with his scabbard to correct their forms.

Afterwards, they were divided into groups as large as six for team exercises. Veronica was put into a team opposing Cheryl's. Disappointed though she was that they would not be working together, Veronica faced Cheryl with the same dedication she had when they were sparring alone. It would have been a dishonor and a disservice to her if she did otherwise, not to mention the fury it would incite from their instructor.

Her team did not coordinate well in the beginning. They refused to cooperate, insisting their way was best.

Meanwhile, Cheryl's team worked flawlessly together. They responded promptly to their appointed leader, cooperating to destabilize their competition. Theirs was a fine performance.

Three times Veronica's team lost to Cheryl's, each failure making her teammates more desperate and aggressive. Veronica offered a few ideas to her leader, but she was shot down, ignored, told to be quiet and not get in the way. Their detest for her was apparent.

Just once, she wished her peers would not treat her like a nuisance.

They were fortunate that this was only practice. There were no chances to make up for mistakes during the enactment. They had to prove themselves stalwart. One misstep was one too many. One would be all it took to turn victory into defeat.

Her team remained on the defensive when the next round began, and waited for their opponents to approach. They stood close together, forming a shield that would repulse the enemies. A few of them saw it as cowardice, but it was the strategically sound thing to do. Not every situation called for taking the offensive.

And once they were close enough, Veronica made her move.

She broke from her group and made the daring move to rush straight at the enemy team at the last moment. Her attack was easily intercepted, but the point of it was not to beat one foe. Rather, it was to disrupt the whole team's formation. They broke apart when she clashed with the leader. She fought him and two others who thought to strike her quickly, giving her teammates the chance to push back against the remainder of the enemy team.

Veronica held her own against the three, defeating two and holding the leader at bay, until her team leader stepped in to help.

The only opponent left was Cheryl, but since victory hinged on which team struck the other's leader first, there was no need to face her.

That did not stop her teammates from continuing to attack her, though. At first, Veronica thought they had just gotten carried away. But her leader jumped into the fray to harass her too.

By the time Veronica moved in to push the boys away, Cheryl had been smacked to the ground. Cheryl's teammates rushed to her aid. Many of them formed a wall in front of Veronica's teammates while Veronica helped her up.

"Not so cocky now, are you?" taunted Veronica's team leader, Nev.

"Nev, that's enough," she scolded him.

"It won't be enough until we're even."

"This is about the exercise? You went too far, all of you! We had already won. There was no need to—"

"I don't need a lecture from you, witch!"

Cheryl was about ready to push through the wall of people to get to Nev when Sir Storn got approached. "Enough of this tomfoolery!" he ordered. "There will be new teams for the next exercise. Come, now."

The pages followed Sir Storn back to the center of the training grounds to gather with the others, though Cheryl lingered where she was for a moment, her vile glare fixated on Nev. The suddenly smug boy returned the bitter look with his own, not willing to break away first.

Cheryl's steely fists closed, trembling with the anger she struggled to contain. But she had a compelling reason to control it.

Unclenching her fist, she followed Veronica, who waited for her, to join the other pages.

Nev snickered and nudged his friend in the arm. "Do you suppose this is how she looked when she ran away from Sacridge?"

Cheryl came to a staggering halt when she heard what he said. Veronica, immediately recognizing where this would lead, looked to her with worry. Cheryl's eyes were opened so wide that they looked ready to pop from her skull, and as the weight of his scornful words sank in, her anger festered into something darker.

"Cheryl—"

It was already too late. She could not hear her.

She bared her teeth malignantly as she faced Nev. "Take that back!"

The snide page looked back to her with a raised brow, acting like he had not heard her. "Say again?"

"Take. It. Back!"

Guided by unrelenting rage, Cheryl dropped her sword and rushed at Nev, and tackled him to the ground. She kept him pinned beneath her, refusing to let him get away, and started to pummel him viciously. He barely put up a struggle, raising his hands only for them to be swatted away with her arm while her opposite fist smashed into his face.

"Cheryl, stop!"

Veronica fought to get her off of him as Cheryl put her fists together, bringing them down on him like a hammer on a nail. She wrapped her arms around one of Cheryl's to pull her away. Cheryl flailed to throw her off. Her rage gave her frightening strength. But Veronica took advantage of her frantic movement to draw her arm behind her back and pull her off of her victim.

"Stop this! This isn't going to solve anything!"

Her words did not reach her. Cheryl was so fixated on harming Nev that she was deaf to much else. Nev's friend helped Veronica pull her off of him as more pages gathered around them.

Nev crawled away from Cheryl. He flinched when it looked like she would break free from their grasps, raising an arm to shield himself. Blood leaked from his nostrils, and his face was swelling, especially around his left eye and right cheek. The heavy impacts left him trembling as he tried to get back on his feet.

He was truly frightened of the girl who nearly beat him senseless, and as he came to recognize as much, that fear turned into rage as well. Losing himself to it, he leaned back down to pick up the sword he dropped and was too startled to use at first.

Before Veronica let go of Cheryl to stop Nev, Sir Storn came back to them. His presence prompted Nev to lower his sword, a wry smirk forming on his face in place of a twisted grimace.

"Enough!" the knight demanded.

Nev put a hand to his swollen cheek while Cheryl struggled to break free. She finally settled down when she realized what went through the battered boy's head, though her rage continued to flare, so much so that Veronica could feel it burning her.

Sir Storn stepped in front of Cheryl to block her from glaring at Nev. "This outburst is completely inexcusable, Page Evaleen!"

"But he—"

"I will hear none of your excuses! I have enough to handle without dealing with your incompetence and childish interruptions." Sir Storn shook his fist fiercely as he stared Cheryl down, plainly showing his discontent. "Do you think a knight will want *you* for a squire when you can't even demonstrate self-control? What knight would want a bratty girl who can't guide a sword or her own emotions? It is a privilege to be able to serve, one that you clearly have not earned." He lowered his fist to fold his arms behind his back. "The ready and able will take part in the enactment—you will not."

Cheryl all but froze from those heavy-handed words. She stood still, her eyes wide open in disbelief.

Veronica was just as baffled by the knight's decree. "Sir, with all due respect, you do not have the authority to make that decision. Lord Estrine alone decides—"

"Do you want to be next, Page Alivvrn?" Sir Storn threatened. "Lord Estrine relies on his instructors—on me—to decide whether or not pages are fit to take part in the enactment. If I find any of you are unworthy of the opportunity, then he sees to it that you do not receive it."

As the knight continued his tirade, the anger in Cheryl built up anew. With each word he uttered, it grew stronger. And when it finally overpowered her need to respect Lord Estrine's instructors, she gritted her teeth, clenched her fists, glared at Sir Storn, and vehemently said:

"Are you kidding me, Stoneface!? You call me out for incompetence when I've whooped *everyone's* arses here? While that little dastard insults my home and calls me a coward!? I will not take it, and I won't take anything from you either!"

The knight's eyes drew open wide. The creases on his face broadened, making his forehead look soft, and his thick chin hung from his mouth gaping. "S-Stoneface...?" His eye twitched and his brow quivered.

A few pages could not help but chuckle at that epithet and how his face looked, but they stifled their laughter when his chiseled face hardened from frustration.

"Storn!"

The knight flinched upon hearing his name called. He looked back to the chateau with a somewhat composed face and proper posture.

Veronica was surprised to find Lord Charleston approaching. He did say he would be around for a while longer when she delivered a message to him the other day.

But what was he doing out in the training grounds?

Sir Storn put his fist over his heart to salute him. "Lord Charleston, sir! Ho—" He paused to clear his throat. "How may I be of service?"

"What is this about?"

"Nothing to concern yourself with, milord. It's just a misbehaving page."

Cheryl groaned and looked ready to lash out again, but she held her tongue when Lord Charleston looked to her. Talking back to Sir Storn was one thing, but she could not show disrespect to, or even in front of, one of the Six Champions. She glanced away from him.

Sir Storn seemed haughtier when he saw that. He must have thought that she was relenting and now felt shame for her actions.

But Lord Charleston looked to suspect otherwise. "Just a misbehaving page. And yet you've let her rattle you so."

Sir Storn tensed up. "I-I was merely deciding on how she should be disciplined."

"There is nothing wrong with the traditional way."

Veronica gasped when she saw Lord Charleston reach for the sword on his back. He took it in hand with the blade still housed in its scabbard. Then he looked to her. "Page Alivvrn, give her your sword."

She hesitated a moment, but when Cheryl looked to her and nodded, Veronica gave her the sword, as well as a worried look, as if to say, "Be careful."

Everyone backed away from Lord Charleston and Cheryl as they took their stances. Discontent was evident in the champion's heavy stare. His eyes, hard and fiery, bore into the page before him. Brave and confident though she was, even Cheryl could not mask the unease she felt caught in his sights.

"Your name."

"Cheryl Evaleen of Everspeak, sir."

"And you are from Sacridge?"

The very mention of that name caused her valsara to flare, and the fear in her eyes became buried by anger. It was not directed at him exactly; there was no malevolence in his voice when he said it. The memory of the scorn she received always emerged whenever it was said.

"You are angry. Good." He drew his sword forward, and Cheryl immediately followed with hers for them to cross. More force was used by her, though it did nothing to startle the champion. "Use that anger."

He pulled his sword away and quickly hurled it back down at Cheryl. She blocked it promptly, and did as she was told when they pulled back for the next swing. Their swords clashed with great force, both guiding all of their strength into their swings. Cheryl was not as strong as him, but she stood her ground and kept meeting his attacks with everything she had. Above. Below. Above. From the left. She defended herself aptly until she finally caught an opening and thrust.

But Lord Charleston saw through her attack and brought his sword against hers, grinding it against the dull blade, and slew it across her chest. Cheryl fell to the ground with a loud, painful *thud*. Miraculously, though, her weapon remained in hand.

She did not get up right away. The impact was so strong that she could not ignore the pain crushing her from both sides.

Lord Charleston looked down at her with the same hard eyes, then glared at the crowd. "What are you playing at?"

The pages were distraught to find he was referring to Sir Storn. "Sir...?"

"Incompetence? Can't guide a sword?" He marched toward the instructor, pointing his sheathed sword at him. "I've been watching for some time now, and I am appalled by what I've seen.

"Her form is perfect—strong, stable. Her timing is appropriate for one with her experience. Yet you focus on her and ignore those who need correction. Such as ..." Lord Charleston approached one of the boys from Cheryl's team and, without warning, thrust his sword. The page quickly raised his sword to guard, but was swatted to the ground with one swing. "His legs must be further apart to promote balance." Then he went to one of the onlookers from the other teams, who defended himself just as well and lasted just as long. "His arms are too rigid. They must move fluidly with his weapon."

It was impressive of him to notice so much in such brief instances.

And finally, he glanced at Nev. "And this one..." He moved toward him quickly but did not actually attack. He only feinted a swing that looked like it would go into a downward chop. That was all he needed; Nev fell back on the ground, cowering from that alone. "This boy fears a challenge, a trait unbecoming for a knight."

Veronica looked Cheryl's way when it seemed Lord Charleston made his point. Opportune as it was for her to learn, even indirectly, from the Champion of Duty, she could not simply ignore her. Cheryl took a heavier hit than the boys. It was well deserved, for she lasted much longer than them.

Though she was still lying on the ground, Cheryl fought to lean forward and sit up.

"I trusted you with my former position for the same reason I picked you for my squire: you knew to keep a sharp eye on everything around you. I see that has changed."

"N-No, milord! That's not true."

"Then you are showing them favoritism." Disgust grew in the champion's deep voice as disappointment spread in his valsara. "These children are not your squires. It is not your place to put one above the others. And you cannot be allowed to let something as trivial as their sex dictate how you teach them."

"That is an absurd accusation! ...Ahem, sir."

The strict stare Lord Charleston gave the now trembling Sir Storn did more than command respect. If he felt the need to respond to his subordinate questioning his eyes, what they saw, he would have. But instead, he slid the sword and its scabbard into place on his back.

"I will be taking over here. Report to Lady Biancore, tell her you were sent to relearn the Maidens' Call to Arms. Once she is through with you, you will report to Lord Estrine for your reassignment."

Sir Storn was shaken and aghast, his stony composure now crumbling from being chipped at so thoroughly.

The pages were in awe at the display before them. Never had they seen anyone treat Sir Storn like a child. They did not expect that he would do as he was told. But he did, with his head hung in dejection.

"Page Evaleen, report!"

Cheryl picked herself off the ground and joined the other pages at the champion's behest. Her face twitched and scrunched up with every move made. When she stood beside Veronica, Lord Charleston began.

"Pages, you will all be led by me until a replacement instructor is determined. Know that I am not as careless or as patient as Sir Storn. Mistakes will not be tolerated. Step out of line, and you'll receive *proper* correction."

That last sentence was said with a glance in Cheryl's direction, and the pages looked her way as she hastily moved her arm back to her side, hiding her attempt to ease her pain. Making a mistake became all the more worrisome, especially for those he already called out.

"We will begin with single combat again. Pair up!"

The pages split up and picked partners they had not sparred with previously, getting to work right away.

Veronica did not yet leave Cheryl's side. "Are you all right?"

"Yeah... It's just a few ribs."

"Would you like me to take you to the medical ward?"

The offer was tempting, but Cheryl shook her head. She wanted to stand out in a better way after getting reprimanded and smacked around. Continuing to train despite a few fractured ribs and the risk of receiving more was a good way to start.

The least Veronica could do was give her a nice, easy workout.

"Page Evaleen."

The two stood at attention when Lord Charleston approached.

"Begin with the boy," he said as he glanced over his shoulder to Nev.

Suddenly, Cheryl perked up and wore a wicked smile. She moved to follow the order, but stopped when Lord Charleston's hand rested on her shoulder.

"Use your anger; don't let it use you."

The page nodded and went on her way when he let go.

Although she worried for her, Veronica could tell she was in higher spirits. So long as Cheryl could stand, she would try not to fret for her, but she knew to keep an eye on her in the meantime. She always pushed herself so much.

~ Ninth Chapter ~

The Enactment

Training under Lord Charleston was, as promised, more strenuous and unforgiving than it was with their former instructor. He was much more direct than the other Estrine knights and very forceful, both with words and correction. Those qualities were appreciated by some but loathed by others, perhaps because more pages were corrected than before—about twice as many.

Nevertheless, it was a rare opportunity to be had. They were being trained by one of the Six Champions, the greatest knights in the kingdom. Many yearned merely to be seen by such grand figures, let alone be taught, however briefly, by one.

The sessions with him ran Veronica ragged, but it meant the world to her to be able to learn from him.

Veronica was returning to her bedchamber one late evening after serving the Estrines their meal. When she stepped inside, she found Cheryl at their desk, looking at an open book. Cheryl looked up to give her roommate a quick "Hey!" before turning back to it.

Veronica walked to the desk for a look. It was the one she kept beside her bed. Its pages had no text. What rested between them instead were flattened, dried out flowers.

"Did you find a new one?" she asked while leaning over her shoulder.

Cheryl shook her head. "Nah. Just wanted to look at them."

Collecting flowers had been a hobby of hers since she came to the chateau. She did not know how to at first, but when Veronica noticed how much she liked them, she taught her how to press and preserve them. She got so upset when she first tried it. After she got the hang of it, though, she had been pressing every kind of flower she could find.

Veronica giggled. "To think you used to hate flowers."

"Yeah..."

That was what she said when she first started. But she came to love them. That newfound love served as a connection to her family.

Before coming to the Estrine Chateau, Cheryl lived with her mother and two elder sisters, Lily and Violet, in a humble village. They had a garden that her mother grew from seeds she collected. Her children often tended to it while she worked. It was not a task Cheryl liked, but it was time spent with her wonderful sisters, and when their mother was with them, it was perfect.

Alas, that happy time came to an end when her village, when Sacridge, was attacked by the Renegades. The village's defenses crumbled before the enemy forces. The knights were wiped out and the civilians captured.

Desperate to save her family, Cheryl fled Sacridge to find help. She ran for days until reaching Brigadier. The city, too, had been attacked and remained on high alert. The child pled for the knights to save her home.

And that was exactly what they set out to do.

But they were too late. Sacridge had been destroyed. Everything was burned to the ground, the earth left scorched. No survivors remained.

With Sacridge's fate sealed, Cheryl decided on her own. She swore to become a knight and avenge her family.

To that end, she learned of how children were groomed to be knights and went straight to the Estrine Chateau. She shouted at the gates for them to let her in and begin her training. The guards turned her away many times, thinking her a nuisance. But her resolve had impressed Lord Estrine. He took her into his care and began training her personally to see how far that resolve would go.

Many had heard of what brought her to the chateau, and some of the pages came to pick on her for it. They called her a coward for running from Sacridge and associated that cowardice with weakness.

Cheryl became lost in thought when she flipped to the next page, where rested a pressed golden alcea, a flower that once grew in Sacridge.

Veronica knew what was going through her mind. She slipped a hand onto her shoulder, giving it a gentle squeeze.

There were nights when Cheryl had been haunted by her family's fate. She thought that perhaps she should have stayed behind with them. In those times, Veronica comforted her and tried to ease her suffering.

After four years, her valsara remained serene in thinking about them.

"It won't be long now..." said Cheryl. "Soon, we'll be knights, and we can avenge our fallen loved ones."

When she was finished looking through her flower book, Cheryl stood to get some water. Veronica flipped through its pages for a little bit longer. She eventually stopped when she saw a familiar shape pressed against the parchment. It was a white orchid with lovely golden anther.

She gasped when she saw it. "When did you get this one?"

Cheryl was just putting the pitcher back on their dresser when she noticed what Veronica was doing. The wooden container slipped from her grasp and fell to the floor. She leaped away from the spill, then groaned at her mistake.

Not much water was spilled, so it was easy for Veronica to dissolve it into mist with her power.

With the mess gone, she hopped back onto her feet and looked Cheryl squarely in the eye. "Cheryl, that is a pearl orchid."

"So?"

"So? Do you know what this flower is?"

"Pretty, yeah. I know that."

Many flowers were made into symbols and given meaning for more than their beauty. This particular flower was a token given to someone the giver was in love with.

Veronica had seen what power that flower had. One who gave a pearl orchid gave a piece of their heart.

And the rosy color of her cheeks and the uneasy fluctuations of her valsara proved Cheryl recognized that.

A beaming smile sprouted over Veronica's face, and it made Cheryl all the more nervous.

"You picked it for someone!"

"No, I didn't!"

She was skilled at many things, but Cheryl could not lie well. Her voice wavered and her gaze fell short of Veronica's, just like when she tried to hide something.

"You like someone!"

"No, I don't!"

Veronica leaned in closer to Cheryl and looked into her flustered eyes, her own aglitter.

"Who is it? You have to tell me. Come on, please."

"No one! It's no one, okay? Just stop talking about it."

Cheryl marched back to the desk and slammed the book shut, picking it up and holding it protectively in her arms. It had been some time since she was so wary about Veronica touching it. She looked at her so fervently, like when they first met and she was reluctant to let her in.

After all this time, there were some things she was afraid of expressing even to her. Poor Cheryl was always so worried about letting her feelings show. Plucking the pearl orchid in a moment of realization and pressing the flower, concealing it, because she was afraid of what the response would be was certainly something she would do.

But Veronica did not want her hiding anything from her.

She feigned acceptance for a moment, giving Cheryl time to put the book back under her bed, then moved in and swiped it.

"Hey, give that back!"

Veronica leaped away from Cheryl's reach before she could grab her. She laughed in delight while being chased around their room, treating it like a game.

Cheryl had her cornered atop her bed, but the spry girl kept bobbing this way and that, ready to bolt the other way when she pounced. The constant back and forth got on her nerves quickly, and she leaped at Veronica, but she jumped over her, legs tucked in to avoid hitting her friend's head, and landed on her own bed.

But when Veronica looked back, Cheryl had already gotten up and had pinned her against her covers. Veronica still laughed even after getting caught. If that was what it took to get her to play chase, she would have done it a long time ago.

"Give me the book!"

"Uh-uh. You have to tell me who you like first."

"Give. It!"

"Hm ... okay. I'll give it back if you call me Verrie."

Cheryl tensed up when she heard that. She always reacted so adversely when she asked her to be called by that nickname.

It was something her siblings always called her, and she came to think of Cheryl as the sister she never had—this she told her before. But Cheryl always said she felt it was silly and never said it once.

So when it sounded like she was muttering it under her breath, Veronica could not resist leaning in to hear her better. She let her guard down. Her arms loosened up around the book, allowing Cheryl to swipe it back.

"Hey, no fair!"

"Says the girl who stole my book."

When she got off of the book thief, Cheryl went back to her bed and slipped it back underneath.

Now that she had her fun, Veronica sat up to give her some encouragement. "Come on, Cheryl, you can tell me. If you can't even tell me, how are you ever going to give the orchid away?"

No answer passed Cheryl's lips. She remained where she was even after putting her book away. Strife and frustration sparked from her valsara in a frenzy. It was so intense, lashing out from the depths of her being. It had to be troubling her for some time.

Perhaps it was best not to press the matter further.

After taking a breath to calm down, Cheryl turned around to face her again. "...I'll tell you ... after we become knights."

Veronica blinked. "What? But that'll be such a long time away."

Cheryl put a hand on her hip. "Tough. If you want to know, you'll have to become a knight."

Happy as she was that she would tell her, it was disappointing that she would have to wait for so long. Still, this was the first time she liked someone. Veronica had to know who it was.

"Fine then. I'll just have to impress the knights by outdoing you in the enactment."

Cheryl grinned and laughed, letting the awkward moment pass. "You're welcome to try."

The long days of rigorous training passed in the blink of an eye. All of that preparation finally led them to the day that the pages long anticipated: the day of the war enactment.

The instructors spent the morning preparing their pages with brief refresher courses on geography and strategy. There was much to absorb in a short time, but those with the most experience were able to retain the knowledge well.

Upon the afternoon, the pages were all called to gather behind the chateau. A veritable army of children had amassed before the Estrine family. Some of the Estrines looked upon them with harsh scrutiny, others with pride. Regardless of their outlook, they were all eager to see what effort their pages would put up against one another.

It was easy to distinguish the first-years from the more experienced pages. They were looking around the empty field for equipment, horses, anything to give them some inkling of what they would be doing.

Their ignorance tickled Veronica. They were in for quite the surprise.

She remembered her first time seeing it for herself, and how thrilled she was to test her abilities. After five years as a page, though, she stopped looking at it as an opportunity to measure her skills and saw it for what it was: a trial judged by their spectators.

Looking down at them from the windows of the chateau were the knights visiting for the enactment. They all came to see to results of the Estrine family's work. Among them were knights looking for a squire. Being chosen by one of them was what determined how far a page with her experience had gone.

Knowing all of those knights were watching her, that they would see her every move, tore at her confidence. This was her fifth enactment, her fifth attempt to impress. She always told herself it was fine if she was not chosen, that she could use the next year to keep searching for her brother's spirit. But she had been training all this time to become a knight. If no one would continue her training, that would never happen.

"Pages!"

Veronica shook off her dreary thoughts as Lord Estrine made his announcement. The short man stood proudly with his arms behind his back.

"Much has happened since the dawn of spring. A terrible plague came to make this city a graveyard. But not only have you withstood its deathly touch, you drudged to protect the lives of your fellow pages, your instructors, and the hundreds of innocent people throughout Brigadier. We, the Estrine family, commend you all of your struggle and ruth."

Many still thought about the suffering brought about by the plague and the lives it took. They glanced away from Lord Estrine, sorrow and grief in their hearts. But what they endured did not diminish their fighting spirit. No, it only stoked the fires in them to burn brighter.

Veronica felt it. It was intense. Basking in the warmth of everyone's valsara inspirited her to reclaim her own confidence. She had an enactment to fight in—and win.

"Dark times will befall you. Uncertainty and despair will endlessly continue to temper your resolve. But we will not falter, for we are

Vermalians! And *you*, my pages, shall be the beacons of hope, the rays of light that shall peel away the darkness, for our people! For that is your calling. That is what led you to walk the path to knighthood!" His loud, profound words further stirred the flames burning within everyone, exciting them all the more. "Are you worthy of being part of this light? Are you fit to be the spears and shields that protect Vermalio? We gather here today to determine that."

Lord Estrine unfolded his arms and held up, for all to see, the smallest shard of glass. "For this enactment, each of you will be divided into two 'armies' and do battle with the other. And *this* will be your battlefield."

Whispers were shared among the first-years as nothing else was said or done for a moment. The pause was to deliberately get a reaction from the inexperienced. It was as entertaining to the other pages as it was for Lord Estrine.

This tradition of not sharing what happened during the enactment was all to capture their wonder and amazement in the next moment.

Lord Estrine turned to hurl the shard high into the air. Light gathered into the glossy stone as it soared toward the sun until a brilliant flash engulfed the fields. Veronica peered through the stabbing light with her magic sight to witness the illusory magic reshape everything within its gleam. Grass receded into the ground. Trees spurt forth. Water flowed along the surface. The earth piled upon itself to form hilly terrain and tall cliffs.

Once the light faded, the pages opened their eyes and took in what was now before them. The first-years were utterly baffled by what happened. They thought that Lord Estrine had completely changed the expansive fields into something else entirely.

What they saw, though, was but a manifested illusion, a series of spells that gathered magic into a projected shape and granted it a stable physical form. So many such spells were imprinted into the charm tossed by Lord Estrine, allowing it to create the magnificent tableau before them.

This year's battlefield looked to be rough, rocky terrain for the most part, sudden hills and slopes on all sides. Within them were clusters of trees, which in certain spots would undoubtedly be hiding the bases for both sides, and a small, dome-shaped mountain standing above it all in the center. It had such an aesthetic appeal.

Lady Abeel always put so much effort into crafting these illusions.

Everything was explained to the pages while Veronica was lost in thought looking at the symmetrical terrain. The two sides the pages would be separated into were decided.

As they were divided, a few Estrine knights called out the magic users, Veronica included, and gave them each a bracelet with a charm embedded into them. The pages slipped them around their dominant wrists, then returned to their designated groups.

Once each side was informed of their respective bases, they marched into the battlefield.

Veronica paced through a verdant clearing by her lonesome. She surveyed the area before advancing quickly and quietly, careful to leave nothing unnoticed. Adhering to caution, she took everything in with her magic senses before moving forward.

She stopped to wipe the sweat from her brow and looked up to the trees. Shimmering golden streaks peered through the branches, the air almost aglitter. It was a hot spring day. Having trees to provide shade was a great comfort.

But the branches above her did not block the sunlight. No shadow was cast beneath them apart from her own, the sunlight beaming directly through the seemingly solid forms.

She had gone a long way since leaving her army's base, and it seemed she was perfectly alone. So Veronica decided to take a break and sat against the tree beside her. Its trunk was as hard and smooth as a rock. She spent a few moments there until jumping from her spot. It was startling how the wind brushed chillingly against her neck, almost as much as how it blew through the tree.

There were always some notable flaws in the illusions, likely due to the number of spells imprinted into the charm that created them. And

Lady Abeel was always hard on herself whenever she noticed them. Still, being able to reshape such a vast area with magic alone, even temporarily, was a testament to how powerful the sorceress was.

Veronica looked down at the bracelet on her wrist, wondering what Lady Abeel had found thus far.

That charm bracelet had an enchantment that affected the magic of its wearer. So long as she wore it, her power would be repressed, unable to inflict significant harm upon those she turned it against. Instead, those she struck with it would be overcome by a spell designed to keep them from getting back up.

It was like the enchantment on the sword she was given; should she strike someone with its shaven blade, the magic would bind their mind and force their body to partially shut down, simulating death.

Those enchantments were key to replicating actual warfare. It gave the pages a glimpse at what it would be like.

Some lost the will to continue their training after seeing bodies that would not move, or experiencing what it was like to have their minds submerged into nothingness.

Veronica recalled her first time being struck down by the enchantment. It was not swift or pleasant. For a brief time before drifting off into a deep, empty sleep, she felt her senses slipping away one by one, until there was nothing. Remembering what happened after she awoke left her shaking. It was as if she actually died, and that terrified her.

But what terrified her more was seeing it happen to Cheryl.

She gazed to the sky as her thoughts drifted to her friend. They were placed on opposite sides this year. Moreover, she was the enemy general. If Veronica hoped to win, she would have to strike down her dear friend, or allow someone else to do it.

After taking part in the enactment four times before, she found some solace in knowing this was only a test. None of it was real. No one actually died. It was all to prepare them for what was to come.

Telling herself that was all that kept her from dwelling on what she had to do to succeed.

Deciding that she rested long enough, Veronica stood from the tree. The brief moment her eyes fell shut, switching subconsciously to magic sight, allowed her to notice something ahead. She saw the valsara of people moving in her direction.

An enemy party, without a doubt. Perhaps scouts.

She took her sword in hand. Rather than rush back the way she came, though, she looked every which way, perturbed. She could not decide which way to go.

By the time she figured it out, an arrow flew at her. Veronica swerved to the side before it could hit her and ran back the way she came.

Raucous jeering and the heavy beat of boots hitting the ground followed her down the twisted path. Gatherings of bushes and trees forced her to take several turns, but slowing down to make them was difficult given how steep the path was. Thankfully, she was more familiar with the terrain than those chasing her. She timed her turns while keeping at a favorable running speed.

She made it down to the foot of the path and nearly lost her pursuers. But just as she was about to slip out of sight, she stopped in place. She could have gotten away if she remained decisive. Instead, she remained where she was, hesitant about which way to turn again.

Veronica took the path up the next hill by the time her pursuers caught up. They drew near as she reached the top. Greeting her was a long, foreboding slope that plummeted into a shroud of overgrowth.

She turned back as the enemy faction moved to subdue her, barely able to hide her impish smile.

It almost hurt to hold back her laughter.

Before they got close, she dove down the slope, rushing into the overgrowth. Upon breaking through the wall of foliage, she saw the glittering pond at the bottom. She met the crystal clear water and used her power to keep it from parting enough for her to stand atop it.

Veronica turned back to the overgrowth above as the enemy party broke through. They saw what awaited them, but it was too late to retreat. The slope was much too steep to climb back up.

Her trap sprung, Veronica drew forth the water around her and launched it at her enemies like cannon fire. The spouts of water crashed into her enemies, the immense force sending them tumbling down the slope and into the pond.

Only a few enemies managed to escape the downpour by throwing themselves off the slope to escape down the hillside.

Veronica watched her adversaries retreat down the hidden path until they were out of view, then walked across the pond to those who had fallen. They floated lifelessly along the water's surface, the enchantment subduing them. Not wishing to leave them there, she brought them to the shore, then stepped back onto dry land to see what became of the rest.

She ran halfway up the path they escaped down to find them collapsed on the ground, her own party standing triumphantly over them.

Her captain turned her way and waved. "Good going!" he called. "They completely fell for it."

Veronica's smile turned gleeful. She enjoyed fooling the competition.

While scouting the area, her faction worked to reduce the enemy numbers quickly and decisively. Happening upon that pond made their task all the easier. The Evaleen army, as expected, saw Veronica as their biggest threat. They proved much too eager to remove her from the enactment when they caught her alone, seemingly unaware and hesitant.

Underestimating the enemy was one of the most dangerous things a knight could do.

The party's navigator ran down the hill to meet them. "We should reach the border soon."

The captain grinned. "Good. Once we're there, we'll meet up with the other scouts and advance into enemy territory. Before the sun sets, we'll have Evaleen's army on their knees."

He was certainly enthusiastic about this, as were the others. But they had every reason to be. They all wanted to win the enactment, after all.

The party returned to the path they left, reaching the clearing where Veronica rested, and continued onward. Soon, they reached the top of the hill; it was the tallest one they climbed thus far. The earth rose and fell almost like waves throughout the entire battlefield, undulating wherever the eye may rest. Climbing so many hills gradually shaved away everyone's stamina, but they forged on, fueled by their resolve.

They crossed at least seven more hills before meeting more of their comrades in a level field. Altogether, there were easily a hundred pages ready for a major clash.

A messenger returned to base to notify the main force of the best path to take. While the captains of each party discussed the final aspects of the invasion, the other pages rested. Veronica kept an eye out for the enemy in the meantime.

"If you are planning something, expect the enemy to be plotting too."

Of the many things Lord Tamsilac taught them, that was perhaps his most important lesson. Opportunity presented itself to friend and foe, good and wicked alike. In gathering together, Veronica's allies gave a perfect chance to their enemies for an attack.

Their opponent was Cheryl, a girl who took the Estrines' teachings to heart. And being made a leader, more was expected from her than anyone else. So much rode on the results she would reap—being made a squire, proving herself to the one who took her in, one day facing and defeating the Renegades. She would not let her foes do as they pleased.

Soon, the main force arrived. Their army doubled in size. Once the commander decided on a course of action, they were on their way.

The stretch of flatland continued around the mountain, offering an unobstructed path into enemy territory. While it was the quickest possible route to take, it was also the most obvious place to put up a strong defensive front. Everyone was ready to charge into battle at a moment's notice.

But no troop stood guard to hinder their advance. The field was clear of any threat.

It seemed too easy.

Veronica's comrades marched past her as she came to a sudden halt, suddenly feeling her balance falter. Upon steadying herself, she looked around to see if anything had caused her to trip. There was nothing.

Rather than put too much focus on that, she went to catch up with the others.

Then it happened again. She caught herself before losing her footing, standing like her feet were caught in a pool of mud.

Something was off—if not with her, then with the ground underfoot. It felt like, for the briefest moment, everything around her shook.

Curious, she took a knee and pressed her hand to the ground. Her eyes closed, she began to read the energy flowing underneath. The magic that made up the battlefield obscured the valsara of the land, although that was always something she struggled to perceive. The flow continued in its ever-shifting cycle to keep the illusions solid.

Everything seemed to be fine until Veronica lifted her head. There was another energy flowing underneath the ground other than the magic of the illusion. It was faint, barely noticeable, but grew immensely as her comrades walked over it.

Veronica jumped back to her feet. "Get back! It's a trap!"

Her voice reached them too late. They were directly above the energy upon its discharge. A strong pulse swept across the field, ensnaring dozens of pages in a net of wild, crackling sparks. Many fell to their knees, overwhelmed by the power. Some were resistant to the spell, but many succumbed to its pressure and became incapacitated by the enchantment.

Similar spells activated all around them, but the army retreated out of their range before falling victim to it themselves.

And their enemies came out to take care of the rest. Parties of the Evaleen army leaped from their cover and rushed at the fleeing pages from all sides—from up the mountain, from behind the trees, from the hills they walked past.

Veronica's allies regrouped upon recognizing their situation and stood their ground. While thrown off balance by the ambush, they remained strong as they fended off their attackers.

Veronica charged to face the enemies that came from the trees. A great many of them closed in, eager to crush them. Unwilling to let the battle end as soon as they'd like, she gathered water from the air to form along her blade and flung it at her foes. It struck them like a whip, staggering most and knocking a few off their feet.

As one recovered, she closed in and thrust her sword. The enemy was knocked to the ground, and the enchantment spreading across his body kept him there.

Two others tried to rush her from the sides, but she was ready. Droplets still clung to her sword, and were cast at her foes with another swing. The beads of water pierced into them like needles, disorienting them. Seizing her chance, Veronica thrust at the one on her left, striking his chest, then turned to arc her blade into the other's ribs.

Her allies stayed clear of her as she fought, perhaps worried about being struck by her power themselves. Unnecessary though it was, it gave her the room to perform.

Water continued to gather around her sword as she repulsed the enemies circling her. Its mass grew with each wave sweeping more moisture from the air. It became arduous to guide the more she moved; the water followed her guidance, easing the weight put on her, but making more movements in succession became more difficult. The next swing hurled the water from her sword, a massive ring forming around her and slamming into her foes.

Some of them struggled to get back up. But that would not do.

Veronica raised her sword and used the tip to draw a circle in the air. Water gathered into the space to form a dense sphere hovering in place. A giddy smile on her face, she turned to deliver a swift kick to the sphere, sending it crashing down on them all.

The enemy party was down. Her magic sight showed her that the enchantment had claimed them all. With that taken care of, she returned to her comrades to aid in getting rid of the rest.

Many of her allies had fallen, and those still fighting were losing momentum. A flash similar to the discharge that crippled the army went off near the crowd.

The mage who set the trap was among them. That was who she had to face next.

Some of the water she used trailed after her as she returned to her comrades, forming three barbed spears. She turned her sword around in her hand as she ran, gripping the handle tightly. Hurling it forward sent the spears flying at the rear of the enemy vanguard surrounding her allies. Droplets scattered into the air, sunlight glimmering off them, as they struck their targets.

Upon turning her sword upright again, she had been beset by enemy pages who broke from their ranks. The first to reach her was the first to fall. His sword had been ripped from his grasp from Veronica's parry, and hers struck his ribs. Two more blades thrust past the boy's head, his comrades using his defeat to catch her off guard. Veronica leaped back before they could graze her.

She stood in place, her sword held before her, her smile teasing them to act.

They, too, were struck down, but by her commander. He left the fray upon her intervention to get to her.

He shook his buckler to let her know he had her back.

The help was greatly appreciated. While the rest of her allies fought on, those two circled the clashing forces, picking off the enemies that came their way, to follow the flashes of power tearing through their army. Veronica sliced through those in her way with blades of water. Her commander kept others from circling and harrying her.

Soon, she found the enemy mage. Or rather, he found her. Alerted by the cluster of magic, Veronica hurled a water sphere at the lobe of light that flew her way. The light vaporized the water in a fit of sparks, vanishing thereafter.

The mage glared at Veronica and took a tighter grip of his sword. Energy crackled between the fingers of his empty hand.

It was a rare opportunity for her to use her powers against another magic user, and one she would enjoy.

Rather than carelessly charge ahead, Veronica feinted to spur her enemy into action. When the next spell shot from his hand, she pulled water into a wide barrier before her. The barrier broke apart upon intercepting the blast, turning into a cloud of mist. The mist spread throughout the area, blinding those caught within.

Under the cover of the mist, she crossed the field and closed in on her foe. Her blade drew forth, parting the mist, and fell upon the mage as he lifted his sword to block.

Such quick reflexes. He clearly had not been dodging weapons' training in favor of magic.

The mist parted as they clashed. Veronica pressed her foe hard, swinging her sword at him in split-second strikes. The mage guarded well, giving himself time to ready another spell. He launched another lobe of light at Veronica the moment he saw a break in her attacks. But her limber form swerved around the blast before so much as a spark touched her. That cost the mage. His loss of balance gave Veronica the perfect chance to bat him away with the flat side of her sword, knocking him against the mountain wall.

Ready for the finishing blow, she gathered more water along her blade and thrust it at the mage.

Her smile broadened with the thrill of victory, but quickly fell apart when she saw the charm on her bracelet shatter.

Panicked, Veronica turned her wrist for the water to curve away from the petrified boy, piercing into the rock wall beside him. Flecks fell from the surface, leaving behind a clean, deep gash.

Had she acted a second later, that gash would have been in him.

The mage stood against the rock wall breathing haggardly as the water at his side plopped to the ground. He and Veronica remained perfectly still, both frightened by what they witnessed.

"Look out!"

Her commander warned her too late. Someone came at her from behind and slew their sword across her back. She gasped and fell to her knees. There she sat, overwhelmed by the sensation rushing throughout her body. But it was not the enchantment. It was simply pain.

Her arm moved around her abdomen to brush against her back, which shocked the one who struck her. He raised his sword to try again, and watched it fly from his hands when it was hit by a lobe of light.

The mage ran from the mountain wall to his comrade. "Knock it off!" he chided. "You just saw that it didn't work, yeah?"

Veronica nursed her bruise as she stood back up. It was still difficult to understand what happened. That she was able to process it at all unnerved her. The enchantment on that weapon should have sealed her mind and put her in a false death state. But there she stood, able to feel the throbbing pain shooting down her back.

The mage walked up to her after bickering with his ally. He looked down at her wrist and saw the state her bracelet was in. He then lifted his arm to look at his bracelet. It was broken, just like hers.

This was not right.

Though it aggravated her spine, Veronica dropped back to her knees and closed her eyes. Her magic senses again picked up the magic that created the battlefield. For a moment, she thought her injury was affecting her focus, but the longer she focused, it became harder to detect the energy beneath. It moved in smaller traces than before. By the time she noticed the flow had been obstructed, she realized that the physical shells they projected, from the specks of dirt to the grand mountain, were becoming unstable.

Veronica opened her eyes and stood. When looking to the one who struck her, she glanced at his sword. The energy inside was barely enough to maintain its appearance.

The other pages had stopped fighting when they noticed no one else fell to the enchantment. They bickered with one another, accusing the other side of cheating somehow.

Tensions were running high. Both sides looked ready to settle this even without the enchantment.

Before that could happen, Veronica gathered a large mass of water directly above them. The enemy mage caught on to what she was up to and hurled a lobe of light at it, vaporizing the water in a loud burst. The lightest drizzle fell on the warring pages, who looked up to see what happened, then turned to the spell casters.

Veronica stepped forward. "Everyone, listen! Something is wrong with Lady Abeel's spell. The magic maintaining the battlefield is wearing thin; that's why our weapons and charms are losing their enchantments."

The pages turned to one another, muttering their disbelief.

"This is just the start of our problems. We must leave now before—"

The fragile state of the battlefield kept her from saying any more. The ground shook, this time vigorously enough for all to notice. A few trees split in two and fell to the ground, their mighty bodies then glowing and breaking apart into flecks of fading light.

The commanders from both sides immediately called for a truce. They ordered a few captains to lead their troops off the battlefield. The others were to return to their respective bases to warn their comrades.

As for Veronica, she followed the Evaleen army to their base.

There was resistance met when the Evaleen army returned to their base. They saw Veronica among them and thought they had turned traitor. They did not even realize such a thing was not permitted in an enactment, but it did not matter.

They had seen the changes in the battlefield too. No one understood what was happening. It terrified them, and their fear made them act rashly. They attacked their own and ordered them to leave.

There was no time to indulge in their squabbling. Veronica rushed past them the moment she saw her chance and ran straight for the enemy base. She fended off anyone that got in her way with swordplay alone, not wanting to risk harming others with her power.

She, too, was being driven by fear and impulse. This chaotic situation they found themselves in made her worry terribly for her friend. If she used her power and let her anxiety direct it, it might inadvertently injure another page.

This was no war, and they were not her enemies. It was not something she was willing to do to them.

She followed the directions memorized from the map and soon made it to a fort equally identical to her own. It was a modest stone fort, its walls tall and strong, without a proper gate or additional defenses. Many pages were about, though they were scattered, unorganized and confused. Several trees had fallen over their stone walls, tearing through them like parchment, and were still fading away. The tremors grew more violent, enough for a nearby hill to crumble like a sandcastle on a beach.

Veronica took the direct approach and made her way to the gate. If she tried to sneak in, she would be treated with suspicion. The only way they would take her warning seriously was if she went to them as a messenger, not a warrior.

The few who remained on guard saw Veronica's approach and held up their spears. One of them, to her luck, was Sashan.

"You're a fool to come alone," said the mistrusting girl.

"I didn't come alone. Your allies led me as far as they could."

"Led you? Surely, you don't think me—"

"We've not the time for this!" Veronica interrupted. "The battlefield is falling apart. You must warn Cheryl. We need to evacuate immediately."

"We're not leaving until we've won."

As stubborn as ever, even under the circumstances. The Estrines have done too good a job with her. The most respected soldiers followed their roles no matter what happened. Theirs was to keep Cheryl safe. The only reason she had not yet seized Veronica was likely because she was so cautious of her.

The ground beneath them shook again. They could barely keep from falling over.

"Don't you see what is happening? It is much too dangerous for any of us to remain here. We must go, now!"

"Then go!"

"Not without Cheryl. Not without all of you."

"Enough!" Her patience at an end, Sashan thrust her spear. Veronica held her sword up to deter it, the blade grinding against the shaft. But the force used in the attack threw her off balance, enough for Sashan to shove her against a tree. She then swung the spearhead at Veronica's neck, swatting her to the ground.

That weapon had lost its enchantment too. She was able to pick herself up just as she had during training. Sashan's eyes spread so wide upon seeing that.

"Do you see? The enchantments are fading. And so is everything else. It's only a matter of time until the battlefield collapses. We have to leave before that happens."

"Sashan, maybe—"

"Shut up!" she interrupted her comrade. "She can't be telling the truth. There's no way. Everything she says is a lie!"

A terrible pang rocked Veronica in hearing those words. They were so callous, so spiteful. Her hands trembled in trying to withstand it.

"Then why am I here? What possible reason would I have to come here like this now? ...Sashan, I don't want to see you get hurt."

"Shut up! Shut up, shut up, shut up!"

Sashan swung her spear at Veronica with abandon. Veronica followed the sharp pull of her reflexes and blocked, parried, and stepped away from Sashan's frenzied attacks. She relied on her senses and training to defend herself, her swordsmanship almost second nature by now. With the anxiety raging within her, it was all she could rely on.

She had genuinely been concerned for her. She wanted her to be safe, and showed her that she wanted to help.

But all Sashan did was spew venom and treat her like a monster.

That's it!

Veronica's stance suddenly changed in between Sashan's attacks. She took her sword into both hands and threw it aggressively against the spear's shaft, then slammed it into Sashan's chest.

"Stay here if you want then! But I came all this way to get her out, and that's exactly what I'll do."

She left Sashan to lie in the dirt and marched toward the gate. The other guard was alarmed by Veronica's sudden change and held his spear at her.

"Out of my way!" There was no attempt to wait for a response. She went through him just like she did Sashan.

There was a gathering in the fort's courtyard. Everyone was likely trying to figure out what to do. They became alert when someone saw Veronica coming.

Sashan and the other guard followed her inside, but they stopped at the motion of their leader. Cheryl stepped from the gathering, a sword in hand, and looked to Veronica aghast. "You!"

Veronica smirked as she stepped closer. "Oh, you remember me? How flattering. And here I thought you only cared about your little friend."

Cheryl took her sword in both hands, adopting the same stance as her apparent friend. "I take it you want to settle the score?"

"Believe me, frump. I'd love nothing more." It was so tempting to charge at her then and there, but instead Veronica tossed her weapon aside. "But now is not the time. The illusion is failing. I don't know what will happen if we stay here, but it won't be anything good."

Cheryl lowered her weapon and listened to what she had to say. She seemed conflicted, as were the others surrounding her. But seeing Veronica stand before her as she was, refusing to fight like this, made her relent and sheathe her weapon. "Right then. Next time."

Veronica smirked again and nodded.

Before Cheryl could give the order, the ground shook once more. The tremor was so strong that the fort's very foundation was shattering before their very eyes. A section of the wall collapsed. Before it could crush them, Veronica tackled the boy beside her, knocking them out of the way.

Her vision became hazy when she hit the ground. She lifted herself off the boy she saved enough to see his sword had jabbed her in the gut. Her muscles were getting heavier. Its enchantment was still active.

No! No, not again...

She fought the cold grip of the enchantment and struggled to push herself back up, but it was to no avail. The crumbling of rubble and the clamor of voices around her became muffled. Her breathing became weak.

Soon, everything faded.

~ Tenth Chapter ~

Schism

Veronica awoke in a panic, a frightened gasp escaping her as she bolted upright. Everything was hazy at first, but as she calmed down, she found herself behind the chateau again.

A nauseating ringing filled her head, blocking out all other noise. The first thing she heard as it parted was her dear friend's worried voice. Cheryl was beside her, holding her steady until she was steady again.

Veronica held her pounding head as she reassessed her predicament. The last thing she remembered was running through the forest to warn her competition of impending danger.

When she turned to the fields, she found that all that remained of the battlefield flew into the air as flickers of dying light.

She stood to take a look at the aftermath while Cheryl filled her in.

True to her fears, the manifested illusion had become unstable. Lady Abeel had lost all control of the spell, her connection to the charm she crafted inexplicably severed.

Several knights led search parties into the crumbling battlefield. Lord

Estrine himself had found them at the Evaleen army base shortly after Veronica was put into her false death state.

Even as the illusion collapsed, the effect of its enchantment would not lift. The inflicted pages remained unresponsive. It was all Lady Abeel could do to wake them one by one.

They were very fortunate. Everyone made it out safely, and those under the enchantment's influence were all awoken.

Everything remained disorganized for a time. The Estrines were at a crossroads as to what to do, leaving their pages to wait for their judgment. Nothing like this had happened before.

As the sun sank over the horizon, they announced their ruling.

That night, the traditional banquet had been held. Everyone gathered in the banquet hall for a bountiful feast of the most succulent meat, the richest fruit, and the finest bread. The grim ambiance from earlier had been virtually erased within those walls. The food provided, the merriment had, and the music played lifted everyone's spirits.

Since the war enactment had been unexpectedly interrupted, theirs was not a celebration of victory. Neither side surmounted the other. But they all faced a disaster and came out unscathed. This banquet was to praise their tenacity and quick thinking.

Veronica did not feel much like celebrating. It was not because of the enactment's results. Some battles ended without a winner, whether it amounted to the scale of the casualties or that neither side took any ground. It was what led to those results that troubled her.

The charm used to simulate warfare gradually lost its power. And it had been crafted just recently.

Everyone in the chateau had learned at some point that magic was disappearing from the world. The topic was prominent in several of the Estrines' lectures. Some had seen the phenomenon firsthand in witnessing once powerful charms become drained of their power, or even mages themselves.

Over her five years in the chateau, Veronica had seen numerous pages training in the arcane arts fall ill and become comatose from magic deficiency. Every one of them suffered before the witch god of death claimed them, and the few who survived were never the same.

No one understood why this phenomenon occurred. And it seemed to worsen with each passing year. It was why some were hesitant to develop their gifts and chose to repress them instead. Those with greater magic power were more susceptible to developing magic deficiency, so many thought the best solution was to keep it weak, limited.

But even that was not so simple. When people with powerful magic kept it repressed, it often resulted in uncontrollable and volatile discharges of their power.

What was once a sign of might had become an omen for one's doom.

Even so, mages were still highly desired individuals.

Many of the pages sitting around Veronica were of Cheryl's army. Her own comrades did not keep her company. They were glad to have her in battle, but once it was over, they avoided her as always. She was not lonely, though, not when Cheryl invited her to join her group.

The incident troubled Veronica, so she did not speak much that night. But when spoken to by one of Cheryl's comrades, she gladly listened. They were all very impressed with their leader's planning and execution. It amazed Veronica as well; her defensive measures were very thorough and would have given her enemies a lot of trouble.

Had the enactment continued, Cheryl's army might have won.

Veronica watched Cheryl interact with her former subordinates while noshing on a sweet apple. Seeing her grin and boast of her feats made her very happy.

Her confidence had grown considerably since she first arrived. She used to carry so many doubts and worry over whether she had what it took to be a real knight. Now she was personally aiding the head of the Estrine family, taking charge as a leader, and proving herself as a warrior. There was no doubt in Veronica's mind that she would go far in life.

And what about her?

Five years in the Estrine Chateau... The more that came to mind, the more it weighed on her.

Veronica looked down to her tea, slipping into deep thought. The torchlight gleamed beautifully off the tawny drink enough for Veronica to see her frowning face in it. Even the clamor of joyful voices around her was not enough to cheer her up.

That clamor quickly went quiet as Veronica's drink came to reflect an unexpected visage.

"Don't stop now. I love hearing pages gripe about the Estrines."

She thought the little ripples in her drink had distorted the image, but upon turning around, she saw exactly who she thought it was.

A tall woman in armor stood beside their table. She had a black mane neatly arranged into a ponytail draped onto her shoulder. Her posture was casual, a hand on her hip. She looked to the pages with proud hazel eyes. And her lip, fuller on the bottom, curled into a shrewd smile.

One of the boys lowered his head. "Forgive our rudeness, Lady Knight."

"What for? I told you that I love it." She tilted her head in another direction, her smile broadening and showing some teeth. It was at Lord Charleston. "What do you have to say about Charlie over there?"

The Champion of Duty was looking their way from across the hall, his gaze as stern as ever. It looked like he noticed the knight speaking to them, and it made the pages go rigid.

"He can't hear you from all the way over there," the knight reassured. "Go on, tell me. I'm in the mood for a laugh."

Those who seemed to be having a few jabs at the Estrine family now found it hard to speak. More of the Estrines were looking over at their table now. They must have thought they sent her to command their respect and end the jokes.

But Veronica could see this woman genuinely wanted to hear more.

After quietly clearing her throat, Cheryl spoke up. "H-He's a very admirable knight, ma'am." It seemed she had said a few things as well.

The knight groaned and crossed her arms. "So much for my laugh." She shook her head, then glanced over to Veronica. "You there."

Veronica felt her heart pound against her chest. She confronted her nervousness and stood to salute the honorable knight. "Ma'am."

The knight looked to be mulling something over a moment, then spoke. "You know how the Estrines know everything that goes on during the enactment, right?"

"Yes, ma'am. There is a crystal ball through which everyone can see any place on the battlefield simultaneously."

Her smile became one of content. "The image was pretty fuzzy after that mishap, but I still saw what you did when you followed the other side to their territory." Her slight pause allowed her words to sink in, as if to make an accusation of sorts. "Why didn't you leave with your side?"

Veronica swallowed. "I had to make sure they would get out safely."

"And you did so without using your power."

"I couldn't use it. I mean…" Veronica hesitated when she realized she had interrupted her. "My charm was broken. I did not wish to take the risk of harming the others with my power."

"You were concerned with harming your enemies with water?"

"A weapon of any shape guided improperly can be the death of any around you. And … they were not my enemies, ma'am. That stopped being the case when the spell began to fail. We're all pages of the Estrine Chateau. I knew their leader would listen to me, so … I had to warn them, all of them. I would not abandon them."

The knight did not respond right away. She stood there, silent.

Veronica felt vulnerable under her gaze. It was as if her eyes were peering beyond the layers to uncover her every secret.

It was only now that Veronica realized how quiet the banquet hall had become. She was so focused on answering the knight to the best of her ability that she failed to notice more people had their eyes on them.

"What's your name?"

"Veronica Alivvrn of Illuascove, ma'am."

The knight unfolded her arms. "Well, Veronica, I am Lady Victoriah Kronas of Southern Valley."

Her breath became trapped in her throat. "Victoriah Kronas?" It was a name known throughout the kingdom. She knew this person to be a knight of character, but she had no idea she was one of the Six Champions.

"The Champion of Heart?"

That astonished reaction brought the champion's smirk to broaden. "Your caretakers had good things to say about you. I was not so sure at first, but now I know." Her hand planted itself back on her hip. "You're coming with me."

"Pardon?"

"I've made up my mind. You're going to be my squire."

Noise filled the banquet hall once more in following the Champion of Heart's proclamation. The pages, the servants, even some of the Estrines themselves were surprised by her words. Exchanges were made between them while Veronica stood in a daze.

She could hardly believe what she had been told. Someone had finally chosen to make her their squire—and it was a champion, no less. It was a dream come true.

"Your answer, Veronica?"

Her fist fell from her chest at the rapid percussion of her heart. Her arm slid back to her side, gone limp. A heavy gasp escaped her, pushed out of her throat by the gratitude welling in her breast, inundating her entirely.

Wanting that gratitude to show, Veronica humbly bowed her head. "Milady, it would be an honor."

It finally happened. Someone had chosen her to be their squire at long last. And everyone knew what that meant.

Once a page was chosen by a knight, there was one last trial for them to face, a trial that allowed everyone to recognize them as well. The Rite of Chivalry. Acting in the rite was a longstanding tradition for young Vermalians striving for knighthood. Their potential was revealed to them, and the result determined whether they were worthy of the honor of serving the kingdom.

Preparations usually took a couple of days, but Veronica's new meister knight was not one for patience. At her behest, her rite had been set up by the afternoon the next day.

Veronica was taken across the city by Lady Victoriah. They were followed by select members of the Estrine family, including Lord Estrine, Lady Abeel, and Lord Charleston, as well as a few bystanders who had taken interest. They knew who they were, who *she* was, and what was happening; it was not every day a champion took a squire.

They soon arrived at the cathedral, a grand building standing tall among the humble dwellings. It took one's breath away just looking upon it, the structure both beautiful and imposing. Many went to the cathedral for comfort, guidance, and to heal the spirit. And when it came time to test a young soldier's mettle, there was a special ritual carried out within.

Veronica followed Lady Victoriah up the steps of the cathedral while the others remained outside. Atop the stairway awaited four maidens in ceremonial vestments. They were the vestals of the cathedral tasked with aiding Veronica in the Rite of Chivalry.

The page bowed to Lady Victoriah, excusing herself as she followed the vestals inside.

The vestals guided Veronica through their hallowed halls in silence. She remained close to them while taking in the surroundings. Rare were the times when she was permitted to visit this holy place. The air was always so inviting, comforting, like she had stepped into another realm, one of understanding and belonging.

And the vestals she followed were as angels sent to guide her. Clad entirely in heavenly robes, their heads and faces concealed beneath hoods and veils, it was as if they were enveloped in light.

They came to the heart of the building, where a chamber had been readied for them. It was a shallow room lit in an indigo glow from sunlight creeping through the stained glass on the ceiling. A delicate layer of magic reverberated throughout the room upon them entering. Shivers shot up Veronica's spine upon coming into contact with the energy, and she finally felt the weight of importance that her trial carried.

She knew what would happen to her if she failed. It was well worth facing that risk.

The vestals directed her to the center of the room. There, an unusual symbol had been carved into the floor. They circled around the symbol, each vestal coming to sit at different corners of it.

Veronica walked before them and sat directly atop the symbol. The magic circulating throughout the room concentrated on that spot, making her hair stand on end. The vestals raised their arms, the lengths of their sleeves drawing open like wings. Their gloved hands were held to one another, their magic gathering in their palms. The sudden surge of power in their valsara startled her, but Veronica remained still and silent.

Once the vestals were ready, they recited in sync their eldritch chant:

"We beseech thee, Divine Cural. Guide this brave child."

*　*　*

An otherworldly light shone down on the land. It was not the light of the sun, but rather the spiritual radiance of the plane of phantoms.

Try as she might, Veronica could not disengage her magic sight. Everywhere she looked, she saw wisps of ghostly flames glimmering across the air. It started to make her dizzy. She sat on the edge of a nearby stone fountain to relax, rubbing her temples, then leaped to her feet and turned around to look at it.

She knew this fountain. The wave-like basin, the small statue of lovers reaching their hands out to one another at the top—this was the fountain from her family manse, from the garden she used to play in.

It was hard to believe, but as her gaze shifted past the fountain, she circled it and made her way to the modest rock wall at the end of the gardens. It was little more than décor; the other taller walls down the hill served to protect the abode. From there, she had the perfect view of the vast, vast ocean, and at the inlet, she could see the beautiful harbor city of Harnola veiled in fog. It looked almost exactly as she remembered it, except the harbor was devoid of ships.

The need to further convince herself pestered her until she turned around to gaze upon the majestic manse she called home.

It had been years since she returned to Harnola. She had the chance

~ 166 ~

to every summer, but rather than taking it, she always remained at the Estrine Chateau, accepting the family's offer for extra training, so she could search for Wally. She believed it to be the right choice.

Yet she always yearned to return, to see her home and family again. That yearning pulled her toward the manse, and she entered through the gate past the fountain.

Exploring the halls, guided by the memories made in them, filled her with nostalgia. It almost seemed like yesterday she was playing games with her brothers, pulling harmless pranks on her father and the servants, nary a care in the world.

How times have changed. How she had changed.

As she crossed the hall, Veronica could hear someone crying. In following the sound, she realized whose voice that was, and immediately went into a sprint. She had only seen him cry, heard his dismay and heartbreak, once. And it was as clear to her now as it was then.

This was not a moment she wanted to relive.

She followed the crying sound to a small room she knew well. The door had been left wide open, granting her a look inside. In a way, she was relieved, and in another, confused.

Past the door was her old nursery, and hunched over the cradle was a man garbed in familiar robes. It was her father. He stood over the cradle with his head hung, his left hand tightly gripping the wooden frame, his right pressed to his face as he fought back the tears.

He looked much the same as when she walked in on him after being shown his youngest son's corpse. Proud to a fault he was, always trying to portray a man of pure strength. But even he could not stand the despair of losing a child.

Veronica stepped inside and reached a hand out to comfort him.

"Why...?"

His tattered voice shook with such pain, such ferocity, that it made her stop in place.

"Why did this happen? Why did I have to lose her?"

Puzzled by his words, Veronica peered past his strong form to the little one resting in the cradle. It was strange to look upon what had to be herself as a baby, and stranger still was that the baby did not even move.

A frightened gasp escaped her. Before she could call out to her father, he became surrounded by a menacing black aura. His features melted as his shadow clung to his form, merging with him. The eyes that turned to her were glowing blood red.

"If it wasn't for you—!"

Veronica stepped back when the shadow that was once her father lurched forward, his hands reaching out to throttle her. The shadow, however, froze when the vase by the window shattered. The water inside had shot from it, shaped into a long, narrow blade, and pierced its chest.

Seeing her father turn into a monster and go on the attack was terrifying, but that was not what shook her the most. The blade of water, it was not being controlled by her.

"I already told you. Stay out of it!"

The water blade twisted and sliced open the shadow's abdomen, parting into droplets as the monstrosity fell to the ground and dissipated in a cloud of smoke.

Aghast, Veronica turned around, following the new voice, only to find something she could not comprehend. The one facing her was Veronica.

Her mirror image stood at the doorway with her left arm out, having just used the same power she had. She looked exactly the same as Veronica, but while Veronica looked to her with a wide gaze frozen from disbelief, this other self of hers had a countenance harsh and imposing.

"W-What is this? How... Did I—"

Her other self groaned. "Are you still adjusting?" She then folded her arms, looking more condescending. "Try to think. You were brought here by the vestals' spell."

"Spell? What are you talking about? This is my home! That man was—"

The memory of entering the cathedral returned to her mind as quickly as the reality she was in resembled a dream. She held her head as her focus reset and barely kept from tottering backward.

She understood what had happened once the light of the vestals' spell flashed in her mind. Their magic brought Veronica into the world of her soul. This was not Harnola, only a replication of the city built from her memories.

It was explained to her beforehand that she would confuse that world for the real one. It was a consequence of her consciousness being suddenly thrown into her inner world, forced to perceive it in a way unfamiliar to her. Everything became clear again as her mind adjusted, after that shadow was cut down. That thing must have been a part of the rite.

Her weakened reaction made her other self click her tongue. She looked to her with disgust.

This second Veronica was different from the shadow. She appeared as real as Veronica herself, though when she saw her, it was like looking at a stranger. Something told her that she was not invoked by the spell.

"*Your* home, huh..."

What she said went unnoticed. While Veronica came to accept the world she found herself in, the presence of her other self bewildered her.

"I do not understand. How can I be talking to myself?"

"You're not."

"Huh?"

"I am not you; you are me."

What she said made no sense. It only confused Veronica all the more.

Seeing this, her other self sighed and looked past her. "This actually happened, you know."

"...What did?"

"That."

Her other self unfolded her arms to point at the cradle. Veronica, wanting to understand, turned back to the cradle and approached it, although not without hesitance. The need to turn away, to look away from the still baby swaddled in blankets, rose and slowly overpowered her, pushing her like a wave. She did not understand what this was, why this crippling fear tormented her so.

"Have you ever wondered where our power comes from?"

Veronica faced her other self again. She seemed as pale as she now was, though there was clear frustration, anger in her expression.

"I had it for as long as I can remember. Mother and Father said I had it even as a baby. They told me how bubbles formed when I laughed, how dry the air became when I cried."

"You always had that power. But not me..." Her other self hung her head and clenched her fists until they trembled. "I got it after I died."

"D-Died...?" Veronica felt the need to glance at the still baby again, but her fear overpowered her and kept her from acknowledging it.

"I was so young when it happened. I couldn't even realize it back then. Even now, I don't understand how it happened." Her other self lifted her head, looking back to Veronica with pure malice. "But as the years went by and my consciousness grew, I recalled my moments under the waters my soul was swept into. It was so dark, so cold, and every minute spent under them was suffocating." Her voice was riddled with pain, and it became heavier as she went on. "But then someone pulled me out."

Something about her words captured Veronica. When she mentioned waters, her mind began to wander but remained focused on what she said. And somehow, she soon came to think of those words before her other self said them.

It was faint and difficult to contemplate, but what she said brought something in her mind to resurface. Veronica did not know when or how, but she felt she had once experienced what her other self had. She remembered being under the dark waters and was slowly pulled deeper and deeper into an undersea abyss. At some point, something cradled her, supporting her back and head, and as the water pushed a little harder against her, light came to peer through the void. She could not make out who it was that carried her and brought her above the waves.

All she knew was she had been saved.

"She plucked me from death's embrace, breathed life back into me. But it didn't mean anything. How could it? This second chance at life wasn't even mine to have, not when it was given to you."

"I do not understand."

"Then let me spell it out for you: you took my life from me, fake!"

Veronica felt herself petrify upon registering those venomous words. She could only shudder.

"F-Fake...? How could you say that?"

"I was alone here before that spirit revived me. There was no other Veronica. But in the years I've spent 'alive' in this Second Verse, I realized I had no control. The words that left my mouth weren't my own. The actions I've taken were against my will. Everything that was done, it was all you.

"I spent fifteen years trapped within my own soul watching someone else live in my place. And in all that time, I've only stolen back mere minutes from you."

Shivers shot down her spine and freed Veronica from the shackles of dread. "It was you." She took a step forward, coaxed by the frustration and woe she held in for years. "You are the reason I black out all the time."

"If only it was all the time," said her other self. "Spending so long here gave me a decent grasp of the soul. I couldn't do it whenever I wanted, but I found a way to take control when you were at your most vulnerable. And when I finally had it, I did what you were too cowardly to do."

Veronica took another step forward. "I am no coward. And whatever you may think of me, I am not a fake. I *am* Veronica."

"You've been Veronica for my entire life. But no more."

At the snap of her other self's fingers, their surroundings changed in an instant. Veronica looked around to find they were outside again, this time in the training grounds where the guards helped her practice swordplay.

When her eyes fell back on her other self again, she had a sword in hand. "Now everything changes."

Veronica shook her head. "I do not want to fight."

"I don't care." She waved her sword, then held it in both hands, pointing it at Veronica. "I want my life back, and the only way that will happen is for you to disappear. You want to be Veronica, fake? Then pick up a sword and fight for it. Show me how real you are!"

There was nothing she could say to dissuade her. Her mind had long been made up. All that kept her from acting on her malice right away was her pride.

She remained where she was while Veronica remained unarmed, refusing to attack. It was a knightly quality. It showed that she had the reason to know honor.

But that did not mean she would remain idle and listen to Veronica should she choose not to act. To her other self, she was a villain, the usurper of the kingdom of her soul. And she had fifteen years' worth of anger to deal out.

She had experience aplenty with individuals so proud that they would not speak, that they had to fight to sate their egos. The only chance she could reason with her was to knock the fight out of her.

That was not what brought Veronica to take a sword in hand.

Many cruel things were said about her over the years, but hearing her other self call her a fake ignited something in her. This slight was too much for her to let go.

She had to— No, she wanted to respond in kind as befitting a knight. For Veronica, too, had her pride.

Her opponent sprinted into action the moment Veronica took a proper stance. She held her sword to the side and waved it into a wide arc. Veronica leaped back, avoiding the slash, then pressed her heels against the ground upon landing to push her into a strong thrust. Her other self drew her sword back in time to meet Veronica's blade, and pushed back with fierce strength.

Veronica held her sword in both hands once she thrust and pressed against her other self's with all she had, but her muscles relented and she stepped back before her foe could run her through.

How strange that she outdid her in a show of force. They had the same body and the same strength, yet her other self used hers so differently than Veronica had. She was stern, forceful, and relentless.

She rushed after Veronica, keeping her from retreating, and brought her sword down on hers in a heavy swing.

Having grasped her opponent's strength, Veronica blocked the blow and expertly parried, forcing her other self aside. She lunged forward, keeping the pressure on, but with a quick turn, her other self managed to block her attack. She threw around more power, but her swordsmanship was not as refined as Veronica's. She made up for that with her fluid reflexes.

But Veronica was more in tune with her body and used her reflexes more effectively than her counterpart.

"You call me fake. But I'm still a match for you."

Her other self, reacting vilely to her taunting, pushed Veronica back when next their swords met. She was thrown off balance for only a second, but it was enough for her to get the jump on Veronica. Veronica held her sword up to block and became overpowered by her foe's excessive use of force, steadily backing away while her other self pressured her.

"I've not even begun, *fake.*"

Her pestering affected Veronica just as much as Veronica affected her other self. She seized more strength and fought back for control of the battle. Veronica held her sword in one hand again and lashed at her in blinding fast slashes. Her other self blocked each swing of the blade just before it could meet skin, and pressed her sword firmly against Veronica's when she saw her arm slow. She shoved her weapon aside, then moved in to tackle her, ramming her shoulder against her chest.

The air had been knocked out of her, but Veronica caught herself before she fell to her knees. She barely managed to roll out of the way before her other self swung for her head.

Veronica quickly got back to her feet and turned to block another incoming attack.

"What makes me fake?" she found it in herself to say upon repulsing her other self. "I learned, I loved, and I grew to better myself. I lived the way I knew how, did what I've done for those I care for, and you mean to tell me all of that was not real? That what I've done was a lie?"

"You took my life!" Her other self rushed at Veronica. She hurled her sword at her but kept missing as her target sidestepped around her. "My identity, my family, my volition." Her swings carried more force with every lost attribute she elaborated on. "All of that was supposed to be mine, and you took it for yourself."

"You know it is not like that!" Veronica stopped dancing around her foe and brought her sword to hers, gliding its blade along hers, then pushing down once it neared the hilt. It was enough to keep her in place momentarily. "You say you've watched me. Then you've seen what I do, even after you took control of me. I never knew what happened in that time. I never remembered. I didn't understand because I didn't know about you. I could not have taken from you when I did not know you."

Her other self would not stay still and listen. With a vile growl, she pressed against Veronica's blade and forced her back.

"No one knew," she said after catching her breath.

Dismay was written all over her face, her eyes narrowed and red, her teeth clenched tightly together. And she would not remain still to let it fester. She charged straight for Veronica, more malicious than before.

Although she did not respond with that same passion, Veronica kept fighting back. She stepped around the throw of her sword, then thrust at her side. Her other self deftly deflected her attack with a mighty swing, a brush of air almost cutting into Veronica. There was barely time for her to block and keep from making that cut real.

"No one knew about me!" Her other self used such force that it threw Veronica off balance. "No one realized that I died." The next swing threw her to the ground. "They never mourned for me because they had you!" She seized the chance to end her vulnerable enemy, closing in to drop her sword in a harrowing chop. Veronica rolled out of the way just in time. Sparks flew as metal met stone, bring the wielder's arms to shake upon impact.

"I was always here, but I could never do anything. I saw everyone, but they never saw me, never heard me. I don't exist to them. That's no different from being dead!"

Veronica froze as her other self charged her way again. She had the opportunity to evade, but instead she chose to stand firm and defend against her next swing. Her muscles ached from the sheer force brought down on her. It took all of her strength to hold her back.

"I won't stand for it. I *am* taking back my life. No one is taking my place anymore!"

She could hear it in her voice. The words she spared derived from loneliness. And with every swing they threw at each other, that loneliness crept through her sword and flowed into Veronica.

With all the power she had flung around, her other self came to tire herself out as much as she exhausted Veronica. Her swings became less passionate, and her muscles grew heavy.

It gave Veronica the chance to step back before her legs gave out. Her other self held back. She stood with a slight slouch and gasped harshly.

They truly were different in many ways: demeanor, perspective, even their favored techniques. And there was something else.

As the wroth Veronica lifted herself up to keep fighting, the gentler Veronica straightened only to drop her sword.

"We're not done yet," her other self growled. "Pick it up."

"I will not."

"What?"

"I told you, I do not want to fight."

"Are you daft?" her other self barked. "If you don't fight, you die!"

Veronica folded her hands, holding them against her abdomen. "Tell me, who are you?"

"Huh?" Her other self stood there with her mouth hung agape, the picture of bewilderment.

"You say I am a fake, someone who has taken your place. But that is not who I am. Perhaps you are right; I did not come to be as one normally would. But I am here, and I am real. And I would like to help you."

Her other self did not offer a response. She remained silent, her face rigid with rage.

It was always Veronica's intent to understand this part of herself, and she certainly did. Working her up allowed her to see where her anger lay. Loneliness became the foundation, and it grew as her existence became overlooked, until she came to question it herself.

She had been a phantom in her own life. It was agony.

And as the source of her woes, however unintended it was, Veronica earned the brunt of her ire.

"I do not understand how this happened. But know that I am sorry for the agony it has caused you. It is a terrible fate, being a shadow in the world you inhabit, in your own self." Her eyes glazed over with sorrow. She closed them briefly to keep it at bay, then looked back to her other self with a weary smile. "I don't know what I can do, but I can start by getting to know you. We already know our name. So please, won't you let me know you?"

Her last words left her other self distraught. She was unsure of how to act, her expression twisting uneasily. The sword trembled in her grasp as her hands shook, but she forced it to remain still. Her face again showed her anger, and she howled a heinous scream before charging once more.

Veronica did not move. She remained where she was, standing tall with hands clasped together. She would not allow fear to overcome her and convey to her other self. Instead, she closed her eyes, resembling a pious vestal at prayer.

If that was to be her answer, then she would accept it. She would not reject her anymore.

She kept her fear repressed as she heard these harried steps close in and a blade tear through the air.

She winced. Her breathing stopped. Her skin stung from the feel of air brushing against her left side. But there was nothing more than that. When she found the courage to open her eyes, Veronica saw the sword hanging at her side mere inches from her arm.

Her other self remained motionless, still as a statue, until her breathing became haggard. She shouted by her ear and tossed her sword, letting it roll across the ground.

"Why...? Damn me, why!?"

She threw a shaky fist at Veronica, striking her clavicle. It was a hefty punch, harder than any she ever took, but Veronica withstood it.

"Why? Why? Why? You took my life from me. I hate you, blast it!"

More shaky punches were thrown at Veronica, and she endured each one. Her legs wobbled as she fought to remain standing and nearly gave out when her other self stopped punching to slap her face.

When she finally stopped lashing out, her other self was gasping, her voice broken from sadness fighting its way to the surface. She held her hand up to slap her again, but it fell back to her side as she crumbled into Veronica, burying her face into her shoulder.

Her face ached so much that it hurt to smile, but smile she did, and held her other self in a comforting embrace. Her anger conveyed, Veronica allowed herself to drop to the ground, bringing her other self with her.

"Why?" her other self sobbed. "Why can't I bring myself to kill you? ...I'm so weak."

Veronica brushed her fingers through the grief-ridden girl's hair. "You are anything but weak, Veronica." She caressed the back of her head like her mother had for her so many times. "This is a heavy burden you carry, but you carry on, and you do so without sacrificing your heart, no matter how much it hurts." She paused to allow her other self to calm down enough to catch her breath. "I rely on that strength too. I see it now. You are the reason I got this far. Without you, I doubt I ever would have gotten through losing Wally.

"I need you to endure hardship, but you need me, too, to remember compassion. We are not as strong as we can be without each other."

Veronica sat on the ground with her other self, holding her as she let out all of the strife she held in for so long. Her other self, moved by her counterpart's kindness, wrapped her arm around her, returning the hug.

A particular warmth welled up in her as the two embraced. And as it did, Veronica noticed something. There was no one else there, yet she felt a hand caress her as she had her other self. It was not unpleasant or even alarming; she thought the touch familiar. And it held them both dearly.

It was her, the spirit who revived them.

When she let go of her woes, her other self released Veronica and stood. "You should have kept fighting." She had taken Veronica's sword in hand, turning to face the family manse. "They would have stayed quiet if one of us vanished."

The air suddenly became heavy and hard to breathe. Dread flooded the area, drowning all familiarity and comfort. Veronica got back on her feet as more shadows of people emerged from nowhere, each one armed.

"They're our angst, yours and mine both, invoked and empowered by the vestals' spell. They're driven to push us to our limit, and consume us should we fall." Her other self handed the sword back to Veronica. She would not have taken it and left her unarmed, but seeing so many approach coaxed Veronica to accept. "They wouldn't have all come at once if I hadn't interfered with the rite and held them back."

Veronica stepped in front of her other self, giving her a chance to go back for the sword she discarded. "Then we face them all, together."

Rather than retrieve her weapon, she instead held her hand out and gathered water into a sphere. "Fine by me," she said with a smirk.

The veritable army of shadows charged at the two, unfazed and eager to crush to them. Veronica's counterpart lobbed spheres of water at the shadows. They struck with the force of cannons, causing those hit to fade into smoke. After thinning the herd, she turned to the few that got in close. She slammed her hands to the ground, drawing the water from it to form an expanding ring. It slowed them down when cast, allowing Veronica to step in and cut them down.

The measure only worked for so long before they became overrun. Veronica fought off two shadows and was about to face a third, but she hesitated when she saw that one had Cheryl's face.

A snap of the fingers brought their surroundings to change once more. They were back in the garden.

The shadow resembling Cheryl, having leaped at Veronica, smacked straight into the fountain. It never had the chance to get back up; the water that flowed from the fountain ensnared it as it shot into the air, falling upon their foes in the shape of a massive sea serpent. The serpent charged at the shadows, mowing down a great many, then rose to strike and swallow one in particular.

They fought valiantly, but there was no end to the army of shadows. And the pressure put on them quickly became too much.

The serpent broke apart, the water splashing over the ground, when one shadow impaled Veronica's other self with a spear.

Desperate, Veronica took the water in the air to form and thrust a blade from her sword, destroying the shadow, and rushed to her side. Waves of the sword cast darts of water at the enemies closing in, fending off those that moved to surround her.

She was nearly there when an arrow struck her shoulder, bringing her to drop her sword and collapse beside her other self.

The shadows cornered them against a wall. They closed in on them, slowly, as if to taunt them, letting them know they had lost before making the final blow.

Veronica crawled over to her other self. She found the strength to sit up and take her other self into her arms, pulling her away from the shadows. So many had come from her—she could feel it—and they were intent on taking her away. But she refused to be parted from her again.

She kept scooting back with her other self in her arms, trying to last as long as possible. Then her other self opened her eyes. She still held a fierce gaze when facing the enemy, but as she sensed the power building in her counterpart, an impish smile crossed her face.

With a snap of her fingers, they were at the harbor—the girls at the edge of a dock. The shadows came to a halt, almost exhibiting fear of their own, upon witnessing the tidal wave formed by Veronica's power.

In a last-ditch attempt, the shadows charged at the girls, drawing near as the colossal wave came down on them all.

* * *

Veronica was barely aware of her actions upon awakening. It was a struggle in itself to follow the vestals off the floor and out of the chamber.

The vestals supported her as they walked through the halls, making sure she did not fall over. Their words, the first they spared her, were soft and hard to hear, but they were enough to help Veronica cling to consciousness.

Setting sunlight stabbed her eyes once they emerged outside. It almost led her to fall backward. She remained still until her vision returned. Only when she saw her meister knight did Veronica start her slow, dizzying descent down the stairway of the cathedral. The world spun with every step. It made her nauseous.

But she kept going, and soon reached the bottom.

When she walked up to her meister knight to present herself, her new squire, she tripped over her own foot. Before she could hit the ground, her meister knight came up and caught her by the shoulders, holding her steady.

"Good work, Veronica," she praised her squire.

It was a pleasure to hear her say that.

~ Eleventh Chapter ~
The Next Stage

Foggy as her mind was, certain things became so much clearer to Veronica. The lost moments from when her other self assumed control returned to her, as though she shared them with her. She learned of the brazen things she did in that time, as well as something more profound.

It was true that she died in her infancy. She did not know why, only that she owed her new life to the spirit she met. This spirit, Fonus, restored her body so that it could again support life, returned her soul, and gave her the power to control water—resurrecting her as a Nascitte.

But something happened during the process that caused Veronica's budding consciousness to divide, separating it into two identities. While one lived as the child everyone knew, the other remained within the soul to learn of the fate they shared and the power bequeathed to them.

The Second Verse, dominion over an element of nature itself.

Absorbing such impactful knowledge took its toll on her, especially after going through the Rite of Chivalry. Thankfully, her meister knight was gracious enough to help her back to the Estrine Chateau.

Veronica leaned against Lady Victoriah for support, barely able to stand, let alone walk. She felt apprehensive in her current state. Her doubts and worries came flooding forth.

"Milady?"

"Mm?"

"Are you certain ... you want me for a squire?"

"Why doubt yourself now?"

"Look at me, I can barely walk."

The Champion of Heart chortled. "That'll happen after a battle, in or out of the soul. Anything else?"

Veronica did not want to say what came next, but she would not deny how it troubled her. She was going to be a champion's squire. Who she picked would reflect on her. "The other pages... They call me a witch."

"Yeah, I heard whispers about that."

The knight reaffirmed her grip on Veronica's wrist to pull her up, keeping her upright as much as she could. The way it made her bounce almost made Veronica lose her breakfast.

"Do you know what they used to call me? She-devil. All because I had more muscle than anyone else."

Veronica lifted her head to look at her meister knight. It was hard to believe anyone would say such things about her.

"I picked you because I believe you're worth it, Veronica. Petty little things like that can't sway me." She glanced down to the weary girl, a grin on her face. "If those runts fear you, let them. It's not something you can control. Follow your heart and your training, and you'll make a fine knight. Got it?"

"...Yes, Lady Victoriah."

The rest of the day was spent resting. And upon the morrow, Veronica prepared to leave the chateau with Lady Victoriah.

Her meister knight gave her until the lessons began to take care of whatever business she had left. She spent that time searching for Wally one last time. Alas, he was nowhere to be found, as it had always been.

It was hard for her to leave like that. Not finding Wally meant accepting that he was truly gone, that the last time she saw him would be as a corpse. But she knew she could not keep her meister knight waiting, and she begrudgingly ended her search to return to her.

She remained strong when she met Lady Victoriah at the chateau entrance, but she did not need to act for long. Cheryl was waiting there too; she gave her best wishes to her best friend and saw her off with a smile.

Those few moments together filled Veronica with joy. They promised to meet again, and that no matter where they were, they would always be friends.

Normally, when a champion took a squire, they were to be introduced to the king. However, with King Faustign attending to matters away from Brigadier, they instead began their journey together forthwith. They mounted Lady Victoriah's mighty warhorse and rode out of the city.

As she looked back at the capital one last time, she saw someone. Rubi stood at the gates, watching her as she rode away. The phantom seemed frustrated, but after locking eyes with Veronica, she brought herself to smile and waved goodbye.

Had it been safe to let go of Lady Victoriah, she would have waved back. But she knew Rubi. That she went out of her way to see her off showed she cared and that she knew Veronica cared for her. Veronica looked her way until she no longer saw the phantom's glow and watched as Brigadier's grand walls sunk over the horizon.

The knight and squire rode for many miles. Their mount ran at breakneck speed for much of the way, slowing on occasion only to catch his breath. At top speed, the winds lashed vigorously at Veronica, even with her meister knight sitting in front of her. If her arms were to part from Lady Victoriah's sides even for a second, the momentum would have thrown her off, tossed to the wind.

It was a relief to feel the breeze still when they stopped to rest.

Veronica was getting used to the gear her meister knight bought her: new clothes not so dissimilar to her old uniform, simple armor plating, comfortable boots. She occasionally looked down to the exquisite rapier at her hip and marveled at its rings, how they twisted around like tree roots. It was a weapon befitting of a devoted acolyte of Great Gaia, the mother goddess of life. Beautiful as it was, it must have cost more than everything else she procured for her.

Lady Victoriah chuckled every time she caught her looking at her new sword. It was a meister knight's responsibility to see their squire properly equipped, and she made it clear how vital having a suitable weapon was. "You should see what other champions got their squires," she plainly put when her squire fretted over lev on her behalf.

No expense was spared on the sword, but her clothes were charmingly simple. Her cotton shirt was protected beneath a sturdy breastplate. The leather trousers were durable but hugged her hips a little tightly.

They rode again until sunset. They made camp within a fair copse, using the trees for cover. And after enjoying a cooked hare, they slept under the stars.

They rose early with the sun. First, they collected their few belongings and scattered the campfire's ashes, careful to save any useable charcoal. Then, once their horse was fed, meister knight and squire got ready for the day with a sparring session.

Veronica was eager to start the exercise, the picture of enthusiasm. Lady Victoriah, on the other hand, was still rubbing sleep from her eyes. That did not mean Veronica did not need to be at her best. She was going up against the Champion of Heart, after all.

Veronica stood with her nimble sword in hand, waiting for her mentor to start them off as she drew her weapon. Lady Victoriah looked down at her coldly before moving in to attack. She was fast, barely giving her time to react. Veronica lurched backward from the attack, then moved in the direction the swing came from. Her meister knight's sword came back for her before she could make another move, forcing her to block it.

The sword Lady Victoriah carried was thick and looked heavy, but she swung it as if it were a butter knife.

Veronica attempted to circle her again, only to meet the same results.

She needed to get past her sword. All she had to do was scratch her armor, and their session would be over. To do that, she needed to take the offensive.

She lunged at Lady Victoriah when she held her sword low. A swift flick, and their swords met again, and the mighty Wolverine shoved her to the ground.

"On your feet."

The squire obeyed. When she attempted to dust off her clothes, her meister knight admonished her.

"You'd have more than dirt on you if this were a real fight." Lady Victoriah held her sword at her. "If the enemy won't let you past their weapon, knock it out of the way. Give it a go."

Veronica nodded and readied herself, then moved in and brought her sword to Lady Victoriah's. She was met with unyielding resistance and moved out of the way before the knight knocked her down again. Following her instructions, she kept striking at the sword to weaken her grip and swat it aside. But Lady Victoriah proved too strong.

The attempt did not impress. Lady Victoriah swatted her aside like a bug. "Why are you holding back?"

Her words stunned Veronica. "B-But I'm not."

"Yes, you are. I can see it. Now tell me why."

She hesitated, unsure of how to respond. Veronica looked down at the rapier in her hand, staring at her reflection in the slim blade. It seemed like a reasonable concern in hindsight. Withholding an answer would only anger the Wolverine, so she simply spoke her mind. "It's just ... I don't want to break my new sword. You were kind enough to spend the lev for it, and ... I'd hate for it to go to waste."

Her answer did not upset her, but Lady Victoriah did look somewhat puzzled. She cracked a smile and shook her head before holding her sword at her again.

Immediately reacting, Veronica rushed forward to strike, only to end up with her rapier being pulled from her grasp and dropped to the ground. She moved to retrieve it, but had been ordered to stop.

Lady Victoriah walked up to her squire, handing her thick sword to her. It was not as heavy as it looked—it was heavier. Even after taking it in both hands, it very nearly pulled her to the ground.

Lady Victoriah picked up the dropped weapon and looked it over. "Do you know why I bought you a rapier out of all of the other weapons?"

"Because swords like the rapier are better suited for swordsmen who rely on speed more than power. It's light enough for the wielder to leave their mark without sacrificing speed."

Her smile remained the same, so that was likely a right answer. Maybe not the one she wanted, though. She took a moment to look at the blade as she circled her squire.

"Slender frame, elegant appearance. It's a lighter weapon, yes, making it easier for those with smaller muscles to wield. Some call this 'a woman's weapon' for that reason, and they think that it'll break easily."

Her eyes turned hard again, and she stopped to hold the sword at Veronica. The exercise was not over yet.

Veronica took a breath, lifting the thick sword with all of her might, and charged at her meister knight. Her muscles trembled, but she kept going to prove that she was strong too. When she swung, Lady Victoriah threw the rapier to intercept, holding back the much larger weapon with ease. Her grip had loosened she was so startled, allowing her meister knight to tear that sword from her grasp as well.

The slender sword flew at Veronica and was held barely an inch from her nose. Her eyes remained frozen on the blade as it vibrated, singing its song. It remained there until its song ended.

The knight pulled the rapier away, giving Veronica a good look at the intact blade, her reflection showing her surprise.

"And as you can see, it holds together just fine."

When she was done showing her, she tossed it back to her squire, who stumbled to catch it without cutting herself. "Weapon's break. When they do, I'll pay for them to be replaced. Or I can just swipe one from anyone fool enough to mess with us—take a page from the Marauding Knight."

Veronica laughed. It had been some time since she heard of her third eldest brother's title. "I'm certain he would be flattered."

Lady Victoriah bent to the ground to retake her sword.

"Lady Victoriah?"

"Mm?"

"Who says this is just a woman's weapon?"

The knight stood and flashed a toothy grin, chortling. "Dumb men who never held one."

Veronica smiled as their session ended and they finished getting ready to depart.

"Are you ready to go, Timberhoof?" Veronica stoked the warhorse's mane before mounting with her meister knight.

They departed when Lady Victoriah gave her mount's side a light tap, and the proud warhorse went into a full sprint once the path was clear.

Their journey continued for many days as they crossed the majestic landscape of Vermalio. They passed through many small towns, stopping only to restock their provisions. The nights passed with them sleeping beneath the glimmering starry sky.

Lady Victoriah always kept Timberhoof going until they came across something they could use for cover: trees, hills, cliffs, anything that could conceal their presence. It was just the two of them traversing the kingdom; they had to be resourceful to avoid getting ambushed by brigands and other unsavory malcontents.

It was a very peaceful march, though, and in ten days' time, they arrived in the vibrant region of Southern Valley. There, they came to a fair farming village called Russalin. Vast stretches of cultivated fields lined the way there, its people hard at work tending to the crops. Their efforts supplied an abundance of food for themselves and well over half of the kingdom.

Russalin's renown was familiar even to Veronica. Many merchants that relied on their business carried goods purchased from its farmers as far north as Illuascove.

Timberhoof moved at a steady trot upon entering the village, mindful of the people roaming the streets. Plenty of knights were out on patrol, offering a sense of security to the civilians. Men and women were hard at work and children out at play, a lively atmosphere encompassing all of Russalin.

And everyone made way for the mighty warhorse marching through.

Many looked to its riders with intrigue, but others appeared unnerved, afraid. A couple of mothers even pulled their children back their way when they expressed interest in either the proud beast or the knight atop it.

Such was the reputation of Victoriah the Wolverine—admired by those she protected yet feared by all.

A few eyes, however, rested on the girl with her arms around the champion's torso. It must have been a first for them to see someone else in the champion's company, let alone someone of her age.

Veronica offered the onlookers a smile and a wave. While wary of the Wolverine, they were friendly enough to return her greeting.

"I can show you around later if you want," Lady Victoriah offered. Before that, she wanted to return to her home.

She led her mount through the marketplace and plaza, taking a direct route through the village. Once they passed the last gathering of houses, they went up a tall hill overlooking the entire area. Timberhoof moved faster without having to worry about running into people. The path before them was long and twisted like a serpent. Along the trees, Veronica saw these small monkeys with fuzzy manes swinging happily on the branches.

And as they neared the hilltop, a structure could be seen not far from the cliff. It was impressive, to be sure, but it was no mansion or castle or even a keep. Atop the hill sat a fairly-sized cottage with a stable built beside it.

Although Veronica had been told that her meister knight lived humbly, it still surprised her that this was it. The Six Champions held more power and standing than anyone in the kingdom next to the royal family. So she assumed a humble home for the Champion of Heart would have been more luxurious than what was before her.

"Well, here we are."

Lady Victoriah dismounted after her squire let her go. She guided Timberhoof to the stable, Veronica following behind.

The stable was relatively small, with only two stalls to house horses. One of them was occupied by a lithe, black-furred mare that moved around in excitement at the sight of them.

"Good to see you too, Nightshade."

The mare poked her head out of the stall and sniffed the knight's outstretched hand enthusiastically.

Veronica liked her energy. It reminded her of Amber.

As she approached to greet the friendly animal, the door to the cottage had opened. A young brunette woman in a leather dress stepped out. She walked to the stable with a basket along her arm, and stopped when she noticed her company. "Lady Victoriah!" she exclaimed with delight.

The knight looked to the woman with a smile. "Hey, I'm back."

The woman held her hands before her and bowed to Lady Victoriah. "So I see. I wish you had sent word that you were returning. I would have gone to the marketplace earlier."

"It's more of a surprise when I don't, though."

The woman turned from Lady Victoriah to Veronica, looking at her with intrigue. "Oh? Who have we here?"

Veronica bowed her head to the young lady. "Veronica Alivvrn, miss."

"A pleasure, Veronica," she said while returning the gesture. "I'm Lyn." She was polite and cordial, and her smile was very amicable.

Lady Victoriah finished securing her trusty steed into his stall beside the black mare's. She gave him a few comforting pats on the back to thank him for his hard work, then turned to the brunette. "Where's my husband?"

"Inside. Shall I fetch him?"

"No, that's fine. Come in with us. The market can wait."

A giddy smile drew to the woman's cheeks and she stifled a giggle behind her hand. She seemed to understand the situation and looked forward to where it would lead.

Lyn led them inside the cottage. "Sir Jerrell!" She waited for a voice to call back to her, then gestured for the lady of the house and her guest to follow her in.

The interior looked rather cozy. A couch draped with fluffy pelts sat near a fireplace protected by a captivating, branch-like fireguard. On the other side of the room sat a table and chairs, where family meals must have taken place. From their design, they were likely made by Ederean craftsmen.

It was certainly humble by a noble's standards, but the Kronas family lived very well, it seemed.

"Lyn, is something the matter?"

The man on the couch grunted as he stood, a hand lingering on his upper leg. He was well-built but had a slight paunch. The light from the window and open door made his blonde-gray hair shimmer. And when he limped toward the door, a crescent scar could be seen carved into the flesh by his right eye, reaching up to his bangs.

He seemed worried for a moment, but when he noticed who else was with her, his countenance shifted into one of joy. "Victoriah."

Lady Victoriah gave the man a sly look as she walked up to him. "What, is that how you greet your wife after months apart?" She put a hand on her hip, looking to him condescendingly.

A chuckle passed his lips. "Oh, so sorry, darling," he spoke as curtly as his wife, playing along with her game. "You're right, though. It should go a little more like *this*."

The man wrapped his burly arms around Lady Victoriah. One hand held her steady at the back close to her shoulder, the other brushed along her hip. Veronica blushed when she saw him pull his wife in, drawing closer to her with lips puckered.

But he stopped when Lady Victoriah drove a fist into his left side, making both her husband and the girl watching wince.

"Ow! Easy, easy!"

Lady Victoriah chortled. "Don't give me that. I know that's not your scarred side." She leaned in a little, her wicked leer locking with his eyes. "Or are you just getting brittle in your age?"

"Either that or your hands are turning into cold steel."

The retort elicited a lighter laugh from his wife. Their banter amused her greatly.

As she stared at the married couple, Veronica caught a glimpse of something in Lady Victoriah's valsara. It went away as soon as she noticed, but in its place was an ardent emotion: the love for her husband. She looked to him gentler after their interesting greeting but recaptured her proud demeanor upon turning to the other two in the room.

"I have someone I want you to meet."

The man looked to Lyn, then noticed Veronica standing beside her. He expressed surprise to see a third girl in his home, though he seemed as intrigued as the brunette was.

"Veronica, this is my husband, Jerrell. Jerrell, darling, this is—"

"Veronica Alivvrn of Illuascove," she finished the greeting for her meister knight. "It is a pleasure to meet you, sir. I am Lady Victoriah's squire."

Her words surprised Jerrell more than her very presence. She could not tell what went through his mind; it made her a little nervous. But he soon expressed enjoyment with a smile and laughter, then turned to his wife.

"So you finally decided to take my suggestion, huh?"

Lady Victoriah looked the other way and shrugged, grinning. "Honestly, I had forgotten all about that." She stepped up to Veronica, putting a hand on her shoulder. "I didn't do it for that, though. She's not like the other runts. I see promise in her, so I'm going to train her."

Veronica beamed with pride hearing her meister knight had such faith in her.

The smile Jerrell wore showed how endearing he thought it. "Well, Veronica, it's nice to meet you. You'll be in good hands with Victoriah here." He approached her and patted her other shoulder. "Just be careful that they don't break you."

She knew he only meant to tease, perhaps more his wife than her. It did not leave her unnerved, though. Having already gotten a taste of the

Wolverine's strength, Veronica knew she would be in for another trial when she decided to use more.

But like the rapier given to her, she would not break so easily.

She would have reassured Sir Jerrell of as much, but rather than direct Lady Victoriah's focus to her, it seemed best to have it kept on him.

"Veronica," said Lady Victoriah, a touch of whimsy in her voice, "do you still want to see the village?"

Her squire nodded. "I would love that, milady."

Lady Victoriah let go of her shoulder and looked to Lyn. "Lyn, be a dear and take Veronica to market with you. And be sure to introduce her to some of the shopkeepers. I'm sure they'd love to meet her."

Lyn seemed to understand well where this was leading. "Of course, Lady Victoriah." She led Veronica out the door without looking back.

Veronica could not resist taking a peek, though. Lady Victoriah had an uncharacteristically jolly smile as the door closed, one that betrayed the glimmer of mischief in her valsara. With her magic sight, she saw through the walls Lady Victoriah closing in on her husband, exhibiting delight for a brief moment, then letting her wicked intent be known.

Lyn and Veronica rode down the hill on Nightshade before she could find out anything more.

The villagers were very friendly. Many passersby greeted Lyn with smiles and waves. She seemed especially popular with the men her age, perhaps ones hoping to court her. The grocers in the marketplace were just as pleased to see her, saying how she always lit up the plaza.

A few people asked who her lovely new friend was, and were surprised when they were introduced. It was hard for many to understand how Veronica, someone so chipper and polite, came to be squire to Victoriah the Wolverine, who everyone in the village knew as the beast living up the hill. They saw it as quite the contrast, but Veronica could only laugh when she was told as much and said she thought her meister knight an admirable woman.

And when it seemed that someone would say otherwise, Lyn finished their business and moved on to their next stop.

They met nearly every grocer in the marketplace before Lyn found the ingredients she needed. After that, she showed Veronica around and introduced her to the captain of the village guard. She was keen on giving her lady as much time with her spouse as she could.

Soon, though, they made their way back up the hill and found Lady Victoriah outside with Jerrell. She was wrapping bandages around his left arm when they noticed the girls' return. A sword lay by Jerrell's feet, the handle pointing to his left hand.

Lyn was worried about Jerrell, but he assured her that his scars were not troubling him at the moment.

She explained his condition to Veronica during their stroll. Jerrell suffered from terrible injuries he received defending his home years ago. The scars they left behind kept him from putting too much pressure on his right arm and leg. When he did, they failed him.

Yet Jerrell agreed to spar with Lady Victoriah anyway. It was the only form of physical therapy he enjoyed, but he could not tolerate it for long.

He got a few cuts, but other than that, he seemed perfectly fine. He even followed the others inside without limping.

Lyn went to the kitchen to prepare dinner, and Lady Victoriah joined her. In the meantime, Veronica kept Jerrell company. He wanted to know a little more about the girl his wife picked to be her squire.

She told him a fair deal about herself: her home in Harnola, her family, her time in the Estrine Chateau. The topic shifted with Jerrell's focus, though, when he occasionally glanced at the painting near the fireplace. It was of him and Lady Victoriah years ago, and in Victoriah's arms was an infant with tufts of blonde hair.

Before she could ask about it, Lady Victoriah called Veronica to take her place in the kitchen for a bit. She never cooked before, so Veronica was glad she had Lyn to rely on for guidance.

When she stepped out of the kitchen to fetch her meister knight, Veronica caught a very interesting sight. In contrast to her earlier moments with her husband, when her demeanor was brash and her words blunt, Lady Victoriah held him close, her touch gentle as she caressed his sore muscles. And her eyes reflected such affection as she leaned in for a tender kiss—a kiss she halted once she realized they were not alone.

Seeing Veronica peek around the wall at them made her push Jerrell away. Her countenance became tense and cold while her valsara rippled with frustration.

Try though she did, Veronica could not stop a giggle from escaping her. She had no idea Lady Victoriah was so shy about showing affection.

She was sure she would demand a sparring session to pay her back, but Lady Victoriah instead returned to the kitchen to finish cooking.

Dinner was well worth the wait. The food was so delicious that it made Veronica melt. The stew in particular, loaded with onions, beef, and potatoes, had an uplifting flavor that invigorated the mind and body. She praised the two chefs for their work, but Lyn gave much of the credit to Lady Victoriah. The recipes she learned all came from her.

It was not difficult to believe. The food she cooked while en route to Russalin tasted so good. She knew how to coax flavor out of the food she had with the basest ingredients available.

She was a woman of many talents. Veronica looked to her meister knight with admiration, knowing there was still more to come.

After they ate and drank to Lady Victoriah's new squire, to Veronica's successful graduation from her status as a page, and to more good times ahead, they turned in for the night. Veronica slept on the couch, using the pelts to keep warm after the fire went out. Lyn had offered her the room she was staying in, but Veronica declined. The considerate girl did not feel right about taking another's bed.

She was sound asleep for a time, but awoke later on. It was not because her accommodations were unpleasant. There was this odd ripple in the air that tickled her magic senses.

It was hard to tell where it came from or what caused it. The ripple had faded as soon as she noticed it. She did not dismiss it as a figment of her imagination, nor did she believe it to be the doing of a phantom. But whatever it was could not have been a threat.

As Veronica was about to rest her head again, she found something else while her magic senses were still active. She looked above the fireplace, where the portraits she saw earlier hung. With it being so dark, she could barely see with the naked eye, but that allowed her magic sight greater acuity. With it, she saw a thin layer of energy around the painting of the couple and their baby.

She was not sure what sort of magic it was. It was spread out, not very concentrated, making it difficult to sense, let alone examine.

Curiosity guiding her, she stood from the couch, a pelt drop to the floor, to get a closer look. Walking up to the painting did not make the magic any clearer. Its frame seemed to be made of a material that concealed much of it, but the magic gathered in the stone at the bottom.

As she tried to determine its purpose, her hand slowly reached up to the stone.

"Paintings are not for touching, Miss Veronica."

Startled, she pulled away and looked to the hall. She was so focused on the magic that she failed to hear Lyn walking across the wooden floor. The young woman held a candle, its petite fire revealing her face and the nightgown she wore.

"I'm sorry, Lyn."

She smiled and walked up to Veronica, her candle now making it easier to see the painting. "You've noticed the magic inside?"

"Yes. ...How can you tell?"

"I have my ways." Her eyes drifted up to the painting. "The spell on it serves as a security measure. It creates a field that stretches past the perimeter of this cottage. If someone breaches it, it relays that to a stone Sir Jerrell keeps on hand."

A fine measure. With their home so far from the village and the only people there being Jerrell and Lyn most of the time, it was prudent to have something in place that would alert them of threats.

"Lady Victoriah's infamous name alone is not always enough to keep trespassers at bay."

Veronica turned to Lyn. "How come you are still awake?"

"Oh, I've had trouble sleeping some nights. More so tonight, with the good sir and lady reconnecting."

Veronica tried to hide her reddening face, which elicited a laugh from the young woman. She had thought Lady Victoriah's behavior with her husband to be her way of flirting.

Not wanting her thoughts to linger on that, she turned her attention back to the painting. "This painting is a catalyst for that spell, yes?"

Lyn nodded. "That's right. What better way to protect a home than with its family?"

A lovely way of putting it though it was, it made Veronica think of how Jerrell looked at it earlier.

As if knowing Veronica wanted to talk about it, Lyn directed her to sit while she got some water from the bucket in the kitchen. She brought back a cup for each of them and sat beside her on the couch. Her silence urged Veronica to speak her mind.

So she did. "That baby in the picture, Jerrell said that it is of his son many years ago."

"That it is."

"Where is he now?"

"Did you hope to meet him?"

Veronica looked from the painting to Lyn and smiled. "Someday."

That answer tickled Alicalyn. "I am sure you would like him. It's a shame he is in another country."

"Another country? Why has he left Vermalio?"

"Much has happened since the attack on Brigadier."

That day, stained forever by the memory of a gruesome and savage attack, certainly changed the lives of many people.

"Did you know I used to work as a maid at the Estrine Chateau?"

"Really?"

"Really. Until that very day, in fact. One of my charges happened to be their son. I was very fond of him; he reminded me of my younger brother when he was still alive."

"It must have been hard to see him go."

"That it was, though not as much as it was for his parents." The joy she expressed talking about her former charge faded as she turned to the painting. "They arrived after the attack, concerned for their son's safety. There were ... things said after they reunited. Jerrell was upset with him, and would not give his best wishes when it came time to say goodbye."

It startled Veronica to hear that. When he looked at the painting, it was not animosity she saw in Jerrell's valsara, but grief.

Noticing her disbelief, Lyn retook her smile after sipping her water. "Whenever he looks back on that moment, it is with regret. He still loves his son, and wants nothing more than to tell him that."

It made her feel better knowing that. Sir Jerrell seemed a very kind man. She could not imagine him still carrying resentment toward his son.

He was his father, after all.

Veronica took a drink from her cup, then asked, "So ... how did you come to be here?"

"Well, I looked after Sir Jerrell during his stay at the Estrine Chateau. His scars gave him more trouble after his son left, so he could not travel home so soon. His recovery was slow; Lady Victoriah herself said he never had such difficulty with them before. The three of us connected in that time—Jerrell when he confided in me, Victoriah when she spoke with me during her rest. When it came time for him to return, they believed he would need someone to look after him, so they offered the job to me."

Veronica's eyes widened in perceived surprise. "And you accepted?"

A giddy laugh passed Alicalyn's lips. "I was proud of my work at the chateau. But ..." She closed her eyes, thinking back on the moment she decided to leave the capital to come to Russalin with the crippled man. "I grew rather fond of them. And since they put such trust in me after our short time together, I thought it best to take their offer."

The changes in her voice as she spoke were so evident that Veronica did not need to gaze into valsara. It was an emotional time, without question. But in that time of unrest and uncertainty, she found something she wanted to protect in the remnants of the Kronas family.

Lyn rubbed her eyes after recounting those moments.

Veronica felt ready to sleep again too. "It might be best to turn in for the night."

"Yes." Lyn took the cup from Veronica once it was empty. She stood and looked down to Veronica with a smile. "Sleep well."

"Good night, Lyn."

When she was alone again, Veronica rested her head on the pillow and closed her eyes. Thoughts of her new adventure filled her head before it steadily cleared and she drifted off into slumber.

Veronica and Lady Victoriah rested in Russalin for two days. After that, it was time for them to return to duty.

Veronica got up at dawn to prepare her meister knight's steed. When she finished, she brushed his mane. Nightshade kept huffing and snorting all the while. Jealousy was usually not pretty, but on her, it was adorable.

After Timberhoof's knotted mane was clean and kempt, since she had been taken in by her charm, Veronica climbed into Nightshade's stall to brush her.

Soon, Lady Victoriah called Veronica.

Her squire dutifully responded, returning to her side. "Your mount is ready, Lady Victoriah."

Lady Victoriah walked over to the stables. She checked Timberhoof to see if his saddle and protective gear were on correctly, and wore a pleased grin when she finished. "Not bad."

Her praise put a giddy grin on Veronica's face.

Jerrell and Lyn came outside to see them off. The man went Nightshade's stall with a slight limp, probably to get her ready for Lyn when she needed to run errands. Lyn presented Lady Victoriah and Veronica each with a meat pie wrapped in cloth for their journey.

"Mm, smells good, Lyn," Lady Victoriah complimented.

"Uh— Yes, lovely," Veronica added. "I can't wait for a taste."

While Lady Victoriah went to guide Timberhoof out of his stall, Lyn cupped a hand at Veronica's shoulder.

"It was very nice meeting you, Veronica."

The chipper girl smiled. "Likewise. I do hope we can return soon."

A knowing look rested in her eyes. It might be longer than she had hoped, but Lyn loved the sentiment. "I'd like that. Perhaps you can regale me with a few stories when you do."

"Absolutely! I'm sure there will be plenty to tell."

"With Lady Victoriah teaching you, I have no doubt."

Hooves clopped against the sturdy ground. Veronica turned to see both Lady Victoriah riding Timberhoof and Nightshade being led by Jerrell, her reins in his hand.

"Before you go, we have something for you." The gentleman walked up to Veronica, presenting the reins to her.

She thought she misunderstood for a moment, but his hand remained extended while she stared at it.

"Go on, Veronica. Every knight-to-be needs a horse."

She faced Lyn when she spoke. "But doesn't she help you with your errands? Won't it affect your work if I take her?"

"Oh, I can get to the village and back on my own. Besides, she will be much happier on the road with you."

"That little trek isn't enough for her," Jerrell continued. "Nightshade can be a handful. She likes to run fast and hates to stop. Neither Lyn nor I can give her the exercise she needs, and it's made her restless. But you are serving a knight. You will face many dangers you will either have to run toward or retreat from—fast. She won't get her adrenaline rush in staying here, but she will with you."

"Not to mention I won't always be able to wait for you to climb on Timberhoof with me," added Lady Victoriah. "We'll have to respond to situations as fast as possible. It will go a lot more smoothly with a mount of your own." She leaned forward to scratch her warhorse's mane. "This was their idea. They want to help us so we can come back in one piece."

Veronica took in what everyone told her. She remained hesitant for a moment, but after seeing Lyn's pleading eyes and the insistent nudge from Jerrell's hand, she accepted Nightshade's reins.

"She will be well cared for."

Jerrell smiled and patted her shoulder. "So long as it's better than how Victoriah treats her horse."

"Oh, you are in for it when I get back," said his wife with a wicked look.

He looked back to her, his smile droll. "Promise?"

Their affectionate display made Veronica laugh. So as not to let the goodbyes last too long, she climbed atop Nightshade, careful not to smush the meat pie against the saddle.

"Take care, you two," said Jerrell.

"You too," Victoriah answered.

Their horses trotted down the hill. Veronica turned back to wave to the ones they were leaving behind.

Eventually, they reached the village and crossed through its peaceful streets. And upon reaching the last house, they went into a full sprint, the fields soon rolling behind them.

Their adventure together as meister knight and squire had begun. And what an adventure it would be.

~ Twelfth Chapter ~
Oblige and Greed

The Six Champions were tasked with traversing Vermalio to ensure its peace was upheld. Their duty was to protect the people—their lives, their prosperity, their well-being—so that the country itself may thrive from them. It was a challenging role with more than its fair share of hardship, but it was theirs to bear, as the king's most trusted vassals.

And as the Champion of Heart's squire, Veronica aided her in carrying out that role.

The months passed with them travelling from region to region, doing anything needed to keep the peace wherever they went. They handled issues as small as lost pets to crises that threatened innocent lives. Once they finished their work in one area, they moved on to the next.

Every moment of their journey together had been a form of training for the eager squire.

Veronica sparred with her meister knight every morning. Lady Victoriah was gentle for the first few days but gradually became more aggressive, forcing her to learn quickly.

When they were on the move, Veronica assessed their surroundings, and when they stopped, Lady Victoriah questioned her to see if she was paying attention instead of just following her. Nightshade did not always make that easy. As Jerrell promised, she was a handful. She often ran past Lady Victoriah when they were supposed to follow her and Timberhoof. And when she ran, she was so fast that the wind ripped the skin from her rider's face.

She was antsy and inpatient, quite unlike the docile Amber.

It took some effort to get Nightshade to behave. Whenever she did so without trouble, Lady Victoriah would propose a race, much to her squire's dismay. But she always accepted the challenge to reward Nightshade's obedience, and so Lady Victoriah would not think less of her.

Much time was spent riding across the plains and fields of Vermalio, just them and their horses. Their days were spent advancing to the next settlement. And at night, after a small meal of whatever they could find, they sat by the campfire and shared stories.

They first spoke of lighthearted things, like of times before Veronica became a squire and the places Lady Victoriah visited, and that her squire soon would. One cold night, though, when they made camp beneath a cliffside to keep out of the rain, Veronica felt compelled to speak of the time when she lost her brother.

"It was horrible, like I was living with a hole in my chest. An important person in my life was just ... gone.

"I hid in my chambers for days. I thought I knew what I wanted to do after I finally stepped outside, but there was still doubt. And from that doubt, my grief narrowly returned anew."

She did her best not to dwell on her heartbreak and instead told her meister the story with a smile.

"Then I went to see Father, and found him speaking to you."

Lady Victoriah had visited Harnola once before. At the time, Veronica did not know who she was or why she was there. She was standing outside her father's study, peering through the door left cracked open and listening to the resolute words of the visiting lady knight.

A promise was made then—a promise to stop those tragedies from repeating. And unbeknownst to them, Veronica took it to heart.

Long had Veronica cherished the principle of noblesse oblige taught to her by her mother. To aid those in need when able was a sign of valiance, as well as an obligation to those with wealth, power, and prestige. And though that code never mentioned acting in battle, she understood then that defending others was an act truly noble, something she knew she had the power to do.

It surprised Lady Victoriah to know that Veronica was there. "I had no idea Lord Alivvrn had a daughter, let alone that she was eavesdropping on us."

Whatever the meaning behind her teasing, it made Veronica laugh. She had not seen her that day because Veronica left for the training yard after hearing her promise. There, she took a practice sword in hand again, and would not put it back down.

"I had to give my condolences," Lady Victoriah explained. "I owed it to him, to all the families that lost children because of him."

She blamed herself for Xanlir's betrayal as well.

Still, that she was there at that time gave Veronica the hope she needed. She found a mission, a purpose, in the words she heard: to prevent tragedies like those from befalling the innocent.

She told her that to thank her, to let her know how grateful she was.

It was no coincidence that Lady Victoriah became more brutal in their sparring sessions the following morning. This mission Veronica was on, while noble, was an impossible one. It would take impossible strength to face it, and she intended to instill it in her the only way she could.

Much was accomplished within a few months, and there was still more for them to do. Their journey eventually took them to the town of Csekentil, where they found its populace in unrest.

The town was in ghastly shape. Damage to the buildings was being repaired upon their arrival, while a barricade was being set in place at the town entrance.

Soldiers guarding the gate greeted Lady Victoriah and her squire with hostility and raised spears. But upon being presented with her name and shield, they immediately lowered their weapons and profusely apologized.

"What's going on here?"

The lead guard approached the Champion of Heart and held his fist over his heart in salute. "Apologies for my men's haste, Lady Victoriah. They have been on edge since the brigand attack."

"Brigands?"

"Yes, milady. They came under the cover of night and waylaid our forces. Havoc spread throughout the town. Many good men were lost and a few women were taken, along with our reserves of food and lev."

They were terrible atrocities, committed to sate their base desires. It was not unexpected but still very troubling. Veronica saw other such deeds done since becoming a squire. Some stole simply to survive. But the destruction before her showed that this was done with malice.

No matter how many times she had seen the aftermath of banditry, it still left Lady Victoriah infuriated. She looked to the lead guard with fury as she heard his tale. "Where is your mayor?"

"At his hall. Shall I escort you to him?"

"No. Stay here and remain alert." She was about to nudge Timberhoof to move forward when she turned west, an empty path between houses catching her eye. "And get someone stationed at that opening there. We can't have any more weasels slipping through."

Her orders were carried out as she and Veronica led their mounts into town.

The destruction became more evident as they rode down the empty streets. Several buildings had been broken into, their doors busted down and their windows shattered inward. They were ransacked, nothing of value left behind. Before they reached the center, they found a couple of them that had been set ablaze, their remains charred black.

Veronica tensed up and pulled her reins to stop Nightshade when she noticed a corpse among the burnt wreckage, crushed beneath a beam of wood.

The recently deceased sometimes left traces of emotion lingering in the air. Even without getting too close, she could feel the dread and terror that smothered the memory of a once happy home.

It was hard to turn away, but she did so and followed Lady Victoriah.

There was no land without crime and criminals running amok, but the brigand hordes had long taken advantage of Vermalio's conflict with the Renegades. With each year, their opportunities grew, as did their spoils.

Things did not look any better when they reached the mayor's hall. The once impressive building, roughly three times larger than the ordinary homes, had been scarred by weapons blunt and sharp. Its walls were stained in crimson, dreadful impressions of people left behind. The struggle became fierce here, brigands and soldiers clashing over everything inside.

Guards stood at the door to the mayor's hall. They were tense, gripping their spears like they expected trouble to return at any moment.

It was a bit of a relief to see them relax when they saw Lady Victoriah. That was not the usual reaction she received from others.

One of the guards showed her and her squire inside while another looked after their horses.

The inside was a wreck. Broken furniture and shattered pots littered the floors. A few servants were in the middle of cleaning it up when the guard walked by with Lady Victoriah and Veronica. When they reached the mayor's study, they found a bearded man writing something at his desk. He was a stalky gentleman with a long nose. Panic filled his eyes when he looked to the door, perhaps wondering what else had gone wrong, but like his guards, he relaxed upon seeing the champion among them.

"Oh, Lady Victoriah! Thank the gods you have come." The mayor stood and circled his desk to greet his guests. He clasped Lady Victoriah's extended hand in both of his, shaking it vigorously.

Upon turning to the young girl beside her, he seemed intrigued. "This must be the squire I heard many a rumor about."

Veronica extended her hand to greet him as her meister knight had. It was shaken with just as much enthusiasm. "I am Veronica Alivvrn, sir. It is a pleasure to meet you."

"A pleasure indeed, young Veronica. Though I do wish I had the honor of meeting you under more uplifting circumstances."

"Speaking of which, Joam," Lady Victoriah spoke, "care to fill us in on the situation?"

"Of course, of course." The mayor walked back to his desk to retrieve the parchment he was writing on. "I am sure you have already been informed that we were beset by brigands just recently."

"We were told they snuck into Csekentil at night and caused havoc."

From what they had already seen, it might not have been difficult for her to determine what had transpired. But it was always best to get the most accurate information they could before speculating on anything.

"Quite so, and they did it with timing and planning. Once they had infiltrated the town, they set fire to some of the residences. Then when the town guard was deployed to restore order, they made their move. A group of them assailed the guardsmen the moment things began to calm while the rest pilfered whatever they could on this side of town. They raided our food store, the money for the town stored here in my hall, and whatever else was nearby. They even kidnapped some of the women, even my dear wife, Elanor. Once they were done, they disappeared."

"Did you learn where they went?"

"I'm afraid not, milady. Many of my guardsmen were killed during the raid, and the survivors were either too injured to act or protecting the rest of the civilians. A few brave soldiers attempted to give chase, but lost sight of them not far from town."

"Can you point me to those who followed them?"

"Certainly."

"Good. I can start with that." Lady Victoriah looked down to the parchment the mayor held in his hands. "What were you doing before we entered?"

Joam looked a little uncertain for a moment. Perhaps he just picked it up to hold something, following a nervous reflex. "I was making a desperate attempt to plea with Constan for aid in our dire hour," he said while handing the parchment to Lady Victoriah.

Constan was the town to the northeast of Csekentil. It took only a day to reach by horse, assuming the weather proved favorable. The main road between both towns often became buried by heavy mudslides when it rained. There was another route by the nearby river, but it took two days more than the main road.

"The attack left us short on manpower and supplies, so we will need their help to recover from this and pursue the scoundrels who kidnapped our people. But they are still wary of us since that dastardly Floyd tried to rally those bands of lowlifes several years ago."

"He had some of them raid Constan for supplies so they could try their hand at killing me," she stated bitterly. "Yeah, I remember."

"I fear they may not help us."

"Oh, they will." Lady Victoriah looked to the letter in her hand, reading its contents, before returning it to him. "Ask for an additional fifty soldiers."

"They will never agree to that," Joam fretted, "especially since Csekentil doesn't have the funds to compensate for that extent of aid."

"They won't have a choice," Lady Victoriah said with confidence. "Notify me when you've finished. I'll swap your seal for mine, and they'll come running."

The Six Champions often handled matters they could not settle on their own by calling for the aid of available militia. When such a request was made, it could not be denied. The champions were the arms of the king. No one held more authority save the ruler they served. Anyone who should receive a message with the seal of a champion was obligated to follow it to the letter.

And for Lady Victoriah to accomplish this task, she needed more soldiers—to protect the vulnerable town and help in suppressing the brigands once they tracked them down.

The wrinkles around Joam's eyes straightened out as relief replaced the anxiety plaguing him. "Oh, thank you, Lady Victoriah! Thank you ever so much."

"Don't thank me yet. We still have some abductees to rescue and some brigands to crush. I'll take your thanks when this is over and your wife is back here with you."

"Right then," Joan said, eager to get started. "I'll have Geoffrey introduce you to the men who gave chase. Please let me know if you need anything. I will do all in my power to see it done."

The mayor called for the guard who brought his guests in, the one he called Geoffrey, and immediately returned to his desk to compose a new letter. Meanwhile, Geoffrey escorted them back to the town entrance, where he had the lead guard assemble those who tried to pursue the brigands. They were a few bold, young recruits.

They gathered in the guards' barracks to show Lady Victoriah where they followed the brigands on a map.

The recruits chased the brigands eastward before losing their trail ten miles from town. The plains east of Csekentil were flat and clear, the grass short and the trees scarce, for a good thirty miles. Northeast of the plains, the land built up into a rolling mountain. To the south grew a dense forest.

One guard speculated that they ran for the mountain and relied on the caves there for shelter. Another believed they went to the forest to conceal themselves among the trees.

Both seemed to be viable options. Either area would have been ideal for hiding a large number of people. Lady Victoriah said nothing as she was presented with information and kept her eyes fixated on the map. As someone who travelled Vermalio more than anyone, she was familiar with the aspects of every region and the purities within them.

There was much to consider and little time to decide on action. They did not know what the brigands had done since their raid or what they had in store for their captives.

Even so, they had to wait on their support from Constan before they could do anything.

When the mayor had finished his letter for aid and had it notarized with the champion's seal, Lady Victoriah set out with a small search party to comb the plains for signs of brigand activity.

In the meantime, Veronica remained in Csekentil. While she thought she should have been with her meister knight, the humble squire understood why she had her there.

Rather than question her orders, she did what she could to alleviate the town's troubles.

For a time, she helped set up fortifications around town. But the soldiers insisted that she look after the civilians after she began suggesting ways to strengthen the plain wooden walls. They did not seem impressed with her Estrine education.

She found her time better served in aiding the civilians.

There was a mother who was too afraid to leave her home but needed to get food to feed her children. When called on for help, Veronica gladly served as her escort. The grocer had a limited stock since the raid and could supply little more than wilted vegetables and dried meat. It would not fill anyone's bellies, but what they had would provide some sustenance for at least a couple of days.

As the mother was deciding on what to purchase, a small boy came up to the stand asking for something to eat. "Please, mister," he begged the man. "We're hungry... We got to have something."

But the grocer could only show a pained expression as he tried to shoo the boy away. Veronica looked to the poor boy, then noticed a younger girl waiting by the alleyway he came from.

She did not judge the grocer too harshly. Although he gave very generous prices for his shriveled goods, he was still a merchant. His business was his means of survival, and the attack compromised that as much as anyone else's.

Still, Veronica could not let children go hungry. She handed the grocer a copper and five gray lev pieces. "Two bags of nuts for the boy, please."

Nuts were a common food in Vermalio, something that could be easily found in any region. The brigands would not have touched them in favor of the meat, eggs, and ale they pilfered. And they were a fine source of protein as well. Fifteen lev normally would not buy much, but the grocer made good on his promise for generous prices during this trying time. He offered enough nuts to fill two pouches that fit in both of his meaty hands.

The boy took the pouches into his arms and turned to Veronica, his eyes aglitter. "Thanks, lady!"

Veronica gave the boy a cheery smile. "You are welcome. Be sure to share with your friend, now."

The boy ran back to the girl in the alleyway, handing one of the pouches to her. They seemed very happy as they retreated out of sight.

She wished she could have done more for them, but Veronica was glad to have helped in some way.

Once she returned the mother to her home, Veronica kept patrolling the town, ensuring things were as orderly as could be. The town was quiet throughout the day, with most of the people holed up in their homes.

Soon, night had fallen with the rise of the moon. Lady Victoriah still had yet to return. Though Veronica worried for her, she knew her meister knight would be well.

She was Victoriah the Wolverine, after all. No one could harm her.

But the town and its people still could be, for they still stood.

The only people still up and about were the guards and those at the tavern. Things had gotten out of hand when two drunken men started having it out in front of the building. A crowd had formed at its doors and cheered them on. The few guards keeping watch at the end of the street thought letting them fight it out would be best. Veronica, however, would not stand idle and let another disturbance fill the streets.

When the guards refused to help her, she marched up to the brawling men to break them apart herself. "What's all this?"

The men stopped when she called them out, and looked to her with amusement. They found how she, a child, spoke to them like they were smaller than her to be amusing. "What's this?" one said. "What're you?"

Veronica did not deign to answer that. "Your town is in a crisis, and you see it fit to rage out here and cause further unrest?"

The men at the bar laughed while those Veronica reprimanded scoffed at her. They acted like she did not understand a thing. "Go on home, girly. This is men's business."

"Men's business? Is that what you call fighting in the street like unruly children?" She then turned to the crowd. "Or goading the frustration of others?" Her eyes were back on the two men, her focus primarily on them. "Is now really the time to be fighting amongst yourselves while your home is in this state, while your families and neighbors are still reeling from the attack you endured?"

The large man with shaggy black hair and a thick beard walked up to Veronica, showing his surly countenance. "Don't go mouthing off to me. I'd hate to mess up that pretty face of yours."

Their arrogance and bravado were almost as unsettling as the anger Veronica felt boiling within her. It never used to be so strong. In coming to know her other self, though, she came to understand—and become compelled by—her feelings. It became harder to resist her own frustration.

It frightened her knowing how strong the temptation to let anger guide her was.

But she was there to quell the unrest, not create more.

"What you're doing here will get you nothing. I am asking you to settle down. This town does not need any more fighting right now."

The nerves in Veronica's body screamed for her to move as the black-haired man, in a throaty growl, threw his fist at her. She stepped out of the way before it even came close and watched as he tumbled to the ground. It was rather sad watching him slide into the dirt and struggle to get back up.

It was then that the guards decided to intervene. They held the drunken man back and blocked him from lashing at Veronica. The other man walked away without another word, a dissatisfied sneer on his face.

The crowd dispersed, many of them scorning Veronica for her intrusion. A number of them returned to the tavern to forget their woes the way they originally planned to.

When the black-haired man tried shouting at the one he fought with, shoving and punching the guards, another sound drowned his voice out. A loud bell rang repetitively through the air from a tall lookout post near the middle of town. Immediately upon recognizing it, the drunk man, the dispersing crowd, even the guards were plagued by fear. The civilians scattered in a panic while the soldiers returned to their posts.

Veronica followed the guards with her rapier in hand until sensing a drastic change in the atmosphere. The discord from earlier and the current panic made it difficult to ascertain at first, but as she got closer to it, she felt the chaos now spreading into Csekentil. From her time with Lady Victoriah, she knew what that feeling meant.

Without delay, she ran toward the chaos.

At the town entrance, she found the guards there clashing with men wielding worn swords and axes around the broken remains of the wooden barricade.

It was as Lady Victoriah predicted.

"Brigands, bandits, pirates—whatever you call them, they're vultures. If they see an easy mark, they'll pick it apart and leave naught but bones. They didn't take everything of value the first time. They may return."

It was bold of the brigands to do so, but as she claimed, this town still held things of value, and had been crippled from the first assault. Help had yet to arrive, leaving Csekentil virtually defenseless.

That was why she had been left there.

The brigands lit torches upon fending off the guardsmen and began tossing them at the houses, having the flames grow and devour them. They were either intent on repeating their strategy, or worse yet, decided to adopt a method used by the Renegades.

Without delay, Veronica gathered water from the air into spheres and launched them at the flames. Dousing them, snuffing out the light, they became enveloped in darkness.

The brigands had no trouble seeing Veronica, though, and charged at her for interfering. But Veronica could see them just as well with her magic sight, their valsara revealing their forms to her. With her magic sight working in tandem with her normal eyes, the light of their valsara illuminated their bodies, allowing her to distinguish friend from foe.

Lord Ralias, guide my hand.

Upon offering a prayer to the god of war and bringer of prosperity, she braced herself for the brigand rushing straight for her, his axe raised high. She leaned low and, her reflexes snake-like, snapped forward, carving her rapier clean through the man's tough flesh. Blood spilled along the blade and its warmth trickled along her arm as his valsara faded.

Rather than clash with more enemies, Veronica made further use of her Second Verse. Taking advantage of their gathered numbers, she guided water along her blade, tracing a circle in the air with the tip. The water flowed to fill the shape she drew, remaining compressed, nearly flat. She then pulled her rapier back and, swift as the wind, thrust incessantly into the water. Lances shot from the mass of water, raining down on the men with tremendous force. They tore through muscles, crushed bones, and sent those hit flying.

When the water nearly dwindled, she reached her free hand out and pulled it back, drawing the last of it toward her, then hurled it in a lash at the brigand hiding behind a ruined cart, crushing his head.

Many of the brigands had been wiped out in her assault. Their bodies remained on the ground, some groaning in pain while others were motionless, without the light of their valsara.

It was not a very accurate attack, but it definitely helped when facing such large numbers.

There were still some enemies hiding behind nearby buildings and the ruined barricade, wary about stepping out into the open. Angst and worry overcame the confidence that they earlier exuded.

She could see their every move and had the power to strike them down without a direct attack, but Veronica did not let her guard down. Her enemies were crafty. They got the best of the entire town once already. All they would need was one opening, and they would be rid of her and could continue ravaging the town.

It was nerve-wracking waiting for the remaining enemies to make their move, but she knew she could not leave her spot. Not a single brigand could be allowed through.

The ones behind the barricade began to move away from the breach they made, perhaps to make another nearby. When she realized what they were up to, she turned to her side and—her heart nearly springing from her chest—took a terrified leap backward.

A broad cutlass nearly decapitated her. Its wielder moved in quickly once she caught sight of him, swinging for her torso. Veronica brought her rapier up to block, but found herself overwhelmed by the brigand's strength. She pulled back before his sword cut through her and tried to move away.

He was relentless, but Veronica read his movements and determined what he would do next. The brigand waved his sword around, grinning like a madman, then angled the weapon with intent to run her through. Veronica dove away from the blade, then thrust her sword, piercing the man's ribcage.

The brigand groaned and writhed, but his body did not collapse. Instead, he snarled, blood spraying from his mouth, and brought the pommel of his sword to slam into Veronica's forehead. She was thrown into a building, the back of her head hitting the wall, and fell to the ground.

The last thing she saw before her dazed vision faded was the brigand pulling the sword from his chest and closing in on her.

When next Veronica was able to lift herself up, the first thing she saw was a lifeless face lying in front of her own. She leaped back in a scream, nearly flying off the ground. It took her a moment to realize that face belonged to the brigand she was fighting.

And still lying in front of him ... was her. She saw her own body lying on the ground, eyes shut, blood trickling from her forehead.

Drawing her gaze downward, she saw that her form was transparent and surrounded in an eerie blue light.

Oh no... No, no, no, no!

She got down on her knees, neither dirt nor stone digging into her incorporeal legs. It nearly made her panic to see her hands phase through her body as she attempted to turn it over.

Getting a hold of herself, she leaned low, examining her face. Although it was quiet, breath still passed her lips.

A heavy sigh escaped her as she sat back up. She was still alive, although she had somehow become separated from her body.

It was very startling to see herself lying in such rough shape, but she forced herself to remain calm. In looking up, she saw the fighting still went on, and to her delight, Lady Victoriah had returned to engage the enemy. Several brigands tried ganging up on her, but the Wolverine was undeterred. She swatted them aside one by one, tearing through them with deft swings of the sword, ribbons of crimson dancing in the air around her. Lady Victoriah fought them all off while remaining in one spot, acting the shield for her unconscious squire.

More flames had spread along the buildings near and far, their light shining upon the resolute knight as she fought. The soldiers she had taken with her fended off a few enemies that seemed to come from within the town. With them fighting together, they made quick work of the brigands around them.

The enemies routed, Lady Victoriah hurried to her squire's side. She turned her over to see if she was all right. "Veronica."

"I'm here, milady."

Lady Victoriah's voice reached Veronica, but Veronica's could not reach her. She kept her focus on the unresponsive body in front of her, worryingly shaking it and calling her squire's name.

"Lady Victoriah, I'm—" Veronica stopped when she recalled she was but a spirit now. She would not be heard, no matter what she said.

One of the guardsmen approached Lady Victoriah. "We should take her to get treated."

Lady Victoriah nodded and stood. "You two," she pointed to the mounted guardsmen. They guided their horses to her as the one beside her took Veronica's body into his arms. "Get this girl to safety and patch her up. Keep her safe while I dispatch the rest of these vultures."

Veronica folded her arms and hung her head. She did not say "my squire," or anything of the like, but rather "this girl." She must have been disappointed in her for losing to a mere cutthroat. She watched, humiliated, as the guardsman brought her body into the arms of his mounted comrade.

Lady Victoriah took the stolen rapier from the dead brigand's hand before calling Timberhoof and mounting up, dashing into the town.

Perhaps she should have stayed close to her body, but shame weighed down her spirit and kept her in place. Her mind was beset by antagonizing thoughts of what her meister knight would say to her when she awoke.

But then, something caught her eye.

Another brigand was hiding in the shadows of a nearby alley. His breathing became loud and haggard once he knew he was alone. He saw the Wolverine fight. Dreading that he would end up like his comrades, he made a break for it out of the village.

Even if she could not fight, there was still something she could do. Veronica felt light as air again as she pursued the fleeing brigand.

His legs carried him in long sprints. Had he not slowed down to catch his breath, there would have been a good twenty feet between him and the spirit he did not know was close behind. He was certainly good at running away.

Without her body, Veronica did not need to stop to cool her burning legs and lungs. She even moved faster than she did with it, unburdened by the heft of flesh and armor.

The flat land suddenly came to a downward slope after they went far through the plains. By the time Veronica noticed, she had already leaped across the air. She expected to come back down, but she didn't. Her spirit remained hovering in the air.

The already bleak world around her spun as she struggled to move from her position. The stars above went below her feet, then at her right side, then circled all around, until she started to move again. Pushing through the air like when she swam was oddly tricky, but she managed.

The brigand had run out of sight while she was disoriented, but the fear in his valsara left a trail for her to follow. Upon making a few strokes, she glided after him again, faster than before.

When she found him again, she saw him push his way into a hillside. She caught up to him as the hole he made was closed back up. Without hesitation, she dove through the ground, phasing through to find a tunnel.

It must be their hideout. They camouflaged a passage they made by placing a bed of grass over a wooden gate. Wavy, hair-like roots stuck out through the small square holes and around the thick fencing put in place. They had been here for some time.

The tunnel stretched far into the hill and broke into various paths. They appeared unorganized at first, but were well built.

Veronica followed the brigand as he called for his comrades, then turned down a different path, waves of anxiety coming from it. It led to a small space with an iron cage at the end. And inside the cage were several women, likely the ones kidnapped from Csekentil.

Returning to town forthwith seemed best, but before she did, Veronica searched the hideout for the brigand she chased. He met up with a man wearing an eyepatch; perhaps he was the one in charge. While vexed by the news he heard, he did not seem concerned.

"If the others get away, they'll know not to come straight here. They'll lead any hounds astray, then make their way back. In the meantime, we lie low. We'll not be found as long as we remain here."

Satisfied with what she heard, Veronica flew through the roof of the hideout, coming out of the hillside, and made haste back to Csekentil.

Upon arriving in town, Veronica knew precisely where to find her body, as if she had been drawn to it. That feeling overcame her during her flight, the need to reunite with her body becoming more pressing by the second. It might have been a homing instinct for the spirit.

She found her body in a bed at the guards' barracks. Returning to it was as simple as lying her spirit atop it. It was not long before she felt the bed cradling her sides and her head pounding. Moving made her headache worse, but she could not remain idle.

Lady Victoriah was in the next room talking to the lead guard and the mayor, discussing their next move, when Veronica entered and told them of what she found. At first, they thought the head injury might have given her a very lucid dream. They remained adamant that she return to bed and recover.

When she went into detail about the hidden tunnels, though, Lady Victoriah had her continue. It was hard to convince her that it actually happened when she said her spirit had been projected from her body.

Confused though she was, Lady Victoriah gave serious thought to what she said and weighed that with the unfruitful results from her search. She knew of her squire's ethereal powers and that she was not one to lie.

Mayor Joam, desperate for a lead, chose to believe her. "Perhaps she was given a vision from Lady Malute. Even she grants boons from time to time." Invoking the name of the goddess of misfortune and bringer of the night sky did not inspire confidence in either his lead guard or the champion. But by his insistence, Lady Victoriah agreed to search the area Veronica described.

The cavalry from Constan arrived not long after sunrise. Though some complained about their timing, their help was appreciated regardless. Most of them remained in town while fifty of their finest riders followed the Champion of Heart to the fields.

Veronica showed them exactly where the brigands' hideout was. She was not sure who was more surprised when her meister knight forced her way inside the covered entrance: the knights or the brigands.

Few enemies remained inside since most of their band had yet to return, making their capture swift. The prisoners were freed and immediately brought back home.

Everyone was delighted to see their loved ones return safe and sound. Joam was in tears when he held his wife in his arms again.

The people of Csekentil gathered to show Lady Victoriah their gratitude, but she would not accept it. "If it's thanks you want to give, it's hers to take," the champion said as she pushed her squire before the grateful masses. "Veronica here is the one who found the bandit's hideaway. This town is safe again because of her."

It filled her with pride to hear her meister knight say that, but having the attention of all the townspeople embarrassed Veronica in a way different than she knew. It felt good but still overwhelming; she was not used to having that kind of attention from so many.

The mayor continued to elaborate on his idea that she was granted a boon from Lady Malute. He seemed rather insistent about it and the people were impressed, so she let him go on without correcting him.

Veronica knew what became of her did not come from a goddess' blessing. It was another power that came with the Second Verse, something she felt should have remained secret.

Lady Victoriah seemed amused by it, but did not say anything. She realized this power of Veronica's was new to her, given how hesitantly she spoke when she first told her about it. If she had questions later, she would certainly let her know. But for now, she wanted her to enjoy her success.

The last of the brigands were soon captured, ambushed in their own hideout by the soldiers lying in wait. Csekentil reclaimed its stolen goods and lev, and order was restored.

~ Thirteenth Chapter ~

Friction

The course Lady Victoriah had planned took them in a circle around the kingdom. With eastern Vermalio in a peaceful state, enough for it not to need a champion's aid, they rode north around the Ravaged Precipice and gradually made their way west.

Their travels took them near Illuascove. Excited, Veronica asked if they were going to visit her home. Lady Victoriah never gave a straight answer to tease her squire, only promising she would like where they were going. Veronica knew her meister knight enjoyed the honest expressions she made. She thought that if she did not give her meister knight what she wanted, then she would stop teasing and tell her.

But she could not contain her excitement.

Alas, they never arrived at their intended destination.

They received unsettling news about a fierce skirmish at the western border. It was an attack from Pterna.

Pterna, the Land of Renewal. It was a notably aggressive country that once fought Vermalio in a bloody and devasting war. The war ended with

Vermalio as the victor, their peace attained by then Prince Faustign L. S. Vermalio, a mighty warrior blessed by Lord Ralias, the god of war and bringer of prosperity. However, despite Pterna's vow to cease hostilities with Vermalio, their forces continued their attacks on Styne, the fortress city built at the Vermalio-Pterna border after the war to keep Pterna from invading by land.

The Pternite emperor always claimed that those forces were rogue militias that splintered themselves from the empire. Few believed such ambiguous claims. But Vermalio recognized that, after the war, the Pterna Empire had been divided in twain and power struggles became commonplace. What was now called "East Pterna" grappled for control over the empire with enemies in the west. But the ruler of "West Pterna" denied that she had any influence in the east or further interest in Vermalio.

There was much they did not understand about the situation, but since Vermalians were not permitted to enter the divided empire, they had little more than the words of the rivaling warlords to go on.

The Pternites did not concern Lady Victoriah. But the Vermalians at Styne did, so she raced to the region of Teterbelt immediately.

Soon, they came upon a citadel standing in the gap between two unscalable mountain ranges. Towering walls stood tall around Styne, connecting the mountains and cutting off the pass from the outside. The only way through was to enter the tremendous steel gate in the valley.

Those standing guard opened the way for Lady Victoriah once she was recognized.

Past the foreboding maw of the gate was a beautiful city. The path from there led downward, granting them a marvelous view. Tall, pristine buildings stood around clean yet bustling streets, and all around them stood the barriers, both natural and man-made, that kept them safe. Toward the southern mountain was the residential area, where a grand cathedral stood over the humble dwellings. The area near the northern mountain looked to be a militarized zone, with many of the facilities clustered around the wall separating them from Pterna. Several large manors stood among the empty fields used for training purposes. And at the center of the city, down the path directly from the Vermalio gate, was a grand marketplace where many civilians roamed.

Lady Victoriah and Veronica rode down the street to the marketplace. A lively atmosphere filled the area, footsteps echoing over stone pathways and voices spreading idle gossip. Everyone seemed to be living their lives in content, without anything to alarm or upset them.

It was as though they were a world away from violence and war.

But the attacking Pternites had to pose some threat if the Vermalian forces engaged them.

Seeing the peace did not make Lady Victoriah any less intense. "If that blasted informant brought me here for nothing..." she muttered to herself. It was difficult to hear over the clamor, but once Veronica noticed her angst, it was impossible to ignore.

Her countenance became all the more stern as they neared the western wall, then suddenly loosened up. "We're taking a break." Lady Victoriah led her mount to a tavern at the edge of the central district.

It was unusual for her to want a drink in the middle of the day. She was always so diligent, putting their daily goals and Veronica's training before all else. Rest and indulgence were rewards she allowed herself only at night, if at all.

She was to follow her lead, though, so after tying Nightshade's reins to the post by the water trough, Veronica went inside with her meister.

The tavern was overcrowded by soldiers—its tables, walkways, stairwell, and bar all occupied. The armored men and women managed blithe countenances only with the influence of liquor, and even with it, their morose valsara affected the mood around them. Their loud voices sounded empty, and their laughter gruff, tired.

Lady Victoriah looked around the gloomy tavern, shook her head, and marched inside with a hand on her hip. "You folks still know how to ruin the atmosphere, looks like!"

The soldiers all lifted their heads when her proud, boisterous voice filled the tavern. Some looked to her with confusion, but the grizzled veterans beamed with excitement.

"'ey look, it's Vicci!"

The majority of the patrons raised their mugs and hollered in cheer. Suddenly, the tavern's tired atmosphere became electrifying.

It was such a startling change that it baffled Veronica. She followed Lady Victoriah through the cheery crowd, careful not to get separated from her.

A spot became available at the bar once they reached it. The lady who stood for Lady Victoriah then noticed the girl in her shadow. "Oi, who's this little thing?"

"That's my squire, Della."

The lady gasped. "So the rumors were true? Blimey, I never thought you'd take one for yourself, Vicci." Della turned to the man in the seat beside her and grabbed his shoulder. "Where're your manners, now? Come on, offer the little lady a seat."

Lady Victoriah chuckled. "It's all right. She can have mine. I'll just sit where I used to." Not minding the approaching barkeep, she grabbed the counter and lifted herself to sit on top of it. "Now, this is a familiar view. Brings back good times. But I can't say time has been good to any of you—or is that just Harvey's doing?"

Laughter boomed throughout the entire tavern. Her crude joke made those who recognized her chortle uncontrollably and those who did not crack a smile. Nearly everyone raised their drinks to that regardless of how they felt.

Her meister knight's behavior made Veronica blink in disbelief. She had never seen her act like that in the other taverns they visited.

Speaking curtly about someone who may or may not have been there did not surprise her as much as her sudden sociability. She always refrained from speaking to those who did not approach her and drank in peace. And while she was never ladylike, per se, she never sat on bar counters or shouted at the barkeep for whatever she needed.

Something about this place made her a different person entirely.

Worrying she would anger the barkeep, Veronica tried to convince Lady Victoriah to get off the counter. But rather than berate her, the barkeep brought the rowdy knight a mug of rum. Seeing that he did not mind, Veronica quietly took the seat offered to her meister knight.

She sat in silence, nursing the cup of ivory juice offered to her, while Lady Victoriah interacted with the soldiers that came up to her. When she began introducing her squire to them, Lady Victoriah told Veronica that they were old friends she made during the war with Pterna.

During the war, Lady Victoriah was but a gutsy squire eager to rush into battle. She fought alongside the soldiers stationed at Styne until joining a lancer unit to push back the invaders. Her strength and guile made her well-known, and the valor she showed in saving her meister knight won her the battle and everyone's respect.

The veterans and her peers in the tavern were the first to call her Victoriah the Wolverine, and said the name with admiration and pride.

It was pleasant to hear about Lady Victoriah's squiring experience. She rarely talked about her youth.

Focusing on the now, on what was right in front of her, was always best for her.

"Oh, Vicci was always such a scrapper. Tough as steel and hardheaded to boot. It made her a real terror, even when she was only your age." Della seemed especially close to Lady Victoriah and was not shy about singing her praise.

She then leaned an elbow against Veronica's shoulder, giving her a shrewd look. "Makes me wonder what she'll make you into, little lady. No doubt you have your hands full with training."

"She handles it fine, Della. Look." Lady Victoriah grabbed hold of Veronica's wrist, pulling it high to make her arm sway. "I haven't broken her yet. Don't let her innocent face fool you; she's tougher than you were in your squiring days."

"Oh ho! Is that right?" Della leaned into Veronica a little more, grinning. "I'll have to see it to believe it. What do you say, little lady? Want to show me what you can do?"

"Leave her be!" Lady Victoriah said in a laugh. "We're here to get a little leisure in before we get to business." She took another swig of rum, smacking her lips parted from the mug. "Or if you want, you can tell me what happened here, and you all can have a go at both of us later on."

Her old friends grinned at the offer. It had probably been some time since they had the chance to catch up. If they were all as competitive as her, sparring together seemed like a great way to do it.

The knights began to brief Lady Victoriah on what happened in their skirmish with the Pternites, all the while cursing the name she uttered earlier, when Veronica noticed something odd. She excused herself and walked across the crowded hall.

Everyone was in a much better mood after Lady Victoriah's entrance. There was, however, a flare of hostility that rippled through the pleasant atmosphere. It was not mere irritation. She felt whoever it came from was on the verge of spilling blood.

Upon approaching the staircase, she saw a few squires on the upper level surrounding someone. When she climbed it to get a better look, they scattered. A lone girl remained and watched the others go, then looked Veronica's way when she approached. Her eyes, hard and heavy, bored into her the hostility she sensed.

This was no place for angst. Veronica wanted to see if she could lighten her spirits, but after getting so close, she froze.

The girl noticed her sudden rigidness. Her eyes narrowed, glimmering with rage, and she turned to walk away in disgust.

Veronica did not expect to see one of them here. It was quite a shock. But realizing that she upset her even more made Veronica regret letting it show.

She was familiar with that sort of hostility. There would be nothing she could do to ease it.

Awful though she felt, she could not focus on that for long. The entire tavern had fallen silent in an instant, its lively atmosphere snuffed out. Veronica looked down from the railing to see everyone focused on someone standing at the entrance.

It was another knight, a man donned in beguiling silver armor. His black hair gleamed like obsidian from the sunlight beaming inside until he entered, and his stern eyes darted around the place until resting on three nervous soldiers.

"I do not remember giving you the day to rest," he hollered. "Back to the base at once!"

The soldiers dropped their mugs to salute the knight, then left in a hurry, careful not to get too close to him. His fierce stare lingered on the doorway before turning to the bar.

"So here you are again. As dignified as ever, I see."

His attention was on Lady Victoriah, much to her chagrin. Her squire felt the animosity she tried to drown boil over merely from the man's presence.

Despite that, she had enough liquor in her to force a wry grin and sound somewhat chipper. "This *is* a tavern, Harvey. People come here to loosen up, not get a lance stuck up their arse."

The name Lady Victoriah uttered and the unease from the soldiers told Veronica much about the man. She watched the scene unfold as she slowly descended the staircase.

"And just as eloquent..." A conceited smirk crossed the knight's face as he approached the bar. He kept a fair distance from the women he scowled at but acted as if he owned the place. "What brings you to my city, Sister?"

Sister? Veronica halted at the middle of the staircase, her eyes drawn to her meister knight.

A vile anger reverberated from her valsara and reflected in her eyes. Though she may have tried to appear relaxed, her stare became fiercer the moment he uttered that word. It revealed their resemblance to one another.

"That's Lady Victoriah to you."

"Falling from nobility does not change your blood, *Sister*. But fine. You will address me as Commander Archave then."

"*Fine*, Archave. I came here to take a look at your mess."

The commander scoffed. "As you can see, the citadel still stands. The Pternites have been repelled. My defenders survived the assault, and are being rewarded for their work with rest and relaxation. At least, until you came along."

Perhaps so she would not trouble the soldiers she got along so well with, Lady Victoriah let it pass how it was the other way around. "Then my stay will be brief, won't it?"

"Let's hope so. We wouldn't want to keep the Champion of Heart away from where she is supposed to be, would we?" He spoke with venom as he addressed her title. Upon deciding it was time to part, he turned his back on her. "Do try to interfere with the soldiers as little as possible. We have an intricate system to uphold here." With that, he took his leave.

Lady Victoriah let her smirk turn into a twisted scowl as he left. She faced the bar again, slamming her mug against it. "Barkeep, another."

Veronica returned to her meister knight's side as her company tried to put her in a better mood. She downed her mug upon getting a refill and immediately asked for another.

Despite her curiosity, Veronica knew not to ask about what just happened. That had to be why she insisted on visiting the tavern in the first place.

Assessing the damage from Pterna's attack came before all else. Lady Victoriah was able to deduce what transpired from the soldiers' reports and the available documented information. Afterwards, she surveyed the western wall at the points the enemy made contact.

Scaling or circling Styne's wall was futile, that much Pterna knew. Their attacks, however, often focused on breaking through it.

The wall was a hundred feet tall and half as thick, and made of the strongest of stone. Ordinary methods would not even scratch it. But Pterna's imperial army was cunning and resourceful. They commanded one of the world's largest orders of mages and often used them in the allegedly rogue attacks on Styne. Their magic was uncanny; whatever sorcery they used weakened the structure of the wall, enough for them to bore into it.

Fortunately, there was no damage this time around.

It had been some time since Lady Victoriah saw her old comrades, so rather than leave immediately, they stayed in Styne for another day.

Even though they were on standby, the soldiers still needed to train in the morning. They found it a treat to spend that time sparring with Lady Victoriah and her sprightly squire.

The rest of the day was Veronica's to enjoy. When asked what she wanted to do, she had them show her around the citadel. A couple of soldiers, including Della, acted as guides, but they steered clear of the military district at Lady Victoriah's behest.

She likely wanted to avoid him.

When the day neared its end and the skies turned golden, Lady Victoriah took Veronica to her favorite place in the region. They rode to an outlook along the southern mountain that offered a breathtaking view of the border. The city rested comfortably tucked between the mountains. The plains of both nations glistened magically in the late day sun, the rolling hills of Pterna and the verdant fields of Vermalio, although separated, sharing in its brilliance.

Styne itself was beginning to settle down. They could see the streets clearing even from so high up. Soon, everyone would be at rest, at peace in their little shell.

The majesty of the view and the gentle caress of the air comforted Veronica, but her troubled thoughts came to resurface. It did not go unnoticed by her meister knight, who told her to share them.

Bringing it up might not have been best, but since Lady Victoriah insisted, she had to obey. "That man from the tavern yesterday... He said you were his sister."

Bitterness arose from the knight's valsara. Her gaze became hard and cold. While not angry with her squire, she could not help but feel it.

"Is he ... the reason you—" The words became caught in her throat before she could finish. Simply saying them proved too difficult for her.

Veronica had been told that Lady Victoriah was a fallen noble—that, for whatever reason, she had been cast out of her family and lost her status and inheritance.

Fallen nobles in Vermalio were seen as disgraces, rejects, scandals. Their very names were mud, their fall from nobility made known through slanderous rumors. Rebuilding their reputation often led to undertaking labors that left many broken.

Veronica never saw Lady Victoriah as a fallen noble, nor would she say in any way that she was. It would have been a terribly callous insult to a knight as fine as her.

Lady Victoriah understood what Veronica was trying to say. She knew her squire to be a kind soul, one that could not comprehend why family, a bond unquestionable, would forsake one of its own.

Lady Victoriah mulled over her thoughts while looking down at the city for a bit, then when she decided on what to do, she distanced herself and ordered Veronica to draw her sword.

Her anger had settled. She did not make the order to discipline her.

Whatever the case, Veronica drew her rapier and took her stance.

Lady Victoriah armed herself, "The longer you last, the more I'll tell you," and crossed her sword with Veronica's.

Her arm shook when it met with her meister knight's force, but Veronica held strong. A smirk from Lady Victoriah let her know to be on her guard—she was going to get serious fast.

Lady Victoriah drew her sword away and brought it back down in three quick, heavy swings. Veronica blocked them all and moved to her opponent's side to thrust. A deft swing met her rapier and threw her off balance, but she quickly recovered and blocked again just in time.

"Don't misunderstand. House Archave didn't disown me; I turned my back on them."

Had she stopped to ponder on that brief statement, the thick sword looming over Veronica would have torn through her. She retreated backward before the sword fell, trying to put some distance between them. But Lady Victoriah would not let her get away. She closed in and threw a horizontal swing, prompting Veronica to step back and block.

"My parents had a lot of children, hoping our success would help build the family name. My brothers and I never got along—you could probably tell from how I treated Harvey. Those three obnoxious arses always acted like they were better, that they knew best because they were boys.”

Her swings became exceedingly aggressive the more she thought about her siblings. Even when she dodged and parried, Veronica could almost feel her blade cutting through her. Had she not faced Lady Victoriah before, her heart would have stopped from the imposing force she exuded.

Her family certainly brought out the worst in her, as her enemies did.

But as her thoughts changed, she became calmer, less frightening, almost serene. “The only one I could ever relate to was my sister, Laryn.”

It was a good thing Veronica kept her guard up. When Lady Victoriah moved in to strike, her movements became almost unreadable. Her stride was quick and silent, and the waves of her sword true. She was even more dangerous when composed.

“The two of us were inseparable. We always stuck by each other, always encouraged each other to chase our dreams.” The memories of her beloved sister kept her voice and valsara calm. It was like she called on them to soothe her. “It was because of Laryn that I knew I could be a knight. She was the one who motivated me to leap at the chance once it presented itself.

“We sent each other letters when I left for the Estrine Chateau. Reading her words wasn’t the same as hearing them from her, but they were what kept me going throughout my training.”

Veronica was left fighting for breath and barely able to keep standing when Lady Victoriah let up. She knew that she had been going easy on her before, but she never realized just how much strength she held back. And there was still more she had yet to let loose—she could feel it.

But then, Lady Victoriah lowered her sword and became lost in her memories. She stared past her squire, her gaze somber.

After reflecting on them for so long, she lowered her sword. “Eventually, after I became a knight, the letters stopped coming. And later on, I got word that she disappeared, outright vanished without a trace.”

Veronica’s caution faltered. She, too, lowered her weapon as she looked upon Lady Victoriah’s valsara. It was a painful memory she shared.

Though her countenance remained as stoic as possible, Veronica could understand what she felt from that time.

"I fulfilled my dream. I became a knight of the realm. My duty was to the kingdom. I was to be where I was ordered to be, in body and mind. But because of that, I couldn't look for my sister. She was out there somewhere, and I couldn't do a thing for her."

Terrible pangs struck Veronica once she became attuned with Lady Victoriah, the waves of emotion assailing her. Her free hand rested over her chest, nursing her heart from the grief she read.

The resonance between them was abnormally strong. She was typically not so heavily impacted by the emotions of others.

"You wouldn't believe how overjoyed I was when I saw her again." For a brief moment, there was joy, but that became immediately eclipsed by something else. "To think, all that time I worried about her, feared what had befallen her, and I found her in the sleepy little town I was stationed in. And when I did ... she was murdered right before my eyes."

Horror inundated Veronica. It felt like her heart had been ripped from her chest. Dreading what may come next, she shut off her magic senses before Lady Victoriah's valsara could overwhelm her.

She shuddered when she looked back at Lady Victoriah, and found that their eyes met. The champion charged while Veronica was off guard, the squire barely able to react before she came in close. Their swords crossed over a dozen times until Lady Victoriah overpowered her squire, knocking the rapier from her hands, and jabbed her with her elbow.

Veronica tumbled to the ground. She went rigid upon opening her eyes, seeing the sword of her meister knight point to her neck. Lady Victoriah had not forgotten what they were doing, and she wanted to remind her squire of that. Every moment was one to learn.

When Veronica yielded, Lady Victoriah traded her sword for an outstretched hand. Sighing in relief, Veronica accepted the help up.

"The rest ... isn't very pleasant, nor is it important. What matters is, I lost Laryn. Without her, I had no family left. She mattered to me, not the Archaves. So I cut my ties with them and became a fallen noble."

Leaving it at that was rather unsatisfying, but she did say she would talk for as long as Veronica remained standing. Giving the tale some sort of ending was a courtesy on her part.

They sparred a little longer until the sky darkened and the sun rested on the horizon. The cool evening breeze felt good against their skin.

It was pleasant just following the path down the mountain and breathing in the crisp air.

But it seemed others had come to train at the outlook as well.

The crude sounds of grunts and a body hitting the ground drew Veronica's attention to the lower cliffside, where she saw two knights overseeing a bout between squires. The knights appeared relaxed as they watched their squires have at each other in hand-to-hand combat.

There was a third, however, between the two boys. And when she noticed that, she realized they were not sparring.

Concerned, Veronica broke from her meister knight to act. She gathered water and lobbed it at the boys, knocking them away from the girl they were beating. At her rider's guidance, Nightshade brought herself between the squires and the girl. The mare let out a loud *neigh*, as if to frighten them off.

"What's the meaning of this?" one of the knights snarled.

"That's for me to ask!"

Lady Victoriah caught on to what her squire was up to and followed her. This was not the first time she went her own way when she saw something was wrong.

The knights lost their fire when Timberhoof's thunderous clopping drew near. They stood upright to show respect for the esteemed knight atop the steed's back, for whatever it was worth.

Their squires stood down immediately when their knights had. Noticing this, Veronica looked behind her to see if the girl was okay. Her black hair bun was a mess and nearly coming undone, and her olive skin was marred with dirt and bruises.

It was the girl she saw at the tavern the night before.

"T-They were just—"

"If the next word to leave your lips is *training*, I'm tearing them off!" The ground shook when Lady Victoriah dismounted.

The knights struggled to offer an answer. And as they saw her close in, baring her fangs, the one who had yet to speak panicked. "What does it matter if the boys are being rough? She's just a Pternite!"

What he said was outrageous, though sadly, it did not surprise Veronica at all. That girl was indeed a Pternite. But she was also young, perhaps no more than a year older than Veronica.

That piqued Lady Victoriah's interest but did nothing to quell her anger. She noticed that the girl wore the same uniform as the squires. "And what is a Pternite kid doing here?"

"The girl's a refugee. She enlisted in the army for food and shelt—"

"You stand by and watch your runts beat another comrade-in-arms into the dirt?"

By the time the knights' instincts warned them to retreat, Lady Victoriah grabbed them by their helms and slammed them together. The squires tensed up in watching their meisters drop to the ground, likely fearing what she would do to them.

"Who's responsible for her?"

"Commander Archave, ma'am!"

"Harvey!?"

"Yes, ma'am! He has the lot of us watch her since he's always busy."

The knights thought she was going to pounce. Her teeth grit together so tightly, and her armor rattled from her fists shaking so.

"On your feet!" She grabbed the knights by their collars before they dared move, pulling them up so they would not be so slow. "You're taking me to see your commander."

"Ma'am, yes, ma'am!"

Lady Victoriah turned back to her squire. "Veronica, get her looked at. Make sure she's in fighting shape." Her glare rested on the squires returning to their meister knights' sides—an unspoken threat for if she was anything less than that. They trembled but dared not slow down, hurrying to the knights if only to hide behind them.

As they went on their way, Veronica dismounted her horse to get to work. She took a cloth from her saddlebag, then bent down to the Pternite girl's side.

She was not looked upon with kindness, only scorn and distrust.

But Veronica gave her a friendly smile nonetheless. "Don't worry. I'm here to help."

The girl was surprised that she had spoken to her in Pternite.

Veronica held up the cloth to eye level. A bead of water formed just above it. The Pternite girl watched with intrigue as the bead grew, the water slowly pouring onto the cloth.

Seeing the trick calmed her a little, Veronica reached out for the girl's hand. Just before she could grasp it, the girl's hand snapped up, grabbing Veronica by the wrist. For a moment, Veronica feared that she might have misspoken. Her grip was tight and firm, and strong enough to keep her in place while she snatched the cloth from her. When she let go, Veronica pulled her arm back and watched the pink marks on her wrist fade.

The girl cleaned the dirt from her face and arms. She kept her eyes averted from Veronica, trying not to pay her any heed.

It likely had to do with her being a Vermalian.

Rather than pester her further, Veronica looked over the girl's exposed arms, neck, and face. She was covered in bruises fresh and old, though she did not even wince when touching them. There were a few cuts, one more noticeable at her lip, but they seemed shallow.

"There doesn't seem to be anything serious. Thank goodness."

The girl glanced at her, but turned away when Veronica smiled again.

Perhaps there would be no way for her to trust in her. Even so, Veronica did not leave her.

"...Why ... did you help?" the girl finally spoke. Her words were a little forced and said quietly.

Veronica tilted her head. "Why? Because you needed it."

The girl made no response. She just sat still.

"Why did you let them do that to you?"

"Let...?"

Veronica leaned in. "Your reflexes are sharp. And you look like you know your way in a fight." She did not wish to think of what came to mind, but they already let their disdain known. "Could it be ... because of the knights?"

The girl stared at the ground, trying not to look like she was fazed by what happened. Under the surface, there was no fear or anxiety, just anger. "Those boys act like I disrespect them. They lie about me, make excuses to hit me—they can't do it in a real fight. If I resist, the knights punish me, take my food or lock me up."

"Why would they do that?"

"They like to, and don't like me. I am a Pternite. They don't trust me or want me here, but they will use me. That is just how it is."

Veronica was not sure she wanted to ask anything else, but ignoring this was out of the question. The soldiers there were mistreating her, and it was being overlooked even by the one in charge. For something she had no power over.

"Don't worry. I am sure Lady Victoriah will straighten this out. After all, you are one of us."

"One ... of you?"

"Of course," said Veronica with a chipper smile. "You became a soldier of Vermalio. That makes you one of us. And it doesn't do a unit good for its soldiers to hinder each other. Lady Victoriah knows that. Once she is done, those knights won't get away with harassing you anymore."

The girl did not look at all reassured by Veronica. If anything, she seemed to sink more and more into herself.

"So long as I can fight the empire. That's all I care about."

The more Veronica tried to understand her, the more she saw how she tried to hide herself away. Though she acknowledged her and answered her questions, the Pternite girl did not truly open up. She was only doing what was expected of her by a Vermalian soldier. Her anger settling only made her seem heavyhearted. It was as though she kept her other emotions locked away to avoid hurting.

She must have been so lonely.

"What is your name?"

The girl glanced in Veronica's direction. "Why do you want my name?"

"So that I can be your friend." Veronica scooted a little closer and held out her hand. "My name is Veronica Alivvrn. May I have yours?"

Again, there was no immediate action from the Pternite girl, apart from a mild look of surprise. Her arm budged a little, perhaps suspecting she would strike her like the others had. When the outstretched hand made no contact, she stared at it, unsure and untrusting.

After moments of stillness, she raised her head to look Veronica in the eyes for the first time. Hers were a beautiful blue. It was like staring into two pristine springs. The way they shimmered revealed hints of worry.

Opening up to others was not always easy, and it must have been harder still for one who was rejected by many. But she found the courage to raise her hand and take Veronica's in it.

"I am Chi'en Tzu."

It was a tremendous relief to know she had not given up on herself. The smile Veronica wore spread to her rosy cheeks as she shook her hand. "It is a pleasure to meet you, Tzu." She kept their hands locked as she stood, pulling the wary girl up with her. "Come on, let's go to the tavern. I think Lady Victoriah will want to meet us there."

Tzu followed her without argument, seeming not to mind that their hands were still connected. Her new friend led her to Nightshade, letting go only to mount up. She struggled to climb on with her, but she managed and sat behind Veronica.

The ride down the mountain was rough. Without Timberhoof guiding them, Nightshade got antsy and flew down the path like an arrow. Veronica tried to get her under control, but her mount would never slow down for long. Tzu did not make much noise. She just clung to Veronica so she would not fall off.

Once they neared the bottom of the mountain, Nightshade finally settled down. Her passengers were on edge from her constant outbursts, expecting her to run at breakneck speed again at any moment. But she never did. Her pace remained steady as she trotted back to the city.

As much as they would have liked to relax, something made the hair on the back of Veronica's neck stand on end. From atop the cliff they were on, they heard a commotion coming from the city.

Proving herself a dutiful soldier, Tzu said they should investigate. Veronica agreed and, steeling herself for another hair-raising run, nudged for Nightshade to speed up.

Panic spread all throughout Styne. The Pternite forces had infiltrated the citadel.

They had stormed the residential district, killing every Vermalian in sight, be they man, woman, or child. The streets became a field of corpses as they further advanced toward the military district.

The soldiers scattered in the panic, but Veronica and Tzu braved the streets to protect the civilians. They led as many as they could to the nearby armory, Tzu explaining that it was the most fortified building in the vicinity, and protected it with their lives.

Few soldiers stood with them to guard the armory, but they would not yield to the enemy.

Veronica held off the most enemies with her Second Verse. The armor worn by the Pternite warriors was relatively thin and not as bulky as the Vermalian iron, allowing her plenty of openings to strike.

Tzu acted as her support, fiercely cutting down those who got too close with skillful waves of her axe. Even when her weapon had been torn from her grasp, she did not relent. She fought on, outmaneuvering the enemies' weapons, disarming them, and striking back hard with her bare fists. She was well versed in some form of Pternite martial art.

Veronica and Tzu fought valiantly together, but the enemy kept coming without end. They were nearly overwhelmed until Lady Victoriah joined the fray with a cavalry squadron riding at her command. With their help, the enemy had been routed.

Once they managed to secure the armory, Lady Victoriah took a few soldiers to meet up with those fighting in the military district. Veronica remained behind, though not to protect. She used her new ability to project her spirit from her body so that she could soar above Styne and watch the battle unfold from the air.

From up there, she saw the Pternite warriors' retreat. The Vermalians did what they could to keep them from getting away, but a few enemy factions still eluded them. They retreated toward the southern mountain—to a tunnel hidden between the crevasses of the mountainside.

The attacks made on the wall were but distractions. They strived to keep all eyes on the west, where the Vermalians expected the danger to come from, while the tunnel had been dug from Pterna.

Unfortunately for the Pternites, they were not as prepared for their siege as they anticipated. The presence of the Champion of Heart tipped the scales enough for the Vermalians to emerge victorious.

Although, many did not see the battle as a victory.

Pterna had breached Styne. They found a way past the wall that the Vermalians never saw coming. It was a terrible blow to the people's confidence. They no longer believed they were safe from the enemy.

Nevertheless, Styne was still their home. Restorations were underway once the tunnel had been found and sealed.

The residential district and marketplace were in complete ruin, while the military district remained nearly untouched by the conflict. The contrast revolted Lady Victoriah, who now stormed the halls of the central command center. She and her squire were working to help restore the proud city when a soldier gave her a message from Della. Whatever it was made her livid; she looked ready to skin someone alive.

Even without the order to, Veronica followed her. She knew who she was going to see.

"Harvey!"

Lady Victoriah threw the door to the commander's quarters open. The loud slam spooked the man at his desk, causing his hand holding a quill pen to flick and spill his vial of ink.

Gritting his teeth made Commander Archave look as irritated as his sister. "What is it now?"

"You're planning to attack the Pternite encampment."

In following the Pternites through the tunnel they dug, Veronica found a massive encampment on the other side. Their numbers easily matched that of the Vermalian soldiers inside Styne before the attack.

Learning of the enemy numbers dissuaded Commander Archave from ordering a counterstrike, at least at first. It did not seem to be a problem now.

"Naturally. After the damage they caused, retaliation is in order."

"Are you insane?"

"What is this? I did not think Victoriah the Wolverine would lose her taste for blood." His soldiers said that name with admiration, but Commander Archave used it to spite her.

"You know how many troops were lost in the attack."

"All the more reason to retaliate."

"There were too many! As of now, they have more soldiers than we do. There aren't enough men to form a suitable strike party and leave Styne protected."

"We had the tunnel sealed. With that, the citadel is all but secure."

"You—" The fury in Lady Victoriah's valsara sparked into a heavy blaze. Pretending not to notice or care, the commander took out a new slip of parchment. Lady Victoriah marched up to the desk and ripped the quill pen from Commander Archave's hand before he started to write again. "You would send all of your soldiers to strike against the Pternites?"

Commander Archave stood and glared at Lady Victoriah. "You would have me do anything less?"

"You pigheaded arse! Styne will be left defenseless."

"We have the wall."

"And they have mages! Mages that can erode and break through it."

"All of which are at the encampment. When it falls, we will have nothing left to fear."

"You don't know that. I've seen the reports; the attacks you sustained for the last half year were made by units that came from all directions. You can't be certain that they all came together. You heard what Veronica said. She couldn't tell how many mages were at that camp."

"So I am to make my decisions based on the findings of one little girl under your command? Because she used 'magic' to see to the other side? For all I know, you told her what to say to keep me from doing what needed to be done."

Veronica blinked. "But, sir, you—"

"Hold your tongue, girl! You will speak only when spoken to."

She knew it would have been best to stay silent, but the words left her before she realized what she did.

The tunnel itself should have served as proof of what Veronica saw; she was the one who showed it to them.

But trust was not a factor in the commander's decisions.

And the scowl Lady Victoriah gave him showed she understood that. "So tell me then. Why did you cancel your initial attack, if not because you relied on my squire's foresight?"

"Why does that matter?" Commander Archave snatched his quill pen back from Lady Victoriah. "The tunnel is sealed. Styne is safe. And the enemy has yet to pay."

Lady Victoriah narrowed her eyes. "It wasn't for your soldiers or your people or even the citadel itself. You just had it closed to keep the nobles here from squawking at you. Right?"

He scoffed and shook his head. "You are being ridiculous."

"I'm the ridiculous one? You gave the soldiers the order to rendezvous at the gates of the military district in advance!" She circled the desk, keeping anything from being between them. "You suspected that the Pternite army would find a way in someday. You had a plan in place for the soldiers to focus solely on the military district. The nobles here have their own paid guard, yet you saw it fit to give them all of the protection and leave the civilians to the enemy!"

Commander Archave made no retort. He stood there, staring Lady Victoriah down, as he crushed the quill in his hand.

"And now you're going to sacrifice their protection again just because the nobles had a little scare. People were killed out there, Harvey. The knights need to be here."

"People are killed every day."

His cold words, spoken so simply, left Lady Victoriah and her squire speechless. Whatever retort would have come from the champion, it was left unsaid. But how her eye twitched as she glared at him spoke volumes.

"We're at the doorstep of the very empire that tried to wipe us out over two decades ago. They have continued in their endeavors while we have done nothing more than hold them at bay. That's all we are told to do, and that won't work anymore." He waved his arm in belligerence. The disdain he felt over the years of inaction showed in his face and demeanor. "Pterna won't stop its attacks until we Vermalians are enslaved or dead. Maybe you have forgotten the horrors they committed in the war, before that wall stood as tall as it does today. But I have not, and neither have the nobles. They see what must be done, and so do I."

Veronica looked away from the commander. She felt sick listening to his tirade as he talked down to his sister like she was mad.

Commander Archave carried himself like a hero would—proud, unwavering. It was likely a desire of his: to be a hero. But this desire had become twisted. He had forgotten what his role in commanding the soldiers of Styne was, and excused the deaths of those he swore to protect as a normality of the world. Whether he chose to overlook his fault in it or became so engrossed in his delusions that he actually believed in what he said, it did not matter. There was no erasing the mistake he made.

And he would not seek to correct himself for it.

The animosity Lady Victoriah held for her brother shifted into something more intense. It was not quite pity, nor was it disappointment. From what Veronica saw, it looked like she was accepting something, something that was painful to acknowledge.

Though she did not think him family anymore, they were still siblings.

"I've heard enough."

"Likewise," answered Commander Archave. "See yourself out."

"I'm not the one who's leaving." Lady Victoriah grabbed his shoulder and shoved him away from the seat he was about to take. "Harvey Archave, I find you no longer fit to lead the defense of Styne and the security of the Vermalio-Pterna border. In the name of King Faustign L. S. Vermalio, you are henceforth discharged."

Those had to be the first words of Lady Victoriah's to leave the man utterly shocked. He quickly recovered, showing resistance as his wide-eyed stare turned into a malign scowl. "You can't do this. You don't have the right!"

"Oh, I'm sorry. I don't have the right?" The ceremonious way Lady Victoriah carried herself for her respected role gave way to the fury she scarcely held at bay. In a quick stride, she shoved the disobedient soldier against the wall. Her right arm pressed forcefully to his chest, pinning him in place, while her left hand rested atop the sword at his hip, keeping him from drawing it. "You have it backwards! Being a fallen noble has nothing to do with it. I am the Champion of Heart, the arm of the king himself. I have more authority than any general from *any* region in the kingdom. If I say you're discharged, then you're discharged!"

Veronica moved away from the door when Harvey Archave was thrown her way. He crumbled to the ground upon crashing into the wall. When he rose, it was with his hand on his sword's hilt.

The only weapon Lady Victoriah needed to keep him from drawing it was her glare. "Here is what's going to happen: either you walk out of here with your tail between your legs holding onto whatever semblance of dignity you have left, or I drag your sorry arse outside and show the recruits what I do to soldiers as pathetic as you. Your choice, *Brother.*"

There was no immediate reaction. Despite what he thought of her, Harvey Archave recognized the strength she had and the power that came with her position. Wariness of both kept him from making a hasty decision.

In the end, he stood up straight and walked out the door. "She-devil..."

Watching him go without a fight was the last thing Lady Victoriah wanted, but rather than sate her desire to rage, she forced herself to calm down. When turning to her squire again, she was as stern as ever. "We're going to busy here for a while."

Veronica shook off the tension binding her to nod. It relieved her to hear that. After what happened, she did not think she could leave so soon.

"Come on. Time to inform the troops. Things are going to change around here."

It was not always easy to decide between desire and duty. And letting either distort reality led to the fall of many great people. But Lady Victoriah, for better or worse, chose to follow what she believed was right. And what was right to her was protecting her people, no matter who or what stood in her way.

~ Fourteenth Chapter ~
Ties of Fate

Upon the removal of Commander Archave, Lady Victoriah assumed control of Styne's militia. With her efforts, the citadel's restoration progressed smoothly and the military protocols were restructured.

The nobles and upperclassmen made many attempts to convince her to take action against the Pternite army, but their arguments went unheard. The safety of the people came first; she made sure everyone understood that.

No attacks were made on the wall since Pterna's retreat, a sign that they were recovering from their own losses.

After two months, a suitable replacement for Commander Archave arrived, a general who Lady Victoriah knew personally. Some orders were left with him so that the nobles would not get carried away. He seemed comforted to know he could refuse them with the Champion of Heart's blessing.

It saddened Veronica when it came time to leave. She had gotten close to Tzu during their time together. They taught each other many things about their home countries and protected each other when pestered by other squires. She was worried about how the people would treat her, but Della promised she and her friends would look after her. They could not let them disrespect someone who fought for their city, after all.

With Styne in good hands, Veronica and Lady Victoriah left to continue their journey across Vermalio.

The colors of the countryside faded as autumn came to an end. The first snowfall of the year arrived while they were between towns. A gentle wind carried the flacks across the mute sky. Watching them fall could lull one to sleep.

But as the fields turned white, travel became more dangerous. Blizzards blew across the land, making the ground and sky blur together. Unable to see what lay before them, Veronica and Lady Victoriah had to remain close to each other and guide their mounts with care. The days were longer for them, too, since they had to keep riding until they found a safe place to rest, which became terribly scarce.

Fortunately, they were very resourceful.

They came to a warmer climate upon travelling to Starscape, a region to the northeast of Vermalio. The air there was eerily still, and snow only covered the ground in thin sheets instead of burying valleys and making hills. Snowfall either remained gentle or stopped entirely.

It was suitable enough to stop and rest in the open.

Veronica built a small fire—nothing too big so they could put it out and leave at a moment's notice. They sat by it and ate a ration of smoked jerky. Since the snow came, they had eaten more dried meat than anything freshly cooked while on the road. It was not as tasty, but it was easy to carry and preserve, and was well appreciated since wild game became scarce.

They rested until the fire started to go out. It seemed like a good time to start moving again. Since the weather was more favorable than it had been in a while, though, Lady Victoriah decided they would spar for a bit.

She had not been able to train her squire as frequently since the dawn of winter. Now that they were not in a hurry to rush through the frigid winds, they needed to make up for lost time.

The exercise warmed them right up, and Veronica lasted a long time without getting thrown into the snow.

It had been nearly a year since Lady Victoriah took Veronica as her squire. In that time, Veronica learned a great deal from the champion. She got knocked to the ground more times than she cared to count, sometimes getting the occasional concussion. Those painful lessons were etched into her muscles and mind. It was not long before Veronica, whether through skill or luck, won a round against her meister knight.

It made her meister knight all the harder on her, and Veronica both feared and delighted in it.

As they began their fifth round, Lady Victoriah became distracted by something above. A bird soared across the dim sun, swooping down as the light nearly blinded Veronica.

"Is that ..." Lady Victoriah set down her sword and took her shield in hand. The bird glided her way, coming to roost on the edge of her shield. It was a scarlet falcon, a rare and very intelligent creature.

Veronica had never seen one before. Its plumage shimmered like fire in the sunlight. She tried to get a closer look when the falcon turned her way, cocking its head to look at her rapier. It subtly raised its wings, looking ready to take flight.

Worried she had frightened it, she hid the weapon behind her back and gave it a goofy smile.

There was a slip of paper tied to its leg, which Lady Victoriah gently took and unfolded. She was oddly stern as she read it, and when she finished, she sighed and crumbled the paper up. "Good work. Go on, now." A firm upward thrust of her shield urged the falcon to take flight. It took off to the southwest, fading into the distance.

"Lady Victoriah, what was—"

"Get everything together. We're leaving now." The knight walked back to the fire and tossed the paper into the dying embers.

Confused as she was, Veronica asked no more questions and gathered their gear.

Once they were all set and the paper had been reduced to cinders, Lady Victoriah scooped up some snow with her shield and dumped it onto the firewood. A harsh *hiss* sounded, a white vapor floating in the air in small puffs.

Timberhoof seemed agitated while they made ready to leave, as if he sensed his mistress' anxiety. "Hyah!" Lady Victoriah nudged him to go into a full sprint the moment she mounted up, and the warhorse raced across the plains, kicking snow and dirt into the air.

As they rode, Lady Victoriah explained everything. Scarlet falcons were raised by the royal palace to serve as messengers of the king. Famous for their unrivaled speed, they were only ever dispatched to reach the Six Champions in times of urgency. The falcons tracked them by following the spells imbued in the champions' shields, an enchantment placed on the birds so they knew which one to find.

An emergency prompting the king to call upon his champion. It excited Veronica to take part in it, but it made her nervous all the same.

According to the message, an envoy from Ederea had gotten shipwrecked along the shore of Starscape. Their task was to secure the envoy and escort them to Cragfill, the region bridging Vermalio and Ederea, so that they may return home.

It was an important task that required more than a knight and her squire. To ensure their mission would succeed, they visited a town en route to their destination to request the aid of a small party. As luck would have it, a troop of soldiers was visiting the town to rest and resupply.

Lady Victoriah and Veronica went to the tavern to meet them.

The building was packed with patrons relaxing and taking shelter from the cold. It was not hard to find the soldiers; they all gathered in a cozy corner to drink and be merry. Lady Victoriah moved past the crowd with haste, but she looked more at ease when she set her sights on two men arm wrestling. The younger man pushed against his senior, smacking his hand against the table with a hard *bang*.

"I'm next."

The winner turned in his chair to face Lady Victoriah, and froze when their eyes met. He retook his smile and stood to greet her.

"Lady Victoriah!" He sounded more excited to see her than most.

The other soldiers quieted down upon hearing him, though the tavern remained lively still.

"Good to see you again, Prince Aeron."

Veronica was standing behind her meister knight when she greeted the young man. She walked in there expecting to see just another soldier, but when she heard him addressed as a prince, she found herself staring. He looked rather handsome. His hair had a luster like bronze underneath the candlelight.

And when his black eyes looked her way, she suddenly felt stiff.

"This must be the squire I heard much about. Father was disappointed to hear he missed his chance to meet her."

Lady Victoriah chuckled. "I'll remember to bring her to him when next we visit Brigadier."

Veronica clasped her hands together before her and made a nervous smile. Being in the presence of one of royal blood, she had forgotten her conduct as a soldier, the rehearsed mannerisms she learned as a noble lady resurfacing. "It is an honor, Your Highness. I am Veronica Alivvrn of Illuascove, daughter of the marquis Brian Alivvrn."

Lady Victoriah gave her squire a rough pat on the back. "Don't get all worked up. He's just another soldier, like you and me."

Color filled Veronica's cheeks in hearing her meister knight say such a thing about the prince of Vermalio. "Lady Victoriah, please!"

"It's all right," Prince Aeron reassured, a kindly albeit humble smile on his face. "No need to be so formal. She's right. Here, I am but a commander to my troops. You needn't treat me like a prince."

"Oh ... okay." It seemed odd for a prince to not want to be treated as such, but so she would not upset him, Veronica complied.

"What brings you here anyway?" asked Lady Victoriah. "I thought you were training your men in Everspeak."

"Father received word of Renegade activity in the region and sent us to investigate. Sadly, we were unable to find anything."

"In that case, would you be willing to help us before you return home?"

"Of course. How can we help?"

"We received word from your father via scarlet falcon."

That was all Prince Aeron needed to understand the gravity of the situation. "We'll leave immediately then."

"Where are we going?" asked someone who pushed their way through the walls of drunken men. It was a young girl clad in armor as regal as the prince's, who looked to them in disbelief. "Veronica?"

"Cheryl!"

With a beaming smile, Veronica ran up to her good friend and caught her in her arms. She laughed and, overcome with joy, started jumping around with her, all the while Cheryl tried to get her off. Public displays of affection always embarrassed her so.

Veronica let go. "What are you doing here?"

"You haven't heard?" Cheryl said with a proud grin and her hands on her hips. "Prince Aeron made me his squire."

Now Veronica looked to her in disbelief. She turned to the prince when all Cheryl did was grin. She first thought this a prank to get back at her for all of the times she woke Cheryl by pouring water on her face. But Prince Aeron smiled and nodded, bringing back her radiant smile.

"You and the prince?" she asked. "How did that happen?"

"Plenty of time for you two to catch up later." Prince Aeron made sure their attention was on him before turning to the rest of his soldiers. "We have another mission. Make ready to leave at once."

The soldiers raised their mugs in cheer before downing what was left and standing to leave. They were ready for action.

Veronica and Cheryl held their fists over their hearts in salute. "Sir!" They looked to each other, smiling, and laughed. It had been some time since they did that.

Preparations were made for the party to depart straightaway. There were at least fifty soldiers, not including the champion, the prince, and their squires. While they made ready, Lady Victoriah went to purchase some extra provisions, leaving Veronica with the prince.

Veronica helped Cheryl ready hers and the prince's horses. It surprised her how readily Cheryl entered the stables, and watching her walk by the other horses and approach the prince's mount without flinching or showing the slightest signs of anxiety made her chuckle in disbelief. When asked what happened to her fear of horses, Cheryl would not say much, only that the prince showed her that they were as much their comrades as the other soldiers.

They talked while they worked, Cheryl explaining how she became Prince Aeron's squire, unable to resist her friend's pleas.

Knights as young as him did not typically take a squire, and he was apprehensive about the idea at first. It seemed, however, that Lord Charleston had been insisting he consider it for some time.

The young prince did not have much confidence in himself as a leader. It was only by his father's order that he assumed the role of commander of his own platoon, modest though it was. The king wanted his heir to accept that he was and would be a leader, and his Champion of Duty, further proving himself worthy of the title, believed he would grow if he took a squire. It was a more intimate responsibility than simply leading soldiers; he would teach her, guide her, help her to grow as a warrior.

It came as a shock to Cheryl when Lord Charleston introduced her to the prince, but she proved to them both that she was the one best suited to be his squire.

Hearing that her friend impressed both the prince and one of the Six Champions filled Veronica with pride. She wanted to hear more about how Lord Charleston came to favor her, but Cheryl said not more. Veronica took the hint and began to tell her what she had been doing.

The party led by Lady Victoriah marched east, eventually coming to a dense forest near the coast. The message from the scarlet falcon informed her that the Ederean envoy, wary of potential threats, used the trees for cover and refrained from moving inland.

Many found it odd how the envoy took such elusive measures. The town they left was not even a day from there, yet the envoy chose to remain hidden and somehow established contact with the royal palace without alerting the nearby militia. It seemed so strange, even to the ever-trusting Veronica.

But Lady Victoriah assured them that their objective was there.

The forest was quiet, with only the faint sound of rustling tree branches to accompany them. A few patches of snow could be seen here and there, but they were small and crumbled just by looking at them. The open path had several twists and turns, but everyone kept a straight course toward the shoreline.

There were no signs of activity. Nothing else was there. Yet Veronica could not shake this feeling that they were being watched.

She thought it was just the crow she saw perched on a branch. When she looked down from it, though, she saw a silhouette hidden among the trees. And it was armed.

Another soldier also noticed and, in his alarm, fired an arrow at it. A man in full body armor dove out of hiding and got in their path. The soldiers in the front moved to surround him, but the armored man rushed through them, cutting their spears at the shafts when they got close and smacking one of the soldiers aside.

Lady Victoriah had Timberhoof charge past the others. Just before coming upon her target, she let go of the reins and rolled off the saddle. She recovered quickly upon landing, watching her mount dash at the armored man. Just as he moved out of the way of Timberhoof's thundering charge, she brought her sword down on him fast as lightning.

Her blade met with the armored man's pitch-black sword, a harsh cry resounding from the impact. They both appeared evenly matched, but then Lady Victoriah was forced back. The armored man lurched backward, remaining alert.

If he had the strength to oppose Victoriah the Wolverine, they could not take him lightly. Veronica moved forward atop Nightshade, ready to use the Second Verse, as the others rushed at him.

But everyone stopped when Lady Victoriah held her free arm at them. She seemed to want him all to herself.

When the soldiers held back, the armored man lowered his sword.

Timberhoof came charging fiercely back, the ground shaking from the *ptump, ptump, ptump* of his hooves. But when the stranger turned to face him, Timberhoof stopped dead in his tracks.

Seeing the ferocious warhorse that charged fiercely into battle to trample his foes suddenly and hurriedly come to a stop baffled Veronica. She could not believe it, but it looked like he stopped just from the armored man's gaze, masked beneath a helm though it was.

All eyes were on the enigmatic man. Every part of his slick gray armor looked sharp. His helm resembled the skull of a noble beast, with only these slim slits for eyeholes. The gauntlets on his hands, grasped around his sword, its scabbard held in his left hand, looked like claws. Whatever had not been covered by metal hid behind black leather, completely masking his identity.

Upon facing the party, the armored man raised his sword—everyone flinched—and put it to rest in the scabbard, its rim stopping just as it met the large blue gem by the sword's guard.

"My apologies. I mistook you for the ones after my charge." The stranger's voice sounded menacing, but it did not seem like he meant any harm.

Thus, Lady Victoriah lowered her weapon. "Your charge?"

The armored man slid his sword through the loop at the left side of his belt, and kept his hand resting on its pommel. His other hand made a fist over his heart. "I am the Azure Knight, guardian to Her Highness, Princess Camellia du Joiec of Ederea."

A firm introduction. But it did nothing to ease their caution. He may have worn fine armor, but that did not make him a knight—of Ederea or otherwise.

"You're Camellia's guardian?" While the others remained tense, Lady Victoriah kept her sword low and spoke as if to toy with the stranger. "So where is your princess then?"

The Azure Knight let his fist fall from his chest. "At the cove, with the rest of the survivors. We lost our food supply after becoming adrift at sea. We had nothing when we washed ashore, so someone had to forage. Of our soldiers, I am the best hunter. I had hoped to find suitable game." He turned his head, perhaps to look past her to the other soldiers. "But 'tis just as grand to see King Faustign's rescue party in my hunting ground."

Some of the soldiers let their guard down. No one had mentioned King Faustign's name or what their objective was. That, however, only made the others more cautious. There were two reasons he would know either of those things, and they feared the less savory one.

Prince Aeron dismounted his horse and approached the Azure Knight, much to Cheryl's worry. "Your shield, if you please."

Without delay, the alleged knight reached for the round shield latched on his back and took it in hand to show the prince. It had gold trim around its edges, and in its center was the crest of the sea drake, the same crest used by the Ederean royal family.

"Titaei metal," noted the prince. "Rare metal mined only in Ederea, and only forged into equipment for military use." He allowed himself to relax as his eyes drew along his armor. "Your armor is made of it as well, indicating you are a knight of high standing." With a smile, Prince Aeron pressed his flat palm between his ribs, a diplomatic gesture made by a noble rather than a knight. "Forgive us for the suspicion, Sir Knight."

Upon the prince recognizing the knight to be who he claimed, everyone lowered their weapons.

"'Tis always best to be on your guard." The Azure Knight secured his shield back where it was.

Lady Victoriah stepped forward as she sheathed her sword. "Is the princess safe?"

"Aye, otherwise I would be by her side this very moment."

"You don't need to worry about hunting anymore, friend," Prince Aeron assured. "We have rations aplenty for your charge and all of her hungry vassals."

"Let's not waste time then." The Azure Knight went back to where he hid to pick up a hare carcass, the scant game he managed to find. With that in hand, he led the party through the forest.

Prince Aeron walked alongside the Ederean knight, asking him a few things about the voyage he and his allies were on. The Azure Knight was a reserved sort. He said little more than they were on the way to Petrine, the independent island nation between Vermalio and the country of Brungo, when disaster struck.

Most of the soldiers kept their distance from this enigmatic knight. They were still wary of him. He did have quite the effect on those around him. Even the very air seemed chiller with him there.

But Nightshade remained close to him. It was not by Veronica's guidance. She was very interested in him, as was Timberhoof. And though his demeanor was somewhat distant, the Azure Knight was quite gentle when he petted their manes.

He might have been dangerous, but he was not a threat to them.

Veronica overheard a few of the soldiers whispering about him. Many heard rumors about a mighty warrior being trusted to protect Ederea's beloved princess. But they were not familiar with the name of the Azure Knight. Someone claimed her guardian was a man called the Blood Beast, and another said she heard he was the Dancing Blade.

Before Veronica could make sense of what that meant, they arrived at the edge of the forest. Voices were heard toward the clearing, and as the foliage parted, they could see soldiers standing lookout. The Azure Knight went ahead so he would be the first they saw, then signaled for the rescue party to follow.

The weary Edereans became at ease once they realized their visitors were allies. They cheered jollily, drowning out the dread that lingered in the air. The soldiers were all men larger than most of the Vermalian knights and even the Azure Knight himself.

The rescue party followed the Azure Knight as he neared the cove. He came to a rock on a sandy hill. Sitting upon it was a petite maiden of starlight silver hair accompanied by three young women, all of them looking curiously to the excited soldiers.

Something small ran from the maiden's lap to greet the Azure Knight. Veronica thought it was a dog, but as they got closer, she was surprised to see it was a white fox. He gave the hare to it, perhaps as a treat.

The maiden stood from the rock, helped up by the pull of one of the young women in frilly attire. The woman tried to dust off her seafoam green dress and make her look presentable. Even with her dress tattered and shriveled up, her doll-like face dirtied, and her hair an unruly mess, the maiden still proudly carried herself in a manner befitting royalty.

"We're sorry to have kept you waiting, Your Highness."

The maiden's smile grew when Lady Victoriah spoke. Her lovely eyes, big and bright like that of the moon, shone with delight. "Lady Victoriah! I am truly relieved to see you have come in our time of need."

"And I brought someone else too." Lady Victoriah stepped aside to make way for Prince Aeron.

The prince stepped forward and bowed his head. "I regret that we must meet under these unfortunate circumstances, Princess Camellia. I am Prince Aeron K. G. Vermalio."

"The Vermalian prince. Well met, good Aeron." The princess let go of her help's hand to curtsy, but took it back upon coming up. "'Tis grand of you to come. Vermalio honors us in sending its heir to our aid."

The woman holding the princess' hand scowled at the Azure Knight and said something in Abioan. "Why are you still in your helm? Go on, take it off. You should greet them too," it sounded like.

The Azure Knight slowly took his hand from his sword and drew it to the crown of his helm.

Lady Victoriah's smile became gentler. "It's all right," she said in Vermalian. "I'm sure the prince can overlook my son's rudeness."

His hand lingered a moment, then continued to slide the helm through a few latches connecting it to his armor. Upon removing it, he showed a pale face that reminded Veronica of Jerrell, though it was not as long and rugged. His blonde hair sheened nicely beneath the sun, and his glacial blue eyes reflected its light. He gave a thin smile upon facing them. "And here I thought I sounded Ederean enough to surprise you."

Without the helm on, his voice sounded quieter and carried a fine tenor. It made him much less menacing, more approachable.

"You could sound like a drunken old codger, and I'd still recognize you." Lady Victoriah stepped past the princess and her handmaiden to wrap her arms tightly around her son. He returned the hug with his free hand, then stood still when she let go to grasp his shoulders. "But my, how you've grown. And into such a handsome young man! The Ederean girls must not be able to keep their hands off you."

He took a step back from Lady Victoriah but kept his smile.

"Van?" The prince spoke up. "Is that really you?"

"It's been a while, Aeron. Good to see you've grown into a leader."

Veronica had dismounted from Nightshade when they arrived. She tried to keep her mount from wandering off but lost her grip on the reins. The mare trotted over to the unmasked knight, greeting him with a loud neigh, and rubbed her snout against him.

The knight allowed himself to show more joy as he stroked her snout. "I missed you too, girl." He petted her a little more before turning to Veronica. "And who is this guiding my old mount?"

Veronica blinked. "Huh? Your old mount?"

Lady Victoriah stepped around the horse. "I bought Nightshade from the Estrines after Van left. It didn't sit right with me leaving a horse he loved so much with them." She turned to her son. "Van, this is my squire, Veronica Alivvrn."

His eyes widened. "Your squire? How things have changed." He composed himself as he stepped up to Veronica. "Veronica... I'm Vandelas. It's good to meet you."

Veronica recaptured her smile and nodded. "Likewise, Sir Vandelas."

"Vandelas, that is no way to greet a lady," chided Princess Camellia.

Sir Vandelas tensed up. "With all due respect, I don't think that sort of greeting is appropriate for another—"

"No, she's right, Van," Lady Victoriah interrupted. "You *are* an Ederean knight, after all—and a high-ranking one at that. You have to act by example. You wouldn't want to disappoint your charge, now would you?"

Though she sounded serious at first, Princess Camellia tried to hide a smile as Lady Victoriah goaded him on. The brief moment Veronica saw it, she knew it to be a playful one.

They were both quick to work together in teasing him.

Perhaps knowing he could not get away with ignoring it, Sir Vandelas took a breath and relented. He took Veronica's hand in his, showing her a gentlemanly smile. "Well met, fair Veronica. I am Vandelas Kronas. I do hope we will get along well."

Veronica felt heat rush to her cheeks and her head become fuzzy when the young man leaned down to plant a kiss on the back of her hand. She thought she could remain calm in knowing it was an Ederean custom for a man to formally introduce himself to a woman in that way. But knowing that did her no good.

A boy had never done that to her before. She hid the spot he kissed behind her other hand and felt her heart beat rapidly when pulling it close.

When she saw his cheeks redden like hers, they both looked down to his feet, where the white fox stepped from to put itself between them.

"I see your pet still clings to you, huh? Don't tell me she does that with every girl you meet."

"Mother...!"

The Ederean soldiers within earshot all chortled seeing the Azure Knight so anxious. He scowled at everyone he heard, as embarrassed by this as the girl he greeted.

Even Prince Aeron found his agitation amusing. "As much fun as this is," he began before looking more serious, "there are some things we must discuss, You Highness."

Princess Camellia pulled her hand away from her smile when she managed to retake her refined composure. "How we came to be here being one issue, aye?"

"Indeed."

The moment they made for a laugh did wonders for the fair princess. But as it passed, her countenance straightened out into a solemn one. She raised a hand to cover her mouth, clearing her throat, then told her tale.

"Well, you see, good prince, we were on our voyage to Petrine to make contact with a person of importance who escaped from Pterna."

"From Pterna?"

"Aye. Our sources in Petrine confirmed this person was being pursued by our mutual enemy. As a soothsayer, he brandished magic that made him a threat to the empire after he refused to cooperate with them. Seeking sanctuary, he fled to Petrine, then established contact with our forces. He promised to be of aid to us if we permitted him entry into Ederea. Once my father weighed his options, he decided to accept. I volunteered to go in place of an envoy as a sign of goodwill."

More signs that there was significant unrest in the Land of Renewal.

It was not unfathomable for a refugee to go through so much effort to get to Ederea rather than head for the Vermalio-Pterna border. Perhaps they fled from West Pterna and could escape easier by ship instead of braving the trek through East Pterna. Or it was just as likely that they wanted to avoid Vermalio altogether.

Vermalio had been an enemy of Pterna for so long, and many Pternites lost family and loved ones in the war. To escape cruelty and persecution took compromises, but sometimes a grudge was just too strong.

"It was meant to be a simple mission. We would arrive in Petrine, our forces would escort the soothsayer to our ship, and we would all return safely to Ederea." A dark foreboding overcame the princess as she reflected on what would have been and what had been lost when it all went wrong. "But we were attacked."

"Was it an ambush made by Pterna?"

The princess' eyes nearly slid shut as she lowered her head. "I know not. Everyone says the flags had no colors, no means of identifying them, and that the ships did not look to be of Pternite design. Mayhap it was not them. But then..." Her voice grew quiet. She seemed unsure of what to believe, or perhaps even what she wanted to believe.

Anticipating what she meant, Prince Aeron nodded and changed the focus. "Thank Lady Untae that her waters guided you here."

The sullen uncertainly of Princess Camellia washed away as she raised her head again. "Aye, I thank the goddess of the sea for her kindness." Then she turned to her Azure Knight. "But thanks should also go to Sir Vandelas, for ridding us of the enemy fleet and making us a means of remaining afloat when our ship sank."

The Ederean soldiers who heard that cheered Sir Vandelas' name. They shouted of how he tore the enemy fleet apart by turning the sea into spears, and forged a raft of ice for them to ride the rocky waves.

Sir Vandelas gave a smile when Lady Victoriah looked to him in awe. "I learned quite a few things in Ederea," he simply put.

That seemed enough for her shock to turn into pride.

With the situation explained, Prince Aeron showed the princess and her vassals to the soldiers handing out food. "You've all been through a great ordeal. There is still a long way to go before we get to Cragfill. We'll move out once everyone has their fill. You must all be famished."

The arrival of their rescuers brought an air of relief to the Ederean camp. With their allies' help, they had hope of getting home, and were thrilled to revel in it.

The Vermalian rescue party escorted the Edereans through a dense mountain range south of the Starscape coastline. Lady Victoriah and Prince Aeron thought it best to avoid the well-travelled path on their journey to Cragfill. The mountains provided ample cover, its known paths twisting in many different directions.

They made significant measures to avoid being followed. And it was obvious to everyone why they did. But that remained unsaid by those who understood.

It was for the best to avoid creating more tension.

They traversed the rough landscape for three days before coming to an open ravine, where they made camp. The night there was peaceful, a comfort brought to them by Lady Luneste, the goddess of the moon.

Veronica awoke to the sound of crunching grass and shifting armor. It was so quiet that she was almost surprised it disturbed her rest.

The moon still hung high in the sky. Many of the soldiers were asleep,

Lady Victoriah, Cheryl, and Prince Aeron included. The Ederean princess was also at rest. But not her guardian.

As Veronica stood and allowed her eyes to adjust to the darkness, she found Sir Vandelas kneeling over the river, splashing water on his bare face. The moonlight shimmered magnificently off his armor. There he remained, slouched over the waters, before standing again. Instead of returning to the princess' side, he went to the lone tree atop a nearby hill.

He seemed troubled. Unease chimed from his valsara. He must still have been affected by the attack, as the Edereans were. Veronica followed him to see if something was wrong.

The Azure Knight sat against the tree with his faithful fox, Snowflake. Every now and then, he looked over the campsite, then turned back to his sword. He polished the black blade with a worn cream cloth.

Snowflake picked her head up at Veronica's approach. The little thing did not look to her very kindly, but she settled down when her master put the rag down to pet her head.

"Is there something you need, Veronica?"

He must have seen her coming. It was reassuring to have such sharp eyes watching over them. "My apologies. You seemed a bit out of sorts. I thought to see if you are okay."

"I had a nightmare, that's all. I don't want to sleep again just yet."

"Nothing too dreadful, I hope."

"They happen all the time. It's nothing to worry about."

"I see..." It was disheartening to hear that. To be constantly plagued by the horrors of one's mind and accept it as a norm, it must have been very trying, very tiring. "I do not mean to pry."

Sir Vandelas looked to Veronica with tired eyes, but his smile was kind. "It's all right. Please, sit. I had hoped to get the chance to speak with you."

Veronica nodded and joined him by the tree.

Snowflake did not seem to like her presence. The little thing stepped closer to the knight. It was adorable how she kept watch over him. Such a small creature, yet so protective.

Veronica sat beside Sir Vandelas, giving her a good look at the sword in his hands. With the light of the moon shining upon them, she could faintly see her reflection in the lustrous pitch-black metal.

"That is such a beautiful sword."

The Azure Knight gave a slight chuckle. "I've heard others call it many things, but never once beautiful."

"I have never seen anything like it."

The blade had an elegant shape to it, slender around the center while broad at the top and where it met the guard. Its edges looked to be sharp enough to cut through stone. It was difficult to tell with only the glow of the moon, but the black blade was welded perfectly to the guard, which resembled two fangs protruding from its sides. And between the blade, guard, and handle was this enchanting blue stone.

The stone was the size of a man's fist and formed out of both sides of the sword. Its shape was uncanny, like an oval seed, and it was perfectly smooth. And its luster—the longer she looked at it, the more she thought it resembled valsara.

"There is nothing else like it." Sir Vandelas looked along the blade to the stone. "Las'cent is one of a kind."

Veronica's smile grew. "You named it?"

"Not me. The creator, my meister."

"Your meister knight? He made this weapon?"

"He wasn't a knight. He was an executioner, but more than that, a blacksmith."

"Gaia's breath, that is incredible."

Sir Vandelas looked to her with a slight grin. "What's incredible is what it can do. Las'cent didn't always look like this."

"What do you mean?"

"The metal used to be pure white, and the blade was shorter."

"How can that be?"

"Wolfram called it the Evolving Blade. Its magic reacts to the wielder. If it recognizes its wielder, it can change shape, gain new power."

Veronica held her hand to her mouth to cover a gasp. She never imagined something like that could happen. Merely looking at it, she could tell the weapon had magical properties, nothing like she had seen before. But for something to change shape and grow as a person did, it was unbelievable.

What Lady Abeel would give to study it.

It piqued Veronica's curiosity. She thought about what it might have looked like before, among other things.

"Do you suppose ... I could try it?" She did not normally have interest in weapons simply to use them. It was an excitement foreign to her, but it suited her other self, and it was palpable enough to affect her as well.

The smile on Sir Vandelas' face went away, and he looked to her rather skeptically. Then, as his glacial eyes turned hard, Veronica began to feel she should not have asked.

"Tell me, Veronica. Do you have the strength of will to wield Las'cent?"

The bubbly squire blinked a few times. His question perplexed her, both in how he put it and the intensity behind his words.

"Strength of ... will?"

"This weapon is very powerful, but also very demanding. It requires whoever wields it to have an immense will. Should the wielder be too weak, the blade will reject them and cut them down."

Veronica could not help recoiling. After hearing that, she almost thought the weapon would leap out to strike her for merely wanting to hold it. A look at it, though, revealed the magic inside to be at rest.

That was enough of an answer for him. "I had to make sure. What Wally would have done if my sword hurt his dear sister..."

The unease she felt faded. She calmed down after hearing that name and scooted back into her spot. "You remember my brother."

Sir Vandelas smiled again as he slid his sword back into its scabbard. "I could never forget Wally. He was my best friend."

It warmed her heart to hear him say that.

"I often wondered what I would have to do to meet with his family. And now, here you are."

"I wanted to meet you too. For a long time."

"Really?"

"Wally talked about you all the time. He always wrote in his letters how much fun he had with you."

Sir Vandelas looked a little nervous. "It makes me wonder what exactly he told you."

Veronica giggled. She heard a great many stories about him. They were all very entertaining. Though he did not play many jokes on him, Wally always did have the funniest things to say about his best friend. She remembered the nights when she read the letters he sent and how she always laughed.

"Nothing unflattering, I promise you," she said with a wink.

Her words did nothing to reassure him. But he still smiled with mirth. He remembered well how Wally was, and it showed how he held dear his time with him.

When his eyes set on her again, Veronica felt a little flustered. The moment when his lips pressed against her hand kept popping in her head. They may have only been teasing him, but thinking about it made color speckle her cheeks again.

"You remind me of him."

"Hm?"

"Of Wally. You kind of look like him."

Veronica blinked again. No one had said that about her before. "Really?"

"Yes. Especially when you smile. It reminds me of when we first met."

The warmth in her cheeks made it a little harder to keep her smile, but being told that kept it from leaving her. "He told me how it happened. You were eating by yourself. He thought you looked lonely, and he could tell you were far from home. So he sat with you, and you started talking. He thought you were very entertaining. And he said that after that, he decided to 'stick with you and keep you out of trouble.'"

Sir Vandelas' grin twisted as he let out a hearty laugh. Veronica laughed with him—they both knew full well who really needed to be kept out of trouble.

When he calmed down, he seemed to be in better spirits. But that did not last. Sir Vandelas rested his head against the tree as he looked up to the stars. "The reason I wanted to meet you ... I owe you an apology."

Veronica tilted her head. "Whatever for?"

"For Wally. It's because of me that he's—" He paused and closed his eyes, looking pained. His fox sensed that pain and crawled into his lap, rubbing her head against him. Petting her soothed him enough to speak his woes. "If I was there, like I should have been, I could have saved him."

Grief shook his words and reverberated in his valsara. His eyes were dark and heavy as he spoke. This pain was deep-seated. It troubled him terribly. Perhaps that was what haunted his dreams.

It was difficult to understand how he felt, holding himself responsible for the loss of a friend.

Veronica cupped a hand to his shoulder. "Wally wouldn't want you to blame yourself for what happened. And neither do I."

Sir Vandelas turned back to Veronica. Their eyes locked, and as she stared into his, she saw how they shimmered like sheets of ice. They had the faintest glow, something spiritual. Her words did not sway him, that much she saw. But her kindness touched him enough to ease his pain.

He smiled again. "You are very kind, Veronica."

She returned the smile. "I only say what is true."

"Maybe you aren't much like him then," he said with a slight laugh.

He must have been feeling better to make jokes like that. It was true, though, that Wally had a habit of fibbing to cover up his antics. Veronica wondered what sorts of things he told Sir Vandelas back then.

The need to sleep again washed over her like a wave, bringing her to rub her eyes. "I should return to camp. Please do try to get some rest, Sir Vandelas."

She did not even take three steps before hearing him say, "My friends call me Van."

Veronica halted and turned around, thinking she might have misheard. But when she looked back to him, she saw only sincerity.

It was not often that someone said they wanted to be friends with her. It was still as thrilling as she remembered—and as overwhelming.

"And mine call me Verrie." She was not sure if that was the right thing to say, but she felt she should.

"All right. Good night, Verrie. Sleep well."

Her heart beat more erratically when he called her that, a name she only heard her family call her. She did not think it would sound so unusually familiar coming from him.

"Yes, you as well."

She hurried down the hill, unnerved but excited all the same. It made her so happy to know he wanted to be her friend. Though they only just met, it felt like she knew him for some time.

It was nice to learn he was as kind as she thought he would be.

Feeling she would sleep better, Veronica returned to camp eager to bask in the moonbeams giving it that serene feeling.

~ Fifteenth Chapter ~

The Enemy Within

The route they took across the Starscape countryside taxed the will of
the rescue party. As it was the path less travelled, so was it a more
arduous one.

Crossing the mountains to the neighboring region, they came to an
amber canyon, where they quickly learned they were not welcome.

The area was home to a pack of wolves, proud and territorial beasts
that did not take kindly to intrusions. They moved as silent as shadows,
surrounding the entire party, cutting off any chance for escape.

But escape they did, without any loss or struggle, because of Van.

When the pack closed in, the Azure Knight captured their attention
with a terrible roar. It stopped them in their tracks, snuffing out their
hostility and, in its place, inspired fear.

His valsara reflected the fury they once showed, as if he became one
of the beasts himself—and surpassed them.

With but a command from him, the wolves turned tail and fled.

The Edereans were ecstatic over this feat, but it left many of the

Vermalians daunted. To intimidate a beast, let alone an entire pack, while impressive, was itself frightening.

Prince Aeron did say he had a way with animals. It certainly showed.

It bothered Cheryl how much attention Sir Vandelas was getting. She seemed to warm up to him at the beginning of their journey, only to turn aloof and dismissive a mere four days later. She would not say why. For one reason or another, his presence affected her much like the pages at the Estrine Chateau used to.

That was their last day on the road before reaching their destination.

Cragfill was divided between the Vermalian and Ederean kingdoms in recognition of their long-standing friendship. The eastern half belonged to Ederea, the western half Vermalio. Though few towns lined the region, the main western city, Heveilon, was heavily populated by both Vermalians and Edereans. It sat on the edge of the Vermalio-Ederea border, not even thirty miles from its sister city on the other side, Velrut.

Heveilon served as a nexus for the two countries and their cultures. The peoples' customs, fashion, cuisine, and teachings were all shared. And everyone who lived there spoke both Vermalian and Abioan.

It was not without discord or strife, with the many cultural differences separating them, yet they chose to exist together and learn from one another regardless.

Upon entering Heveilon, the city guard escorted Princess Camellia and her entourage to the duke's manor for rest. It would be the safest place for her in the entire city. The duke was an ambassador of Vermalio who worked to secure his country's relationship with their neighbor. As such, it was in his best interest to help the Ederean princess in her time of need.

His hospitality was made known upon their arrival. The gates to the manor were open, the noble's soldiers lined to guard his guests' way as they marched down the path.

"Vandelas, is something the matter?"

Veronica was in the front, so she did not notice Van stop until the princess spoke. He remained still in front of the gate, almost a statue. Although his face was covered, there was a noticeable ripple in his valsara.

"No. Sorry." Whatever troubled him, the guardian pushed it aside to walk beside his charge.

The doors of the manor opened for them, and waiting inside was a gentleman of flaxen hair wearing scarlet robes.

"Princess Camellia! It is a tremendous relief to see you safe and sound."

Princess Camellia curtsied in greeting the nobleman. "You have my utmost thanks for receiving us, Lord Ivanstronge."

"Please, it is my pleasure." The duke approached the princess from the center of the foyer as the doors to the outside were closed. His face was the picture of solace. "When I heard from Duchess Gaelica of Velrut what befell Your Highness' fleet, I feared what became of you. But I never gave up hope that you yet live. Praise be to the gods for your safe return."

"I apologize that you had to hear of my disappearance from another. Were the circumstances more favorable, I would have sent word in advance. But good Prince Aeron and Lady Victoriah insisted on remaining unseen and unheard until we arrived."

"Then your assailants were—" Duke Ivanstronge finished his thought in silence. It was as unsavory to him as it was to the others. "Mm... Then that was best. All that matters is, you are safe." He turned his attention to Lady Victoriah and Prince Aeron. "And that is thanks to the two of you. Champion of Heart. My prince."

The duke bowed his head to them both in a show of appreciation. Lady Victoriah merely smirked with her arms crossed while the prince bowed in return.

When facing Princess Camellia again, he could not help, Veronica noted, giving a faint look to the knight beside her. Duke Ivanstronge paid Van no attention in glancing past him once, but in seeing him a second time, he seemed disquieted, if only for the briefest moment.

Shrugging it off, he smiled at the princess and her entourage. "You must all be weary from your long journey. I invite you all to rest and enjoy yourselves here in my home until preparations are made to escort the fair Princess Camellia to Velrut. My servants will see to your every need. If you require anything, you need only ask."

With that, Duke Ivanstronge excused himself to make the necessary arrangements. At their lord's signal, the servants waiting along the stairwell went to escort the soldiers to the guest chambers. The princess and her retinue all left together with Prince Aeron, perhaps to someplace suitable for royalty.

Lady Victoriah and Veronica were being shown to their chambers when they came across a distinguished woman standing by a window overlooking the open field behind the manor. The woman noticed their approach and, with a smile, went to greet them.

"Good to see you again, Rauva," hailed Lady Victoriah.

"Likewise, milady." The woman bowed her head to the champion. "Forgive me for not being with my husband to greet you. I had been rather preoccupied as of late."

"Don't worry about it. I understand. You may want to pay the princess a visit, though."

During their exchange, Veronica noticed something about the woman, who Lady Victoriah seemed acquainted with. Her red hair, beautifully braided into the ponytail placed over her shoulder, made her think she had seen her before.

Rauva ... Ivanstronge?

A gasp escaped her when she made the connection.

"Um ... excuse me, milady." Veronica spoke up when there was a slight pause between them. Both Lady Victoriah and the duchess looked to her, uncertain of who she meant to address. "You are Rauva Ivanstronge, yes?"

The noblewoman seemed puzzled yet intrigued. "That I am."

"By any chance, did you have a daughter named Rubella?"

Her question came as a shock to the duchess and Lady Victoriah both. They looked at her as though having heard a taboo word.

"How do you know of my daughter?"

For a moment, Veronica was not sure of what to say to put her at ease. So she simply told her the truth. "She was a friend of my brother, Wallace Alivvrn."

That seemed to calm her somewhat. She blinked, something coming to mind. "Wallace... Ah, yes. I remember her mentioning him. She always had very ... honest things to say about him."

Veronica put on a rueful smile. "I'm sorry for asking, milady. It's just—"

"No, no, it's quite all right, dearie." Lady Ivanstronge turned her attention to the champion. "Lady Victoriah, was Wallace one of them?"

Lady Victoriah nodded, then looked down to her squire. "Veronica, why don't you go rest in our chambers? I'll catch up."

The squire took her meister knight's hint and followed the butler down the hall.

The conversation continued once she was on her way. A hall opening at her left tempted Veronica to slip down it so she may listen in on them. But Lady Victoriah's eyes faced that direction, and she would be upset if she caught her squire disobeying orders.

She did as she was told and remained in the chambers shown to her. The main room was quite comfortable. Plenty of light came in from the outside, the glass window stretching from floor to ceiling and granting a magnificent view of the gardens. There was enough there to suit a soldier's needs: a few beds with nightstands between them, a decent-sized dresser, a small table, and a tall mirror.

Since she would be resting, Veronica took off her armor, setting each piece orderly on one of the nightstands. After kicking off her boots, she took her hairbrush out of her satchel, pulled a chair up to the mirror, and sat herself before it. It had been a while since she brushed her hair. She had not as many opportunities to maintain her blonde locks as when she was a page.

With every day an adventure spent crossing the countryside and training until she dropped, it was pleasant to slow down and do something so simple, so relaxing.

Lady Victoriah joined her before long.

When Veronica stopped what she was doing to greet her, she apologized for bringing up upsetting things to their host. Despite what the duchess said, she knew it left her uneasy.

But Lady Victoriah also claimed it was no bother; it actually reminded her to inform the duchess of something. When asked what, she did not say, and instead asked for the brush.

She did not want to stop just yet, but she obeyed. She expected Lady Victoriah to undo her ponytail and tend to her own umber locks, but Veronica felt the tug of the brush against her hair again.

It puzzled her why her meister knight suddenly wanted to brush her hair, but Veronica did not oppose it. The last time this had been done for her was when she was a little girl still at home with her mother.

While she was tending to her hair, Lady Victoriah asked why Veronica had such an interest in Rubella. In all the time she spent as her squire, Veronica never told her of her ability to see phantoms—and she did not find it appropriate to bring it up now. So she repeated what she said to Lady Ivanstronge, expressing a desire to know about the people in her lost brother's life.

Whether or not Lady Victoriah believed her, she did not let it show. The brush kept gliding down Veronica's hair, slowly and gently.

"Be careful who you ask about her," she advised. "Not many mention her around here since her murder. I'm sure you understand why."

Veronica gave the briefest nod when the brush pulled away. It was not so different from what happened in her family manse.

Silence filled the room now and then as they shifted between topics. It had a comforting effect that complemented the faint sound of the brush dragging down her hair.

When she finished, Lady Victoriah braided her hair in a way different than she usually wore. Her bangs were tied away from her forehead with locks from the sides. They were looped around her head twice to resemble a crown. The long locks behind her head remained as they were, flowing unimpeded past her shoulder blades.

"Want to give this style a try?"

It was not often that she let her hair down except to brush it. Lady knights and their young pupils typically did not have their long hair flow freely since it could get in the way during combat. Tying it into a ponytail was the most popular choice. Some kept their hair short for convenience.

But with the way it was held up now, that would not be an issue. She loved what her meister knight did. "I do. Thank you, Lady Victoriah."

After the trying expedition, it tempted them both to lie in the beds for some well-deserved rest. For reasons their own, though, they both left their appointed chambers to explore the manor. It was likely that Lady Victoriah sought out her son, who she had little time with personally during the march.

Though she knew to heed her meister knight's advice, Veronica still wished to see the duchess. She had a feeling Rubi was still roaming Brigadier in search of the answer that would free her from the phantom plane. If she could find a way to bring her peace, then Veronica felt she had to. For Rubi and her family.

The gardens were an excellent place to start as any.

An open space, bright and sunny, filled with vibrant plants—what a fine place to go to calm the mind. A cobblestone path led from the manor to a garden with an elegant fountain at its center. Shadows crept from the arches standing opposite of the garden patch. Past the gardens, the grounds were more open. Sturdy trees stood in formation like lines of soldiers near the manor, and past that, they were more spread out.

Quite a few people roamed the tranquil space, and many of them went to and left the tall hedge walls not far from the manor. Curious, Veronica went to see what was inside.

There was enough space between the gaps of the hedges for several people to walk through. A dozen flowerbeds grew within their borders, and in the center of it all stood a grand oak, its branches canopying nearly the entire space while keeping out little sunlight.

It looked to be a popular meeting place in the manor. Servants, soldiers, and envoys alike were about, talking gossip and sharing other such pleasantries, just having a good time.

As she explored the area, she saw a familiar face by the tree.

A grin on her face, Veronica crept slowly toward her, careful not to alert her too soon. When she was close enough to reach out and grab her shoulder, she spoke Cheryl's name.

The tall girl turned around in a fright, calming down only when she noticed it was her good friend. "Veronica! Gods, I wish you wouldn't do that."

Veronica could not resist letting out an impish laugh. It was rare for her to catch Cheryl off guard, and each time she did was always a delight. "Sorry, sorry," she said. "What brings you here? Are you exploring the manor too?"

"Yeah. Just thought to see what it's like around here."

Cheryl seemed oddly tense as she spoke. Her freckled cheeks were rather red as well, though Veronica first thought it had to do with being startled.

"Cheryl, is something wrong?"

"Wrong? What could be wrong? I'm here talking with you."

Veronica recalled that she was looking at something before she made her jump. She leaned to the side to peek past her. The only thing she saw from there were two gentlemen having a conversation.

In facing Cheryl again, she looked tense for a moment, but she loosened up shortly afterwards.

"Were you eavesdropping on them?"

"Me? No, why would I?"

Her voice wavered, and she did not look Veronica in the eye. Still as poor a liar as ever.

"That's very impolite, Cheryl. You'll make those men uncomfortable."

"R-Right. Sorry, I won't do it again."

Veronica smiled and took her friend by the hand. "Come on." She wanted to take her elsewhere so she would not continue staring at the men minding their own business.

As she inadvertently gazed their way again, though, she saw something that made her pause: the two men sharing a kiss.

It kept her attention for a moment more, but then she smiled and continued tugging Cheryl along.

Public displays of affection were uncommon and typically frowned upon by many, but where they were, it did not matter as much.

While Vermalians were a reserved people, Edereans were much more open with their feelings, good or ill, and were not shy about expressing them publicly. Since the social customs of both peoples were included and accepted in Heveilon, that sort of behavior was not unusual.

And neither was it for a man to be romantic with another man.

Once they were alone, out of the hedge garden, Veronica turned to Cheryl. "That's something between them, you know. It's not something to stare at."

Cheryl, her face redder than it was before, nodded. "So ... you're not shocked by that at all?"

"I was surprised. I mean, I haven't seen something like that before."

"You seem pretty calm about it."

"Why wouldn't I be?"

Veronica knew exactly what Cheryl meant, but Cheryl understood that she pretended not to. She was not one to object to the love of others.

She did not find Lady Ivanstronge, but since she was with her friend, Veronica decided to spend as much time with her as she could. The two went off to explore the gardens, happy to enjoy each other's company.

With the preparations for Princess Camellia's return to Ederea in Lord Ivanstronge's hands, the Vermalian knights who escorted her enjoyed a comfortable respite in his manor.

Resting in a bed felt strange after the nights spent sleeping on the cold, hard ground. Having a roof over their heads and walls to protect them was a comfort many appreciated.

And the food was heavenly. Veronica nearly passed out after the exquisite supper she had. It had been some time since she ate like that.

Their second day in the city was calm. Though many were excited about their royal visitors, they saw little of the Ederean princess, who took it slow after her eventful journey, and only saw the Vermalian prince when he went to the field to spar with his squire.

Veronica and Cheryl spent more time together after they trained, and their meister knights did a little catching up as well.

The winds were rather strong that day, the occasional gust offering a refreshing touch. It felt good to just sit still, take it in, and look down at the city from the hilltop the manor rested on.

And then, the peace fell apart.

Veronica felt the chaos spreading before the messenger arrived. The Renegades had infiltrated the city and were causing havoc.

The knights of Heveilon were deployed to repress the threat, but it was not enough. They needed help.

Lady Victoriah took half of Aeron's soldiers to put an end to the madness quickly. They joined the battle raging at the center of the city. By the time they arrived, the Renegades had already wiped out Heveilon's protectors.

No quarter was given to the merciless turncoats. Their formation was broken when struck by Veronica's Second Verse, a large sphere of water thrown their way. Thereupon, Victoriah the Wolverine and her comrades charged straight at the disorganized troop. They mowed down the enemy until none remained.

More enemies leaped from the buildings, attempting to catch the knights by surprise. The prince's soldiers, familiar with that tactic, moved out of the way before they were hit. The others then moved in to strike them down.

Lady Victoriah was bold enough to remain where she was when one Renegade fell atop her. She remained still until he came close, then hurled her sword at his axe, knocking it from his grasp. When he fell to the ground, her mount slammed his hooves into his chest, crushing his ribcage.

All was quiet after that.

Lady Victoriah scanned the area, her stare grim. "Something is not right."

The younger soldiers were unsure of what she meant. They thought her overcautious, though none could blame her given the carnage around them.

Those familiar with the ways of the enemy, however, knew better.

"This can't be it," she stated firmly. "Veronica."

Her squire nodded and closed her eyes. Cutting off her vision, submerging her mind in darkness, allowed her to strengthen her magic senses. In doing so, she could detect the valsara of those in the nearby vicinity. She only sensed her comrades around her. In a few nearby buildings hid a great many people, but their valsara projected fear, suggesting they were civilians.

She found nothing unusual, but kept looking. It strained her mind to expand her perception to the outer reaches of Heveilon, but as she did so, she sensed more activity. There were a great many amassed around the manor, ready to protect it from attackers. But more kept coming together.

Small groups that were once difficult to trace marched on the manor from all sides, and quickly the valsara she sensed came to glimmer and fade.

"No!" Her eyes flew open. "The manor is in danger!"

Lady Victoriah looked back to the manor. The chorus of battle echoed from there. "Damn, a diversion. Move! We can't let them face the Renegades alone."

They hurried back up the path without delay. The horses ran with all they had, moved by their riders' urgency.

A loud *bang, bang, bang* shook the air as they rode. The knights needed only to keep their eyes forward to know what that was. Even from afar, they had a fitting view of the uppermost part of the manor, and they watched in horror as the front had been impaled by pillars of stone jutting from the ground.

"Earth mines!" a knight exclaimed.

Lady Victoriah told Veronica of the destructive spell once before. It was used by a mage of the Renegades, an elementalist. He rarely appeared, but whenever he did, disaster followed.

An obstacle got in the party's way. Three factions of Renegades leaped from the shadows to bar their path. One of the men among them took the lead, carrying an orb that fit in his palm. Upon striking it to the ground, a cloud of black smoke burst forth. As the black cloud rolled up to the knights, it spooked their mounts.

The horses panicked at the sensation of the ground moving with the cloud. The only one to leap bravely through it was Timberhoof, and his rider held her sword out to impale the man who cast the spell.

It was not easy, but Veronica managed to soothe Nightshade before she shook her off. The others were not so lucky. Nearly every horse threw their rider off them they were so frightened, and ran away in a panic.

Victoriah the Wolverine and Timberhoof fought off most of the enemies before her comrades rose to their feet to take care of the rest.

The interference cost them time, and that was the point. That was a calculated move following the series that already passed—cause a disturbance, lure the Champion of Heart and her allies away, bar their path from the manor.

The Renegades were hell-bent on killing the princess.

Only five of the knights had their mounts. Those without argued for them to go on ahead and help the others. But Lady Victoriah would not have it. If they left them behind, the enemy would pick them off.

The knights knew that, but they also knew what their mission was. They staked their pride on ensuring the Ederean princess survived, even if it meant giving their lives for it. The longer they tarried, the worse it would be for her.

Their argument became all the more compelling as more earth mines were cast. Two more stone pillars sunk into the manor from the sides; they were as claws entrapping their vulnerable prey.

Still, Lady Victoriah refused to leave her comrades behind. The situation was dire, that she could not deny, so she went ahead with those still mounted to scout the path and slay every enemy in the way. But the men and women on foot were ordered to advance as quickly as possible. She was determined for them all to see this through to the end.

More Renegade warriors were lying in wait, and they were as determined to halt their advance as those they followed. The same trick used to startle the mounts had been implemented again and again. But it did not slow them down. The climate was perfect for Veronica to disperse the water in the air as a heavy mist. Though it did not brush away the black smoke entirely, the bursts were strong enough to intercept it and weaken the spell.

The knights on foot caught up as their mounted allies struggled to tear through the blockade. With their help, they were able to fight off the enemies rushing their way.

But more Renegades kept coming. Over a hundred warriors had already fallen, and a hundred more came to take their place.

No matter their efforts, the path would not clear.

As another faction rushed the knights' way, something else flew from the street the Renegades came from—and tore right through them. A man collapsed to the ground as his arm was ripped from his torso by a white blur. It moved as fast as an arrow and curved right back at the enemy faction, upon dropping the limb, to strike another down.

One by one they fell, until a single Renegade stood alone. He tried to flee but did not get far. Whatever butchered his allies rammed into him hard enough to leave a bloody impression on the stone wall behind him.

Upon slowing, the blur was found to be a small yet monstrous beast. It shook its head from the impact it made, and roared a shrill, heinous cry at its victims, revealing fangs sharper than daggers. Its eyes were a steely blue. And its pure white fur was coated in the blood of its enemies.

Everyone remained on guard as the beast looked their way. Even the horses were afraid of it.

At least, most of them were. Nightshade tried to trot up to the bloodstained thing, bringing Veronica to tighten her hold on the reins. In the few steps she took, though, she caught a glimpse of the cerulean stone in the beast's forehead.

There was something about the energy in the stone that allowed curiosity to override caution, and when she saw into its valsara, she understood why. The beast's valsara somehow resembled Van's.

"Lady Victoriah, I think that is Snowflake."

"What?"

It was even harder for her to believe after saying so, but looking to the beast again only made her more certain. Its shape was indeed that of a fox, and although somewhat bigger than the plush pet they recognized, its fur and eyes matched Snowflake's.

The malformed fox did not attack. Instead, it made an abrupt sound, then turned around. It stopped at the path it came from to look back at them.

Rraw! Rraw! the beast barked.

It seemed to want them to follow.

More Renegades came from the path to the manor, bringing the fox to turn their way and snarl. Whether or not it was who Veronica thought, it showed who its enemies were. Sometimes, that was enough.

The knights on foot held the Renegades off for their mounted comrades to escape. As much as Lady Victoriah did not want to leave them behind, they were running out of time.

They followed Snowflake, who remained in the lead. This new monstrous form was startling. Not only was she strong enough to wipe out an entire enemy faction, but she also outran the horses.

They raced through the streets, avoiding enemy forces, gradually nearing the manor. The route they took brought them to a group of Renegades clashing with a party of knights. Among them were several Ederean soldiers.

Snowflake leaped into the fray, beginning another frenzy. While the malformed fox carved a path through the rear, Lady Victoriah led her soldiers to attack from the side. The knights' morale was bolstered by the champion's arrival, and together, they routed the enemy.

"Victoriah!"

Emerging from the party of knights was none other than Prince Aeron:

"So you escaped," answered Lady Victoriah. "What of the princess?"

"She's with us."

The prince showed Lady Victoriah to a house across the street. Its door barely hung by the hinges. Opening it invited a sword to fall.

The prince expected his squire to be on edge, and blocked her swing. Cheryl backed away upon realizing who she almost decapitated. "Sorry, Aeron."

Several other soldiers were inside. Most of them suffered terrible injures that would keep them from fighting.

In the far corner of the room sat the fair princess. She was hunched over one of the wounded, his chest bare and stained crimson. A soft light filled the space, a light that glowed from the princess' hand. Once it faded, the bleeding had stopped and the wound was closed.

Such a potent form of healing magic.

But alas, there were some that it could not help. Several dead were laid together in the shadows, their bodies straight and their hands placed over their chests. Some were soldiers, some civilians. One of them was that of the princess' faithful handmaidens.

Princess Camellia turned to the new arrivals as her last handmaiden helped the soldier to sit up. Her eyes reflected relief. "Lady Victoriah! Thank the gods you are safe."

As the door was closed, the malformed fox scampered inside and hurried over to the princess. Rather than be fazed by the beast, Princess Camellia was overjoyed.

"So that is where you went. Well done, Snowflake."

That dismissed their doubt about the fox, but it raised many questions.

"What happened?" Lady Victoriah asked.

"The Renegades infiltrated the manor. They very nearly had us."

Princes Aeron stepped in. "They were among the guards."

"Ivanstronge was compromised too?"

"It would seem. But they found out shortly before the attack took place. Lady Ivanstronge warned me just in time to get to the princess."

"Sir Vandelas believed it was not safe there, so we made our escape."

"But where is Van?"

He was not, as Veronica mentioned, among the soldiers either in the house or on guard outside.

"I am afraid ... we became separated when the manor was hit by magic. The floors broke apart and—" Worry kept the princess from finishing. She merely hung her head and gripped at her dress. "I ... I did not wish to leave him. But he told us to escape."

Lady Victoriah leaned in and cupped her shoulder. "It's all right, Princess. We'll find him. But first, we have to get you to safety."

While her words did little to reassure her, Princess Camellia conceded with a nod.

"We have more company. A lot more!"

Cheryl's warning brought the air to thicken. Fear overcame the injured and the noncombatants, all the while stoking the fury in those still able to fight.

It would not be safe there for long, but they were not going to let the enemy through. Lady Victoriah, Prince Aeron, Veronica, and Cheryl left the house to see a massive enemy party charging at the knights of Vermalio and Ederea.

They came from the path Snowflake led them down.

Letting wrath guide her, Lady Victoriah led her allies on the attack.

Veronica fought alongside Cheryl and the prince. The two squires acted as support for the royal knight, keeping enemies off his sides while he struck down the ones before him. Veronica quickly disposed of her foes with speed and precision, her quick swipes slicing through gaps in their armor and spilling blood. When only the Renegades stood before her, she gathered water into a large sphere to spike at them. Cheryl dove after those who fought to get up, finishing them off.

One Renegade came at Cheryl from behind. She reacted immediately, waving her sword to intercept a falling axe. She struggled for a moment, but managed to push the axe back and move in to slit its wielder's belly open.

Her time with the prince served her well.

The Vermalians fought fiercely, bringing the battle to a daunting impasse. But the scales were about to be tipped.

The ground shook and debris scattered upon a concussive bang sounding from behind. When looking back, Veronica saw soldiers at the rear knocked to the ground and a few burnt black, smoke wafting from their bodies.

From the path behind them came a larger platoon of Renegades lined in formation. In the lead was a man whose valsara exuded sheer power. That man reached his hand to the heavens, sparks flying between his fingers, forming a massive fireball in it.

It was him. The elementalist.

Acting quickly, Veronica drew water to create a bubble barrier around her comrades. The thin layer it formed popped upon intercepting the fireball, but the resulting burst pushed her back. She tottered backward as two more fireballs flew at them, one striking her comrades, the other setting the princess' hiding place on fire.

Assailed from the front, smote from the rear, all the while the princess and the injured were being circled by growing flames.

Dread coiled around Veronica's lungs, crushing them slowly. They were cornered and outnumbered. She could not foresee a way out of this.

But the call of her leader rallied them to hold strong their resolve. "Ederean knights, hold these dastards back! Soldiers of Vermalio, with me!" Lady Victoriah charged directly for the elementalist and his brood. The soldiers who could break away abandoned all fear to follow her into the line of fire.

Veronica kept her eyes off the battle and on the housefire as she acted to put it out. She expanded her area of influence as far as she could, gathering every drop of water to douse the flames from the roof down.

Her actions caught the attention of the elementalist, who tried again to smite her with fire. The spell did not even fly halfway to her before Lady Victoriah got in the way, taking the blast instead. Her shield protected her from the worst of it, though it left her staggered. Like that, she was left open to another spell. The next one did not brew fire in his hands, but rather a rampant web of lightning.

The moment the lightning flashed its brightest was the moment it faded away. Before the spell could be cast, the elementalist was impaled by a spear, one that reflected the harsh sunlight. He struggled to keep standing as death cries were screamed from behind, his comrades hitting the ground. The one responsible closed in on the elementalist like a phantom and brought his head to roll.

The Renegades around him backed away in fear.

"It's alive... The Blood Beast is still alive!"

The Azure Knight had returned with sword in hand.

Overcome with joy, Lady Victoriah rushed to his side, as had Veronica. They cut their way through the enemy to him, and together, the three rent the Renegade party asunder.

Upon coming together, their backs were to each other, facing the enemy at all sides and ensuring no one would strike them from behind. Then they went on the attack.

Assured that she did not have to worry about the Azure Knight or Victoriah the Wolverine, Veronica lashed at her foes with a whip of water formed from her rapier. Once they were disoriented, she hurled the water at them and closed in to cut them down one by one.

As the herd thinned on one side, Veronica caught a look at how Van fought. His swordsmanship was uncanny. He held his sword in his right hand and used the scabbard in his left as a shield. His feet looked to glide along the ground with each step. With every swing of the sword, his body moved in a lithe fashion that made him appear to be dancing.

Every move the enemy made had been anticipated and countered, as if he read their minds. Never before had Veronica seen such a vibrant display of swordsmanship.

When the fight died down, she came to realize how intense his valsara was, and it frightened her. Pure fury exuded from him, the flames of his spirit raging against the shell that was his body.

He was not that fierce even when they were attacked by wolves on the road. It was as if this man before her was not the same Van.

His foes disposed of, Van waved his sword, splattering the blood along the blade on the ground. The thick substance clung to his armor, but not a drop stuck to the slick metal of Las'cent.

The three warriors returned to their allies as they fell back to the house they protected. Princess Camellia and the others stepped out into the open, wary of the house's failing structure. They watched as more Renegade reinforcements rushed in from the eastern road.

The fighting seemed endless, but the soldiers did not waver. They formed a line, ensuring they would not reach the princess. Lady Victoriah took the lead upon her return.

Stepping past her and the other soldiers was Van. Lady Victoriah moved to stop him, but she held back upon witnessing the light coming off of his sword. The jewel at its guard was alight with a brilliant, piercing glow—an intense azure.

Slowly, he drew his sword to the side and waited for the enemy to make their approach. When their vanguard came within thirty feet, "Roar, Las'cent!" he swung it, casting a trenchant wave of the azure light, sending it crashing into the enemy party.

Those caught in its radiance came to a screeching halt and struggled to make sudden moves. It was as if they were shackled by fear.

The Ederean soldiers, screaming their mighty battle cries, broke formation and rushed at the enfeebled enemies, and the Vermalians followed suit. They tore through the Renegades with ease.

Lady Victoriah fell back with Van as he returned to the princess' side, seeing that her allies handled themselves just fine.

The princess was so pleased to see her guardian safe that she broke from her handmaiden's side to meet him. "Vandelas—"

"It was the duke!"

"What?"

"Riverin Ivanstronge is responsible for this. He called the Renegades here. He planned the attack down to its last contingency."

Prince Aeron joined them as Van told them what he learned, and he was as shocked as the others. "Van, are you certain?"

"He told me everything when he had me surrounded. That dastard is after the same thing Xanlir was: war between Vermalio and Ederea bought with Camellia's life."

His claim was a heavy one, but one that everyone took seriously.

Veronica did not want to believe it, but she could tell from his valsara that he spoke the truth.

"Then nowhere in the city is safe," the prince concluded.

"Van, take Timberhoof and get the princess out of Cragfill," ordered Lady Victoriah. "She's safest with you. We'll deal with Riverin. Once we—"

"I will not go."

All eyes fell on the princess. Her stare, once riddled with terror and disbelief, now burned with defiance.

"Your Highness, you must understand. If you remain here—"

"Nay, I will not go!" she firmly repeated. "I cannot run now that I know who orchestrated this madness." Her gentle, kindhearted persona fell apart as she trembled with anger. She was enraged, humiliated, by the betrayal of the duke who spoke such lies to her. "This would not have happened if'n I never came here. There are good Edereans and Vermalians suffering right now because of this attempt on my life. I cannot— I will not abandon them to this charlatan to save myself!"

The mighty warriors of both kingdoms stood in awe of the young maiden before them. She showed such zeal and passion. Although small and frail, she displayed a will of pure strength.

"Then you won't run." Her words moved Prince Aeron as well. "My deputy commander will escort you and your guard to the shelter north of the city. Have your knights protect the civilians as they would you."

"Aeron, that isn't—"

"Lady Victoriah, I order you to stand down!" Prince Aeron always spoke softly and with sensitivity, but now he was loud and stern. He demanded compliance from his subordinate, for he understood what led the princess to her decision. "As you said, the princess will be safe with the Azure Knight. We'll take care of the traitors and that dastard Riverin."

Lady Victoriah glared at the prince, but once she saw his will was as strong as the princess', she relented with a smile. Neither of them, she knew, would be denied. "Understood, my prince."

After the princess made her escape to the shelter, the Vermalians fought to rout the Renegades loose in the city. Prince Aeron led his soldiers to the manor, where the majority of enemy forces remained.

With valiance and fury, they eliminated the enemy and freed Heveilon.

The traitor Lord Ivanstronge was found hiding in a secret room of his manor, though not of his own volition. His own guard held him captive.

Having discovered her husband's plot, the duchess swayed the soldiers with grudges against the Renegades to follow her and stand against Riverin. They captured him and kept him out of reach of the enemy until the prince's arrival.

Ever on the hunt for the elusive princess, the Renegade commander's troops did turn to the shelter, but they were deterred by the Azure Knight, who blocked the way by creating walls of jagged ice. The only way in was through him, and all who charged at him were slain.

The perimeter was secured, but one last contingency remained in play. A few enemy agents hid among the civilians inside the shelter, and moved to strike when exposed by Snowflake.

The Edereans knights fought them off—with some unexpected help. The last surviving agent, who threatened to slit a child's throat in his mad attempt to escape, had been stabbed through the heart by a blade connected to a long silver chain. The one controlling the chain was a Pternite man in sage robes.

The one the princess set out to find had found them, guided by his skills as a soothsayer, and he saved an innocent child in the process.

Lord Ivanstronge was brought before his people in shackles, his crimes revealed to all. The princess got a good look at the traitor on his knees before making her departure for Velrut with the prince's party.

As Heveilon began to recover, Lady Victoriah took it upon herself to question the traitor. The interrogation went on for hours, and no one saw her leave the dungeon since it started.

Veronica was curious. She was ordered not to interrupt, but she could not help herself. A lot was happening, and everyone was so frightened.

The soldiers guarding the dungeon did not permit her entry at first. But when they saw she had brought bread and water for her meister knight, they caved and opened the way for her.

The sound of hard fists tenderizing meat reached the doorway. Hoarse groans echoed throughout the dungeon, its closed space twisting the agony it carried. The space was lit by four torches hung from the corners of the walls. Stairs descended from the entrance down beneath the ground, offering an uneasy feeling of walking into a grave.

In the center of the room was a large post. The prisoner had been strapped against it. His back was pressed to the hard wood, his hands bound behind it and his legs tied together. His feet did not even touch the ground. And his bare skin was battered black and swollen.

Lady Victoriah stood before the prisoner, glaring at him. Her fists were clenched tightly, blood dripping from her gauntlets. It seemed she was doing the job with her bare hands instead of using the startling array of tools that sat on the table underneath the stairway.

She looked Veronica's way when she made it to the bottom of the stairs. "I told you to stay out." The severity in her eyes and voice did not lessen even when directed at her.

"I'm sorry, Lady Victoriah. I thought you might need—"

The Wolverine groaned. "Leave it and go!"

She knew the interruption would not be taken kindly to. Veronica placed the tray of food on the table with the tools and turned to leave.

Lady Victoriah did not wait for Veronica to go before continuing. "I've got all day, Riverin, and this was just a warm-up. Tell me who you serve, or I stop being gentle."

The prisoner lifted his head, every move making him tremble, to look his captor dead in the eye. In his stare lingered a hate that grew with the spite he fed it. He spat blood at Lady Victoriah, undaunted by her promise.

She did not bother wiping away the blood. It would only amuse him.

Lady Victoriah did not grin as she had in battle. The challenge was not what concerned her. "Just like the cannon fodder you threw at us. You only care about victory." She waited for an answer that never came. "Does everything else mean so little to you? Even your daughter?"

Veronica stopped moving as she reached for the door and slowly looked back at the prisoner.

The man grimaced. He looked more irritated at the notion than anything. "My daughters were safely hidden away during the attack."

Lady Victoriah threw her fist into his gut. "You know who I mean! Rubella! I'm talking about your youngest, Rubella Ivanstronge!"

The duke recovered and let out a throaty groan. Just hearing that name made his spite grow. He looked at the Wolverine again with a cold gaze. "And what of her?"

"What of her? What of her!?" Lady Victoriah took the man's skull in her hand and squeezed it like a vise. "They killed her. The Renegades murdered your daughter! They infiltrated the Estrine Chateau and cut her down. You know this and still turn your back on the kingdom you served all your life, for them! For the monsters who killed y—"

"That was on her!"

What he said was enough to shock the Wolverine into losing her grip on her prey. She looked at him horrorstruck, as did Veronica.

His eyes remained fixed on his captor even as she let go, judging her, thinking her weak. He struggled to keep his breathing steady enough to speak again.

"I had her arranged to be married. I could have had her brought back here the moment the Ederean princess arrived in Brigadier. Then your son got involved. He had to invoke that outdated tradition, where the boy ignorant of the world meddles in organized affairs and violates them through trial by combat, so that Rubella could remain a page, when I forbade her to return to the Estrines in the first place! She died because she wasn't where she was supposed to be—because your son took her hand from the Ginnstom boy. Her death was on them."

Veronica could not believe the hate-filled nonsense coming out of his mouth. The one he spoke of was his own daughter, someone he was supposed to love and cherish. But there was no love in his words. He abandoned his daughter, resigned her to the fate she suffered, a fate he knew would happen.

What hung there was not a father. And as Veronica took in his horrifying words, he stopped looking human altogether.

You ... disgusting clod!

She turned away from the door and marched down the stairs.

"And let's not forget who cut her down," he went on with maniacal delight. "It was by one of your own, a champion of the supposed king. Even his most loyal soldiers do not accept him. You may have the country, but you're the ones fighting a losing battle. When he finally takes what belongs to—"

Lady Victoriah snarled and raised her fist, but hers was not the one to silence him. It was Veronica who rammed her fist closed in anger across his jaw before he could utter one more venomous word.

Her meister knight was so bewildered that she could not even admonish her for her disobedience. She stared at her, unsure of whether it was truly the same girl before her.

It made Veronica's blood boil just looking at the despicable man, and she clenched her teeth when he snickered at her.

"You think a child can make me divulge any—"

Veronica slipped her hand around his throat. Her grip was only tight enough to keep him from shaking her off. Nothing kept him from speaking. Even so, he squawked like a dying animal and spasmed against his bonds.

"I bet you didn't know your body is mostly made of water," she taunted the thing squirming in her grasp. "And I can control water!"

He looked like he wanted to retort, but he crumbled against the waves of Veronica's power. The water that made up his muscles and organs convulsed and fought against his solid form, inflicting nightmarish pain throughout the body without destroying anything.

"My meister knight asked you a question, worm. Who do you serve?"

The duke now showed great fear after experiencing that pain, but he did not answer. Veronica punished him by strengthening her power, squeezing a gargled mess of throaty screams out of him.

"How do you get your orders? Letters? A charm? Talk!"

To show she was not playing games, she wrung his muscles harder. It made his eyes open so wide they looked like they might pop out of his head.

Lady Victoriah was about to make her stop when she got results.

"A messenger!" the duke squawked. Veronica loosened her Second

Verse's hold on him when he finally spoke. "A liaison receives the orders. They then deliver them to me."

It was not what she wanted, but it was a start.

Deciding that this may prove worthwhile, Lady Victoriah stepped back into the prisoner's focus. "And who gives the orders?" she asked. "Who do you serve?"

Veronica stilled her power for the duke to breathe easily, giving him a brief rest, before having it strangle him again.

The duke thrashed against his bonds, desperate to escape the pain smothering him. But there was no escape. It would not stop until he gave up the information he so stubbornly withheld.

"You will tell us everything," Veronica stated. "This power of mine, it can make you experience the pain of death in all of its forms a thousand times over, and you won't be any closer to it. All you get from holding back is suffering without end. You want it to stop? Then talk!"

Using the water to claw at him from the inside out was just the one thing she could do. Her Second Verse could dehydrate his body enough that he would not be able to lift a finger, shrivel out his eyes and make him go blind, attack his brain until his mind drowned.

And Veronica would not care. She would squeeze the life out of him if it brought them closer to destroying the Renegades once and for all.

When it sounded like he was trying to say something, Veronica let up. He was indeed struggling to tell her something. But he only shook his head and babbled. Tiring of his nonsense, she reapplied the pressure.

It was then the duke slammed his jaws shut. Blood spattered from his teeth as something flew, hitting Veronica's cheek. It was his tongue.

She took her hand from the duke's throat to cover her mouth. Fighting back the bile rising in her throat, she tottered to and leaned against the wall. She writhed from the burning sensation until it finally passed.

A hand rested on her shoulder as she struggled to catch her breath. It led her up the stairs and out of the dungeon for some fresh air.

Lady Victoriah remained silent until she felt better, then drew her hand along her back, giving it a light pat.

"So, you're the other Veronica."

That was something she had been told about when they were travelling. She had seen this wroth Veronica before, but she was too drunk at the time to remember. She actually laughed when someone told her that her squire put someone in a headlock and made them beg like a dog.

Hearing her say that made Veronica smile. "What gave it away?"

"Everything." Lady Victoriah patted her back again.

"Disappointed?"

"No. You're pretty fiery—I like that." She took her hand back when it seemed she could sit up without wobbling. "But it looks like neither of you have the stomach for torture."

Veronica blushed and glared at Lady Victoriah. "I-It was the tongue!"

"Relax. It wasn't something I wanted my squire learning. And yeah, that includes you too."

Feeling embarrassed, Veronica looked away from Lady Victoriah. She focused on the sunset. "I know ... I know I should've walked away, but..." She tightened her fists in remembering what she heard. "I let you down. Now we can't get anything from him."

It was astounding. He was more afraid of his leader than he was of the torment he suffered.

Someone that terrifying was out there, creating havoc unimpeded.

A hand was propped atop her head, rubbing it. "No one ever gets anything from the Renegades. That's how it's always been." Lady Victoriah comforted her for a moment before standing. "Are you feeling better?"

"Yeah."

"Good. Then you'll come spar with me for a bit. I still have some anger to let out."

"Yes, Lady Victoriah." She understood that was how she would be punished for disobeying her. But still, sparring with her sounded good.

She was looking forward to personally getting to know Victoriah the Wolverine. Her gentler self was not the only one who looked up to her.

~ Sixteenth Chapter ~
That Which Slowly Kills

Since the attack in Heveilon, the Renegades have become more active. They appeared in nearly every region across the country to commit atrocities large and small, seen and unseen. Wanton destruction left in their wake, they spread fear and chaos across the land.

Whatever purpose it served, no one knew. But the sudden increase in activity heralded a grave fate for Vermalio.

And the kingdom, after two decades of internal conflict, still knew next to nothing of their enemy within.

The Champion of Heart raced across the country to prevent many a catastrophe by their wicked hands. It led to many battles, some with grave odds. In some such times, she cooperated with her fellow champions, their combined efforts making quick work of the threats to their kingdom.

Never was she alone, though, not with her trusty squire by her side.

In the several passing months, Veronica had grown stronger. Her swordsmanship was further tempered by Lady Victoriah's training.

Even her control over the Second Verse surpassed her expectations thanks to the guidance of her other self. They had grown much closer, understood each other better.

It was with her phenomenal powers that victory was attained time and again. Her control over water, the ability to project her spirit from her body, even summoning her wroth self when needed most—they made her a forced to be reckoned with and a vital asset to the kingdom.

And the Renegades came to recognize that as well.

While resting on their way to their next destination, they were ambushed by rogues. Cloaked in black, they blended in with the cover of night. But Lady Luneste, goddess of the moon and bringer of the night sky, watched over the two warriors, and her twin, Lady Malute, amused herself in waking Veronica with a cawing crow so she may notice them.

Despite the scare, she looked at it in an oddly gleeful way. Sending assassins after her meant she was considered important. It made her wonder how her eldest brother, Siron, would react if she told him.

Hm... Perhaps I shouldn't. It might irritate his missing eye.

After they killed the rogues, they went to find someplace else to rest for the remainder of the night. As if guided by Lady Luneste herself, they happened upon a military encampment. Though it was well into the night, the party's captain welcomed them into their camp.

Upon being graced by dawn's radiant glow, the party gathered their equipment and readied to march. They were en route to the mining town of Feilor to suppress a revolt.

The Champion of Heart joined them, deciding she would take the lead.

The revolt was, as she feared, a result of Renegade activity. They incited violence and convinced the people to take up arms against the knights. In the ensuing chaos, the captain of the town guard was murdered and the mayor taken prisoner.

That the military had to deploy troops from other areas meant the situation was dire. If worse came to worse, the casualties would be immense, and what followed would create further rifts in the kingdom.

Veronica did not want to fight the townspeople. They were not warriors trained in combat, just miners armed with pickaxes and hammers.

The people were being used by the traitors who worked to topple the current reign. But if left alone, they would continue to defile the king's name and bolster the Renegades' cause.

Doubt plagued her thoughts as the party arrived in Feilor. She strived for knighthood to protect the people, not to put them to the blade.

Alas, there was not the time for doubt or hesitation.

The violence had escalated drastically. The other parties sent to quell the revolt arrived before them and had taken the initiative to engage the threat.

It irked Lady Victoriah that they did not wait before making their move. Some soldiers were too overzealous for their own good.

Their party marched quickly into town. The outskirts were littered with corpses from the most recent skirmish. Most of them were young men.

Feilor's gate was unguarded. An uproar came from the town square.

When they found the townspeople and knights embroiled in combat, Lady Victoriah gave the order to have them separated. Her soldiers, well equipped with thick armor and large shields, got to work immediately, pushing them back and defending with the sword only when necessary. Caught in the heat of battle, the other knights were as irrational as the raging populace, but the soldiers under her command fought hard to avoid any needless taking of life.

Once both sides were separated, Veronica pulled the water from a nearby trough. Gathered with the moisture in the air, she shaped it into a large bird of prey, its wings flapping frantically. All looked up to the terrifying figure and were awed into silence. Having gotten their attention, Veronica had the bird swell into a bubble, then it popped, scattering the droplets everywhere. Underneath where the bird once hovered stood Lady Victoriah. With all eyes on her, she made herself known.

"I am Victoriah the Wolverine, the Champion of Heart!"

Everyone's valsara trembled upon recognizing the champion, be it from reverence or fear. Their malice waned, their will to fight fading with it.

"I have come to put an end to this madness. People of Feilor, lay down your weapons and bring me your leader."

"We won't bow to a dog of the king!" a man wielding a large hammer was bold enough to say.

"Didn't you hear me?" asked Lady Victoriah as she turned her sword the man's way. "I'm a wolverine!"

That motion stopped him from saying any more.

"There will be no more needless bloodshed, nor will you further slander the name of our king." Her expectations given, Lady Victoriah lowered her sword. Her eyes pierced through everyone before her, showing no compassion. The time for that had long since passed.

But that did not mean she wanted the conflict to continue.

"What reason would a mining town have to revolt against the kingdom you served since its founding? Your prosperity comes from the gems and metals harvested from the earth. Your labor may well have been what gave the smiths the metal to forge my sword." That sword was raised only so she could admire its luster, the blade gilded by the shining sun. Drawing it downward, setting it under the long shadow cast by the mayor's hall, she set her sights on the people again. "And what now? You turn your tools on the knights that have protected you, that you have supported all this time, and shed blood instead of stone?"

"The knights are pawns of the king, a king who has abandoned us!"

"Yet here I am!" Lady Victoriah's howl commanded silence once more. No one else dared to speak, lest they rile up the Wolverine. "Unrest came to Feilor, and I followed—a champion, one of the arms of the king himself." She paused to shake her head. "Abandoned you? Here I stand, keeping these streets from becoming rivers of blood, dividing the conflict rather than fueling it further." She glared at one soldier who looked to be responsible for the other parties. "King Faustign values your lives. And more than that, he wishes for your happiness. That will alone is what brought me here. If that's not being taken care of here, then leave it to me to set things right.

"Listen to me now: lay down your weapons."

The civilians looked to one another in their confusion, sharing in their hesitancy. They saw that Lady Victoriah still held her sword in hand. Though some still wanted to fight, they knew it would mean fighting her too. And that would not end well.

Clank!

A young man dropped his axe at his feet. Others followed suit, putting down their weapons one by one. In turn, the knights lowered their swords and spears to show they were not a threat to them.

It never ceased to amaze Veronica how her meister knight managed to compel others.

Just like that, the fighting was over. ...Or so it seemed.

Someone in the crowd tried to hide their malice, but it failed to escape Veronica's notice. As she sensed it spike, an arrow flew. There was no time to use the Second Verse. Before it could meet its mark, she threw herself in front of Lady Victoriah. The tip tore into her upper arm.

Lady Victoriah caught her as she fell back. Her touch let Veronica experience the rage building in her. "Lady Victoriah, wait!" She was an admirable knight, but her anger often got the best of her. If she were to lose herself now, the people would react accordingly.

But it was not her that led the situation out of hand.

"They shot her! The rebels shot a squire!"

"They tried to shoot Lady Victoriah!"

"How dare they!"

Before either the champion or her squire could protest, the soldiers rushed past them to go on the attack. The civilians, still riled up, took back their weapons and fought them off.

A couple of soldiers went to help Lady Victoriah get Veronica away from the clash. They took her into an alley beside the square and sat her against a wall. Then Lady Victoriah shooed them away. "Get your captain to call off his soldiers now."

"But milady—"

"Just go, both of you!"

They followed her orders and left posthaste.

The arrow in Veronica's arm started to burn. "Lady Victoriah…"

"Steady there, soldier." Lady Victoriah held up her squire's arm. She put her sword down to reach her other hand for the arrow. "This is going to sting." That was her only warning before she pulled it free. It almost ripped through her as painfully as when it first pierced her.

"Thank you," she uttered with a twisted face.

Lady Victoriah held the arrow close to her nose upon removing it. Then, with a growl, she discarded it.

"I'm fine now. Please, put a stop to this."

But she did not leave her side. Instead, Lady Victoriah grabbed her by the other arm to help her stand. "Stay close to me."

"But—"

"Shut up and stay calm, or the poison will spread faster."

Veronica all but stopped breathing when she said that. Poison. The arrowhead had been coated in poison? Knowing that made it nearly impossible to remain calm, but the moment she began to shake and stutter, Lady Victoriah urged her to relax by gripping her shoulder.

What happened angered her, but she did not panic. She must have known about that particular poison, and perhaps an antidote as well.

Lady Victoriah guided Veronica away from the fighting. A few townsmen tried to go after her, cursing her name, but the soldiers protected her and her injured squire so she could get away.

They did not make it far before Veronica came to a halt. She felt something shoot up her spine, causing her muscles to stiffen.

"Come on, Veronica. Keep moving! We can cure you if we make it back to the supply convoy."

"Something is wrong…"

"Stiff muscles, I know. That's what the poison does to you first."

If the poison was the cause, she might not have been able to break free of Lady Victoriah's grip. She was just fine. Her muscles did not weaken. Pain only pulsed in her arm as numbness settled in.

With a dazed look, she turned her head downward.

"Something … something is happening below us."

The conflict might have kept her from noticing it before. She might not have felt it now were it not growing more tumultuous by the second.

If she hoped to dismiss that as a poison-induced hallucination, she could not anymore.

The ground started to shake, subtly at first, then violently. The clashing men and women took notice as well when the hard stone ground beneath them began to chip and crack. From those cracks, the earth breathed a foul gas in clouds thick enough to force those fighting apart.

The townspeople looked at the phenomenon in horror and scattered in a panic.

A soldier fell to the ground upon taking a burst of the gas. He struggled to claw his way back to his feet and catch up with his retreating comrades.

The air quickly became discolored. A thin purple fog enveloped the square and spread throughout the area.

"Fall back! Fall back!"

The soldiers returned to Lady Victoriah's side following her call. They fled the square with her to regroup, hopefully to figure out what was happening.

The situation was grim. The gas spewing from the earth, a deadly miasma, had spread throughout all of Feilor by the day's end, and had killed dozens of people who breathed it in. The soldiers had little choice but to flee the town.

But Lady Victoriah would not allow them to leave without the civilians.

Several frightened people, particularly mothers and their children, brought themselves before the knights begging to be transported out of town. They did not care who they served; they just did not want to die there.

The rest of the townspeople required persuasion, and they were not easy to convince. They were in a panic after seeing the miasma emerge. The hysteria from the earlier clash only fed their dread.

Grown men babbled about how they would not let themselves be tossed back into mines from whence the miasma came.

Fear shook their voices and etched into their rough faces. They knew well how it eroded the body from the inside out, how it made their bones harden together, how it turned the victim's skin a stony gray, until all they could do was cry out in a dry, gravelly voice their agony.

The miasma had been a problem for some time, it seemed. Perhaps that was what the Renegades used to inspire a revolt.

Fear kept them from realizing that staying in Feilor would lead them to the same fate as those miners who died before. They did not trust the knights, who they believed were there to continue their suffering.

But the knights managed to convince many of them that they were safer following them. They used wagons to transport the townspeople to the hillside east of Feilor. The pure air there would help cleanse them of the miasma.

Veronica was supposed to be on the first wagon out of town, but she snuck away to help round up the civilians. The concerned squire refused to stand idle while Feilor was being destroyed. They had not the time to worry about one soldier.

Even after receiving an antidote, she needed to rest for it to eliminate the poison. But she felt as fit for duty as the moment she arrived.

So long as she could be of help, she would.

As she searched for the townspeople, she found a soldier had fallen unconscious, a squire from the looks of it. She must have gotten separated from her meister knight in the confusion. Veronica hurried to her fellow squire's side and picked her up by the arm.

She froze upon seeing her face, but Veronica shook off her hesitation and pulled the squire's arms over her shoulders. Whether or not she wanted her help did not matter—she needed it.

When she made it back to the knights gathered at the edge of town, Lady Victoriah had found her. She was angry that her squire had gone off on her own, after she had been poisoned no less. But she could not raise her voice very loudly to express it.

The miasma was weakening her too.

Seeing that her squire had more energy than her, Lady Victoriah relented and let her squire work. "The moment you slow down, you're out of here." With that said, Lady Victoriah rejoined the effort to finish the evacuation.

It did not seem to be a problem. As Veronica worked, she remained healthy and able. Her heartbeat only fluctuated from exertion and worry, her muscles weighing only from fatigue. She listened with a heavy heart to the people moan over their lungs melting from the ghastly vapor, and began to feel guilty that she could not understand their agony.

It dawned on her how odd that was. She spent as much time running through the miasma as anyone else. Many had already died from it, yet she remained perfectly healthy. Her insides did not burn. Her skin stayed creamy. The polluted air did not even slow her down.

Her thoughts stopped as she felt the air ripple. That had been happening since the miasma began spewing from the ground. And she was rattled every time it did.

She opened her mind and concentrated her magic senses to find out what it was. There was something about it that did not seem natural. She tuned out the low hiss of miasma leaking through the cracks in the ground, and as the world began to quiet around her, she heard something when the air rippled again. It was a scream.

"Veronica!"

She returned to reality to feel Lady Victoriah shake her shoulder. Veronica looked at her with pity as she took her hand in hers. The mighty Wolverine did not look so good. Her face had gone pale. Even when she stopped shaking her, her hand still trembled.

"I am sorry, Lady Victoriah. I was in thought."

"You can be in thought on the road. We're leaving."

More civilians were boarding the wagon behind her. Many of them were low on energy and collapsed immediately upon getting inside. They were coughing violently, barely able to catch their breath without wheezing.

They would not last long if they stayed.

"Lady Victoriah, I think I know what is happening."

"I heard from the civilians. Miasma—" she paused to cough, "—coming in from the mines. It's made them dangerous for months, and now it's spreadi—" Another angry cough made her stop altogether.

"I mean, I think I know what is causing it."

Lady Victoriah somehow managed to stifle her hacking voice to listen.

"I've been feeling magic pulse through the air for a while now. It's coming from the mine, along with the miasma. I think it might be causing it to spread."

She was not certain about that until now. She tracked traces of energy emanating from the vapor as it flowed into the air. She swore that she recognized it, but she could not recall from when. All she could tell was that it seemed to be guiding the miasma.

Magic flowed freely through the world, but it was not strong enough to cause such disorder on its own. It had to be guided by something.

Lady Victoriah seemed skeptical, but she always put faith in her squire's perception. "From the mine, huh?"

"Yes."

Her gaze remained on the caverns toward the opposite side of town, intrigued but troubled. "Then there's nothing for it now," she said ruefully. "The miasma will be all over the mines. No one can explore them without succumbing." She looked her squire firmly in the eye. "All we can do is get out of here alive."

It was true. If an ordinary person were to delve into the mines, they would be a corpse before long. But Veronica was not an ordinary person.

"I can."

"What?"

"Look at me—I am perfectly healthy. The miasma isn't affecting me at all. I can go into the mines and find the cause. If I can dispel it, the town will be saved."

"No, that's too great a risk. I'll not have you go on a suicide mission."

Lady Victoriah tightened her grip on Veronica's shoulder and urged her toward the wagon. It was fairly tight, but not enough to keep her held in place.

"With all due respect, milady, I do not see how you can stop me."

Before a rebuttal could be given, she slipped free of Lady Victoriah's grip and ran straight for the mines.

"Veronica!" Lady Victoriah tried to pursue her squire, but she fell to the ground gasping for breath. "G-Get ... back here...!"

A pang beat against her chest for leaving Lady Victoriah to hack her lungs out. Ignoring it induced another, but she had to keep going.

If anyone could save the town, it was her.

The air inside the mines was stained violet from the thick clouds of miasma. It remained steady, swirling only when movement cut through it.

The darkness parted from the glow of the lantern Veronica carried. Several were left near the entrance by the previous workers, and the one she borrowed had plenty of oil left inside.

The path was straightforward in the beginning. After going so far, though, there were more to choose from. One wrong turn would waste too much time, and there was no telling how deep each path went. Thankfully, the energy that lingered in the miasma became more potent in one direction in particular, creating a trail for her to follow.

The vapor became thicker the deeper she went, but no matter how much miasma she inhaled, Veronica was perfectly fine.

How it unnerved her every time she recalled she was different from ordinary human beings. It was only because she was a Nascitte, however, that she managed to press on.

When revived by their spirit, a Nascitte developed a powerful resistance to what first killed them. Finding herself immune to elements that would erode her from the inside out, it stood to reason that she died from an illness of some sort.

She had been told she was so frail as a baby.

Though it would not kill her, the miasma had such an acrid flavor. Every breath she took was enough to make her eyes water. For once, she was thankful that she could not smell; it would have overwhelmed her otherwise.

The burgeoning fog blocked out the lantern's light after going so deep. Soon, the cavern walls and the uneven floor had been erased, leaving only a violet void.

Perhaps this was what it was like to descend into the gate of the seven hells.

She had already gone so far. Turning back was not an option, even if the two-faced gatekeeper himself was the cause of this.

Suddenly walking into a wall made her think she had lost her way. Veronica tottered backward, rubbing the bruise forming at her forehead from bumping into a pointed stone. In putting her hand before her, she felt a bumpy surface. The ground shaking must have caused a cave-in.

The trail only led one way, and it was right before her.

Time was running out. Rather than consider an alternate route, Veronica put the lantern down and began pulling the stones out of place. She picked up and hurled them behind her one by one until her fingers could no longer pry them loose. She could feel something on the other side. All that stood in her way was a thin layer of rubble.

Taking the chance, Veronica backed up several steps before running at the wall, ramming into it shoulder first.

The thinned wall broke apart, and she went tumbling down a rugged slope. Her body was battered once she reached the bottom, sliding along gravel. Upon pushing herself up on her knees, she found what she had been searching for.

It was as she feared. That scream she heard belonged to a phantom.

Its silhouette, surrounded in a glaring blue light, was huddled in the corner, arms wrapped around its legs, its head buried in its knees. Slender in shape, it appeared to be of a young man.

Veronica stepped toward him slowly so as not to startle him. He seemed vulnerable, but the energy he exuded was pure malice. It spread through the air, possessing the miasma itself and causing it to amass.

It was the same as what happened to the conjoined phantoms. This one became powerful enough to affect the physical plane in some way.

"Hello? What are you doing here?"

No response.

"My name is Veronica. What is yours?"

All that came from her speaking was the phantom's malice continuing to grow. The miasma flowed forth from the earth more intensely.

He can't hear you.

Veronica did not want to agree with the voice echoing in her mind. It was not often that her other self spoke directly to her; their knowledge was usually just imparted unto one another.

It was true, though. Malice had consumed him. All she could feel from him was a haunting hatred.

The revolt must have awakened him, and I don't think it reminded him of anything pleasant.

Veronica raised her head. "What can we do now?"

What we must. If we don't, then everyone else will die.

Again, she was right. This one's malice was great. It would not fade even if he succeeded in destroying Feilor.

Tragedy begat tragedy, and from it would come more suffering, more that would seek vengeance, even from beyond.

Perhaps he could not be given peace, but he could not be allowed to rob others of their peace either.

Her arm felt heavy as she reached it for her waterskin and opened the cap. In raising her hand, the water flowed from it.

Her Second Verse was the only thing that could end his suffering. Veronica continued to tell herself that as she shaped the water into a short spear.

"I pray that you may forgive me."

With a thrust of her arm, the spear was guided through the phantom's head. The eerie blue light surrounding him scattered upon the exorcising blow, turning a bright silver. As his silhouette faded, so, too, did the silver light, glimmering like stars until flicking away.

Veronica sat in the darkness for a few moments. Even after saying her piece, she felt it necessary to pray. She always pled with Lady Cural to guide the souls of those who departed from the world, and for those slain by her hand, she also begged forgiveness from Great Gaia for harming her precious lambs.

As she finished her prayer, she stopped hearing the *hiss* of miasma leaking through cracks in the earth. When she opened her mouth, the polluted air was still foul, but the taste was thinning.

In crawling up the unsteady slope back to her lantern, she saw its light beam through the vapor once again. Without the phantom's influence, the miasma was starting to dissipate.

Her mission done, she returned to the surface to face her punishment.

The town was empty by the time Veronica reemerged. The only soul left to greet her was Lady Victoriah, who remained behind to wait for her squire's return.

She was more than furious. Were she not so enfeebled by the miasma, she would have grabbed her shoulders and shaken her like a rag doll.

After barking at her for being disobedient and negligibly reckless, covering the girl's face in spit, Lady Victoriah asked about what happened down below. As upset as she was, she knew the miasma disappearing was her doing.

Her meister knight would not accept anything less than the truth. But convincing her that the cause of their turmoil was a phantom, that they were real, was much easier than expected. "After everything I've been through with you, it's not something I can dismiss outright," she put it.

After hearing that, telling her the rest felt less troubling.

With their work done, Veronica and Lady Victoriah rode to meet with the survivors. They had their horses move at a steady trot so they would not overexert themselves. Lady Victoriah spent the night listening to her squire speak of her encounters with phantoms. It amused her enough to make the time go by faster, and help her forget about her weakened state.

When they arrived at the encampment at sunrise, the knights and townspeople were elated to see Lady Victoriah's safe return. The civilians were very apologetic upon greeting her. It seemed the one who tried to shoot her was a Renegade, the one that riled them up in the first place.

There was still much to address. Though weak and weary, Lady Victoriah prolonged rest for a little longer to hear about what the knights learned, including what incited the violence. The mayor of Feilor himself seemed nervous about speaking with the Wolverine.

In the meantime, though, Veronica had been ordered to rest. She obeyed so as not to exhaust her meister knight any further. Curious though she was, she would hear about everything later.

Lady Victoriah was not in any danger. There were no more Renegades among them, just tired and agitated people.

There were many tents to rest in, but she chose to visit one in particular. With the directions she received from a knight on guard duty, she learned of which tent the squire she rescued was in.

She was nervous when she found it. She took a deep breath to calm her nerves. And upon entering, she found the squire was asleep. It tempted her to leave, but she remained, sitting beside the squire and waiting for her to wake. If nothing else, Veronica had to know she was okay.

"Veronica?"

In hearing her name called, she realized she had nearly drifted off into slumber herself. She opened her eyes and saw that the squire was the one to call her. "Oh ... hello, Sashan."

It had been so long since they last met. Veronica still felt apprehensive about being near the girl who treated her so callously during their time as pages. The lingering silence between them made her feel all the more awkward.

"Excuse me."

Now fully awake, she realized there was no more need for her to be there. She was alive. That was all she needed to know.

"Wait."

Although hesitant to do so, Sashan sounded concerned. Her hand tense against the tent flap, Veronica ignored her better judgment and looked back to the girl lying in the animal skin blankets.

Sashan's lips pressed together, but she pushed herself to speak. "You were the one who got me out of the miasma."

Veronica nodded.

Sashan's uneasy gaze settled and her shoulders sank, letting go of her tension as best as she could. "...Thank you."

Veronica turned around, her hands clasped together. "You are a fellow soldier. I could not just abandon you to your fate."

"No, I mean ..." The words failed her. Welling frustration contorted her face as much as fatigue. One of her hands clenched around the blanket covering her legs.

She was still as proud as ever, reluctant to offer a kind word to someone she so deeply detested. But that very pride would not allow her to leave silent what needed to be said when it was owed.

In the past, Veronica protected her; now she saved her life. Her pride demanded that she let the due gratitude be known.

"I'm sorry. For everything."

Her words stunned Veronica. Of all the things she thought would pass her lips, an apology was not one of them.

Having put that in the open, Sashan was able to better articulate. "You have always been nothing but kind and cordial to me. And I've repaid that kindness with venom and spite. You didn't deserve it. I'm sorry."

It would have been prudent to accept her apology, but instead Veronica said, "But ... you have always said it was only an act."

Sashan nodded and averted her gaze, still feeling awkward herself, but she looked back at Veronica. "When you left with the Champion of Heart, your friend told me about your ... split personality. I did not believe her at first. I told her that she was madder than—" She turned away to cough a husky cough. Her eyes wandered and would not look her way again. "Anyway, I thought it made sense after a while. You became so different then. Your behavior. Your voice. Even your swordsmanship."

Hearing that Cheryl told her about her other self was hard to swallow. She always told her not to say anything about it, for it would only sound like an excuse.

But at least Sashan came to understand. "So, I am sorry. I hope that you can forgive me for the abhorrent way I treated you."

Even after everything that had happened, Veronica never held it against her. She knew that she had her reasons.

And now that she knew about her other self, she had something to say as well. "I can't fault you for being angry for your friend. What happened to him was rather brutal, after all."

Sashan looked back at Veronica, perplexed. "I thought you don't know about what the other you does."

A guilty smile drew along her face. "She and I reconnected during the Rite of Chivalry. I learned quite a lot, even about the things she did." Her smile vanished. It was not a pleasant thing to remember, but after all the anger it brought her, Sashan deserved to know. "Marc was rather taken with me, I understood. But I could not return his affections. I did not know what to say. I was flustered, and he was behaving very brazenly. When he said he would 'not take no for an answer,' that was when she assumed control, and my memory of that time fizzled out."

This new information puzzled Sashan. It remained to be seen whether it enlightened or enraged her. She just stared at Veronica with a restrained expression.

Unintentionally, Veronica peered at Sashan's valsara, and kept herself from wincing at the sight of the storm of clashing emotions in her. The anger was clear as day, as was her grief and uncertainty. But as she contemplated her emotions in silence, the storm dispersed and, slowly but surely, died down.

She took a deep breath. Upon exhaling, her stare became free of angst. "Marc was always a pushy one. It doesn't surprise me that he would make you feel so uncomfortable."

For the first time since hearing her voice, Veronica felt she could breathe easy again. Her muscles relaxed and her apprehension dwindled.

"Still, I'd like to speak with this other you some time." Sashan narrowed her brows, groaning, and shook her head. "...This is confusing. What do you call that shrew anyway?"

She wanted a name so she would not have to compare Veronica to her other self, perhaps as a courtesy as well as a means to simplify this identity crisis. But while they were different, Veronica would not acknowledge her as anyone other than who she was. She deserved as much after being overlooked for so long.

"She is Veronica, just as I am. We are one and the same, even if we do see things differently."

Her answer only made Sashan arch an eyebrow.

"I am sorry if that is confusing."

Sashan tried to smile and appear cordial. "Well, perhaps you could tell me about it. If you have the time, of course."

The smile Veronica wore lost its rigidness and became one of genuine joy. "I would be happy to." She walked back to Sashan and sat with her.

The last time they were so close to each other, they were fighting. Truthfully, Veronica still felt a little skittish being so close to her. But Sashan extended her hand in friendship and tried to get to know her better. It was only right that Veronica gave her the chance to. After all, she wanted to be her friend too.

~ Seventeenth Chapter ~

In Times of War

The unrest created by the Renegades led Lady Victoriah and her squire throughout Vermalio. With the intel collected and relayed to her by Lady Ivanstronge's spies, the Champion of Heart dealt a blow to the Renegades wherever she went.

From repressing full-scale sieges to uncovering plots to wound the kingdom, to tracking Renegade activity, they gave their all to protect their country from those who were actively working to destroy it.

Though they claimed their mission to be righteous, the Renegades have created conflict after conflict, their battles laying waste to every place they hoped to "unshackle from the king's lies." Innocent people were caught in the carnage, the mad warriors drowning their streets in blood.

It was a war of their own making.

In following the latest intel handed to them, Lady Victoriah and Veronica journeyed to the perilous Sperov Mountains. The mountain range was one of the grandest purities in Vermalio, a mountain range perpetually blanketed in ice and snow. Few dared to go there, and fewer returned.

But Lady Victoriah did not fear the pure land, and with courage unrivaled, she tracked the Renegade faction they were hunting to their hideout halfway up the southernmost mountain.

The Renegades would not allow themselves to be captured. They were the informants, more vital to their cause than the fighters that threw themselves at the knights. Desperate to keep their knowledge out of enemy hands, the Renegades called down an avalanche that swallowed them and their hideout.

The intel was lost, as was whatever lead Vermalio might have gained from it.

But what was most important was that the knight and her squire escaped with their lives. Sometimes, that was all that mattered; Lady Victoriah often said so.

They rested at the foot of the mountain that night.

At dawn, Veronica was told the delightful news that they would ride to Russalin for a brief respite. They had not returned to the peaceful village for many months, their travel plans constantly compromised in dealing with the Renegades.

She missed Lyn and Jerrell. They were always a delight to be around.

Since they were already on the edge of Southern Valley, it only seemed appropriate to visit them. They must have been worried about them since the escalation in Renegade activity.

They rode south to the expansive plains that always greeted them before reaching the village. The sun began to make its descent. Seeing as they were so close, they had their horses slow to a steady pace so they could recover from their long run.

The open stretch of land always had a fair breeze going through, cool and refreshing. Its gentle caress made the spirited horses whinny. Veronica stoked Nightshade's mane as she trotted. As much as she loved to run, even she had her limits, and she reached hers about ten miles back in trying to make good time.

Such a faithful horse, just like her senior. "You work so hard. I'll be sure to get you a treat when we get to Russalin."

Lady Victoriah looked to her squire with a fond smile. "We'll have to get you something too."

"You really don't have to, milady."

"Of course I do! We couldn't properly celebrate your coming-of-age while we were on the road."

Veronica had recently turned seventeen, a milestone every Vermalian recognized as a child becoming an adult. And Lady Victoriah was very disappointed that they could not stop fighting to celebrate.

Birthdays were very important to her, something Veronica learned when Cheryl gave her a charm blessed by Great Gaia for missing her sixteenth birthday. How worried she looked back then, so unlike the collected woman she was. She acted like she had broken a sacred rule in front of the gods.

And a child's seventeenth birthday was their most important one.

"Every girl should have something to commemorate their becoming a woman. It's a very big deal."

"Really, you do not need to worry yourself so. I am just happy that you remembered."

"Well, you'll be even happier when you taste the cake I'm going to make you."

Veronica's eyes shot wide open. "Cake?"

Lady Victoriah's smile grew into a proud smirk. "Oh, that gets your attention, huh?" she said knowing full well how much her squire liked sweets. "The best cake is made with Russalin's flour, and baked by me. Soft, sweet, and moist—every bite is a slice of heaven."

Thinking about it almost made Veronica's mouth water.

Her excitement must have shown because Lady Victoriah started laughing. She started to look excited herself, perhaps in thinking about how Veronica would react to the culinary creation she had in mind.

The anticipation made her squire giggle.

There was never a dull day with Lady Victoriah, and Veronica was grateful for every second spent by her side.

While contemplating aloud what gift she should get her squire, maybe to excite her even more, Lady Victoriah kept her eyes fixated on the horizon. The boundless blue sky captivated her, as did its cottony white clouds. No matter where they went, it was always there to relax her.

After looking at it for so long, the calm in her valsara became disrupted.

A dark cloud blotted out the great blue. It was nothing too big, certainly not one that would promise much of a storm. Nevertheless, Lady Victoriah had Timberhoof speed up a little. Veronica had Nightshade followed suit. After going so far, they saw that the dark cloud had a tail, and in following it, they saw the sky becoming smeared black. More trails came from the land, gathering over the hills they rode toward.

It was smoke.

Wasting not a moment more, knight and squire directed their mounts into full sprints. The warhorse and mare, abandoning their fatigue, raced across the plains at breakneck speed. The once pleasant breeze lashed at their riders like a maelstrom, and the once fresh air suddenly felt harsh on their lungs.

The smoke blocked out the sky as they neared the village, with only slivers of light coming through. When they scaled the tallest hill, they looked on with horror. Russalin was under siege.

The crop fields had been reduced to ash, and fires were consuming the houses. The clamor of conflict roared from within the village, dispelling the ominous silence at its outskirts.

Veronica tried not to look upon the fresh corpses they passed to reach the village. There was nothing they could do for them. But the same could not be said for those struggling to survive.

A row of people armed to the teeth with weapons awaited them, and when they saw a knight approaching, they nocked their bows. They were Renegades. Lady Victoriah protected herself with her shield as her warhorse fearlessly charged at their enemies, trampling them beneath his hooves.

The path immediately cleared, Lady Victoriah and Veronica came to the marketplace, where more Renegades were about to torch another house. A man burst forth from the door before they could and charged at the one holding the torch with a hatchet in hand. Another Renegade blocked him with his sword and pushed him to the ground, keeping him pinned there to watch his home be burned.

Veronica hurled a lobe of water their way, putting out the fire not a moment too soon. While they were off guard, Lady Victoriah threw her shield at the Renegade restraining the civilian, knocking him in the head. By the time the others readied to counterattack, the Renegades had been cut down by the knight's sword and pulverized by her squire's power.

Lady Victoriah dismounted and helped the man up. "Where are the other knights?"

"They fell back to the square. There were so many... So many..." The man could not remain calm. He started hyperventilating and tottered backward, coming to lie against the wall of his home. "My grandfather ... he was in the fields. Tell me you saw him. Please, Lady Victoriah."

Veronica felt a pang of remorse in her chest. If he was in the fields, they might well have seen him, but he would not be coming back.

They had not the time to panic. Lady Victoriah grabbed the man by the shoulder, forcing him to remain steady. "Stay hidden. We'll look for him when we've routed the enemy."

"But—"

"We've got a village to protect, but this home is yours. Make sure your grandfather has a place to come back to."

The man was on the verge of a panic attack, but he forced himself to take a deep breath and steady himself. Whatever he feared, he knew she was right. He picked up his hatchet and returned inside.

As he said, the knights took their last stand in the square. They were being overwhelmed by the Renegades' great numbers. A sea of murderous men blocked the Champion of Heart's advance, but the tides of battle were about to change.

With only their enemies before them, nothing kept Veronica from letting her power run rampant. She gathered water into the shape of a massive serpent and sent it into the fray. The water serpent tore through the Renegade forces, mowing them down with its massive body, sending them flying with flails of the head and tail. When it raised its head high, it opened its massive maw and took a bite out of a burly man with a mace. Its body broke apart as the enemy regathered, shooting sharp scales at them.

When the spectacle ended, Lady Victoriah charged into the fray to pick apart those still standing.

The Renegades began to falter as the rear of their party was compromised. Seeing Victoriah the Wolverine's return bolstered the knights' morale, and they seized this chance to push back against the enemy.

Veronica caught up with her meister knight while repulsing the enemies within reach. Continuously gathering the water she used around her rapier, she slammed it against them like a flail, scattering countless droplets into the air.

With her power and Lady Victoriah's ferocity, they managed to level the playing field enough for the knights of Russalin to take charge.

"Lady Victoriah!"

A lone soldier broke from his rank to fight his way to the Champion of Heart's side. He called out her name and lifted his visor when she had her mount stop before him.

"You must hurry home!"

"What?"

"A large group broke from their ranks and circled the village. They're after Sir Jerrell!"

Without another word, Lady Victoriah nudged her mount to run full speed past the conflict. Veronica followed posthaste. At their top speed, they managed to cut through the village in no time. But when they did, they saw the smoke brewing at the top of the hillside.

Panic rushed through Lady Victoriah's valsara. "Timberhoof, hurry!"

Sensing her dismay, the warhorse picked up speed, his hooves beating against the ground so hard it sounded like thunder. Nightshade could barely keep up, but she gave it her all to remain close to Timberhoof.

Their hopes began to darken like the smoky sky above.

More knights were found on the trail. They must have been following the enemy after they noticed where they were going. They put up a good fight, seeing as there were just as many Renegades lying beside them. Valiant until the very end.

Nothing got in their way as they ascended, but the further they went, the more they felt an oppressive force crushing them. A bright light stabbed their eyes from atop the cape, where the cottage stood.

Veronica gripped her reins as her chest tightened around her lungs. She prayed to the gods that it was not too late. She pled for Great Gaia to watch over her poor lambs; for Lord Ralias to protect the war-torn man and the sinless woman; for Lady Sundralla to bless them with the fortune to escape the flames; for Zyleec, child god of the wind, to stir a storm and douse the fire.

The infernal flames had completed consumed the cottage. They had grown so fierce that simply coming to the top of the hill made it feel like they would be burned away.

A corpse lay under its blazing light, pointing to a man and a woman by the cliff.

Lady Victoriah and Veronica jumped off their horses and hurried to their side. Lyn turned to them in shock, perhaps fearing they were a threat. Her hands were covered in blood.

"Jerrell!" Lady Victoriah ran to her husband and fell to her knees.

Veronica froze when she saw the wound Lyn was struggling to treat. Blood flowed ceaselessly from the crevice dug over his right breast.

Jerrell, pale and wheezing, looked to his wife. "Victoriah ... I'm sorry..."

Lady Victoriah took his hand in hers, squeezing it tight. "Don't ... don't apologize. You didn't do anything wrong."

"The last thing I ... wanted to do ... was leave you alone..."

She raised her other hand to his cheek, caressing it tenderly. "But I'm not alone. You're here with me. You've always been with me ... remember?"

Weak though he was, Jerrell still managed to muster a smile. His fingers slowly curled around her hand, fighting desperately to remain with her longer.

The light flickering in his eyes began to dim. "Victoriah..." He said her name again and again, until breathing his last.

Tears fell onto Jerrell's face as Lady Victoriah felt her husband's head become heavy and his hand lose its grip of hers. Grief overcoming her, she let go of Jerrell's hand to lean down and hold him close. His blood stuck to her breastplate as she bawled into his shoulder, her shrill cries drowning out the roar of the flames devouring their home.

Veronica could not look any longer. She turned away, burying her face in her hands. Her tears seeped between her fingers.

Jerrell was a good man. He did not deserve to die. But he had been taken from his family—taken by them.

Those monsters ... will pay!

Lady Victoriah hurried back to the village to finish the Renegades off. Veronica followed with Lyn at her back, not wanting to leave her alone. The safest place for her was with them.

The knights of Russalin had almost entirely routed the enemy by then. They surrounded what remained of the main force as they fought to escape, keeping them in place. Victory was no longer an option for the Renegades, so they simply decided to take out as many knights as they could before being struck down themselves.

Lady Victoriah shoved the knights out of her way until they made an opening for her, allowing her to see that the only one still alive was their captain. The Renegade captain looked to the Wolverine stalking toward him, and reeled from the sheer malice he felt from her.

Her grip tightened around her sword. She raised the blade, making the Renegade shudder, and sheathed it.

The Renegade captain, foolishly assuming she left herself open to attack, charged at Victoriah the Wolverine. His sword fell upon her, missing as she stepped to the side. Before he could react, she grabbed his wrist and twisted it hard, the sound of cracking bones coming before the screams. The enemy's sword dropped to the ground as he fell to his knees.

Lady Victoriah threw her other fist into his chest, knocking him onto his back. She stepped on his stomach to keep him in place, the impact making him cough up blood.

His life was not the only thing she was after. His attack robbed her of her husband—she wanted him to suffer for it.

The knights hollered and cheered as Victoriah the Wolverine beat the enemy captain senseless. They called for more as she grabbed him by the collar and slammed him against the ground. They all craved his suffering. They all wanted him to bleed as their people had bled, to suffer through all of the pain and anguish they had to endure.

Even Veronica, having surrendered to her rage, took delight in seeing such brutality. He deserved it after what he had done, after all of the people he and his allies scarred and slaughtered.

...But—

The longer it went on, the more it began to unnerve her, and as her gentler self assumed control once more, it terrified her. She no longer recognized her dear meister knight, who now resembled the beast she embodied. And the other soldiers, their shadows were distorted by the flames devouring their town, revealing something inhumane in them.

Unable to take anymore, she rushed through the crowd. Just before Lady Victoriah was about to throw her unforgiving fist down at her victim again, Veronica grabbed hold with both arms and pulled her back.

"Stop! Stop it!"

"Let go of me!" Lady Victoriah tried to throw her off, but Veronica held tight with all of the strength she had. "Let go, damn it!"

"He's already dead!"

The enraged Wolverine stopped flailing a moment to stare. She looked at Veronica like she thought her mad, but in turning back to the Renegade, she finally noticed. His face had been pulverized, left nothing more than a massive smear in the dirt.

"You already killed him. You can't hurt him anymore, so please stop!"

His valsara had faded, and she kept pummeling the empty shell anyway. She and everyone else had gotten swept away in their rage to the point they only desired the complete erasure of the object of their hate.

Meanwhile, their village still burned. The civilians still alive were hiding or wandering around, dreading their end.

The moment she realized her folly, Lady Victoriah unclenched her fist. Veronica took a step away from her as she stood. Lady Victoriah looked down at the man she had beaten to death in utter shock; she did not even realize how much damage she had done in her rage. Then she looked to her hand, coated in the blood of her victim, staring at it as it grew cold.

Clenching her fist, she turned to the other knights, who seemed as baffled by what they were doing as she was. "What are you maggots gawking at?" she angrily proclaimed. "Douse those fires! Search for survivors! Get your arses moving now!"

The knights scrambled into action at her command. They scattered in every direction in teams, ensuring no one was alone should any Renegades remain.

Lady Victoriah gasped heavily, then composed herself as she faced her squire. "Veronica."

"Y-Yes, milady?"

"Help these fools put out the fires, then tend to the injured."

"...What will you do?"

The Wolverine took her sword back in hand. "I'm going to sweep the village. If there are any more Renegades here, they won't be for long." Rage still seethed from her valsara, oppressive and unrelenting. And it would not relent until those who threatened her home were gone.

Without delay, Veronica went to handle the fires.

Russalin survived, though as a husk of its former self. Over two hundred of its people were slaughtered. Its fields were left in a state of ruin. A third of its buildings fell to the flames before they finally died out.

The only ones roaming the streets were the knights working to repair the damage and those who lost their homes in the attack. Everyone else was too afraid to come out of hiding.

Lady Victoriah tirelessly oversaw the efforts to lighten the burden of the citizenry. She would not let her losses keep her from helping those still suffering. It was as much to follow her duty as it was to honor Jerrell's memory.

No one wanted tragedy to befall their village, but they were well prepared to weather the aftermath. The food stores, which were thankfully left untouched during the carnage, preserved enough to last the people throughout the month. Requests for aid were sent to the neighboring settlements. Given the importance of their trade with Russalin, they would respond forthwith. Within three days' time, Russalin would have more protection while they rebuilt.

The village had seeds stocked away as well, in case a natural disaster hit and ruined their crops. But unless new plots were prepared, they would have no place to grow. The old fields needed time before they could yield crops again.

It took some effort convincing the farmers to step out of the village and tend the fields again. It could not be helped. This was the first time the Renegades were bold enough to lay siege to Russalin. Most of the people there knew nothing of the terror the Renegades wrought, and to learn of it firsthand left them crippled with fear.

She could not erase that fear, but Veronica managed to sway a few to follow her to the fields. Seeing her power at work put them at ease, and all of her innocent questions about farming made them feel somewhat lighthearted. She even offered to help prepare the new seedbeds.

Once reinforcements arrived, a sense of stability began to return. More farmers left their homes for the fields, reassured by the vast number of soldiers there to watch over them. Many who lost their homes relied on the kindness of their neighbors for shelter and were provided rations by the mayor.

When Lady Victoriah finally allowed herself some rest, she returned up the hill overlooking Russalin.

Veronica worried for her deeply, but she knew she needed time to herself. Losing someone precious, it could crush even the strongest of people. She remained in the village with Lyn, delivering rations to those who needed it.

The kindly woman worked hard to maintain the smile she wore for everyone else's benefit. But inside, Lyn was struggling to hold herself together. No doubt she had grown close to the man she looked after.

He protected her in the attack, and she made her first kill to keep him alive, however long she could.

The soldiers were very accommodating to allow Lyn to stay in the women's barracks with Lady Victoriah and Veronica. Even with the bed to rest in and the roof over her head, though, she could not sleep. She tried not to let it show to keep from troubling her companions, but they became a comfort she knew she needed.

When they finished their work, Lyn asked Veronica to make one last delivery to Lady Victoriah.

"I'm sure she could use some comforting herself."

Lyn always had a way of knowing what her dear charges needed, so Veronica nodded and left to climb the hill.

It was already sunset when she reached the top. She found Lady Victoriah kneeling by the burnt wreckage of her home. Veronica took slow, quiet footsteps as she approached, careful not to alarm her.

Her meister knight was covered in soot from sorting through the wreckage. Her eyes rested on something in her hands. It looked to be the portrait that once hung over the fireplace, the one with her and her family. But all that remained of it was the rightmost corner with her in it. The side with her husband had been burned away, as had the baby she held in her arms. Loneliness rippled in her valsara as she sat there, taking in what was left of the portrait—of the reality she was now in.

Veronica, unable to ignore her loneliness, went to her side.

Lady Victoriah did not even flinch when her squire cupped her shoulder. "How's it going down there?" Lost though she was in her grief, she seemed to recognize who approached.

She would not look her way, and Veronica would not force her to.

"Everything is going orderly, Lady Victoriah. Though unrest is still prominent, the reconstruction is proceeding without incident."

"Good, good..."

Lady Victoriah put down the empty portrait and grunted as she stood. Still not looking her squire's way, she paced over to the cliff, avoiding the spot where her husband died. The grass there was still stained crimson.

Veronica remained close. Whether she wanted her there or not, she could not leave her alone now.

The sunlight glistened beautifully along the fields. The light was heavenly, a boon from Lady Sundralla to soothe them in this trying time. Alas, it had a bittersweet effect on the broken village. The only thing to make the scene less dreary was the farmers at hard work and the knights guarding them.

Knowing her to be a benevolent god with gracious intent, Veronica bowed her head and clasped her hands together.

"Who are you praying to?"

Her meister knight's question surprised her. It was not something she usually asked. "Lady Sundralla."

A dry chuckle escaped her. Perhaps it would seem ironic to pray to the goddess of luck after what had transpired. But, surprising her even more, she joined Veronica in prayer with a fist clenched over her heart.

The times that she offered prayers to the gods were few, though not because she lacked faith. Lady Victoriah always believed in answering her own prayers and not overly relying on divine intervention. Whenever she addressed the gods, it was only for something important.

When they raised their heads again, Lady Victoriah finally looked to her squire. Her face was pale and her eyes red. "Are you doing all right?"

Considerate words, but they made Veronica frown. "Please, milady, do not worry about me."

"And why not?" she asked curtly, trying to sound like her usual self. "You worry about everyone."

Veronica looked to her meister knight, pity heavy in her stare. "I did not lose a husband. Or a home."

Lady Victoriah sighed. "No, I guess not." She took a deep breath and stared at nothing, allowing herself to get lost in her memories. Whatever they were, her face was impassive and her valsara stagnant.

Veronica remained silent while she reflected on her past, watching as she closed her eyes. Processing loss was not easy, not even for a hardened knight.

And Lady Victoriah, she had so little family left in her life.

"I always knew ... that this was how he would go, fighting for someone else. That's who he was—a protector." She paused to clear her throat, keep it from closing from overwhelming sadness. "Every time I left them behind, I always worried that would be the last time I would see them. It ate me alive some days, worrying that I would receive word that they had been killed, and I wouldn't be there for them."

Them. She thought not of just the husband she lost, but also the son she missed with all her heart.

"But I was here ... and I couldn't save him." Her voice trembled a little. She stopped to shake her head. "I failed you, Jerrell... I'm sorry."

For the first time, the indomitable Victoriah the Wolverine looked so fragile, as if she would shatter were something to touch her. Veronica pulled her hand back when she reached out to her, almost fearing that would happen.

But she pushed past the worry to rest her it on her back.

"Jerrell was a fine man, and a true knight—just like you. I'm sure he must have harbored fears of never seeing you again, of something happening to you while you two were apart. But he did see you again." She smiled when Lady Victoriah looked her way again. "He got to see you, the love of his life, before he left this world. I am certain that it brought him peace."

Those soft-spoken words brushed against Lady Victoriah like a cold breeze. She tried to keep from trembling.

Knowing that a loved one had passed was hard, and accepting that they were gone was harder still. But knowing that one had done something for them in their final moments, while bittersweet, brought an ounce of comfort, if nothing more.

Although hesitant, Lady Victoriah turned to the spot where she held her husband's body. Her hand clenched around the grass as it had when she held him. She closed her eyes, fighting back the tears in remembering his last word.

Veronica leaned in to give her a gentle embrace, remaining there for her until Lady Victoriah patted her head.

"It never gets easier," said the knight as Veronica let go. "The role we have taken is never without loss, without strife and heartache. As soldiers, our job is to fight for our kingdom, for our people, and die for them if necessary. The comrades we make become our family—our aunts and uncles, our brothers and sisters, our nieces and nephews. Losing them in the line of duty will always be misery. And if you take one to be something more ..." Her face scrunched up as she kept fighting back the pain roiling in her. "It's like having your heart crumble to dust with them."

Thus was the price of caring for others. Once one let another into their heart, they became a part of it. To lose them was a pain unparalleled.

But what was the alternative? To live with a heart devoid of love, to care for one's self alone? Such an empty existence that would be.

Lady Victoriah lifted her hand to stroke down Veronica's hair. "I won't tell you to dwell on this, but don't forget. This is something everyone must know."

Veronica closed her eyes, giving thought to the weight of that pain while being soothed by her meister knight. "I know it will be hard ... but having such close people in life makes it worth living."

A quiet laugh escaped Lady Victoriah. "Just what I've come to expect from the kingdom's newest knight."

Veronica blinked and raised her head. "Milady?"

She was greeted with a soft smile. "You're ready, Veronica. You're ready to be a knight."

Her throat closed in shock, keeping her from offering a response right away. Of all of the things she expected to hear her say, that was the last to come to mind. "R-Ready? But Lady Victoriah, I do not understand. I have only been your squire for two years now."

"And you think I haven't taught you much in that time, huh?"

"No, no! Far from it. I have learned a great deal from you. You have been a wonderful mentor to me in many ways. But ..." She paused to choose her words carefully, not wishing to contradict herself. "There is still much ... much I do not know."

"You know enough," Lady Victoriah insisted. "You've grown into a fine woman, Veronica. You're strong. You know how to use your environment to your advantage. You're intuitive, brave, committed, and you do what's right. That's how a knight should be."

"But ... but ..."

The smile Lady Victoriah wore became endearing. She could tell what Veronica was thinking.

She was such a wonderful meister knight: strict but fair, tough but kind. It was hard to think that they would part after she had grown so close to her.

And she felt the same way. "Don't get the wrong idea, Veronica. I don't want you gone." Her hand rested back on her squire's head, rubbing her scalp. "You've become like a daughter to me. And the last thing I want, especially now, is to send my daughter away."

Veronica felt warmth calm the tension in her throat and fill her chest and cheeks. It meant a lot for her to say something so sweet. "You do not have to," she insisted. "Most squires remain with their meister knights for three to four years before they reassign them. I could stay with you, and we could keep fighting the Renegades together."

The offer tempted her. She rubbed Veronica's head a little more, then moved her hand down to cup her shoulder. "I wouldn't be a good meister knight if I held you back. I'd only be denying you the chance you deserve." She lifted her other hand to hold her steady, looking to her with a proud smile. "You have what it takes to be a great knight, Veronica. One of the best. You were trained by me, after all."

Her encouraging words brought the saddened squire to smile again.

This meant she and Lady Victoriah would have to part ways. Their adventures together were coming to an end.

But this was what Veronica was after from the start. She was going to be a knight, just as she had been training for since that fateful day.

Sadness about their inevitable parting melted together with the excitement of having reached her goal at long last. Veronica sat back and took one last look back at Russalin. "So ... what happens now?"

"When everything here is sorted out, we'll go back to Brigadier. It's customary for the squires of the Six Champions to be knighted by the king himself. You'll meet with him, he'll instruct you on how the ceremony will go. If we're lucky, I'll get to show you off to Charlie and the other champions."

Veronica giggled. "And after that?"

Lady Victoriah mulled that over for a few moments, saying "Hm..." rather loudly to tease the now excited squire. Then she looked back down at the village. "Should the king agree ... I think I'll have you stationed here for a time."

Veronica blinked again. "Really?"

"Russalin is going to have a cursed time recovering. And now that they know the Renegades are willing to attack them, the people will need someone they can look up to. I need someone I can trust to watch over them while I'm all over the kingdom." Lady Victoriah wrapped her arm around Veronica's shoulder, pulling her close. "I'm sure Lyn will appreciate having you around to talk to."

The idea made Veronica bubbly with excitement. Knowing she trusted her to protect her home while she was away instilled more confidence in her. "I will not let you down, Lady Victoriah."

"I know you won't."

~ Eighteenth Chapter ~
Knighthood

Word of the Renegades' attack on Russalin spread unrest across Vermalio. The discouraged people, realizing their enemy's actions were growing ever more heavy-handed, bolstered their defenses, fearing they would be the next to fall.

But all was not grim in the Kingdom of Valiance, for the people also heard of news that helped foster their hope. The Champion of Heart had decided that her squire was fit to become a knight.

Just hearing that was enough for many on their trail back to the capital to let go of the dread clinging to their hearts, knowing they had another protector fighting for them. Many thought to test this would-be knight's prowess, and were not disappointed with what they found. Veronica felt awkward about fighting before a crowd, but in ceding to Lady Victoriah's insistence, she put on fine shows in every town they visited.

Some were not convinced after seeing her skill, strangely enough. They claimed that she lacked the mettle to be a proper knight; it felt like she was still a page in the Estrine Chateau. And every time that happened, her other self assumed control to show them exactly what they thought they wanted.

Although she still did not enjoy fighting for the sake of fighting, the reassurance she saw in others from witnessing her prowess left her more confident. They saw her as someone they could count on. It filled her with pride and delight.

When Veronica and Lady Victoriah reached the walls of Brigadier, they found that they were expected. Soldiers were lined at the gate, every one of them standing at attention and prompted to raise their spears to form an arch. Meister knight and squire brought their mounts to a trot as they crossed the path of spears to the gate.

A pair of knights in lustrous white armor stood at the end. They saluted them, fists clenched over their hearts. "Welcome back to Brigadier, Lady Victoriah, young Veronica."

The soldiers did not usually greet Veronica when she returned, let alone with such a grand reception. It seemed the matter of their return had already reached them through the rumors spread.

When the gateway opened, the white knights led them inside. More soldiers stood ceremoniously in the street, forming a well-guarded path that led to a carriage. Several more such knights awaited on horseback around the carriage, all armed with spears. A man stood among the soldiery, one clad in exquisite robes made of the finest silk.

Veronica's heart quickened when she saw a vermillion circlet atop the man's head, and she gripped her reins at the sight of the silver gem resting on his forehead. Only one wore such a crown.

She dismounted her horse as Lady Victoriah had.

"Your Majesty," said Lady Victoriah as she bowed her head to him.

It was the Vermalian king, Faustign L. S. Vermalio.

Veronica felt her heart stop when his brilliant red eyes fell on her, and bowed her head to hide her anxious face. She still felt his gaze upon her, but it was not critical, rather a gentle one. And when raising her head to look his way, he greeted her with a kindly smile.

He resembled Prince Aeron, though the king's visage was rather sage.

"The famed Veronica. I am pleased to finally meet you face-to-face."

His venerable presence put Veronica at ease, at least somewhat. She stood straight to look the king in the eye and offered a fair smile. "It is an honor, Your Majesty."

They had yet to meet since the king was always away whenever Lady Victoriah returned to Brigadier and vice versa. Lady Victoriah seemed to feel somewhat guilty about that; she was oddly tense.

"I apologize for not introducing you sooner," she said with her hands behind her back, looking oddly formal.

The king's smile broadened as he let out a soft laugh. "Please, it is all right, milady. We were both where we were needed, as these trying times demand." His attention shifted back to the soldier at her side. "And now we have a new knight to help us face them."

The young lady was grinning ear to ear as she stood before both her mentor and her king.

In boarding his carriage, King Faustign led them through the city. His party of Holy Knights formed a protective circle around the carriage, as well as the Champion of Heart and her squire.

As they marched across Brigadier, the people stopped to watch them go by. Some were in awe of the knights, others excited that they caught a glimpse of the king. But many eyes rested on Veronica herself.

She looked the way of those who saw her, curious at first. Then she gave each person a little wave. It earned a smile from almost everyone. Some of the children at play even waved back.

To think she used to be so nervous about having this kind of attention.

Some people had gathered along the palace gate, all to see the knights and king. They looked to them with delight and hope.

It was reassuring to see so many still had faith in them.

It still felt strange entering the palace grounds, and going inside in tow of the Holy Knights did not make Veronica less uncomfortable. It was not the grandeur of the vast grounds or even the presence of the knights in white. A noble herself, she was used to being in places such as this. Yet there was something about it that made her feel like she should not have been there, that she did not belong.

It is just nerves, she reassured herself. If she truly did not belong there, Lady Victoriah would never have picked her for her squire.

The Holy Knights rode with the king until his carriage stopped before the palace entrance, then dispersed. One took Timberhoof and Nightshade with her so that they could rest in the stables. The king then showed Lady Victoriah and Veronica inside.

Waiting for them at the palace doors was an elegant brunette woman in a verdant dress. She also wore a circlet, hers with wing patterns carved into the sides.

"Queen Selenee!" Veronica greeted the elegant woman excitably.

The queen wore a cheerful smile upon recognizing the young lady. "Hello again, Veronica, dear."

While she tended to miss the king, Veronica was fortunate enough to meet Queen Selenee for the first time when she returned to Brigadier a year ago. They got along well; the queen even said she reminded her of her young niece.

The king and queen walked side by side as they showed their champion and her pupil to the throne room, where the knighting ceremony would take place. They briefed Veronica in detail on what would happen so that she would be ready for it. First, she would be summoned to the throne room, led there by her meister knight. When she arrived, she would march up to the king at his throne and kneel before him. Upon swearing her fealty to the kingdom and her liege, King Faustign would take a shield made especially for her, tap her shoulders with it, then present it to her to signify her accepting the responsibility of knighthood and all that it entailed: protecting the people, her comrades-in-arms, and the name of Vermalio itself.

Their summary, while appreciated, made her anxious. To be knighted by the king was something she could only have hoped for; most squires were usually just given the honor by senior knights they would serve, with no ceremony or people to bear witness aside from their meister knight. It was such a momentous occasion, perhaps the most important one of her life.

Her nervousness showed; the giggle from her queen made that quite clear. Veronica tried to hide her reddening face when she saw her.

"If that is too much for you, my dear, I can't imagine how you will feel when you go to greet the people of Brigadier."

Veronica bit the inside of her cheek when looking back to the queen. "I am very grateful for this opportunity, but is it truly necessary to amass a crowd just to greet me into knighthood?"

"But of course. It is not every day that a champion has their squire knighted. And for you to survive Lady Victoriah no less! It is most certainly something that must be seen by all."

Lady Victoriah crossed her arms in hearing that. "It is not as if I would have broken her, Your Highness." Now that she was only before her king and queen, she ceased to stand on ceremony for appearances. Though she spoke with the proper respect, her demeanor was much like it had been with everyone else.

Queen Selenee held up her hand to conceal another laugh. "With how roughly you treat your own, milady, how could anyone be certain?"

Veronica could not help but giggle at the women having their fun with each other. She knew what they were doing, and was appreciative of it. It helped to forget about her apprehension.

"This is as much to recognize your meister knight as it is to celebrate your success, Veronica," explained King Faustign. "With all that my champions do for the kingdom, it is to be admired when one makes the effort to nurture a child's future as well."

Lady Victoriah glanced back at Veronica. "Especially when one is as much of a handful as you."

Her squire held her hands together and playfully glanced away. There were moments when she had to admit she caused her trouble. It must not have been easy teaching her the ways of knighthood while balancing her responsibilities as a champion, even when they braved so many dangers together.

After all that she had done for her, she deserved the recognition.

The time it took to reach the heart of the castle seemed to slip right by them. There, they came to a hall lined with several suits of ornamental armor, at the end of which were two grand doors made of the finest scarlet birch wood. They led to the throne room.

The king stopped with his queen just where the suits of armor stood guard. "The knighting ceremony will be held tomorrow at midday. Until then, I do hope you will enjoy your stay. If there is anything you require, do not hesitate to ask."

It seemed that was as far as he had planned to take them. It was a bit of a disappointment, after going all that way. Perhaps it was his way of keeping the young lady in suspense of what was to come.

Veronica bowed her head to the king. "You have my gratitude for your wonderful hospitality, my liege, my queen."

Joy reflected in the king's eyes. "It is my pleasure, young lady." His expression began to settle as he set his eyes on his Champion of Heart again. "I must continue with the preparations. If you will excuse me."

So the king went on his way, leaving Queen Selenee with Veronica and Lady Victoriah.

"Shall I show you to your chambers?" the queen suggested.

"Sure," answered Lady Victoriah.

Queen Selenee walked beside her champion and the knight-to-be as they went on. With the formalities out of the way, she sought to enjoy their company.

The queen always delighted in speaking with Lady Victoriah. When in private, they were very open with what they had to say. While the queen was not as blunt as Lady Victoriah, they were actually quite similar. It surprised Veronica when she first noticed, but it was interesting all the same. And the stories they had to share were most entertaining.

Upon getting herself settled in the palace, Veronica decided to visit the Estrine Chateau. She had been escorted there by a pair of Holy Knights, and they remained at the chateau's gates with its guards.

She was rather insistent that she wanted to visit the Estrines alone, which was why Lady Victoriah did not join her. It did not bother them to wait for her; their only concern was getting her safely to the chateau and back, as ordered.

A servant greeted her at the doors, and was escorting her to Lord Estrine's quarters when the august duke himself was stepping out for some air. He was very surprised to see Veronica. She worried that she had come at a bad time, but Lord Estrine assured her that she was more than welcome.

News of her knighting had reached his ears. It made him proud to know that a page his family trained had been accepted as a knight by the champion she left with. As such, he chose to escort her to visit Lady Abeel.

As they walked through the halls of the chateau, Lord Estrine spoke of how they were receiving more recruits in the last two years than they had been annually for a long time. He stated that it was likely in response to the increase in Renegade activity. Many children had arrived from all across Vermalio, notably from places where the Champion of Heart visited during times of crisis.

Veronica was not entirely listening to what Lord Estrine said. Her focus often drifted between him and their surroundings, her gaze shifting every which way when they went into a notably open space.

Lord Estrine noticed and stopped his story to look her way. "Is something the matter? You seem out of sorts."

She looked back his way with a start, giving him an apologetic look. "Please forgive my rudeness, sir. I was merely on the lookout for someone I know."

Fortunately, the Estrine family head did not seem offended. "Ah, I see. You wish to spread the good news to your old page friends."

Veronica nodded. "Yes, sir."

"We can spare a few moments if you see them. But keep in mind, we do not have all day." Lord Estrine turned around to keep shepherding his guest down the hall.

In truth, Veronica was not there to see Lady Abeel. But the Estrines would not have allowed her to traipse through their halls without reason. And they likely would not believe she was there to see a phantom.

If Rubi was still there, she had to see her. What she learned from Lady Ivanstronge and Lady Victoriah could well bring her peace.

Veronica kept her magic senses heightened so that she could detect the presence of phantoms in the vicinity, thinning her focus. If she was there, she would know.

Although, perhaps she would not even need to look for her. Rubi often made a habit of appearing before Veronica on her own accord. When that happened, she would have to find a way to slip away from Lord Estrine.

As she began to ponder that she could use her powers to mislead him, Veronica's mind came to a startling halt. Something suddenly distorted her magic senses, muddling her focus. Her hands drew to her temples to stave off the dizziness it brought.

This feeling was familiar, and filled her heart with dread.

Quickly, she regained her balance and walked past Lord Estrine. Few were the times she felt this unease, but they were times she knew to be afraid. Had her mind not been elsewhere, she might have noticed it sooner. They already arrived in the east wing, where the magic users trained to hone their gifts. Many were practicing spells in the sorcery room they were passing by, unaware of what she sensed.

Concern began to froth from Lord Estrine's valsara as he caught up to Veronica, who was speeding toward the chamber ahead. "Veronica, what is the matter?"

"Something is wrong... Something very, very wrong."

Danger. Someone was in danger. And after going so far from the sorcery room, she feared she knew who.

Unable to go without an answer any longer, Veronica ran to the door of the family sorceress' chamber. Her hand grabbed the knob, and with a twist, the enchantment on it still recognizing her, the door was flung open.

The sight that greeted her made her tremble.

When Lord Estrine came to the doorway, he rushed inside. "Abeel!" He fell to his knees to take the unconscious Lady Abeel into his arms. She had collapsed onto the floor beside a broken teacup. He checked her pulse, then her forehead, then the substance from the cup, desperate to find out what happened to her.

Veronica remained outside the door, paralyzed by what she had seen. Her eyes showed her what normal ones could not. Lady Abeel's valsara, a once powerful presence, had grown faint and weak as it was being eaten away from the inside. The light of her life was dimming and being blotted out by an inky black darkness.

She had hoped, futilely, that what she felt was wrong.

Veronica overcame the dread shackling her and slowly stepped inside. "Lord Estrine, this is ... magic deficiency."

The man became rigid.

Magic deficiency: a terrible ailment that afflicted those who used magic. It drained one of their power—and their very life. Mages were tied to their power physically as well as spiritually. A drastic change in their magic affected their health and, if left unchecked, had disastrous consequences. The pain of having that power sapped from them was often equated to having one's nerves severed, and the more powerful their magic, the worse their suffering.

In most cases, the afflicted suffered until finally perishing. And those few who survived that torture, they became as shells of themselves.

Anguish filled Lord Estrine as he lifted Lady Abeel off the ground. Veronica helped him take her to her bedchambers so she may rest comfortably. The halls were quiet for a while, until the poor woman began to let out these hoarse, anguished groans.

It was only going to get worse.

While Lord Estrine tended to his daughter and other members of his family came after hearing what happened, Veronica waited outside the bedchambers. She leaned against the wall, bereft.

There was no one in the Estrine family she was closer to than Lady Abeel. She was as much of a mentor as she was someone to offer her a kind smile, to counsel her when she felt out of place.

She waited in silence, praying to the gods to have mercy on her.

With the Estrine family in such distress, it was best for her to leave. She could do nothing to help that they were not already doing. If she stayed, she would only be a bother.

As she was escorted out of the chateau by Lord Estrine, Veronica felt deeply ashamed. Seeing what was happening to Lady Abeel, sensing her valsara dwindle away, was truly harrowing. But in turning away from it, it was like she was turning a blind eye to her suffering.

There was nothing anyone could do for one afflicted with magic deficiency, for it had no cure. Only prayer could so much as diminish their pain. Yet she felt she should have been doing more.

A hand gripping her shoulder spooked her out of her melancholy. It was that of Lord Estrine, offering her a gentle squeeze. "It is an agonizing thing—feeling powerless." Tense though he was, the power in his voice did not waver. He retained his stoic countenance and demeanor, projecting an image of strength. "But it is something we all must face. No matter how mighty we may be, we are only human, and we can't protect everyone from everything. Rather than lament what you cannot do, focus on what you can." He softened his grip, then took his hand away to grip his wrist behind his back. "Do that, and Lady Abeel will be proud."

It was then that Veronica felt the weight of her shame and dread gradually leave her. Lord Estrine had to be hurting more than she was. Lady Abeel was his daughter, after all. But he remained composed and stood tall, which made him appear taller than he was. It was no show either. His valsara still shone with resolve.

He would surely grieve when alone, but still he remained strong and reached out to comfort another. The picture of valiance, of a true Vermalian knight—it gave Veronica the strength to do the same.

Sunlight glimmered through the window of the Champion of Heart's chambers. Veronica looked out it from the table she sat at, and saw how the sun hung high over the cathedral. She allowed herself to be lost in the majesty of it so she may clear her mind.

Soon. It was almost time.

Her eyes slid closed. Her chest slowly rose and fell with her steady breathing, her hands clenched over her heart. How it raced. Her heart beat so heavily that it nearly forced her trembling hands away from it.

She had been left alone for some time so that she may have the peace and quiet to reflect on herself, but the solitude only made her more anxious. But why? She had already been through so much, faced trial after trial to prove her skill and resolve. Her meister knight had already dubbed her worthy of knighthood. All she had left to do was swear fealty to the king.

But imagining how that would go made her tremble.

Having knighthood so close that it was within reach made her fear it being denied to her all the more. Her dream was about to become reality, but all she could think about was that it would still be just a dream if she messed up here.

Veronica took another deep breath. It had been such a long time since she felt so nervous. The last time it happened, she reasoned, was when she repeatedly asked her father to let her be a page. She always put on such a brave face every time she tried to convince him, but she was always afraid of being rejected regardless. All she could do when he did was keep training and make him see that she would be a capable warrior.

In thinking back to that stressful time, she remembered why she strived for knighthood. The teachings of the Natural Orthodoxy to do right by their fellow man. The philosophy that her mother taught her and her siblings, noblesse oblige. The stories of valiant knights and their heroism. The loss of her brother Wally. All of those things affected her so deeply, setting her on the path she walked.

She was a knight. All that was needed now was to make it official.

The doorknob rattled and turned. Opening the door was Lady Victoriah. "Veronica."

Veronica quieted her breathing and stood. She joined her soon-to-be former meister knight, who looked down at her with a proud smile. That smile put all of her fears to rest.

They walked together through the halls of the palace. It was very quiet the entire way. Few passed them by apart from a handful of Holy

Knights on patrol and servants scampering to their next task. Preferring not to focus on that, Veronica let her eyes wander. Every hall was decorated with all sorts of valuable things: fancy vases, portraits depicting the purities of the kingdom, ornate swords and shields hung on the walls.

There was always a suit of armor standing within eyesight. Two were together by the staircase they descended, and two more waited at the bottom. Many similar suits were all over the palace, haunting the halls and rooms on every level. Veronica thought they were placed everywhere to offer the visiting nobility a stronger sense of security. The Holy Knights themselves wore more extravagant metal plating, so it seemed odd that the armor would be there simply for looks.

It was certainly interesting to think about.

Once they were on the ground floor and nearing the throne room, Veronica's heart began thumping like before. Lady Victoriah glanced her way upon hearing her let out a shaky breath. Veronica tried to cover that up with a slight cough. Her smile showed how well she saw through her.

This was a moment to be proud, not nervous. Veronica was about to make her first appearance as a knight. It behooved her to show that pride.

Soon, they reached the throne room. Along with the empty suits, six Holy Knights stood before the opened doors. They drew their fists over their chests in salute as she approached, welcoming their new fellow knight. It was very encouraging, but what was beyond them rattled her even more.

At the end of the throne room, standing patiently before the rising path to his throne, was the king. And between them and the new knight, standing along the two sides of the grand room, were dozens of nobles, men and women, all with eyes on her.

Veronica knew many would gather for a knighting ceremony carried out by the king, but to see nearly every guest in the palace there, her conviction began to shake.

She looked back to her meister knight, who gave her a simple nod. Steeling herself, Veronica held her head high and marched through the crowd, passing the Holy Knights that formed a path directly to King

Faustign. The Holy Knights all held their spears steady and saluted her in unison.

Veronica focused only on what was before her rather than the eyes of everyone around her. The king, standing tall and proud before his subjects, graced her with a charming smile. His queen remained close by near the rise in the floor that led to the throne. When she saw who it was beside her, Veronica felt her confidence returning.

It was Prince Aeron and Cheryl. They had arrived to see her rise to knighthood.

A couple of other knights stood near the royalty, both with arms folded behind their backs.

One of them, to Veronica's surprise, was Lord Charleston. That he would come while his dear sister was bedridden showed just how important this was. Their king was not the sort of man who would order him to be present given his current predicament. It was likely that, while the rest of his family tended to Lady Abeel, he was there to serve as a representative of the Estrine family, as well as take part in the momentous occasion as the Champion of Duty.

Another champion stood with him: Lord Astre Just of Condoroost, the Champion of Pride. He stood at a fair height and donned himself in dark gray armor with gold trim. Like many of his brothers-in-arms, he wore a stoic expression on his wizened face, his hard brown eyes projecting strength that commanded respect.

Veronica crossed paths with Lord Astre once before, when she and Lady Victoriah were called to track Renegade activity in the north. He was as relentless as the Champion of Heart when it came to pursuing their enemy, and he was just as strict with the soldiers he commanded at the time. Their mission led them to apprehend a small Renegade raiding party that had no useful intel. But it was not for nothing, as Lord Astre stated, for they spared a poor village from being sacked and burned down.

It was quite an honor, having such noble souls witness her proudest moment.

In crossing the throne room, Veronica had rid herself of her qualms and angst. She saluted her king before kneeling. "Your Majesty," she said as she lowered her head.

"Veronica Alivvrn of Illuascove," said King Faustign, projecting his mighty voice throughout the room. "I commend you for the valor you have shown in the trials faced alongside your meister knight, Lady Victoriah Kronas of Southern Valley. You honor the kingdom of Vermalio, and so you honor me, in performing the duty you have undertaken to the utmost of your abilities. And as my trusted champion has recognized that you are worthy, it falls unto me to see you rewarded the title you have rightfully earned."

A cascade of applause filled the throne room like a heavy rainfall. Hearing it allowed relief to wash over her heart.

As the crowd went silent, Veronica heard footsteps move away from her and stop somewhere close. She saw the king take something in hand before he retook his spot before her.

Her knight's shield. She was so excited that she wanted to dart her head up and take a look at it, but she remained as she was so they could complete the ceremony.

"Veronica, do you swear to uphold the law of this land, to fight for your kingdom, its people, and its ideals, so long as you can take a blade in hand?"

The humble young lady pressed her fist to her heart. "On my honor, on my life, on my very soul, I swear to you, before the gods of this world, that I will protect Vermalio, its people, and the ideals of valiance and truth until the day comes when I must rest."

Her vow was given. At last.

"Then, my child, as king of this proud land, I—"

Confusion was whispered among the nobles when King Faustign came to a sudden pause. Veronica, too, was bewildered, and feared that she had done something wrong. But not long after he fell silent, she felt the air suddenly turn to lead. Her magic senses alerted her of a sudden and drastic surge of energy. She could not quite tell what it was, only that it was strong enough for her to sense it from afar.

King Faustign was a warrior blessed by Lord Ralias, the god of war and bringer of prosperity. He no doubt felt the same disturbance she had.

"Your Majesty!"

A Holy Knight rushed past his cohorts and Lady Victoriah into the throne room. He held his hand to his breastplate in desperate need to catch his breath. When he could finally speak again, he raised his head. "The Renegades have infiltrated Brigadier. They are about to march on the palace!"

Confusion turned into panic at the Holy Knight's words. The nobles and guards were beside themselves, and the champions brought themselves before the king for his orders.

King Faustign hung his head and closed his eyes, the wrinkles at his forehead broadening. His free hand closed into a fist and trembled from strife, but when he raised his head, he looked to his champions with blazing resolve.

~ Nineteenth Chapter ~
Predated Valiance

The Renegades were upon the palace before long. They threw themselves at its mighty gates in full force. The enchantment on the bars held the enemy at bay and repelled the spells hurled at them, but only for so long. Soon, the Renegades forced their way through and commenced their assault.

The Holy Knights guarding the palace grounds clashed with wave after wave of deadly warriors. They held them off while their comrades inside the palace worked to secure it.

Veronica followed Prince Aeron as he led a small party of knights to the north wing. They were tasked with securing a hidden entrance the king believed would be at risk. Though he was reluctant to ignore the fighting at the front, the prince obeyed his father.

From the north wing, they entered a chamber that appeared to be an ordinary storage room. At the end of it was a false wall that led into a dark, dank passage.

During the dawn of the kingdom, when the palace was being built, the first king of Vermalio, wary that the nobles he put his trust in would one day betray him, had an escape tunnel built to keep his queen and heir from harm's way. Should he have fallen, he intended for his heir to escape and one day return to reclaim his birthright.

Fortunately, the contingency never needed to be implemented, so said Prince Aeron.

Only the royal family was supposed to know of the escape tunnel, but King Faustign was as wary of those conspiring against him as his ancestor was. With how much mayhem they caused over the years unimpeded, their knowledge was not to be underestimated.

It was a smart move, given how the enemy operated. Deception was their forte. They had often used chaos to draw the knights' attention away from their true objectives. That they sent such numbers to the palace directly meant they needed to keep the Holy Knights suppressed. And their recent activity across the kingdom all but screamed their intent on taking further action to dethrone King Faustign.

Veronica worried for the king, as well as her meister knight and her fellow champions. When she and her comrades departed from the throne room, they remained.

A terrible guilt possessed King Faustign when he became aware of the Renegades' actions. He ordered his knights to man their stations with haste, urging them to protect the palace and the people within, then ascended to his throne. His queen pled with him to go to their chambers with her, and their champions shared in her concern.

But he would not leave the throne. His guilt would not allow it.

"If the enemy makes it this far," he spoke gravely, "then I will already have failed Vermalio. I will not run from my mistakes. If they come, I will face them as a king."

For all of the harm the Renegades have caused over the past two decades, the king blamed himself. For so long, they ran amok in Vermalio, pillaging and murdering and destroying without rest. Though their sins were unforgivable, the worst, the king reasoned, was his own for failing to put a stop to it.

From atop his throne, King Faustign awaited judgment, whether it be the word of their victory or the sight of treacherous swords pointed at him.

Thus, his loyal champions remained with him. No matter what he thought of himself, he was their king, and they would defend him to the very last.

If things were to unfold as the king predicted, then to prevent the worst, all Veronica and company had to do was stop the enemy from breaching the palace from their side.

After they went so far, the passage spread out into a spacious chamber. They stood atop a risen path connected to a lower level by stairways on both sides. The stairs descended roughly twenty feet to another darkened passage, which would, according to the prince, stretch out farther than the one they crossed. Although ancient, the chamber remained as stable as the day it was built. Centuries must have passed since then. The stairs had a design notably different from the masonry used in modern-day Vermalio. And on the walls were carved simple, albeit captivating, reliefs of the ancient war that resulted in Vermalio's founding.

What allowed them to see such marvels was not the light of the torches held by Cheryl and another soldier, but rather the luminescent moss that had grown on the ceiling. The enchanting light it emitted was bright enough to make it appear as though they were outside. Some spores flittered through the air and flickered from the light of the puffy plant they spawned from above.

Veronica had seen such moss before when they rested at the mouth of Urbon Cave, one of Vermalio's purities. It did not glow as brightly since it was exposed to moonlight, and there was not enough moisture there for it to grow very thick. She wanted to see if she could find more, but going deeper into Urbon Cave was far too dangerous. Legends have said that it led to the gateway of the seven hells.

A brief inhale, and she understood why the moss thrived in the tunnel. The moisture in the air was delightfully palpable. And without outside light to overshadow the moss' properties, it glowed as bright as it could.

They put out their torches and waited there for the enemy to arrive. Veronica took the lead so that she could get the jump on them. Having formed an area of influence that stretched throughout the entire room, she had her Second Verse ready to be used at the first sign of trouble. She withheld from using too much power yet to keep her presence masked. If there were any mages among the enemy, it would be wise to keep from alerting them.

Everyone kept their eyes on the outward passage, observing the darkness clustered at the end of it. The wait was excruciating. Not knowing when someone would emerge or how many there were gave them goosebumps down their sword arms.

After so long, their other qualms began to take precedence. Some were concerned for their comrades fighting on the surface. Others were wary of how the fight in this confined space would turn out. It was hard to ignore how the chamber resembled a tomb; all that was missing was a coffin or two.

Holding onto dread promised an ill fate. To cope, Veronica held onto something else.

She clenched her teeth in thinking about the enemy. Keeping her power limited all the while became more difficult. Her eye began twitching from the stress.

Only when she saw the flicker of another's valsara move in the darkness did Veronica steady herself. Slowly, she pulled water from the air and shaped it into a massive sphere. As the others stirred from her actions and the echoing *ptump, ptump, ptump* of footsteps, she drew her free hand open, pulling spikes from the sphere, making it a mace.

Then, as a leg sprung from the shadows, she thrust her arm forward, shooting the water mace at the men who rushed forth. A light mist sprayed back at the knights as the water splashed over the opposite wall. The Renegades who came out were crushed under the attack and lay unmoving.

A churlish smirk twisted Veronica's face. She was pleased with herself for getting rid of them all at once.

But more were coming—many more.

Clicking her tongue, she gathered the scattered droplets again, this time forming an array of spears hovering in the air.

"You want more?"

The first spear launched jabbed two men into the left wall. The next one was blocked by a shield, exposing its wielder's back, where the third spear struck from above.

Her comrades dared not get too close, lest they get caught in the torrent their ferocious knight-to-be whipped up.

That the capital, the royal palace no less, was being attacked did not surprise Veronica much. After witnessing the carnage wrought by the Renegades, a part of her—the wroth self—knew it would happen eventually. But that it would take place just as she was about to be knighted, to attain what she strived for after so long, even her altruistic half could not deny her rage.

"It's not enough to raze villages and slaughter entire populations for your sick agenda, is it? You just had to strike today of all days!"

The water spears rained down on the Renegades flowing through, striking them down mercilessly. A few stubborn ones managed to stand their ground behind thick shields.

"You want to be the first to face me? Then come at me." The scattered droplets gathered around her rapier as the last of the spears fell, keeping her foes pinned in place. Upon pointing the blade at them, a massive reptilian head formed around the tip. "Meet Vermalio's newest knight!" A quick thrust, and the draconic visage shot at them with the force of a waterfall. Her attack flooded the outward passage, taking with it the Renegades who resisted and snuffing out a few others in the shadows, their valsara flickering out of her magic sight.

An eerie silence followed. Only the sound of water dripping from the walls could be heard.

The knights did not relax. They waited for Veronica's word, relying on her magic sight, before daring to move from their vantage point.

Pleased with her demonstration of power though she was, her eyes told her not to let up. So many of them had gathered. Enough valsara filled her magic sight that it all blurred together. She stopped trying to count all of the bodies they came from when it gave her a migraine.

The enemy remained motionless. They had to be reevaluating their situation. Their biggest obstacle remained out of reach and prone to make quick attacks.

The standoff was becoming irksome, but the knights remained on the defensive. Their priority was to keep the Renegades from breaching the palace. Nothing could be allowed to compromise that, least of all hubris.

Veronica narrowed her eyes when she saw movement, and her power intensified. There was no sense in holding back now that they knew she was there. As she was about form more spears, shock filled her eyes. The valsara of one enemy had suddenly flared.

Two men rushed from the passage, going for both stairways, when a scarlet sphere flew her way. Veronica's spears drew in to protect her, coming together to form a barrier. When the sphere hit, a screaming explosion broke out. The blast threw Veronica off balance, but she managed to dive out of the way when another sphere of energy came flying. The shill sound it made upon dispersal made her skull vibrate.

What a troublesome mage.

Seizing their opportunity, the Renegades rushed up the stairs while their mage kept the Nascitte busy. The knights moved to intercept, keeping them from reaching the top. Veronica hurled a mace of water at the mage, but the gaunt man, nimble on his feet, ran out of the way. He cast the same spell again, hurling another sphere at her.

Before it could hit, Prince Aeron rushed to her aid. He stood before her and intercepted the spell with his shield. The shield's enchantment weakened the magic, allowing him to withstand the dispersal and quieting the harsh screech that resounded.

The mage kept hurling spells at Veronica, but the prince kept stepping in to be her shield. Veronica acted while she could. She formed more water spears above, bringing them crashing down upon the mage.

He moved out of the way of two, three, four of them—each one hitting closer than the last. As the final spear stuck, pinning the mage to the wall, another sphere of crackling energy flew from his fingers, curving toward the ceiling. The resulting explosion sent sparks flying instead of letting out screams.

The moss above head quickly caught on fire. The light that filled the room turned from the gentle green glow into a blazing orange. The glowing spores that blew haphazardly from the stir of conflict dimmed out without the nocturnal light.

The Renegades began to ascend the stairs. Those they defeated were knocked aside, their corpses falling to the cold stone floor. As the flames grew from devouring the moss, the enemy appeared much more murderous, their eyes reflecting the malignant red.

They were losing ground. Even as Veronica used her Second Verse to thin the enemy numbers, more came through the passage. Her comrades were falling one after another, and nothing she did put a stop to it.

"Fall back! We need to fall back!"

If the fight continued there, they would all surely perish. There were too many Renegades, and Veronica could only delay their advance for so long. The only chance they had left to stop them was to return to the palace and finish them in the north wing.

Hearing the prince's order, Veronica gathered all of the water she could from the air. She shaped it into the form of a much larger beast than the last, a massive dragon. She guided its serpent-like body to swerve and smash into the Renegades at the stairs, careful not to hit her own. The knights took advantage of the confusion and shoved the remaining Renegades over the ledge before retreating.

Veronica let her comrades go first while she kept the Renegades busy. The water dragon flailed about madly, brushing its victims away and smashing them like ants.

It was about to come down on a heavily armored man when something knocked it back. Steam brewed from its sides and jaws.

Another Renegade mage had come, and this one knew how to oppose her power.

Desperate to be rid of him, Veronica directed the water dragon to dive after the pyromancer just as a blade of condensed flames spewed from his hands.

Someone grabbed Veronica from behind just as the water scattered. It was one of the Holy Knights. "Come on, now. We're not leaving you behind," she said to Veronica as she urged her down the passage.

They had to hurry to the end, otherwise they would be trampled by the Renegades' sheer numbers. Veronica joined her comrades in a long sprint down the dark passage. It was hard not to look back when she felt the entirety of the enemy party closing in.

War cries and twisted laughter echoed from behind, warping into a cacophony of wicked delight.

It was as if they were being hunted by demons.

That impression only grew starker as a glaring flash darted through the darkness. It narrowly missed one soldier and crashed into the wall. Just as the knights reached the end of the passage, a second flash followed suit, flying straight for its mark.

The Holy Knight behind Veronica pushed her onward, and she and two others stood their ground to shield their comrades.

The blast sent Veronica flying from the storage room. As she pushed herself up, she saw the room ablaze, its door blown from its hinges.

She got to her feet to help the prince stand and joined what little remained of their party. Cheryl remained beside the prince so that if she fell, it would be beside her meister knight. The soldiers faced the open chamber with weapons at the ready.

They had to stop them there.

The disturbance seemed to alert others to join in their struggle. Veronica turned to see soldiers marching down the hall. Theirs was not the armor of the Holy Knights, but instead the modest suits of armor that stood throughout the palace.

Her eyes drew wide open in shock.

She thought at first that some of the devoted servants recklessly decided to don the armor and defend their masters. But she saw no faces in their open helms, nor did she sense valsara from them.

She did, however, sense magic. It was a spell to make the empty suits into someone's marionettes.

And Prince Aeron's delight confirmed it was someone on their side.

"I was wondering when Aggres would send reinforcements."

The empty suits of armor marched past the knights to form the first defensive barrier, their shields up and their swords out.

"Whatever happens here," the prince said to the young women beside him, "know that it is an honor to fight beside you both."

"Save your praise for when we win."

The prince gazed at Veronica with a look of surprise, eying her carefully as she gathered more water around her sword and flatted it to form a broad, sharp blade. He smiled from seeing her resolve and turned to Cheryl. "And you said this Veronica would be trouble."

Veronica looked to her rival, her brow arched in curiosity. Cheryl locked eyes with her and just shrugged, which made Veronica grin.

Though they had their differences, both felt something about the other that they respected.

The clamor of the Renegades' charge closed in.

"Oh, I am." Veronica turned her fierce gaze to the doorway. Her valsara flared and her power surged. It was do-or-die time. "Good thing trouble is on your side."

Emerging from the flames and smoke, the Renegade warriors rushed forth.

Most of the empty armor withstood the attacks inflicted on them. They ignored being impaled and getting their helms knocked off, and raised their swords to strike back. One enemy was too frightened by that to avoid getting beheaded. But a few suits fell to heavy strikes and stopped moving altogether when their chest plates were broken open.

Once they found the weakness in the empty armor, the Renegades made quick work of them and moved to rout the rest of the knights.

Outnumbered though they were, the knights faced their foes valiantly.

Cheryl took charge to protect her prince and meister knight. Veronica remained close to them both; Aeron was their prince, after all, and she would never hear the end of it from her gentler self if something were to happen to Cheryl.

Their clash was fierce. These Renegade fighters were different from the cutthroats that rampaged across the kingdom; their skill took down as many of the Holy Knights as the knights did them.

As the battle reached a stalemate, the second enemy mage reemerged. He hurled fireballs at the remaining empty armor, melting them.

Not willing to let him act anymore, Veronica pushed aside the enemies confronting her and, seeing a clear opening, hurled her rapier. The water around her blade flew at the mage, striking his dominant arm.

He screamed as his arm fell to the floor. By the time he recovered, Veronica had already closed in and, swift as the wind, pierced his heart.

The bodies of both knights and Renegades littered the hall. Both sides had taken terrible casualties.

After the enemy numbers became significantly thinned, the Renegades suddenly began falling one after the next. It was for but an instant that the knights saw who struck them down, then his movements became a blur. At least a dozen Renegades were cut down in the blink of an eye.

Only a handful of Renegades remained when they saw him clearly.

What stood against the Renegades was a dark-skinned man clad in leather armor. The amber scarf around his neck and face complemented his dark attire. His steps were almost silent as he attacked, and his blade struck the enemy swift and true.

It was astonishing enough to watch him cull the enemy, but he came from the same passage they had. That space once blazed with the light of the Renegades' clustered valsara. Now it was dark, devoid of life.

When Veronica again looked at the stranger, she froze. The malice he exuded drew her attention to his valsara. Her ferocity dissolved when he finished the last Renegade, and in its place rose disbelief.

It ... can't be...!

She was so distraught that her gentler self reassumed control, though not to confront what she saw. She took three unsteady steps back, barely stopping when Cheryl came to her side.

When the stranger turned their way from the passage and his eyes locked with hers, flickering a crystalline blue, it became harder to deny what she saw. That valsara, those eyes—they were unmistakable. "...Van?"

Cheryl looked at her as though she thought her insane. "Veronica, what are you on about? That guy doesn't look anything like—"

"Cheryl, look..."

At the prince's behest, she turned to look at the weapon he held. Immediately, she saw what they did.

The sword was pure black, and embedded between the blade and guard was an uncanny azure stone.

The Evolving Blade, Las'cent.

"...Van, why are you here?"

A more prudent question might have been, "What happened to you?" But it was not his physical changes that baffled her. She looked not to his now russet skin or white hair, but to his valsara. The malice he exuded from slaughtering the Renegades now swept over them.

Those eyes of his were like that of a malevolent beast. They showed no compassion—only rage. Whatever he was there for, it could not have been out of the goodness of his heart.

"Stand aside." His words were cold and heavy.

It was not a request. One way or the other, he was getting past them. And the longer they denied him, the more his vehemence grew.

But they could not do as he said.

Picking up on his ally's apprehension, Prince Aeron confronted Van. "What happened to you? Why aren't you with Princess Camellia?"

When Van narrowed his eyes, their glimmer reflected a growing hostility. "I have nothing more to do with her. Her, or anyone else."

That he said it so dispassionately rocked them all. He, who served the Ederean princess so dutifully, had forsaken her. It was too absurd to be true.

But he appeared before them without his armor—without his shield. He was a knight no more.

"Last chance," he warned. "Stand. Aside."

A gasp escaped Veronica. Shivers ran up her spine. The breath that left her was a puff of white. The air had suddenly become frigid, enough that they could watch it freeze in front of them.

It was Van's power in resonance with his burgeoning rage.

That surge of energy from earlier, it came from him. And being so close to the maelstrom of power now, Veronica could only imagine what havoc he caused with it before.

They did not have to for long.

In keeping their weapons raised to him, Van went on the attack.

The remaining Holy Knights charged at the intruder together. Van moved past their attacks as though they were not even moving, and when they surrounded him, the azure gem in his sword started glowing.

"Get back!"

The prince warned them too late. "Roar!" In a spin with its wielder, Las'cent hurled a trenchant wave of light that blew the soldiers away. They flew through the air, like they had been cast aside by a fierce wind.

The azure light crashed into Veronica, Cheryl, and the prince, all but shackling them. They fought to keep their weapons raised as their muscles turned to stone. Their breathing became heavy and harsh, yet they felt their windpipes closing shut. It was as if their bodies were reacting to fear, yet their minds remained unshaken.

It was hard to move, but they forced themselves to anyway. The Holy Knights had been incapacitated. Those three were the only ones left to stop him.

Van closed in. As he rushed their way, Prince Aeron fought against the power enfeebling him to stood before him. He raised his sword to meet the blade of Las'cent as it drew close. Their eyes met, their wills clashing briefly, before Van shifted backward. Las'cent drew back at the prince in a sharp arc, hammering down at him with crushing force.

Shaking off the energy shackling her, Cheryl rushed into the fray to aid Prince Aeron. Her sword met the scabbard in Van's left hand, pushing against it until he pushed back, curving the scabbard ever so slightly. She staggered, looking to be tugged by his movement.

While Veronica recovered, she used her Second Verse to aid her friends. She gathered water to form swords and hurled them Van's way. But when they got close, they froze solid, and with but a thought from him, the ice shattered.

Unrelenting, Van swept aside both the prince and his squire.

Had Veronica not stepped in when she did, Cheryl would have lost her head. She barely had enough strength to block and hold Las'cent back.

Getting close to him only made moving harder. His very presence froze the air around them. The light from Las'cent's gem gleamed off her sword, and it let her catch glimpses of the frost clustering along its thin blade.

The longer the clash lasted, the colder it became, and the harder it was for Veronica to pull water vapor from the air.

But she refused to give in. "Why are you here? Tell me!"

When she saw an opening, she gathered all of the water she could around her rapier and hurled it at his side. The water blade quickly froze and broke apart when Van's scabbard blocked it, sending white power flying. Las'cent carved through the cover just as Veronica leaped back. Before the black blade could run her through, she used her foe's power to her advantage and gathered water into a small barrier. It froze in time to block the attack, shattering after it successfully protecting her. She lurched to his left side and swiped, only for her rapier to be batted away by Las'cent.

Prince Aeron stepped in quickly to intercept Van's next swing while Cheryl came at him from behind.

The white vapor wafting from their foe thickened, and his power suddenly spiked. "For Faustign!" Upon throwing his left fist down, the floor froze solid, and a gust of frost and ice shards forced them all back.

The air had been dyed pure white. Veronica picked herself up, looking this way and that with a start. She could not see Van, nor Cheryl or Prince Aeron. Even her magic sight failed her.

Only when she heard a soft step in front of her did the fog part. In an instant, Van was upon her.

Too slow was she to block his attack. Las'cent fell at her rapier, the force behind it tearing the weapon from her grasp. Van's hard elbow knocked her into the wall. And in dropping his scabbard, he pinned her in place by her clavicle, his icy fingers curling around her neck.

"And you will not keep me from him."

His chilling presence snuffed out the last traces of warmth she had left. Her limbs became stiff. Her lungs felt like they were petrifying. And slowly, her mind failed her.

If she could lift her arms, if she could grasp his wrist, then she would have used her Second Verse to twist the water in his body and force him to release her. But her arms had been bound in place by the ice clustering over her.

It froze over her limbs, then her body. And as the blistering cold crept its way up her neck and around her head, Veronica could only focus on the glacial eyes boring into her very soul.

Her last thoughts were of despair, wondering where the kind guardian she knew had gone.

Veronica's mind was so groggy that she did not even realize she projected her spirit from her body.

Even as a spirit, she shook from the cold. It should not have been possible, yet she still had a link to the material plane. What she felt must have been from her body being in such a precarious state.

Separated from her body, she was more sensitive to the energy rippling throughout the area. She still felt the violent surge of Van's valsara.

The sound of metal bashing against a rough surface reached her. Behind her was Cheryl, desperately striking the frozen prison that trapped Veronica's body. She kept going until her sword snapped in two, the blade falling before the spirit of the girl she struggled to free. Even without that tool, she would not stop, and started bearing the ice with her bare hands.

Even if Veronica returned to her body, all she could do was wait until the ice thawed, or— She shook her head upon thinking of the alternative.

There was nothing she could do. So rather than lament and speak words her friend would not hear, Veronica hovered off the ground to trail the energy her attacker exuded.

What was he after? Why was he doing this? If nothing else, she had to know that much. She had to know what he had done.

"Stop!"

A voice echoed across the phantom plane. It brought Veronica to pause. It was not often that she heard someone's spirit scream. After realizing where it came from, Veronica darted through the palace.

A trail of carnage littered the central halls of the palace. Ice clustered over the floors and walls, entrapping brave soldiers as it did her. Frozen blades and blood-soaked weapons and armor led the way to the throne room.

The grand doors leading inside have been demolished, broken down by an avalanche of clustered ice. A hazy white vapor lingered in the air, only to be parted and shifted from the waves of blades.

Upon crossing into the throne room, Veronica could not bring herself to go further.

Three noble champions remained to defend the king; only one still fought on. Lord Charleston had fallen, so had Lord Astre, both bound by chains of ice clinging to their freshly cut wounds. Already, they looked pale, and the valsara flowing through them was faint.

Lady Victoriah opposed Van as fiercely as she had the Renegades. She had no choice, not when he charged at her with intent to kill. They clashed with one another, their swords vying for control of the battle.

Pain and angst flickered in their valsara. Carrying a heavy heart into battle often proved fatal, but how could they fight each other any other way? Lady Victoriah could never have imagined her son would come before her like this and threaten her comrades and king. And Van, despite whatever he decided, faced the women who raised him. They both loved each other; that plainly showed as their pain grew the more they fought.

A mother, bound by duty, resisted her child's destructive impulses. A son, possessed by anger and hate, lashed out at his parent. Neither held anything back, fighting for what they sought to achieve.

And as this went on, King Faustign watched from atop his throne, a dark countenance under his circlet.

Lady Victoriah fought Van off with timbering swings of her sword. Her strength was immense, but Van met it with his own. Her sword crossed with his scabbard. Before he could turn to disorient her, she thrust her shield, shoving him away. His heels skidded across the floor before coming to a stop, still standing tall.

His irritation at having been repulsed was as palpable as the remorse he felt at having to fight her. The cultivation of angst only pushed him to fight harder. With a throaty growl, Van again charged at Lady Victoriah.

Caught between the staggering floods of emotion, something else flickered between them. The glow of another's energy flashed over theirs. It moved as if trying to get between them. And when the space between them was great enough, Veronica saw that it was not valsara.

When Lady Victoriah moved to pin Van in place, that energy phased through her.

It was Rubi. She called out to them both again and again, trying to get them to stop fighting. But it was to no avail. Their ears were deaf to the voice of a phantom.

Veronica tried to go to her side, but she could not move. The cold biting into her spirit was growing stronger by the second. She felt herself suffocating ever so slowly. "Rubi...!"

The fighting soon drew to a conclusion. Lady Victoriah, shaking her hesitation, had thrown Van against the wall. He fell to his hands and knees, and a pained groan passed his lips. Lady Victoriah stood over him, struggling to maintain her breathing.

"Stand down!" she ordered in a haggard bark. "...I don't want to hurt you any more." The strife on her face, the instability of her valsara, and her wavering voice all laid bare her broken heart.

As he lifted his head, the scarf around his neck, cut in two during the fight, parted and fell to the floor.

That moment, Veronica was horrified by what she had seen. Under his eyes, resting on his cheeks, were two crimson brands shaped like arrows. The dark skin and white hair were surprising enough, but those brands made her see him as something else altogether.

He's ... a Kindhrin!

The Kindhrin, a dead race from the fallen kingdom of Harah Krid. Everyone knew the stories of how the Kindhrin destroyed their homeland in service to their avarice. Those people—those demons—could be distinguished from others by the brands on their faces.

How could it be that Vandelas Kronas was one of them?

Without a thought to any of that, Rubi hurried to Van's side. She stood before Lady Victoriah, acting to block her way with arms stretched out. "Please stop. Stop this now!" Even though she knew she could not do anything, even though they could not see or hear her, Rubi refused to stand by and watch this happen. "He ... he's your son. Please, Lady Victoriah, don't hurt him. Don't hurt him..."

This was the first time Veronica had seen Rubi so horrified. It caught her completely by surprise. Her thoughts lingered on what she called him and how intensely she stared up at Lady Victoriah. She spoke as if she knew him, and she could not bear to see him harmed.

She remembered him—enough to not be alarmed by his appearance now.

Though he saw her and heard her not, the grief she felt seemed to reach Van. His eyes turned downcast, and overflowed with sadness. "Even after all this ... I'm still not strong enough." His hands gripped his sword and scabbard so tightly. Grief overwhelmed him and brought him to tremble. But when he finally stopped, his valsara flared with malice anew. "So be it." A powerful pulse emanated from his valsara, rippling the air.

"Victoriah!" King Faustign stood from his throne. "Get away from him, now!"

The distress of her king alarmed her. But before she could do anything, the power welling within Van was unleashed. The light of his valsara flared as he let out a mighty howl, blinding Veronica. A massive wave of energy inundated the throne room, crashing against everything within.

When Veronica could again see, she saw glass falling from above, shards of the shattered stained glass windows raining down on them. Lady Victoriah stood much farther away from the young man she had trapped, forced back by the flood of power. When she raised her head to look his way, it was with terror.

His valsara had expanded well beyond his body and took the shape of a monstrous beast. It resembled a mighty wolf three times the size of a man, and its right side appeared jagged and sharp, as though covered in blades. When Van raised his head, its massive, slender skull followed suit. The energy was so immense that even one with normal eyes could see a fraction of its mystifying glow.

The phantom who stood beside him was gone, perhaps blown away by the raging energy.

Van, and the beast within him, stared down Lady Victoriah, his mercy gone. "...I am Feroxis Maveronyn, survivor of the massacre your king orchestrated against the Kindhrin race. My vendetta will be settled, and no one—not the Six Champions, not Veronica, not even you, Mother—will stand in my way!" The radiant azure glow of Las'cent, intensified by the flash of his cerulean valsara, shone so bright that it was almost stabbing. "Prepare!"

Swinging Las'cent brought its roar to be echoed by the beast within, an otherworldly cry that had the force of a shockwave. It pushed Lady Victoriah and even froze parts of her weapons and armor. Van charged while she was still staggered, sword held for a horizontal swing. Lady Victoriah barely held up her shield in time to block, and even then, she could not stand against the attack.

Steadfast, Lady Victoriah fought through the grip of Las'cent's power to oppose Van's newfound strength. So much force fell upon her that Lady Victoriah could no longer meet his attacks head-on. The Wolverine dodged every swing she saw coming, avoiding them however she could, and dove at Van when an opening presented itself.

Frost flew and scattered across the throne room in waves soft and crashing. The air became aglitter underneath the intruding sunlight. The polished floor froze over. And as a white vapor filled the air, swirling from the crossing swords, their paths flashing in this stage of light, Veronica began to realize just what this power was.

When Lady Victoriah tried to get some distance, Van cast a wave of jagged ice at her. She rolled out of the way before the frozen blades could graze her, but left herself vulnerable when Van drew near. Her sword blocked the blow from above, then the next aimed at her side. But in meeting the third swing, the weapon snapped in two. And when she raised her shield to protect herself, Las'cent slammed into it with the incredible might to shatter it.

"No!"

The black blade sliced up Lady Victoriah's arm, and Van's monstrous valsara loomed over her, fangs sunk into her. Blood trickled from her side. She tottered backward. The arm cut slowly reached out to him as ice clustered over the wound. A soft word passed her lips before her gaze turned dark, and she collapsed onto the cold floor.

Emerging the victor, Van turned his back on his mother and stalked toward his intended prey.

Veronica stood there in utter disbelief. Never did she believe someone could defeat her meister knight. And the one to do it was her own son. Her eyes wide, her jaw hanging, she shook her head frantically and let out a harrowing scream.

King Faustign remained standing before his throne, and looked down at all that transpired with a pained gaze. Yet in the corner of his eyes lingered a glimmer of pity.

"You have grown strong, Vandelas. It truly is awe-inspiring."

He remained perfectly stoic as the icy beast came ever closer.

"Such a shame that even after all you have achieved, after all you have sacrificed ... you still have yet to find the one you are after."

Those words he spoke made Van's valsara burn ever brighter and spurred him to strike. He ran up the steps to the throne, the monstrous force he carried crushing them.

He narrowed closer and closer to the still man, until a burst of energy rivalling his own forced him back.

The mass of his valsara mowed down the steps and skidded across the floor, narrowly stopping before he reached the bottom. When Van looked up to glare at the king, he stopped growling from shock.

A roaring flame had ignited, catching fire the throne from which the king stood. And just like Van's had, King Faustign's valsara expanded outside of the shell of his body, a radiant cluster of scarlet flames. The shape it formed was not consistent. From the radiant life energy came these faces, each one trying to surface before falling back into the fire.

That valsara shook Veronica to the core. It was so unnatural.

That fire! That valsara!

Veronica darted her gaze back to the beastly valsara coming from Van. A myriad of voices came from it, all of them speaking in unison. The way they spoke, it sounded familiar.

She was right about him, about his power. He was just like her.

Lantia… What is the meaning of this!?

"Who—" Van shook his head. "*What* are you!? There is no way … no way something like you can be human!"

Disagree though she wanted to, Veronica thought the same. The way it shaped itself, all of those different faces trying to emerge, it was a thing of nightmares.

The smile that the king put on was thin and melancholy. "How right you are." Even though they thought as much, his admission still stunned Veronica and Van. A tired sigh passed his lips and his smile faded. "What stands before you now is not the true Faustign L. S. Vermalio. I am a vita, an existence created from magic in his image."

A great many surprises presented themselves this day. There were many to juggle, but this one was by far the most daunting.

Veronica had heard stories of the vita from Lady Abeel. They were popular amongst mages, fables in which they all indulged. And they could only be believed as fables because no one in history had successfully created a vita before. Countless mages have attempted to chase the dream of creating flesh and blood purely from magic, but none have succeeded.

But if what he said was true, then someone must have.

"Not ... the true Faustign?" The realization hit Van all the harder after saying it aloud. But it did nothing to sway his anger. "Where is he then? Where is that murderer hiding?"

"In a sense, he never was. After all, he has been building an army to use against me for years now."

That announcement disturbed Veronica as much as it had Van. She thought that she had misheard, that the sounds of roaring flames and clustering ice had distorted the words carried by his powerful voice.

"The one who destroyed Harah Krid ... and the Renegade leader are—"

"Indeed. They are one and the same."

The youths before the assumed king looked to him aghast, each focused on a different revelation. Veronica lingered on that the vita said their king, the true Faustign, was the cause of the chaos raging throughout Vermalio for the past twenty years.

"How? How can this be?"

The vita who had posed as king gave a fair nod. "It is quite the tale— with much to take in. And one you deserve to know." The somber expression he wore grew rigid, accentuating the guilt and angst kept hidden for so long. "It began twenty-one years ago with a rumor, a rumor that an ancient artifact had been discovered beneath the sands of Harah Krid. Many relics from the long-forgotten past were known to resurface there. This one, however, was said to be powered by magic."

Harah Krid was a vast, barren land mostly comprised of a grand desert. Its harsh environment proved inhospitable to most. Many knew it by another name, the Cursed Land, for it was a place where magic could never cross. Any charm brought to the Cursed Land was robbed of its power, and if a mage there used a spell, their life was forfeit.

And yet the Kindhrin found a means of thriving there, in a land where even magic could not be. It earned the ire and fear of the Vermalians.

To hear that an artifact still containing magic had been found in the Cursed Land would leave anyone in awe.

"When the rumor reached Faustign, he feared what sort of artifact the Kindhrin had discovered. Relations between Harah Krid and Vermalio have always been tense. Haunted by the nightmare of war, he dreaded that the artifact was a weapon of the ancients. Very soon, he decided he must see for himself.

"The rumor was not common knowledge, and taking a voyage to a foreign land was not unusual. But Faustign's advisors were still insistent that he reconsider. Tensions had grown from recent outbursts on the part of the Vermalian envoys and their guard, word of which reached Vermalio, though what returned was more flattering to the envoys and painted the Kindhrin in an even more callous image. His advisors feared that were he to leave for Harah Krid then, the knowledge that would inevitably get out would bring unnecessary unrest to his people."

Van narrowed his eyes. "They created you to act as king until his return."

The vita nodded. "An elaborate solution, but it was a solution nonetheless." He remained silent for a moment, dwelling on something from the past. When he looked to Van again, it was with a hint of nostalgia. "I received my orders, and acted upon them. Because my nature, as well as my appearance, matched his, our ruse proved successful. And thus, he spirited himself away to Harah Krid without anyone the wiser."

It was quite the story—to create something which no one in history had simply to be as a temporary doppelganger.

But it grew darker from there. "When the khan, the ruler of Harah Krid, agreed to meet him, no attempts were made to hide the truth. Perhaps it was to serve as a gesture of goodwill, to build trust between them and thus their nations. But in telling him that the artifact may have indeed been a weapon, the khan only fed Faustign's fears.

"And when opportunity led him to see the weapon with his own eyes..." Suddenly, the vita's voice became hoarse, a lump forming in his throat. It was at that stage that it physically hurt him to speak anything more. But he forced himself to; to do otherwise, he likely felt, would be to deny what happened. "He had lost all sense of reason. He wanted to seize the weapon for himself, and decided that no sacrifice was too great. Not even the lives of your people, the Kindhrin, Vandelas."

Van looked on at the vita Faustign with horror, as though having learned of this again for the first time. Those last few words were so gripping that it looked like he had witnessed what came next with his own eyes.

Something which did not seem at all unfamiliar to him, Veronica noticed.

"I could not forgive what Faustign had done. Though I was created to serve him, my existence came about not without the conscience, the convictions, the principles he himself once had. So, with his six advisors' cooperation, I continued my façade, and forbade Faustign from returning to Vermalio, lest he pay for the pain he had wrought."

They sounded like noble words, but the disgust on Van's face showed how little he believed them. "You knew all of this. You knew none of what happened was our fault. Yet you allowed these lies, for everyone to call us demons, to blame us for the loss of our homeland, for the loss of their lives! Why!? Tell me, Faustign! Tell me why!"

He denied every word of remorse, every lamented thought, that he laid bare. But the vita did not blame him. He hung his head and left his shame for the lost soul to see. "Because that was his parting ultimatum," he declared. "Even removed from power, Faustign was not to be taken lightly. If I did not do what he said and desecrated the memory of a noble and free-spirited people, I would have endangered all that I have become responsible for in taking his place: the kingdom, its people, and its future."

That was twice now that Veronica heard King Faustign threatened his own kingdom. It was no easier to cope with hearing it a second time, and it raised even more questions that left her boggled.

But it enlightened them both.

Veronica looked to the bereft Van, and saw an ugliness in herself.

The Vermalians hated the Kindhrin for reasons so arbitrary, and it was due to that hatred that they allowed themselves to believe in the worst of them. The lie of what became of Harah Krid became accepted as the truth, and then the Vermalians' suspicion of the Kindhrin fermented into pure contempt.

"That was supposed to be the end. Yet here you are, scion of the Kindhrin, a survivor of the genocide, now a warrior carrying the fury of his fallen brethren."

His tale told and his feelings shown, the vita Faustign quelled his power. His valsara receded into his body as the fires went out. "I can scarcely imagine what you have endured—for all that was taken from you, for all the lies you were led to believe, and coming to know these truths most horrifying..." He again hung his head and leaned back to sit upon the throne. "If you still wish to strike me down, so be it. I accept my fate."

Veronica's gaze fell back on Van, worried about what he would do. Although staggered by what he had learned here, the rage within him had not waned in the slightest.

His malice still burned savagely. He yearned to finish what he set out to do. But just like the vita's had, Van's valsara receded. He raised his sword and housed it within its scabbard.

Upon its guard clicking into place, the chains of ice shackling Lord Charleston, Lord Astre, and Lady Victoriah cracked and crumbled into a powdery frost. The three of them fought for breath as their color returned and their valsara flowed normally again.

Overcome by concern, Veronica hurried to Lady Victoriah's side.

Her wounds were shallow.

"I came here to kill a king, not some scapegoat." Van turned his back on the vita Faustign. His eyes crossed over the three he defeated, and once he confirmed what he needed, he marched toward the exit.

Veronica stepped up to him, wanting to say something, but the words were left unsaid as he passed right through her. In all of the confusion, she had forgotten that she was still a disembodied spirit. When she realized again, though, she felt the cold biting into her had diminished, and she could feel her body calling out to her.

He was not after any of them. Just one.

~ Twentieth Chapter ~

For King or Country

When Veronica returned to her body, she awoke to Cheryl's panicked voice. She had been calling out to her, begging her to open her eyes, something which proved more of a challenge than Veronica had hoped.

Having just emerged from her icy prison, all Veronica could do was tremble. Her vision remained fogged. Every haggard breath she took trying to fill her frozen lungs set them on fire.

Once she finally recognized Cheryl, her friend pulled her into a tight embrace. The hands pressed against her back were ice, but the rest of Cheryl radiated a comforting warmth. Veronica was so cold, her muscles so weak, she could only sink into that warmth.

Cheryl's chest rose and fell rapidly, and she sobbed into Veronica's shoulder. How worried she was for her.

Veronica's tired eyes wandered while her mind readjusted. Not far from the two of them lay Cheryl's broken sword, and close to it was Veronica's rapier. The blade of her weapon, the weapon her meister knight gave her, had been cut clean in two.

Across from them was Prince Aeron, unconscious but breathing stably. As Veronica looked to him, she thought about the king.

Few understood what happened after the battle. The frontal assault on the royal palace severely crippled the Holy Knights' forces, but through strength and valor, they repelled the Renegades. The infiltration had also been foiled, though some questioned how. Word spread of how one enemy ripped through the prince's party and the Holy Knights on the inside without killing a single one. This one enemy was not found among the dead, or anywhere else. He disappeared without a trace.

The whole truth was known only by Lord Astre, Lady Victoriah, and Lord Charleston. Although defeated and shackled by the enemy's power, they still heard the exchange between him and their king.

Veronica saw the astonishment in Lady Victoriah when she came to visit her while she healed. It was clear as day. To know that the man she served for years was not who she thought he was came as such a shock. She did not know what to believe.

Trying to speak about it caused her throat to swell shut. The same thing happened to Veronica. Neither of them was sure of how to feel. They could not find the right words to express it.

But there was one thing Veronica was sure that she wanted to ask. "How long has Van been a Nascitte?"

Of all the things she expected to hear her ask, that was not one of them. But her eyes said she knew what she was talking about. That one word—Nascitte—broke the barrier she held up, and she told her what she wanted to know.

Murdered when he was but a boy. Revived by a power ethereal. How Lady Victoriah described it made it easy to picture his confusion and fear, and her own.

All was quiet in the palace after that day, though the silence only thickened the tension. The king secluded himself in his chambers and would not allow any to disturb him. But everyone was convinced that something terrible had happened; the champions, the prince, and even the queen were all out of sorts ever since.

And that the king ordered for his remaining champions across the country to return boded a dark omen.

A heavy rainfall assailed the capital. The skies were filled with clouds as black as the witch god of death's robes. The forceful winds blowing through the streets carried a chilling albeit saddening moan. It was as if nature itself was in distress.

That bleak mid-spring afternoon, the Six Champions convened in the king's war chamber.

"Tell me this a joke."

The others sympathized with Lord Verring, the Champion of Shield. The stout knight looked to the man he thought was their king aghast. His mouth hung open as wide as his whiskers were long until clenching his teeth together.

He and the other two champions who had been absent from Brigadier stood in utter shock as they processed what the vita Faustign had told them. When he revealed the identity of the Renegade leader, they could not believe their ears. But the vita only portrayed grim honesty, as did the six men behind him, his advisors. Most of the people in the room shared the same expressions of dread, including the queen and the prince.

Queen Selenee stood beside Lady Victoriah at the center of the council table, away from Faustign at the head, and Prince Aeron was at the end opposite of the vita, starring at him as one would a stranger.

They knew it was no lie upon reading the room, Veronica noticed. This was supposed to be a closed meeting between the champions, the royals, and the six advisors. The only reason Veronica had been allowed to join was because Lady Victoriah contested that she knew as much as they did. But in feeling the spiking shock, the welling anger, and the corrosive distress emanating from everyone, she wished she had remained outside with Cheryl.

"I don't understand," spoke Lady Bervon, the Champion of Bravery. "All this time, we've been fighting our king? And you, you're..."

"Two decades you kept quiet about this," stated Lord Pleslo, the Champion of Sword. "Why have you chosen to speak now?"

The one to answer was Lord Astre. "Because he already told this to Vandelas Kronas."

Lady Bervon arched the brow opposite of her eyepatch. "Lady Victoriah's son? The boy in Ederea?"

"He's not in Ederea anymore. He infiltrated the palace during the attack, seeming to take advantage of the Renegades' actions, and came at us with sword in hand. And from what I have seen, he is not her son."

Lady Victoriah clenched her fist and shot a glare at the man across the table. "Don't you dare say that, Astre!"

"Cut the mother bear act! I saw him myself. He's not a Vermalian. He's not yours or Jerrell's blood."

"Why would you say such things?" blurted out Lord Verring.

"Because Vandelas Kronas is a Kindhrin."

All eyes rested on Lord Charleston. As opposed to his unsteady comrades, he remained the most composed and spoke with a steady, unwavering voice, as if it had been no secret to him.

When they looked to Lady Victoriah to make a defense, she hung her head. "It's true." She responded softly.

And suddenly, the other champions seemed ready to go on the attack.

Veronica felt she should be ready to defend her at a moment's notice. Such hate, such betrayal showed in their eyes and valsara. Restraining herself from saying or doing anything unnecessary was a struggle; she was there only to observe, not act.

"I ... came upon him when he was a baby. He couldn't have been more than six months old. He was so small, so helpless. I couldn't just abandon him... We gave him a Shift Pendant, passed him off as a Vermalian, and raised him as our own. He became my son."

"Your son!?" snarled Lord Verring, who a second ago was ready to defend her and Van. "That demon could have been the end of us all!"

A harsh growl passed Lady Victoriah's lips, and she raised her head. "He's not a demon!" she vehemently declared. She stared squarely at the four glaring at her with all the ferocity she had. "I watched him grow; he was no different from the other children. He wasn't a menace. He wanted to protect people. He asked for the chance to be a knight for that very reason. Van held the same convictions and values as you and I had." She shut her eyes tightly, taking a shaky breath and clenching her fists tight, then looked back at the other champions as if looking to scare off a threat. "I am proud to be his mother."

"You've more gall than that beast to say something so heinous!" Lord Astre barked. "Have you forgotten what he almost did? He tried to kill us—to kill you—all so he could kill Faustign!"

"Yeah, he did... He could have killed us all. He had the chance and he had the power to do it. And yet here we are, all of us."

"You keep your faith in him because you got lucky?" Lady Bervon shot a frightful look at Veronica. "Covering up his brands and making him appear as a Vermalian does not change the tainted blood in his veins. It does not change what he is."

"Is that the sin he bears? Being born as he was?"

"That is the sin they all bore!" Lord Pleslo answered. "They brought destruction to their homeland and oblivion unto themselves. You knew this, yet kept him alive anyway. He could have brought that ruin here!"

Their spite and anger grew exponentially the more they spat venom at the devoted mother. All from learning what her son really was. Even Lord Astre, who already knew some of the truth, could not stay his secondhand hatred. What they knew to be true—the stories they were told after the demise of Harah Krid, their understanding of the Kindhrin beforehand—made them appear unlike the noble knights they were. And within, their valsara twisted into things one would only see in their nightmares.

Veronica turned away from the horrid scene, and lamented that she harbored an ugliness so similar. That instant she saw Van's scarf fall, his brands revealed, she became rocked by fear, fear of the demon from those terrible stories. She never gave them much heed, she once thought, and even tried to learn about the people bygone. But that one instant showed her that even she was not left unchanged by those tales.

They all believed in a lie so cruel that it made them as thus.

It was no wonder he carried such fury.

"Enough!"

The champions ceased their shameful bickering at the loud outburst of Prince Aeron and his fist slamming against the council table. They all looked at him with shock, knowing the young man to be moderately reserved and reasonably levelheaded. The revelations brought to them have all but crushed his restraint.

The prince took a deep breath to compose himself before looking sternly to the vita. "Tell them. Tell them what you told us."

What he told them first and what would follow had been carefully considered. Beginning with the truth about King Faustign and himself, knowing that the true identity of Vandelas Kronas would be mentioned quickly, the vita Faustign predicted what would transpire and how his champions would react, what they would focus on foremost. He had hoped that they would see what their hatred made of them.

If they could...

"My apologies, Victoriah. I truly should have begun with this."

She offered the vita no answer. She just looked away from everyone in disgust.

"Pleslo, Verring, Bervon, Astre... Your anger is not for Victoriah to bear, nor is it for the Kindhrin." That hesitation he had when divulging the truth to Van impeded him again, but he swept it away, wearing a look of guilt. "You know well the story: the Kindhrin destroyed themselves and their homeland to sate their greed. It was I who conveyed that story to all of Vermalio. ...And I have been bereft ever since. It was not true. The Kindhrin perished not by their own hand, but by Faustign's."

"Faustign is the leader of the Renegades *and* the ruin of the Kindhrin race? That is what you would have us to believe?"

Lady Bervon's skepticism was understandable, especially when that story was so strongly adhered to for years. Rather than respond to that himself, one of the six advisors stepped forward, the man Prince Aeron called Aggres. "We originally created the vita so that Faustign could depart for Harah Krid during a time of strife between our two nations. He sought to ascertain whether or not they attained a weapon that would make them a threat to Vermalio."

Another of the advisors, a man called Gaelith, continued from there. "It was my idea to create him. At the time, I was only fascinated with achieving that age-old dream of creating a living, breathing being from magic. The result was something truly incredible: a veritable replica with a curious link to the one he was made to imitate. And ... it was that link that allowed us to learn of what transpired."

"If what you say is true," interrupted Lord Pleslo, "how could Faustign have accomplished such a horror? Surely, he hadn't many soldiers with him during this secret expedition."

The vita Faustign gave a slow nod. "Yes, few members of his retinue followed. Even if he recruited a number of mercenaries to his cause, it would not have been enough to topple a kingdom and slaughter its people. He would have needed something that gave him an impossible advantage, something overwhelming, disastrously so." He stroked his beard as he spoke, as if considering something he had not before. It fed everyone's doubt, but his heavy tone let them know his thoughts were not of conjecture. "Something like the power that won Vermalio its war against Pterna."

Everyone looked at him like he was mad. What he suggested was impossible.

"The Flames of Ralias?" It was Queen Selenee to first voice disbelief among the table. "That is absurd! It may be a blessing from the god of war himself, but it is still magic. No matter how powerful it is, magic cannot be used in the Cursed Land. If he did, Faustign would die."

"Magic cannot be used there, that is true. But what you know as the Flames of Ralias is no magic."

"You can't be suggesting—"

The vita nodded at Lord Charleston. "That power is the Second Verse. Faustign is the Nascitte of Fire."

Sharp gasps were sounded all around the table, their throats swelling shut from shock. Everyone there knew precisely what that entailed.

During the war against Pterna, then Prince Faustign faced terrible odds against a cruel and oppressive enemy. His forces were divided and crippled. And when they were most vulnerable, the Pternites ambushed his party. All seemed lost, but then emerged the prince, Faustign the Lionheart, adorned in flames so brilliant they reduced the enemy to ash. This blessing won him the most critical battles against the Pternite army and dissuaded the Pterna Empire from continuing their invasion.

For a Nascitte to come into being, someone had to have died. Someway or other, Faustign perished during the war, and came back to save his country.

The vita looked to the queen with the utmost sympathy. "Selenee, I cannot say I know why he kept this secret from you. All I understand is that he felt it would have been a terrible loss to him."

Queen Selenee raised her hands to her face, quieting her whimpering and burying her dismay. Her head shook every other second. It may have happened long ago, but the shock was not any less devastating.

Lord Charleston himself barely kept from taking a staggering step backward. "That ... that's impossible..." His eyes were wide as an owl's, and his hand cupped the side of his head. Veronica noticed how he fought to keep from glancing over his shoulder, to where the prince stood.

Perhaps understanding what it was he was thinking, the vita Faustign addressed his perplexed champion. "I am aware of your fascination with the Nascitte, Charleston. You've learned a great deal from the records we keep on these individuals who command dominion over nature. You marvel at them, but also fear them. That is why you have become so determined to understand them."

It was not often that Lord Charleston appeared anything less than stoic, but in listening to the vita, he looked like a child who had gotten caught swiping sweets.

The existence of the Nascitte had long been kept a guarded secret by the royal family, for the price for their power was immense, and some were still willing—foolishly—to pay it. It was not something one could give willingly.

"But there are things about the Nascitte that even they themselves do not fully understand." The vita Faustign lifted his hand, looking to his palm. A small flame began to burn in it. From certain angles, it was hard to see the embers, but they were so bright that all could catch a glimpse of their glow. "Such as bringing about my existence... Though I am grateful to my advisors, their formula for creating me was insufficient. Not even they, with their vast knowledge and commendable magic, could recreate the Vita Formula of legend. But when Faustign added his fire into the collapsing spell ..." The meager embers then flared until nearly blinding everyone. Rising from his hand was a fire truly magnificent. The flames were so pure that they were almost golden, the heat they radiated warding off the cold air in the room. "I was able to assume a stable form and sound consciousness."

In closing his hand, the fire dispersed around the table. The scattered embers did not burn, merely glimmering like stars before fading.

"The link that Gaelith mentioned, it is our connection through the Second Verse."

"He also said that is how you learned of the genocide," added Lady Bervon. "And something about a weapon... What is all that about?"

His countenance became regretful. He hung his head, not wanting to face that moment again. "What led Faustign to Harah Krid to begin with was the discovery of an ancient weapon. That weapon was said to still be powered by magic."

Lord Astre, intrigued, leaned against the table. "Was it true?"

"That it was. Faustign laid eyes on it himself."

"What is this weapon?" Lady Victoriah asked.

"The khan of Harah Krid believed it to be Might of Judgment." The name itself made some shudder. "There seemed to be a legend about it among the Kindhrin, about an evil blade that could rival the power of gods. I do not know whether he gave it much thought, but when Faustign beheld the weapon, someone believed it to be true.

"You see, all Nascitte are revived and empowered by a spirit—or a voice, if you will—of the very element they control. Those spirits compel their vessels to seek out and correct anomalies in the natural order. Nothing meager, mind you. The world has a means of correcting itself. But there are at times anomalies that even threaten the spirits themselves. The weapon that Faustign found was one such threat."

The vita paused to press his hand to his forehead. He had such a tortured face remembering what he did. "Faustign believed the weapon would prevent another war from ravaging Vermalio and sought to take it. But the Voice of Fire, Lantia, warned that the weapon was far too dangerous and compelled Faustign to use the power it gave him to destroy it. When Faustign refused, Lantia motioned to shackle his valsara and force him to comply, something the spirits are loath to do to their vessels. What would have broken a lesser man only made Faustign fight all the more, and their continued resistance strained them both."

His other hand balled into a fist against the table. His breathing became shaky, as if taken back to that moment. With their connection, the vita must have seen it all—a battle of the soul between the Nascitte and his elemental spirit. What a horror it must have been.

"When their conflict stopped, I could no longer hear Lantia's voice. And what I heard from Faustign ... That laugh—" He was trailing off in thought, but before he uttered a word more, he shook his head and focused. "I feared the worst and, after convincing my advisors, made my journey to Harah Krid."

The false story told to the Vermalians went that the noble King Faustign, having heard of the plight of the Kindhrin's self-destructive tendencies, sailed to Harah Krid to save them. His aid was rejected, and he and his soldiers were forced to return home.

But in truth, the Faustign they knew had gone to stop his creator.

"Upon my arrival, the worst had already happened. The harbor, the towns, even the capital had all been laid to waste. The desert sands were stained crimson with the blood of the Kindhrin. The only ones left were the warriors that followed Faustign. Or rather, what was left of him..."

"What was—" Prince Aeron could not finish his startled thought he was so aghast.

The vita closed his eyes, looking like he was mourning. "That man was not the same as the one who left Vermalio. The restraint he once had on his destructive power was gone. He set the Kindhrin ablaze simply because he believed them to be an obstacle in obtaining the Might of Judgment. Everything had been burned away without remorse, without care ... and with a triumphant grin."

Even after listening to his tale of woe and horror, it was still hard to believe that their own king was responsible for such carnage, even that against a people they not long ago believed were demons.

"It horrified me to see what Faustign had become. I feared his madness would roll over Vermalio like hellfire. What it would do to the people, what it would do to those who followed him... And so, I made my decision. I rejected my creator and usurped his throne."

From then on, it became easy to understand why events played out as they had. The Renegades formed not long after the fall of Harah Krid, following the true King Faustign, to oppose the rule of the false king, the vita who mirrored him. Their rise was slow, their revolts only provocative at first. With time, they grew into a baleful military force that poisoned Vermalio from the inside.

Agents hid among the masses and even acted as honored knights and benevolent nobles. They weakened the current reign however they could, put it through every possible ordeal, to undermine the people's confidence in their ruler, thus strengthening their cause. Whatever information the vita did not keep to himself was likely hidden or erased by the Renegade spies.

All in preparation for the fallen king's return.

Everyone around the council table slowly surrendered themselves to the truth and began to think about where they stood. But there was still one thing left unsaid, something vital.

"Excuse me, Your Majesty." Veronica waited for the vita to look her way in recognition to be sure no one would object to her speaking. "What was this ultimatum you spoke of?"

Several champions looked to her confused, but the vita Faustign knew what she meant right away. That was the exact word he used when he revealed everything to Van.

"I see. So you were there as well." Upon receiving a timid nod from the knight-to-be, the vita forwent his knowing look to retake his grim countenance. "This lie I told Vermalio, it is unforgivable."

"I doubt the people would have accepted the truth."

Faustign shook his head at Lord Astre. "Yes, I deceived my people. But it is the Kindhrin that I wronged by desecrating their memory. Them, and Faustign's family for concealing this truth. I said nothing to Selenee or Aeron, though I wish I could have."

"Of course you could have!" Prince Aeron shouted. "You could have told us at any time. Why didn't you!?" The prince maintained his composure for the sake of decorum, but the dams broke hearing the vita Faustign act like someone so powerless.

The vita chose his answer carefully, worried about the backlash he expected. Though he did not regret his decision, he understood not everyone would see that what he did was right. Knowing what to say so tensions would not be raised too high and keep them from listening, from understanding, was a terrible struggle.

"My words are my own. But my eyes and ears, they are not. Everything I see and hear, so, too, does Faustign. He wanted Vermalio to believe in this wicked story he weaved for me to tell. If I refused to do so, if I told *anyone* the truth ... he threatened to have you killed."

The horror in everyone was sparked anew.

Prince Aeron shook his head so much it looked like it would fall off. "You're lying. You're lying!"

"I wish I was."

The prince fought to refute the vita's grievous confession. When he looked to his mother, hoping another would call out his lies, he only came to share in her despair.

A king who lost his heir would simply have another child. Faustign, in his madness, used that logic to force some level of compliance from his rogue creation.

The vita everyone knew as Faustign, be it for duty or compassion, clearly cared about Aeron and did not wish him harm. Thus, he submitted to the ultimatum and used the Vermalians' prejudice to bury the truth.

Queen Selenee stared at the vita, rattled by the unfathomable things she heard. "Why...? How could he..."

It pained the vita to be the one who broke the poor woman's heart. "For the Might of Judgment," he plainly put. "Faustign needed time to bring the weapon under his control. He made this gambit to keep me from acting against him for as long as possible.

"But his patience has long worn thin, and Faustign knows that I have revealed the truth to you all. He will soon rally his followers to take further action. Everything done by the Renegades up until now has been only to spite me. From this point forward, it's all-out war."

The Renegades' recent ploys have been their most devastating yet. Their bold attack on the palace showed how confident they were that they could oppose the false king.

As bad as it had gotten, though, they knew it could still get worse.

"Then," Queen Selenee struggled to speak, "we cannot stand idle."

To that, the vita Faustign nodded. "If we do not act, then I fear Vermalio will share in Harah Krid's fate." He looked down the table to his champions, all of them understanding where this was going. "For years, you have fought the Renegades as they came. You know well from your encounters with them how devoted they are to Faustign, to what he has become. They will not stop until he has retaken control of the kingdom. The only way to stop this is to take the fight to him."

None of the Six Champions were enthusiastic about this.

"You realize what you are asking of us, don't you?" asked Lord Astre.

The vita Faustign hung his head with humility. "Yes, I do."

Deciding he had heard enough, Prince Aeron left the table, walking straight for the door. Queen Selenee was about to stop him when Lady Victoriah grabbed her by the wrist. She dared not look her way as she shook her head. It was a brazen thing, telling her queen what to do, telling a mother not to go to her son when he was hurting.

But there was no escaping this path they now walked. He needed to figure out for himself what he would do. And he could not do so there, in a room with people who were deciding if they could bring themselves to kill their king.

He might have been gone all his life, but Faustign was still his father.

And despite what they learned, he was still, legitimately, their king.

The Six Champions were duty-bound to serve the will of their king. It was the sole reason for their existence: to honor his name through their deeds, to defend it against those who would dare sully it. Knowing that they had been opposing the true king and defending his usurper all this time put them at odds with themselves.

And now they were being asked to slay Faustign themselves.

Duty, belief, and reality conflicted with one another in a vicious cycle. To choose one meant to betray another, and no matter the result, their world would change forever.

Lord Charleston, his hand gripping into his crossed arms, raised his head. "We as the Six Champions follow our role to serve the king. To do otherwise is to betray our honor." His were words well befitting of the Champion of Duty. What he said next, though, stunned them all. "But our king, too, had a role to play. And instead, he chose to forsake his people to follow in this twisted ambition. You say that he feared a war, but he brought one to us, after having laid waste an entire country. He turned his people against one another, used them as pawns in his game, and put countless innocents to death. Such a king ... is no king at all."

The other champions looked to him as though he were a different person. Even the queen and the royal advisors were perturbed by his sudden change. But truth rang in what he said.

Veronica turned to Lady Victoriah, wondering where she stood. The Champion of Heart kept glancing toward the vita and looking down. Even she had her reservations about this. But her arms slackened and fists unclenched, resentment and dismay slipping away as she faced him again. "You're the only Faustign that I know, and you've always acted for the benefit of Vermalio. Everything you've done has always been for our sake.

But the real Faustign..." Fury burned brightly in her valsara, reigniting her determined heart. "He scarred Van, killed Jerrell, and made entire kingdoms suffer. I won't stand for any more!"

Their feelings reached their comrades, dampening their doubt.

When they first set themselves on the path to knighthood, they had chosen to put their faith in the kingdom and their liege, no matter the hardships that followed. That faith—that resolve—came into question with the betrayal of the one who ruled over them.

But a country was more than the one who ruled it.

"He's already proven how far he is willing to go," stated Lord Verring. "Killing his own countrymen in the most barbaric ways. Sabotaging international relationships to create further conflict. His Renegade army has done more harm to Vermalio than Pterna ever could."

"Maybe this was about the right to rule once," Lord Pleslo said, "but not anymore. Our country is falling apart. We know who is responsible. If he is allowed to continue, he'll destroy it."

Lady Bervon nodded. "Our people need us now more than ever. It doesn't matter who I have to fight. I will protect them at all costs!"

All eyes were on Lord Astre, the head knight of the Six Champions, who had yet to voice his decision. He remained conflicted, his forehead wrinkled, his eyebrow twitching. Even so, he was not unmoved by the zeal of his comrades.

He took a heavy breath and opened his eyes to face the man they chose to follow. "So, what will our move be, Your Majesty?"

Heartened by the noble conviction of his champions, the vita Faustign put on a dry, albeit reassured, smile. He faced them as a king once more, and conveyed to them his plan of action.

The gardens behind the royal palace were pleasant to stroll through, even during a rain shower. A fair distance from the rear gates stood these tall stone canopies, each spread evenly apart, that lined the way through the path of flowers. The only way to get from one to the next was to cross through the downpour. It did not trouble Veronica at all. When she walked between the canopies, she held her hand up and used her Second Verse to keep the drops from falling on her.

It was rather soothing to watch the raindrops bend away from her as she walked, how the water formed a dome over her as it fell. It led her to stray from the covered path and walk beside the plants.

She was careful to avoid mud. After all, she did not want to trouble the servants by tracking it inside.

The gentle *Shaaaa!* of the falling rain was like a song. While a bit melancholy, it sounded divine. It helped her relax after the meeting with the king. She needed some time alone to process everything.

They were going to war soon, to a faraway land so they may face their dreaded enemy. Faustign was still in Harah Krid trying to take control of the evil blade that could rival the gods, a weapon that even the spirits of nature themselves feared. Harah Krid and Vermalio were continents apart—Harah Krid in the central land of Medie Lith, Vermalio to the north in Dynalis—separated by a vast ocean known as the Cascades.

Many in Vermalio knew the Cascades for its enchanting beauty, but those who sailed the seas feared its very name. Beyond the mainland, the Cascades was a stretch of voracious waters and endless storms. Its sickle winds tore through every sail, and the possessed waves bit through entire hulls. All who dared to cross it were pulled under, into Untae's Cradle.

But the only way they could manage a voyage to Harah Krid was by sailing through it. It would be a voyage to their deaths—if not for Veronica.

According to the king, there was a safe route to pass through the Cascades, and the only one who could find it was a Nascitte. It gave most of the champions a pleasant surprise to hear that she was one. With her, they would be able to reach Harah Krid.

"We'll be fine," her other self tried to assure her. *"We're the Nascitte of Water. A stormy sea has nothing on us. We'll find a way through."*

But she was still trepidatious. The fate of an entire fleet would hinge on her ability to navigate through a hellish sea using her magic senses. If her insight was off in the slightest, their crusade would end before it even began.

It had been years since she was last on a ship. She yearned for the longest time to return to the water and set sail once again. But now, she hoped her long-awaited voyage would not come so soon.

Veronica shook that reluctance from her skull. There was more at stake than just her and her fellow knights.

She had to do it. She had to be ready. For Vermalio.

After going so far into the gardens, Veronica noticed she was not the only one there. And once she recognized who it was, she ran her way.

Her boots dug into the soggy ground. The mud clung to them, almost as if ensnaring her. She eventually came back to the canopies and went to the one at the end of the path, vines wrapped around its pillars and flowers growing over its carved images. And beneath it was—

"Rubi!"

The phantom she saw blown away by Van's unbridled power was there, looking longingly to the north. She did not react to Veronica's call, or turn to her when she approached. It was like she was a world away.

When Veronica spoke her name again, this time in worry, and joined her under the canopy, Rubi hung her head.

"It was him."

"What?"

Rubi faced Veronica. "It was him. Van. I was looking for him."

Only the patter of rainfall followed her answer.

It bothered Veronica how she could not bring herself to say anything. She had realized what Rubi had after the Heveilon incident, when Lady Victoriah told her that Van was engaged to marry Rubi. She offered few details, probably because she knew little about it herself.

She truly hoped she would get to tell her. But after what happened...

"Are you okay?"

Rubi gave a small smile. "Yeah, I'm okay. He threw me pretty far, but it didn't hurt. Really."

"I am glad to hear, but ... that is not really what I meant."

Perhaps the release of energy did not harm her spirit, but she was still so aggrieved.

Rubi turned away in a futile attempt to hide her woe. She understood, but she did not want to. "It's funny, coming to find out this way." Her gaze drifted back to the north. "I was just wandering Brigadier, same as always, when ... I felt him. I never could sense valsara in life, so I never felt his before, but still, somehow I knew it was him."

It was a testament to their bond, to how much he meant to her.

"Everything became clearer the closer I got to him. My last moments... Xanlir had just stabbed me. I couldn't move, or breathe, and with every passing second, I got colder. I was just about to slip away when..." The memory began to overwhelmed her. She tensed up and glared, those moments invoking hostility. "He ran Van through. But Van got back up and kept fighting. And somehow ... somehow, he killed Xanlir." The tension in her diminished when focus of the memory shifted back from one to another. "He still kept losing blood. I wanted to reach out to him, to help him, but ... everything went black. I died fearing he would too."

It was a tragic way to leave the world, only to reemerge as a phantom, lost and uncertain but still tortured by those feelings, and unable to do anything about them.

Veronica stepped up to Rubi, resting her hand on her shoulder. The phantom was comforted by her touch and reached back to grip her hand.

"All this time, I never knew whether he was alive or dead. I didn't even remember who he was. And yet ... I just knew, deep down, that I had to find him."

It was such a beautiful thing to say. It brought Veronica to smile again. "You truly cared for him, didn't you?"

And that made Rubi smile. She shook her head and turned away, a mite bashful. But then she faced Veronica again, looking her straight in the eye. "I loved him." More beautiful words. They were not ones she would share so freely, even with the only person who could see her. But now that she had found what she lost, she could not keep them to herself.

"I felt a little guilty when I tricked him into our engagement."

"Wait, you what?" However she intended to make it sound, it made Veronica smirk and giggle.

Rubi shared in her mirth. "It wasn't easy. He wasn't versed in the traditions of nobles, and I couldn't tell him everything outright. The best I could do was keep his attention for a while and play the princess waiting to be rescued."

"And that worked?" said Veronica after a laugh.

"He was naïve, but still smart. And a real animal in a fight."

From the sound of it, she must have seen what happened herself, and was delighted with the result.

She remembered him so fondly, and when she saw him, she rushed to his side to defend him, no matter the futility, no matter how different he was from before.

"Rubi ... did you know...?"

She needed not go any further for Rubi to know what she meant. "Yeah, I did. I saw what he really looks like a couple of times. It was a shock, sure, but... It didn't matter to me. He was precious to me—and that's all there was to it."

A rueful smile thinned between Veronica's cheeks. She recognized the anxiety laced in her beautiful words.

When she mentioned a fight, her thoughts drifted not to the memory of the duel. Rubi tried to keep thinking about their happier times together, but she could tell from the look Veronica gave her that she was not hiding her concern well. "Now everyone knows. They'll be after him. And I can't do anything to help him..."

It was tragic, but there might not be anything anyone could do. The lies told about the Kindhrin had poisoned the Vermalians' sense of reason.

After years of hiding, Van had clearly chosen to stop. If someone were to see him...

What he did was inexcusable, but Veronica still believed he was good at heart. Otherwise, he would have killed them all, sparing not a single soul between him and Faustign, just like he did the Renegades.

"But I can. I will help him somehow. I promise."

Rubi kept looking at Veronica with mournful eyes. The reality of her powerlessness had always tormented her so. Her desire showed through:

she wished to go to his side, to help him face his troubles and let him know he was not alone. It was hard to acknowledge that she could not.

But slowly, surely, her frown eased into a smile. Small beads of light trickled down her cheeks like tears.

"Thank you, Veronica. For everything."

Entrusting her with this wish, the anguish and woe burdening Rubi finally lifted. The ethereal blue light enveloping her transparent form shifted into a gently brimming gold. Veronica watched, with a pang to the heart, as Rubi's form broke apart into nodes of angelic light.

"Good luck, Lady Knight."

Veronica reached out for the light flickering away into the air. When they were finally out of reach, she pulled her hand back and held it over her chest. She had not known another phantom as long as she did Rubi. It made watching her leave all the harder.

The heavy rainfall above came to a trickle while they spoke, and now stopped entirely as the dark clouds came to part, letting pass slivers of brilliant sunshine.

How the sunlight reached through the parting clouds like a bridge put Veronica somewhat at ease. She was going to be well received in the Elysium.

After offering a prayer for her departed friend, Veronica turned around to return to the palace, feeling her spirits renewed. She made it only a few steps before stopping.

Just beneath the canopy before hers stood Cheryl.

Veronica composed herself. She might have seen half of what happened and thought she was speaking to herself.

As she made her approach, Cheryl stood straight. "Hey."

Veronica smiled. "Hey. Um ... how long have you been here for?"

"Since you started laughing. I thought you were having a bit of fun before you started looking sad."

An awkward giggle escaped her as she tried to act like nothing was wrong. Veronica held her hands behind her back, then glanced aside. It was always embarrassing whenever someone caught her like this.

"Were you just finishing a talk with a phantom?"

A spark shot up Veronica's spine. She looked to Cheryl wide-eyed. That startled reaction bought her a laugh from her friend.

"You know about the phantoms?"

"I've seen you talking to yourself a few times before. I didn't know what to make of it. Until I heard you mention 'other phantoms,' that is."

Veronica drew her chin in, nervous. "And you ... don't find it odd?"

"I used to," Cheryl admitted with a guilty smile. "But I know you a lot better now. You're a sharp girl. You notice things that many people never would. And I do believe phantoms are among them."

It was difficult to believe her at first. Veronica knew she would never say anything to offend her. Cheryl was always a forthright one, though. If she did not feel that way, she would not have said it.

Others have always looked down at her for saying that phantoms existed, especially the children back home. What a great relief it was to know that her friend would not do the same, and that she did not have to hide that from her anymore.

"Is it still here?"

Veronica shook her head. "She is at peace now. I ... won't be seeing her anymore."

The tinge of sadness in her voice did not go unnoticed. Cheryl cupped Veronica's shoulder, then, hoping to make her feel better, pulled her into a tight hug. "You did a good thing, Veronica."

A comforting warmth welled up in her chest. It was the first time someone other than the phantoms she helped acknowledged her deeds. It felt so affirming.

Times were few when Cheryl offered such affection. Having her pull away so soon left Veronica disappointed.

"How is the prince?"

Cheryl had already left her spot in the hall when the meeting had concluded, presumably to chase after Prince Aeron when he stormed off.

Her conflicted face showed how uncertain she was about everything overall.

"He should be fine. We talked for a bit. I don't think he'll get over having to confront his father." What they went over bothered her as well. She fought to get the last few words out, and with a straight face. "But he knows what has to be done. When the army sets out, he intends to go with them. He wants to see this to the end, however that may go."

Trying to imagine how this ill turn of fate affected poor Prince Aeron made Veronica's chest tighten. What must it be like, to suddenly view a parent as a threat, to see their idolized visage stained with their sins?

Cheryl knew what went through her friend's mind, the kind soul that she was. She took Veronica by the hand, leading her back to the palace.

"Come on. We'll be marching off to war soon. Let's take it easy while we can."

Veronica nodded and followed her inside.

~ Epilogue ~

Once everything had been settled, Veronica and company set out for the southernmost edge of Vermalio. They arrived at the harbor town of Farer's Cape, a quaint haven for mariners of all sorts.

The town was unaccustomed to receiving so many soldiers at once and submitting to such strict military regulations. It had been used mainly as a trade port since the end of the war with Pterna. Its citizenry adapted to the change from peacetime well, though, perhaps with the help of veterans who retired there. Rudimentary barricades had been set up around Farer's Cape, securing its most vulnerable points. The local militia cooperated with the knights sent to support them. They were ready to handle any threat sent their way.

The streets had been cleared for the army en route from the capital, offering a straight path to the docks. Civilians gathered to watch the hundreds of soldiers on their march from the sidelines, some with fear, others with admiration and hope.

Upon reaching the docks, the army was presented with a fleet of warships prepped and waiting for departure. Lord Astre marched down from the flagship to greet them. He arrived first to handle the arrangements for their crusade.

As per their king's strategy, three of the Six Champions would remain in Vermalio to resist the Renegades, while the other three embarked for Harah Krid to put an end to their long nightmare. Joining Lord Astre were Lord Charleston and Lady Victoriah. They were to act as the head of the army's command alongside Prince Aeron himself.

The prince addressed Lord Astre promptly, receiving a bow from the head champion before hearing his briefing.

Veronica walked beside Lady Victoriah to join them, taking in the aroma of the sea, when she heard someone call her name.

"Verrie!"

It was a name few called her, shouted by a rough and familiar voice. She turned to a gathering of bustling dockworkers and soldiers to see a tall man with light brown hair. He was a rather charming sort. When Veronica saw him, he greeted her with his heartened smile.

She returned it with a smile of glee and ran to him. "Din!"

She leaped at her third eldest brother, Dougdin Alivvrn, to catch him in a big hug. Her brother returned the embrace in kind before letting her go. "It's good to see you, Little Sister," he said while patting her shoulder, a signal for her to release.

Her siblings were always so strict about showing affection in public. It always bothered her, which is why she clung to him so tightly before reluctantly letting go.

"Good to see you too. What brings you here?"

"I heard the word: you're setting out to hunt down the Renegade leader."

News had spread that the king learned the identity of the Renegade leader. While the whole truth was shared only with a select few, soldiers throughout the kingdom had informed their peers and subordinates of his plan to seek out and subjugate the Renegades. Everyone knew that he was acting to erase the chaos swallowing their country.

Many cast doubt on this, dismissing it as a mere rumor to stave off panic brought about by the word of how close the Renegades came to taking the palace. When soldiers started to be deployed in such large numbers, though, they began to believe.

"Oh. Were you sent to aid us?"

Din's smile thinned. "Not quite. I'm expected back in Illuascove to counter whatever madness the Renegades have in store."

Veronica blinked. "Why make such a long journey here then?"

"Well, I'm not here to aid the army. But I am here to help you."

Before he explained further, Din reached for something behind his back. He unstrapped a leather harness and presented it to Veronica, upon which she beheld a sword. Her eyes widened when she got a good look at the aged hilt, and she gasped when she spotted the ruby at the pommel.

"Is that—"

Din nudged the sword toward her, urging her to take it. And so she did. The scabbard felt cool to the touch and weighed against her with the heft of the sword. Eager to answer her question, she gripped the hilt and drew it upward. Her eyes gleamed at the bronzed blade and its wing-like guard.

"Fíochmar."

Her brother's smile grew back upon her uttering the sword's name.

Fíochmar was a relic blade treasured by the Alivvrn family, said to have been forged in the fabled Old Age. Their family cared for it for hundreds of years and bestowed it unto the members in need of its might most. The ruby in the pommel was believed to contain the soul of a gryphon, a mythical creature that had an indomitable nature. The beast's essence was long thought to empower the one who wielded it.

"He who wields the majestic blade Fíochmar shall never lose heart in battle," Din recited the family saying. "You'll be facing more danger than any of us, dear sister. May the blade serve you well."

Veronica looked back up to her elder brother with an endearing smile. "I swear to use it honorably."

Din leaned in to cup her shoulder, giving it a comforting squeeze.

"Are you certain you do not need it yourself?"

Din's smile twisted into a laugh at his sister's teasing. "Who do you think I am?" he asked enthusiastically. "I am the Marauding Knight! What I need, I take."

Veronica teased him only to hear him say that. He always sounded so confident whenever announcing his title.

The two siblings shared in one last brief embrace before parting ways, leaving for their respective battlefields.

It brought Veronica great peace of mind to hold Fíochmar. Having the treasure of the Alivvrn family was the same as having the blessings and best wishes of her entire family.

With the scabbard slung over her back, Veronica could look to the ruby and think of them.

She enjoyed the legend about the gryphon's soul inside of it, even if she did not believe it. Her eyes never revealed to her any traces of spirit energy, just a lingering protection spell that was likely applied to it when it was forged.

When everything seemed to be in order, Lord Astre showed them to the flagship. Most of the soldiers separated to board the other ships, leaving only the best and most trusted knights to join the champions.

Veronica beamed with delight as she climbed the gangplank. The salty ocean air was all the more palpable now that she was over the water. It felt invigorating to breathe it in.

"How much longer, Astre?"

Someone greeted them upon their ascension to the main deck, a shadow tucked in the shade cast by the stairs to the helm.

His sudden call stunned Lady Victoriah. It was Van.

"Van ... what are you doing here?"

When last they saw him, he was fighting them tooth and claw to slay the king. Now he stood before them perfectly calm, leaning against the stairway with arms crossed. His pet fox, Snowflake, stood at his feet, visibly alert and tense from the people scrambling across the deck.

"I asked him to join us."

Everyone turned to Lord Charleston in shock. Of them all, Lady Victoriah was most surprised. She looked to him like she could not believe what she had heard.

"We are about to face an enemy more dangerous than any we have ever known. Any able fighter willing to aid us is a welcome boon. With Vandelas' power, we have a greater chance of victory. That is why I tracked him down and told him to come here for Lord Astre to receive him."

The Champion of Pride kept his gaze, riddled with suspicion, on the Kindhrin. "Keep out of sight until we've left port."

While he stood beneath the shade, it proved difficult to make out the crimson brands on Van's face. Regardless, Lord Astre did not want to risk their soldiers spotting a Kindhrin among them. At least, not yet.

Knowing well why, Van begrudgingly followed his instructions. He and his fox left them behind, walking down the stairs leading below deck.

"Are you certain we can trust him?"

"He has made it clear who his enemy is, and what he is willing to do to get to him. I would rather have him stand with us than against us."

Of that, the Champion of Pride could not argue, not when none of them could keep him from reaching Faustign once before. They shared a common enemy. If nothing else, that would keep them united.

Lady Victoriah was conflicted watching her son retreat below deck, but she pulled away from her thoughts to focus on the matter at hand.

Soon, everything was ready. The anchor was raised. The sails were unfurled. And the ships made their way out of the harbor.

Cheers resounded from the docks as the civilians gathered to see off their brave knights. Many soldiers stood at the railings of each ship, bidding farewell to their countrymen. Whether they were confident that they would return triumphant or understood that this would be the last time they would see their home, the knights retained their strength and pride for their fellow Vermalians to see.

They needed them to remain as such in their absence, until the new dawn would greet them.

Veronica stood at the railing for a while, waving goodbye to her homeland. As the harbor drew farther and farther away, she went to the bow of the ship. She stood as close to the edge as she could, feeling the ocean breeze brush against her face and through her hair.

Finally, she was setting out to sea again.

With the leader of the Renegades finally revealed, the Vermalian army sets out to put an end to their decades-long conflict.

Their destination: Harah Krid. The homeland of the Kindhrin, who were all but wiped out in a madman's attempt to seize an ancient and terrible weapon lying beneath its gilded sands. There awaits a land in decay, with the very skies marked by its curse.

What will the Aethereal Knights face in this grand quest?

The Siren Knight's Wave

Fourth Book of the Aethereal Knights' Tales